Wendy Robertson has lived and worked in the North East of England for most of her life. Before moving to full-time writing she worked in teaching and in Teacher Education, whilst publishing some short fiction and, in the 1970s, writing a regular column for the *Northern Echo*. Wendy has two grown-up children and lives in Bishop Auckland, County Durham, with her husband.

Kitty Rainbow

Wendy Robertson

HEADLINE

First published in 1996
by HEADLINE BOOK PUBLISHING

First published in paperback in 1996
by HEADLINE BOOK PUBLISHING

10 9 8 7 6 5 4 3 2

ISBN 0 7472 5183 5

Printed and bound in Great Britain by
Caledonian International Book Manufacturing Ltd, Glasgow

HEADLINE BOOK PUBLISHING
A division of Hodder Headline PLC
338 Euston Road
London NW1 3BH

For Bryan, who discovered Kitty Rainbow . . .

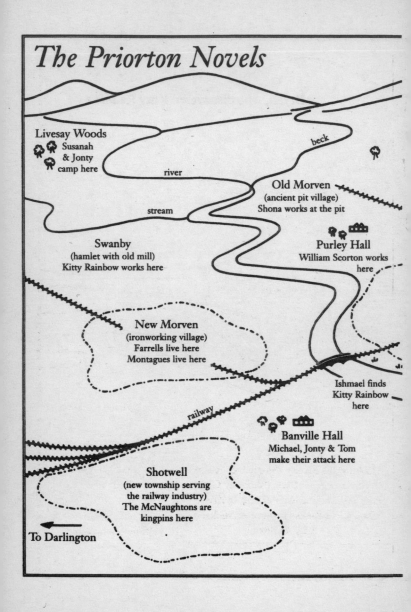

The Priorton Novels

Livesay Woods
Susanah & Jonty camp here

beck

river

stream

Old Morven
(ancient pit village)
Shona works at the pit

Purley Hall
William Scorton works here

Swanby
(hamlet with old mill)
Kitty Rainbow works here

New Morven
(ironworking village)
Farrells live here
Montagues live here

Ishmael finds Kitty Rainbow here

railway

Banville Hall
Michael, Jonty & Tom make their attack here

Shotwell
(new township serving the railway industry)
The McNaughtons are kingpins here

← To Darlington

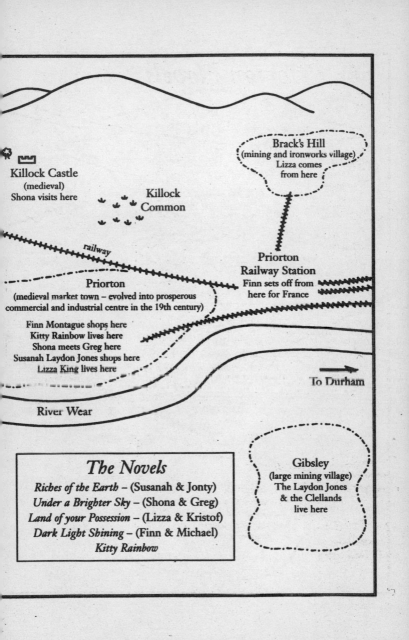

Killock Castle
(medieval)
Shona visits here

Killock
Common

railway

Brack's Hill
(mining and ironworks village)
Lizza comes
from here

Priorton
Railway Station
Finn sets off from
here for France

Priorton
(medieval market town – evolved into prosperous
commercial and industrial centre in the 19th century)

Finn Montague shops here
Kitty Rainbow lives here
Shona meets Greg here
Susanah Laydon Jones shops here
Lizza King lives here

To Durham

River Wear

Gibsley
(large mining village)
The Laydon Jones
& the Clellands
live here

The Novels

Riches of the Earth – (Susanah & Jonty)
Under a Brighter Sky – (Shona & Greg)
Land of your Possession – (Lizza & Kristof)
Dark Light Shining – (Finn & Michael)
Kitty Rainbow

Kitty Rainbow

PLAYERS

KITTY RAINBOW
whose name has to be invented, as she is a foundling

ISHMAEL SLAUGHTER
originally Latvian; ex bare-knuckle fighter, 48 at the beginning

ESME GULLET
Three years older than Kitty

GABRIEL GULLET
Five years older than Kitty

MIRELLA GULLET
Their mother

JANINE DRUCE
'Scotch' draper, sometime prostitute, age 35 at the start,
mother to

THOMAS DRUCE
Seven years older than Kitty, seen by some as an idiot

FREDDY LONGSTAFFE
Kitty's age, her first sweetheart, a miner

JARROLD POMMEROY
Sharp fairground operator, talent-spotter friend of

NED LUMB
Boxing promoter & Ishmael's sponsor

WILLIÁM SCORTON
Manufacturer, watchmaker: 42 when we meet him
Father to Michael (7) and Samuel (5)

TOBIAS HUNTER
Lawyer, Gabriel Gullet's first employer, 60 when we
meet him

MR VAN DIEMEN   Theatre Impresario

MR CULLEN   Theatre Impresario

A Tall Woman

PART ONE

Ishmael

1

A Young Man in Black Velvet

May 1861

'Lucky heather, lady?'

The tall fair woman, her eyes shaded under the deep brim of her bonnet, winced as her hand was grabbed. A squat woman, whose skin was copper brown, tight as a plum and very shiny, her face enclosed by a peacock-blue kerchief which was fighting a losing battle with wild black hair, confronted her. The young gypsy pursed her lips. 'I see a dark man, lady, and a stranger in a great house ...'

'You people always say such things.' The tall woman's voice was flute-like, fine. She wrenched her hand, but the gypsy stood her ground, forcing her to scramble in her bag for a farthing before the gypsy woman gave way with a deep, false curtsy.

Clutching the sprig of heather, the woman walked on, to be stopped by a clatter as the sweep of her long skirt caught a pile of fancy dishes heaped precariously on a piece of sacking. An old woman in a paisley shawl, sitting by the dishes, took the pipe from her mouth. Perched on a wooden box, she screwed her eyes up against the pipe-smoke, which was drifting back into her face on the edge of the skirling May breeze. A child of about seven years sat on the ground at her feet, playing with sticks, making elaborate patterns in the dirt.

The tall woman kneeled awkwardly to retrieve the pile of dishes. The trader bit on her pipe again. 'Jis' leave that, hinney. Thoo wants nowt crawling ower the floor i' thy state. Our Jessa'll pick 'em up.'

The child was already reassembling the pile, balancing one plate neatly on another.

The tall woman shook out her old-fashioned wide skirts over their crinoline, and looked down at herself. She had not thought her 'state' to be evident. She was about to object to the presumption but a look from the pipe-smoker silenced her.

She walked on, pushing her way through the crowd thronging Priorton Market Place for the May Fair. Her nose wrinkled at the smell of sweat and urine, fish and spices, horse and cow manure, apples and milky curds; the music of a penny whistle and the steady beat of a drum found their way to her ears through the cacophony of raucous laughter, the rap of bookmakers and the shouts of traders touting their wares.

A cluster of sturdy young people stood together shoulder to shoulder, watching the crowd with a detached, almost clinical interest. They watched the tall woman boldly as she passed; her eye lingered a second on them. The girls' kerchiefs and the boys' boots showed their chosen destinations of farmyard, dairy and field: they stood there as they did every spring, waiting to be hired for the year by some dales farmer or other.

The tall woman thought about the young man, the one she was looking for, and wondered if he had ever stood in such a line. She knew he'd hired himself as a sailor once. He'd been to America – on a clipper ship to New York. He'd seen the great Frenchman Blondin perform his high wire act across the Niagara Falls – or so he said. And according to him the selling of slaves at auction in America was little different to the hirings that happened every spring in every market town in England, not just here in County Durham. And, he said, those black men knew no difference, did they? He would say that a lot. Declare they knew no difference any more than these farmworkers did.

The tall woman tripped on an upturned sod and stopped to pause for breath. Well, she thought, different or not, those Yankees were sorting that out now. At war with their brothers and neighbours, to stop just such selling of people. She put her hand on her waist to still the tumult inside. Already she imagined the baby flicking against her fingers.

She thought about him, the young man whose child this was. Not much more than a boy himself. Not so very tall really: not as tall as herself. But with heavy shoulders and strong hands; making her happy, showing her how to make him happy. Laughing and singing all the time, liberating her body in its late painful flowering. She thought about the last time in March when, between them, they had made this baby. He had come tap-tap-tapping on her window, having shinned up the medieval drainpipes like a cat.

She strode on. He must be here. Came every May. He said that last September in the river meadow, where he'd come upon her reading as he swished his way with a stick through the long grass. She had read to him then, some piece by the poet John Clare. The boy had liked it. The thoughts of a simple man, he'd said. But he was soon distracted, helping her for the first time through her pain to the point of dazed delight.

He'd said it again, about the thoughts of a simple man, in March when he had sought her out once more on his way to Edinburgh.

Her breath quickened. She must see him.

She strode on, only to be brought to a stop altogether by the heaving mass of people: individuals varying from the most low-life-ragged to the most high-hat-fancy. She stood on tiptoe to see the nature of the hindrance. Her ears were filled by a predatory hum of human anticipation as old as Roman circuses. She flexed her knees and jumped, to get a view over the burly shoulders pressed together and the hats in a dozen styles set at every kind of angle.

Finally she resorted to climbing on to the steps of Handleman's Bank. Now she could see over the heads of the crowd, to a ramshackle boxing ring, set up on the only solid patch of green that graced the Market Square.

The boxing ring was backed by colourful banners and kept clear of the crowd by a hairy rope slung from four posts set roughly into the ground. Inside the ring a man, elbows out, was playing a penny whistle and a woman, dressed in what looked like her underwear, was juggling with hoops. And a young man in black velvet breeches and waistcoat was playing a side drum. Her heart leaped. It was the boy. So he was here.

A hoarse voice in her ear said, 'My dear woman, what in the world are you doing here? This is no place for . . .'

The dry clerical tones made her drag her eyes away from the young man in black velvet and focus blankly on the too-familiar narrow face before her. She shook off the hard insistent hand. 'Leave me, will you?' she said, jumping off the steps. 'Leave me alone!' She thrust past him and plunged again into the crowd around the ring.

Nearer to the front she stopped, her eyes locked on to the dark-haired drummer. Round his neck he wore the thing he called his choker, a deep blue spotted kerchief, wound twice, then tied in a small bow at the front. His dark hair fell in glossy curls to his heavy shoulders and his muscular upper arms were shown off, rather than covered, by his bright silk shirt.

'Mind it, will yer?' Jossy Gullet, a small, hard man, with a bald head, whose non-existent neck sunk into his high old-fashioned stock, turned to glare at the tall woman who was pushing at him to get by. His glare faltered as he saw this woman of middle years had the frayed but unmistakable stamp of a lady. 'Sorry, miss,' he growled, 'but it's crowded down here.'

'I must get to the front,' she said. 'I must get to the front.'

Jossy put out his knobbly, scarred hands, pushed the backs of the people in front of him to make a space, and allowed the woman to squeeze through. His wife, Mirella, corsetted and high-breasted like a pigeon, glared at the back of the woman in the deep-brimmed hat. 'Who might she think she is when she's out? Pushin' through like that!'

'Hold thee bloody whisht woman,' Jossy replied. 'Watch the fight. Here they are! Here's Ishmael. He's on!'

By the time the tall woman got right up to the ringside, the drumming had stopped, the young man had vanished, and a boxing match of sorts was underway, with a short man announcing the fight between Ishmael Slaughter and Gypsy Joe Elliot. Her ears pounded as the crowd roared and dogs barked. Then, interested despite herself, the woman watched as two big men squared up to each other.

The fighter called Ishmael was in his middle years, a magnificent figure of a man with a large open face and a broken nose, his mane of black and silver hair held back with a leather thong. Gypsy Joe was a much younger man with a massive muscular physique. He had the colouring and the flashing looks of his race, not unlike those of the woman with her heather at the edge of the crowd.

Both men moved surprisingly lightly for their huge size, ducking and diving, dodging and swerving so that for several minutes no hit was landed. The crowd was shouting with disappointment, denied their first blood. There was no taste for the new 'scientific' boxing in this crowd.

The woman was reminded of the baying of wolves she had heard once somewhere on the eastern borders of Germany.

'Go to it, Ishmael. Cut the bugger down!' yelled the short man who had parted the crowd for her.

A man standing beside her in a tall hat and a well-cut

7

caped coat was gripping his cane with pigskin–gloved hands muttering, 'Hit him, man, hit him! Blood. Blood.'

Then the man called Ishmael landed a blow which cut his opponent's cheekbone, drawing blood and felling him. The crowd roared its satisfaction, and Gypsy Joe rocked back on to his heels. He uttered a bloodcurdling yell and leaped to his feet, his eyes glittering. He drove forward, forgetting the fancy footwork, piling blow after blow on to, and into, the older man, who finally crashed to the floor at the woman's side of the ring, ending the second bout.

The older fighter grasped the rope in front of her and she could see the bright blood, like the petals of a red rose, on his knobbly hands. He dragged himself to his feet and his eyes met hers. She put her hand to her throat, shocked by the bleak anger she saw in Ishmael Slaughter's eyes. Where she felt she would see fire, there was ice.

Slaughter hauled himself to his feet and turned again to face his opponent.

The woman moved her eyes towards a cluster of men at the far side of the ring. The drummer, the young man in black velvet, had not reappeared. The boxers squared up to each other again and the woman squeezed along the edge of the ring, continuing her pursuit.

The fight lasted forty-three rounds, the obstinate courage of each fighter compelling him to haul himself to his feet each time he was floored. The difference between the two was that the man called Ishmael became colder and harder as the minutes ticked away; he seemed to gather strength out of the air. Gypsy Joe became more and more angry and heated, from time to time reeling with exhaustion.

The rounds followed doggedly one after another, progress slowed because both fighters' fists were broken and bloody and it took greater and greater courage to land a decent punch. Finally Ishmael landed a glancing blow to the jaw and Gypsy Joe, after one final valiant effort, did not get up.

The Market Square resounded with boos and cheers, and clattered with the click of coins landing on the canvas. Ishmael finally allowed his weariness to show as he acknowledged that he had won the fight. He bent to collect his booty, placing half the coins in a neat pile beside the prone body of Gypsy Joe Elliot. Then he came to the side of the ring and spoke to the man with the pigskin gloves, who handed him a round leather purse which he palmed clumsily into the waistband of his sweat-stained breeches.

'Good fight, Ishmael,' said the man, his hands folded again, one over the other, on the knob on his cane.

The fighter met his gaze. 'I would think the betting would be profitable to you, Ned Lumb. Nobody in their right mind would have backed an old hack like me.' The mouth was swollen but the voice was smooth, soft. An outsider would have been surprised at its articulation: more drawing room than boxing ring.

Jossy Gullet, who had shouldered his way to Ned Lumb's side, chuckled. 'By lad, yer don't change, Ishmael. Give no quarter. Never did! Had ter come as soon as I seed the posters.'

A smile lit up Ishmael's battered face. 'While I live, Jossy Gullet!' He turned again to Ned Lumb, wincing slightly as he did so. 'Now here you have a bold fellow, Ned, who knows about this game. I learned all I know from him, bout for bout, in Spitalfield. Fought the great Richmond, didn't you, Jossy?'

Jossy stroked his chin. 'An' got beaten hands down, marrah. Never seen such a fighter. Black as coal, bright as a starry night. Brought out o' the slaves' kitchens in America to fight here by the old Duke o' Northumberland, they say. Little feller, but hard he was, hard as iron.'

'Are you still fighting, Mr Gullet?' asked Ned, the politeness of his question belied by his gaze, which was wandering away into the crowd again, looking for a likely mark.

Jossy roared with laughter. 'Man, I'll be sixty-seven next Easter. Old enough for more sense. Nah. I got myself a pub...'

'Hotel!' interjected Mirella, hard on his elbow. 'The Royal George. Just two minutes from here.'

Jossy grinned. 'An' I got meself a wife who knows how to run a ... hotel. May I present my wife, Mrs Mirella Gullet, who's kept my hands in one piece for ten years now, an' given me two fine children, bless her, to make life worthwhile?'

His wife, a dark voluptuous woman no more than half his age, punched him on the shoulder. 'Don't go on, Jossy. Nice to meet you Mr er ... and Ishmael.'

Ned lifted his hat, his eyes still elsewhere in the crowd. 'Charmed. I'm afraid I'll have to leave you, Ishmael. There's another bout and I have—'

'You go and get your money placed, Ned.' Ishmael looked around. 'I'll have to find somewhere to have a wash, and—'

'Come to the Royal George,' interrupted Mirella, very quickly, her eyes not moving too far from his naked upper body. 'How you can keep standing on your feet I don't know...'

'Yes!' Jossy grinned his gap-toothed grin. 'I wus gunna say come round an' share a drop o' Scotch whisky, Ishmael. For old times' sake.' He draped Ishmael's shirt around his body, shielding it finally from his wife's eager gaze, and put his arm through that of his old friend. 'Come to the Royal George, Ishmael. And welcome too.'

2

At the Royal George

Ishmael winced as the surgeon bound his hands in strips of white cloth. From the other side of the table two pairs of round child-eyes stared at him: a boy with a square head and a girl with wispy hair sticking up from her head like the gossamer seeds of a dandelion.

Ishmael smiled through his pain. 'And how might you be named, my lad?'

The boy took a thumb out of his mouth. 'My name's Gabriel. And she's . . .' He pushed the little girl off the stool and she squealed, '. . . daft. Her name's Esme.'

Mirella Gullet picked up the girl and planted her on the stool again. 'Don't do that, Gabriel,' she said in a distracted voice. She did not comfort her daughter.

Ishmael raised an eyebrow and looked at Jossy.

Jossy chuckled. 'Aye, children of me old age, those two. Why, even Mirella here's no chicken!' He landed an affectionate wallop on his wife's rump.

'Jossy. Behave yourself!' Mirella watched carefully as the surgeon wound Ishmael's bandages. 'Gabriel here's five years old, Mr Slaughter, and the cleverest boy in his class. An' Esme here is a pewling baby still,

11

despite bein' all of three years.'

Ishmael winced again as the surgeon tied his final bow. Then he nodded gravely, not quite sure what to say about these rather unprepossessing children. 'They're the future, Jossy. You're a lucky man.'

'You were not blessed yourself, Mr Slaughter?' said Mirella, complacently adjusting her velvet collar.

'As you say, Mrs Gullet, I wasn't blessed.'

The Royal George Hotel, owned by Mirella and Jossy Gullet, was a superficially genteel hostelry, fronting on to Priorton Market Square. Its Front Rooms, a lounge bar and a commercial bar, had once been finely appointed but were now rather battered. Here self-confident traders, travelling salesmen, and members of the local horse-racing fraternity congregated to discuss affairs of their day: good deals, good bets and occasionally not-so-good women.

Behind these Front Rooms were even more faded Back Rooms, only entered by a side door. Here floated jetsam of this small market town, which was centred on a mining and ironworking district, itself just beginning to boom as the demand for iron and steel blossomed to feed the factories and workshops of the world. At Brack's Hill, only four miles away, the largest steel rolling mill in Europe was under construction. The wives and families of many of the iron-workers would come to the Saturday market in Priorton. And the men would drink in pubs like Jossy Gullet's Royal George and wager their hard-earned money on horses and dogs, foot-runners and fighting cocks.

Ishmael Slaughter, as he boxed his way round the country, had lived in travellers' vans and cheap lodgings. He had once, for a short time, owned a small house in Spitalfields. But he now was glad to accept Jossy Gullet's offer of a home at the Royal George for the eight weeks it took for his hands to heal. In the first two weeks he had to be helped in his eating and dressing, tasks which were willingly fulfilled by the admiring Mirella. As soon as his hands were any use at all Ishmael was helping with all kind of tasks about the hotel. Jossy enjoyed having his old comrade around the place: he relished the opportunity to indulge his penchant for gossip about the sporting world and his nostalgia for the robust, threatening, exciting life of the boxing ring.

Jossy, encouraged by Mirella, urged Ishmael to stay on. 'At least till you're properly fit to fight again, old lad. Somewhere to rest yer 'ead.'

Ishmael shook his head. 'That was my last fight, Jossy, I'm telling you. I only did this last lot of fights, trailing round the North like some ham-fisted donkey, because I needed the money. Ned Lumb wanted a sure bet, matching me against boys who're more fist than brain. Seeing me as an old man, the gamblers think I'm for a fall. But that Gypsy Joe Elliot was a hard nut to crack. Harder than any other I have met.'

Jossy scratched his bald head. With uncharacteristic delicacy he did not question this need for money on the part of a fighter who had won many purses in his time. He knew Ishmael was a restrained man, no drinker or gambler. 'So what'll yer do, marrah?'

Ishmael shrugged then. 'I can mend shoes, Jossy. Even make'm, once my hands're fully healed. You'll remember that was my father's trade?'

Jossy slapped the sturdy table, making Mirella's new china plates jump. 'Then yer s'll stay here, Ishmael, at the Royal George. There's rooms aplenty an' we can jaw on old times when trade's slack. An' yer can mek an' mend yer shoes on the side.'

Ishmael looked around the dark crowded room. 'I'll stay if I can help in some way. Work.'

'Work?' Mirella trilled, fiddling with her new broderie anglaise sleeves. 'There's work for twenty in this place, Mr

Slaughter. And Jossy can't lift a thing since his back stiffened three years ago.' That back-stiffening had coincided with a loss of other powers, which left Mirella Gullet with a raging hunger for a man's touch, which she only just managed to conceal.

In the six months which followed, Ishmael worked for Jossy Gullet and for Mirella. He used his strength to heave barrels, and his massive presence to ensure that the Back Room people stayed just there and did not wander into the Front Rooms. He also prevented any more serious disturbance, particularly on Market Day, when great drinking and consequent fighting frequently occurred.

Wherever he was, Ishmael often found Mirella at his elbow. 'And is there no Mrs Slaughter, Mr Slaughter?' she asked once, not able to believe that such a fine specimen had slipped the matrimonial net. Several times now, she had imagined him naked beside her on the fine bed that had been Jossy's wedding present to her. She wondered if there were scars on that great body from the fighting. Jossy had scars.

Ishmael had nodded slowly at her question. 'Yes. There was a Mrs Slaughter. But she died,' he said. Jayne-Anne had been a milliner, a gossamer fairy of a girl who'd hated the fighting.

Mirella put her head on one side, like a fat pigeon requesting another titbit.

'Consumption,' he growled.

He left it at that. He had, in the end, used all his savings to take Jayne-Anne to a clinic in Germany. And watched her die there. He'd had to fight in fairs in Germany and France to get the money to travel all the way home.

The comradely talks with Jossy before the fire of the Front Room came to an abrupt end in October. Jossy caught typhoid fever in Newcastle, having travelled up there to talk to some people about the purchase of a racehorse. He came back and went to bed and was dead within ten days.

Mirella was dramatically, elaborately 'beside herself' with grief, some of it genuine. After crying solidly for three days she started to tell Ishmael one night how Jossy, a cocky little fighter with gold jingling in his pockets, had come a-courting all those years ago. She had remained unmarried until quite late, keeping the hotel with her widowed father. Jossy was a funny man, lighting up any room he entered. He made her laugh. 'He brought me presents. Exotic things from other countries. Can't think where he got them. Oh, Ishmael!' She threw herself on to him, clutching at his shoulders, her wide skirts swinging round his legs. 'I miss him so.'

After hesitating for a second his arms closed round her and he hugged her to him for sheer comfort. Her stays creaked. Then her spicy sweaty smell filled his nostrils and her lips pressed hard on his.

That night they ended up in Jossy's wide bed, and Ishmael pulled away from her when she fingered the scars on his upper chest. He made love to her as briefly and powerfully as he could, much to her gasping satisfaction, then jumped out of the bed to pull on his breeches.

She put her fleshy arm behind her head, the pull making her heavy breasts move to one side. Her stomach rose white as an egg in the flickering light of the candle. 'Don't go,' she pouted. 'I want you here.'

He tucked in his shirt and pulled on his jacket. 'I'm sorry, Mirella.' He grunted, avoiding her gaze. 'This is not decent. This is all wrong ... wrong, with Jossy not dead ten days.'

She sat up, her slightly greasy curls tumbling about her plump shoulders, and scowled. 'Jossy's been no use to me for years, not since Esme was born.'

He gave her a look of acute dislike. 'Jossy was a fine man,' he said.

She nodded. 'Oh yes, fine man, everybody liked him,' she said bitterly. 'But no use to me.'

15

'I'll have to get away, Mirella. Away from the Royal George. This is all too ... difficult.'

She was out of bed then, clinging to his hand. 'Don't go, Ishmael. Don't go. This need never, never happen ... It can be just like before. I need you here at the Royal George.'

He tried to loosen her grip, but she clung on.

'Jossy would want it,' she pouted. 'He knows I need somebody to look after me.'

He finally managed to get his hand away from hers. 'Well. I'll stay till you ... till you're managing. But not this, Mirella,' he said heavily. 'Not this.'

She pulled on a wrap without fastening it, then nodded. 'All right, Ishmael. None of this.'

He was at the door.

'Ishmael?' she said.

'What?'

'What was your wife's name?'

'Mrs Slaughter,' he said grimly, and the door clashed behind him.

So the two of them fell into an uneasy routine: Ishmael going quietly about his tasks, Mirella watchful and frequently under his feet. The anger and frustration she felt was focused on objects: she broke glasses and plates, clashed pots and pans. She quarrelled with Jossy's barmen, who had served in the Royal George for years, so that they left to work at the Station Hotel and the Phoenix public house. Ishmael put the new barmen in the picture about Mirella's temper, and promised them an extra ten shillings apiece if they stayed for six months.

As well as helping in the Royal George, Ishmael mended shoes for Mirella's customers. It was as a young shoemaker that he had first met Jossy. He had been cheering him on in a fight where the little man's bravery and dogged cunning were winning him a match. It was Jossy who started Ishmael on his long fighting trail, cracking him on his broad back and saying that a well-set-up lad like him would prosper in the ring.

Ishmael's only peace away from Mirella was in the mid-afternoons, between the busy times, when he would take a mug of ale and a plate of meat and make his way out to the stables at the back of the hotel. In this tranquil shady space, with only snuffling horses for company, he would attend methodically to any cobbling waiting for his attention. If there was none, he just sat and watched the movement of shadows in the dust. At least here he didn't have to look behind himself all the time, for the lurking figure of Mirella.

One day in early spring, striding into the stable, he came upon a fine tortoiseshell cat crouched below his cobbler's last. He put out a tentative hand to stroke her, but her ears went back and she spat at him. Even so she didn't run off, just moved two feet away from him and glared. He could see a reflection of himself in her baleful eyes.

'There, beauty,' he said, easing himself on to his stool. 'Did I startle you?' He took some meat from his plate and placed it between his feet. Then he started to work, watching the cat with the corner of his eye. The cat trotted across and put one paw on his boot, pulled delicately at a fragment of meat and then ate it.

Ishmael ignored her, continuing to pare away at a leather sole with his sharp cobbler's knife.

The cat finally finished the meat and settled between his feet. He left her there, surprised how warm her purring presence made him feel. He had never been close to any animal; animals of all kinds had been banned from his father's house. And the mangy hounds that hung around fairs, the poor pathetic bears and the fighting dogs, had always left him unmoved.

The next afternoon as well as meat he brought milk, which the cat lapped up in a second. He fed her in this fashion for a week, then one afternoon he came into the stable to find that the cat was missing. He was amused by his own disappointment, but he sat down to work with his usual steady contentment. After ten minutes there was a rustle and she was gleaming down at him from the top of a stall. 'There, beauty,' he said. 'What is it?'

She mewed and walked the length of the partitions, right to the darkest corner of the stable. He got to his feet and followed her. At first he could see nothing, but then a series of high-pitched squeaks drew him towards the empty stall. He pulled aside some old straw. 'Well, old girl, what have we here?'

There were five of them, delicate mewling things not much bigger than his thumb. Their eyes were still closed. Ishmael laughed out loud. 'Ah, this is what it's about, old girl! I see now! Providing for your family, were you?'

She let him stroke her and her fur felt warm under his hand.

One day when he had settled down to work she brought the kittens to him, one by one. Their eyes were open now, like tiny pansies. There were two tabbies, two tortoiseshells and a white one whose eyes were pink. The mother did not object as he picked up the white one and stroked it with his little finger while the others crawled around at his feet, bumping into his boots and each other, squeaking as they did so.

After that Ishmael walked briskly to his afternoon cobbling, anticipating the pleasure of the cat and her kittens.

One of Ishmael's regular shoe customers was Janine Druce, an occasional customer of the Royal George. Janine was the widow of a Scotch draper, now a draper herself, who travelled the North from the Tweed to the Tees with small bolts of cloth, selling them at markets.

Mirella loathed Janine Druce but Jossy had always had a soft spot for the woman, and wouldn't listen to Mirella when she told him she knew the woman drank, and that, for money, she'd been known to 'oblige' the gentlemen who inhabited the Front Rooms of the Royal George. Mirella was suspicious that Janine Druce may have 'obliged' Jossy at one time, but there was no way of proving it. Pragmatically, though, after Jossy died, the tradeswoman in Mirella accepted Janine. There was no point in turning away such a free-spending customer.

On Thursdays, after closing her stall in the market, when she had some silver in her purse, Janine Druce would sit in the small public lounge at the Royal George, drinking Scotch whisky from a china cup. One day she asked Ishmael to join her and he refused.

'Ye dinnat come fra' round here, mister. Are ye foreign?' she said, picking up the cup and sucking noisily at her drink.

He shook his head, smiling slightly. 'Only if you think London is a foreign land, which some do. But my father was foreign. Came from a place called Riga.'

'Where's that?'

'East. On the way to Russia.'

She screwed up her eyes and looked at him. 'Sit down and talk tae us, will ye? Tell us about London. Ah've had a hard day out there on the market and at ma house there'll be nae talk.'

She was as insistent as Mirella in her own way, but Ishmael felt much easier with her. He slipped on to the bench opposite her. 'You live alone?'

She shook her head in the exaggerated fashion of those just on the brink of drunkenness. 'No. No. I live wi' ma son, Thomas. He's a big lad. Fit as a butcher's dog. Handsome as a prince. But will he talk? Will he hell! Pardon me. That's ma husband. A very profane man, ma husband.'

'You live with him too?'

She shook her head mournfully. 'Very profane and very dead. That's ma husband.' She hiccoughed and stood up unsteadily.

He walked with her to the door and watched as she made her meandering way through the late-night crowds.

After that, he found himself watching out for the Scotch draper woman late on Thursdays. Once he was even obliged to carry Mrs Druce bodily to the narrow house where she rented rooms. He leaned her up beside the door, rattled the catch and left her, ignoring her plaintive calls which pursued him down the narrow street.

Except when talking to Janine Druce, Ishmael was dour and uncommunicative. He was wary of any word or act of goodwill towards Mirella; every time he did the smallest thing for her, she was too eager to capitalise on it, to get nearer to him.

During the third and fourth weeks of April the rain poured down on Priorton, making the grey stone houses greyer and transforming the packed earth of the narrow back streets into liquid mud. The downpour was dreary and unremitting.

Ishmael started to ponder on the fact that he had been here nearly a year, which was much longer than he had intended. Despite the weather, he still plodded across the hotel yard in his great boots to tend to the kittens, under the guise of doing his cobbling. Mirella watched through a streaming window as he made his way yet again across to the stable. What on earth made him leave the warmth of the hotel kitchen for that draughty place?

Gabriel, standing on a chair before the window, looked up at his mother and put his head on one side. 'Mr Slaughter has kittens, Mamma,' he announced. 'I seed them. Crawly things.'

The next day Ishmael made his way across to the stables as usual, to find the mother cat mewing anxiously. She leaped towards him and wound herself round his legs, nearly tripping him up. 'What is it, beauty?' he murmured, catching her concern.

She led the way to a corner of the yard which housed the

water pump. Beneath there was an old tin bath and in it, moving gently as the wind caught the top of the water, were the bodies of the kittens.

'Mirella!' Ishmael roared, the very sinews of his back and his chest tightening.

She was at the kitchen door. 'We want nothing with kittens here, Ishmael. Jossy never liked cats. Only ever tolerated one as a mouser. They'd've been running all over the place in a week or two, we couldn't—' She ducked as his fist came towards her but breathed again as it crashed harmlessly on the door above her head.

He turned on his heel and marched away. Away from the woman with her prattling voice; away from his own temptation to harm her. He was desperate to get her noise, her presence out of his head, afraid of the violence within himself which would lead him to strike her, even kill her.

He strode down the bank, out of the town, on to the river-meadow, his head swirling with potent and lethal aggression – the very *berserk* quality nurtured by Ned Lumb, which had brought so many victories for Ishmael – and so many sovereigns for Ned's own capacious pocket.

Ishmael made his way under the rearing cathedral height of the new railway viaduct and, in an attempt to cool his boiling rage, plodged up to his waist in the swirling river, swollen now by three days' solid rain. Around him the rain suddenly stopped patting the surface of the water, and above him a watery sun filtered its opal gleam through a patch of blue sky.

A high-pitched sound pierced the sullen roar of the water, reminding him of his lost kittens. He looked upward and put out a great hand to ward off a missile which came hurtling down off the parapet of the viaduct. The missile plopped into the water and he reached out and grasped it before it was swept away.

The thing was wrapped in a sodden patterned cloth. He wiped a hand down his coat and drew the cloth aside, then he smiled. It was no kitten, but a bundled baby, red-faced and roaring for all she was worth. Ishmael pulled her to him and tied her inside his coat with his scarf. The roaring subsided to a mewling wail. He looked upwards into the grey, shimmering sky and ran to clamber up the side of the viaduct, only stopping when he reached the parapet.

The viaduct was deserted, its iron tracks glittering in the drenched sunshine. He peered over the parapet, down towards the swirling river, to the place whence he had come. There was no sign of anyone. Then he scanned the riverbank and there, curving over the snaking river, was a rainbow, mirrored within and without with paler images of itself.

'Three!' he whispered. One hand moved to the soaking head of the baby. 'A triple rainbow.'

The little creature had now stopped wailing altogether, and was almost jumping out of Ishmael's coat, hiccoughing violently against his chest. He stroked the streaming hair away from the fat peachy face, soothing her clumsily. He thought of the kittens. 'Can't take you back to the George, little one. Take you back there, and that silly old bird'll have you drowned in the tub like the kittens.'

His feet dragged as he walked slowly back into the town, pondering on just what he was supposed to do with this little dripping, hiccoughing kittenish creature.

Janine Druce surveyed the blank, beautiful face before her, and held up a fustian jacket, ripped from collar to hem, its lining falling out. 'Who did this, who did this?'

Her son lifted his head but did not look at her. Thomas Druce never looked directly at his mother nor anyone else. His own violet eyes were darkening now to dense black, his face smooth and expressionless.

She shook his thin shoulders hard. His body flopped underneath her hand. She slapped his face. 'Ye dinnet know? Then say "no". Just say "no" to me!' Her hand dropped and she pushed her heavy unkempt hair back over her shoulder. 'Will ye not even shake your head at me? If you canna say "no", why can't you show "no"? Ye let those lads dae this to ye, ye'll let them throw ye in the mud, spit on ye and worse . . .'

Her son stared steadily over her shoulder.

Now her hand dropped to her side and the jacket fell on to the dusty floor. 'Aw, son, what do ye know about anything?' She pushed him into his chair and sighed. 'Ye sit down and get your dinner.'

Before she had had her son Janine had never loved any human being in her life, not even Johnnie Druce who'd married her to get an extra pair of hands to help on his drapery stall. Not any of the men she had fallen into bed with since.

She did not know how she conceived him, this beautiful imbecile. He wasn't anything to do with Johnnie Druce, who was never interested in bed after he had that run-in with some drunken miners in Barnsley, which had left him somewhat lumbered in the trouser department. It could have been that Dublin man, that traveller in fancies, who had lain in wait for her one Market Day. But she looked now at Thomas's smooth brown hands, the fine delicate face, the black springing hair. No. Most probably it would be that man out of North Shields, who was so kind, who took her into his dockland shack when Johnnie beat her up, that time his horses lost at Newmarket.

She was forced out of her reverie by a great rattle on the door. She opened it to Ishmael Slaughter.

'Can I come in, Mrs Druce?'

As she opened the door wider, she noticed the bulge in his jerkin: a parcel of some kind, perhaps; a small creature like a puppy. 'What is it ye have there, Mr Slaughter?'

He reached behind him and loosened off his scarf, then very gently lifted his burden into the dust-filtered light by the window. Janine fell back as the small round child's face looked back at her with bright watchful eyes, more lively than those of the seven-year-old Thomas, now stolidly eating his dinner, unmoved by and uninterested in the interruption.

'What in heaven's name is this? Look, the bairn's soaked.' As if hearing her, the baby started to whimper, then cry. Janine took her from Ishmael and brought her by the fire.

'I got her from the river. Caught her like a flying salmon. She landed in the river and almost bounced. Someone threw her. Threw her away like so much rubbish.'

'Her? How would ye know it was a—'

'Look at her face, Mrs Druce. She has a girl's face.'

Janine shook her head stubbornly. 'There's nae tellin' that from the face.'

'Find out then,' he said, tying his wet scarf round his neck again.

Any other woman would have been embarrassed at this but Janine lifted the long dripping undergarments, peered in, and snorted. 'Ye're right, Mr Slaughter. But look, these things are soaking wet.' She sat down in a chair by the fire, and started to strip the child completely of the pretty blue patterned shawl in which she was wrapped, and her sodden clothes. 'Reach me that towel and the shawl beside it, Mr Slaughter.' She nodded at the items, hung to dry on a string over the fireplace.

He handed them to her and she rubbed the baby all over with the towel. The little girl stopped crying and started to chuckle. Janine looked down at her, a smile coming unbidden to her own lips. She was not used to this. Thomas had never, in his whole life, chuckled at anything.

Ishmael was smiling as well. 'She's lively,' he said. 'How old, do you think, Mrs Druce?'

'Three, four months...'

'Ah! Christmas baby!' He put a finger on her cheek.

Janine stood up and laid the shawl on the table, then the

baby flat on top of it, ready to swaddle her in the traditional way. A fat leg flew out and knocked Thomas's thick pottery soup bowl to the floor. The boy looked up in surprise, a sudden light in his eyes, the faintest shadow of a smile on his lips.

Janine felt a ripple of shock go through her. She thrust the baby towards her son. 'Here, Thomas, see the baby. Isn't she nice?'

He didn't look at the child, but he did put a hand out, touch the leg which had disposed of his dinner and nod very slightly.

Janine looked at Ishmael. 'Ye'll be on your way to the constable with this wee'n, nae doubt. They'll have to find her a place in yon Union.'

He shook his head. 'She's going to no workhouse.'

'Then what might ye be proposin' for her?' she said, roughly thrusting the swaddled baby towards him.

He pushed the baby back into her arms. 'I want you to mind her, Mrs Druce. To have her. To take care of her.'

She thrust the bundle at him again. 'Unusual humour ye have on ye, Mr Slaughter. Ah've to mind this bairn of my own, fey as a grasshopper, as well as my rounds and the markets to do. All this means Ah've to leave him wi' ma neighbour Mrs Gordon. How can Ah mind any baby?'

'The boy liked her. You could see that.'

'The boy likes nothing. Doesnae ken his arse from his elbow. A block of lard from a toffee apple. How could he like a scrap like that?'

'He smiled.'

'He did not. He never smiles. Wind from great gulps of ma broth.' But her voice was faltering.

'How much do you make from your rounds?' Ishmael gave the baby his knuckle to suck.

She bridled. 'That's not for ye to know.'

'Well, if I gave you two guineas a week, could you just do

Priorton Market and the shops here? Take the little one with you. You'd see more of the boy too...'

She looked at him uncertainly. 'How do Ah know ye've got such moneys?'

He shrugged. 'I've saved most of every purse I've won since ... since I got back to England after going off to Germany one time. And I get paid by Mrs Gullet. And I earn money from the shoes. You'll get your money, Mrs Druce. You can be as sure of that as you can of the sun rising.' With utmost confidence he put the bundle back in her arms.

The baby, deprived of Ishmael's knuckle, started to whimper again. Janine rocked her to and fro. 'She'll need milk.'

'I'll get some.'

'No, let me. She'll need some kind of titty-bottle too. Ah'll go round to Mrs Gordon's. Ah'll tell her the bairn's my sister's, or the constable'll be round here willy-nilly and have her in the Union.' She paused. 'Ah'll need money right off, mind you.'

Ishmael nodded slowly. 'Just two things, Mrs Druce. I want neither her, nor any other in this town, to know the manner of her finding. Too many questions will be asked.'

'And the second?'

'No whisky, Mrs Druce. No bawling in the streets; no rolling in the gutters. All that might make no difference to that fey son of yours. But with the babe here, all that stops.'

Janine's eyes narrowed as she calculated the benefits to herself. Suddenly Thomas was at her knee, and, without looking directly at the child, had put his knuckle in the soft open mouth in imitation of Ishmael's earlier action.

'Ah'll dae it,' said Janine Druce. 'It might be just the thing for me and Thomas. A change from the driftin'.'

'There is a third thing,' he said. 'You must never come in or near the Royal George. Not ever. I must be a stranger to her, or Mrs Gullet might get ideas. Don't forget this.' He paused. 'And she has a name.'

'And what might that be?'

'She's to be called Kitty Rainbow. No other name. Kitty Rainbow.'

3

The Scrapper

May 1868
Kitty Rainbow decided that walking backwards gave you a whole new view of things. Of course, to keep things in balance, you had to walk backwards for a hundred steps, then turn round and walk forwards for a hundred steps.

Kitty quite liked the backwards world.

Everything looked so different. When you walked backwards, things wrapped sideways into your vision; you could see the whole tapestry rather than bits of stitching. In this backwards world the public houses on the street corners leaned in on you like bulky appliqué; the great hills beyond the street ends looked like green worsted against the stretching landscape of grey-flannel houses, black-velvet pit gantries and a purplish gauzy mass hovering over the coke ovens.

Kitty had played with cloth since she was three years old, when her foster-mother, whom she called Antijan, had plonked her on the shop floor while she was busy with her customers. Kitty was set to practise clumsy stitches in a dozen different kinds of cloth. Not that there was much cloth to stitch these days. One by one, the bolts of cloth had been used up. And they would not be replaced, as Antijan had not managed to pay a supplier's bill for six months.

Kitty liked to wander. Today, the sight of the limping figure of the diminutive six-year-old, waving her hands in the air stroking the imaginary cloth of the landscape, was causing amusement among some Priorton women, who had paused for chat between pegging out the washing and getting their men's dinner on.

The women shook their heads. Mad! Weren't they all mad in that household? That Scotch draper woman, nice as ninepence doing business with you one day and in a rage through the drink the next.

They nodded sagely. That Janine Druce should be well off, but didn't the money go on the bottle rather than the bairns' backs? And then there was that mad boy Thomas lurking on corner ends! No wonder he got a good belting now and then, skulking around like that.

And this little lass! Kitty Rainbow. Queer name that. It was whispered that no priest had christened her. The *niece*, according to Mrs Druce. Well, that's as may be. What counted as family on these back streets of Priorton was something of an elastic notion these days: brothers, lodgers, uncles were being squeezed into every household now, to take advantage of the flush of work that was about. Then there were children of all ages, some of whom were known to share a father and be mothered by their sisters.

'Ninety-nine, a hundred...' Kitty turned around, tripped on an upright stone set on the corner of Salvin Row, and went sprawling. She was winded, but laughed as she hauled herself to her knees, clinging to the stone. Not for the first time she fingered the strange marks, lines and furrows on its worn surface.

She sat on the stone and spread her meagre skirts around her, flexing her toes in the dirt, luxuriating in delight at the brightness and warmth of the May day.

Then her attention was caught by yells and shrieks from

her left, behind Salvin Row. She jumped to her feet, keen to find out what was up.

To the rear of Salvin Row was a dilapidated stretch of land called The Green, where chickens roosted and pigs roamed during the day in snouting freedom, only to be clapped up at night in makeshift huts which were scattered about like pockmarks. The Green was slung about with washing lines and criss-crossed with footpaths, constructed through the years by the various needs of people and dogs, pigs and cats, even the occasional sheep, making pathways to their work, to their play, to food, to warmth.

Turning round the corner of one of the huts Kitty came upon a group of boys dressed in some kind of uniform. They were pushing a spindly girl from one to the other; her loosened white hair ribbons were streaming behind her. Some of the boys were barking like dogs. Others were shouting, 'Spindleshanks! Bag-of-sticks!' as they pushed the crying girl between them.

The boy shouting the loudest was tall and heavily built, perhaps thirteen years old, with thick hair cut in a straight line above his square brow.

Kitty got her eye on him, put her head down and charged, catching him in the side and bowling him over. Then she turned to face the others. 'Leave her! Leave that lass alone!' she shrieked.

For a second the boys stood back in amazement. The spindly girl fled.

Then the gang were on to Kitty, lifting her bodily and throwing her from one to the other, until finally she was thrust towards the boy she had felled. He punched her hard in the face. At that point the watching women came out of their backyards brandishing brooms, yelling at the boys to get off the bairn, get off the bairn.

The boys ran off and one of the women pulled Kitty to her feet, wiping the child's bloody face with her pinny. 'By, yer have a good heart, hinney, but yer want nowt settin' up against big lads like that. Them Grammar School lads, they're the very devil. Torment anything: queen, cat or canary.'

Kitty, holding her breath to stop the tears coming, stood still, swaying, then collapsed against a washing post. 'They were gettin' on to that girl. She had white ribbons. So I . . .'

'Aye, but ye'd be better off leavin' her ter fend for herself, hinney.' The woman looked round. 'Now where is it yer live, pet? Aren't you Mrs Druce's . . . ?'

'I'm all right, missis. Here's my brother. Thomas!' she yelled.

Thomas, always fifty paces behind her wherever she went, came shambling up.

'Crouch down!' she ordered in the loud voice, imitated from Antijan, which was the only thing he would obey.

He did so. She clambered on to his back. 'Will you put his hands round my legs, missis? He won't think to do it.'

The woman did as she was told.

'Now stand up and take us home,' shouted Kitty into Thomas's ear. He set off at a lumbering pace with her sprawled on his back.

She grinned sideways at the woman. 'Thank you, missis!' Her voice was muffled, but filled with triumph.

The women stood a moment, leaning on their brooms, watching the clumsy figure with its lighter burden.

'Well, May,' said one to the other, 'isn't that a bliddy lovely sight? A bairn with the heart of a lion on the back of an idiot?'

As the train made its way home from Darlington Mirella Gullet waited for a favourite point in the journey, where the train entered Shotwell Tunnel. Here the dense darkness transformed the window into a mirror where she could glimpse again her own reflection. She touched the little porkpie hat set at a fine angle over her low chignon. Curls were more fashionable now; she wondered if she should try them. Would Ishmael like them? Jossy always said she had wonderful hair.

Her new purple gown, though, was the height of fashion, with its high waist and narrow skirt tucked up at the back to show the embroidered yellow underskirt. Nobody in Priorton was into that style yet, although she'd seen a woman on High Row in Darlington just today wearing something very similar.

Ishmael was not there at Priorton Station to meet her with the trap, despite it being firmly arranged. He was a law unto himself, that man. Scowling, she scrambled on to the step of Seppy Cornforth's rather grand hansom cab, hauling her shopping with her. Seppy was proud of his vehicle but expected robust independence of his passengers.

Jolting along the half-made road surface, Mirella wondered who worked for who at the Royal George. Through the seven years he had been with her, Ishmael had taken on more and more of the work in the hotel. As well as keeping order, nowadays he did the ordering, paid the scrubbing women and the barmen, kept the books in his neat fine hand, painted and decorated, mended and fixed. The Royal George was a much sounder place than when Jossy had died.

Mirella settled back in the rattling cab, smoothing down her plum velvet cape. And there was more. From time to time, when her nerves were at jangling screaming pitch Ishmael would slip into her bed at night and hold her close, stroking and calming her as though she were a bolting horse. She had learned from him not to take these occasions for more than they were; not to assume they presaged further and more publicly declared intimacies; not to overstep the line he had so carefully and deliberately drawn.

She'd had her offers, from several prominent men from the thriving commercial world of Priorton. These substantial men had their eyes on her widow's mite, and thought that alliances between the Royal George and some grocery store or paper mill would make commercial sense. But for once in her life Mirella was uninterested in 'commercial sense'. All her efforts went towards keeping Ishmael Slaughter close by her side.

Her thoughts returned to the present. She leaned forward to get a better view of the path, then knocked upwards with her purple parasol to get Seppy Cornforth's wandering attention. The cab stopped beside the bedraggled figure of Mirella's daughter, Esme, who was walking in the road, head down, her neat boots muddy and her white ribbons trailing down her back. 'Get in here, Esme. What on earth's been happening to you?'

'Nothing, Mama, nothing at all. I just fell down in the back lane. I just fell down.'

Mirella sighed heavily as she reached down to haul her daughter on to the hard seat beside her, regretting as usual her daughter's lack of sparkle, her whining immature presence.

Janine Druce had had a hard day. Business in her little shop in the shambles under the Market Cross had been slow: one plaid dress length and a packet of pins. And no cash. The cloth was 'on tick' to a dressmaker, who would pay Janine when she in turn got paid.

Janine shot the bolt in the narrow front door and made her way to the little back room which served as extra store, kitchen and living room all in one. She reached into the old cupboard by the range and pulled out a bottle which was disappointingly empty. She shook it and held it up to the light from the dusty window. She couldn't remember finishing it. Perhaps the girl had got at it.

Janine shook her head. No, Kitty Rainbow might be a defiant handful but she was not deceitful. Hide it, yes. Drink it, no. Half the beatings the child got, half the trouble into which she fell, were caused by the fact that she would not back down, would not dissemble just a little to make the other person feel better. And Janine thought that she should know, as she herself was mostly the 'other person'.

She felt in her apron pocket, brought out a single penny and pushed it back again. Ishmael's two guineas, delivered faithfully last Friday, as every Friday, by a messenger boy, seemed always to have melted away by Monday. Once the rent and her bill in the tick-book at Clintock's had been paid, there was little enough to buy anything extra. She was hard put to afford a little comfort herself; Saturday night in the snug of the Centurion, with a little bottle of something to take home. It had to be gin now, for the sake of economy. Then the long wait for Friday again.

Since the day she and Ishmael had made their pact Janine had kept their agreement and never ventured near the Royal George. She had caught sight of his massive figure once or twice on Market Day, but each time she was in that state of drunkenness when matters and their consequences were only too clear, so she had turned down an alleyway to avoid him. Avoiding him was not difficult these days. Priorton was humming with people from the mining villages which spread out from Priorton like stars in a firmament; miners were earning decent money and, thinking the good days might soon end, were keen to spend it. She thought wistfully of the quantities of cloth and patterns she could sell to the wives of the miners and farmers if only her suppliers would let her have more cloth. But they were very stubborn.

At first, she'd thought it was a good idea to come off the road and the markets, into the little ramshackle shop. Ishmael's bit of money had made that possible. It was warm inside, and, from the first, the girl had taken a bit of watching. And young as she was, she wasn't bad with a needle, and that could be handy sometimes. But she had a temper and will of her own. Janine felt she had her work cut out, what with Kitty Rainbow and her own Thomas.

She sighed, pushed the kettle further into the heart of the coal, and measured out the last of her precious tea.

Good thing young Thomas had taken to Kitty Rainbow. Followed her around like a sheep, he did. But there was something about the girl that made Janine edgy. She seemed to know more than she should about everything. Janine's mother would have said she had an 'ould soul'. Worst of all, Kitty would hide gin bottles in difficult places and stand in front of Thomas when Janine, in one of her rages, was consumed by the desire to pummel him into the earth. So Janine was denied even that relief.

She was just scalding the tea leaves when there was a shuffling and kicking at the back door. She went to open it, then drew back with a shriek as Kitty tumbled to the floor from Thomas's back. Janine looked from the bloody battered child to Thomas, who had Kitty's blood trickling down his cheek. 'What's this, what's this? What in Jerusalem have ye been doing today, ye little witch? Have ye got our Thomas in a fight?'

Kitty was watching her warily, her hand on her nose, which had started bleeding again. 'I stopped a fight, Antijan, didn't start one . . .'

'Stopped a fight?' Janine shouted. 'Looks like ye started a war.' She picked up the broom from the corner and started to lay about in the direction of the ducking Kitty. 'Look at the state of our Thomas, blood all over him. Look at the poor bugger. Knows no better and ye get him in a fight.'

'No, Antijan, it wasn't like that.' Even as she spoke, Kitty ducked and dived. Finally, she waited until the broom was at the bottom of its arc and caught hold of it. She wrenched it from the hands of the surprised Janine, shouting at her to 'Leave off, you old cow, leave off!' Then she held it before herself, ready to fend off any further attack.

Janine, unable to strike out, railed on at Kitty, her voice shrieking higher and higher.

'No!' Thomas roared, a sound more animal than human. 'No!'

Startled, Janine stopped her tirade and Kitty dropped the brush. They looked at Thomas who was sitting on a stool staring at the floor, rocking himself backwards and forwards, his hands over his ears, muttering now, 'No-no-no-no-no—'

'That's it.' Janine leaned over and whisked the broom away from Kitty, then grabbed her by the back straps of her pinny. 'You can come with me, miss. It's time you went back where you came from.'

Submitting herself to being hauled across the Market Square, her feet barely scraping the ground, Kitty thought about Thomas, trailing behind them. Never in all of her life had she heard him say a word. She had sat with him many times, her face close to his, trying to make him say even the simplest of words, but the most she ever achieved was a sly sideways look, or a half-smile focused somewhere over her shoulder.

Janine hauled Kitty down the side entry to the Royal George. Without any ceremony she dragged her into the big kitchen and threw her into the centre of the room.

A man, sitting at the table adding columns of figures in a notebook, rose to his feet.

'Ah, Mrs Druce!'

He was the biggest man Kitty had ever seen, as big as those hills outside Priorton she had spied on earlier, on her backwards walk. He had long flowing silver hair and a black and silver beard, and great black brows under which he was now peering.

Swallowing hard to moisten her suddenly dry mouth, she gave the man look for look. But, for the very first time in her short life Kitty Rainbow felt a thread of fear before another human being. What was Antijan up to? What would this mountain of a man do to her?

4

The Beating of the Drum

'There! She's yours. See what you can do with her, she'll do nothin' that I tell her.'

Janine poked Kitty in the back and the girl limped forward, clenching her hands to stop them trembling. Her sore nose itched in the heat of the vast pub kitchen, tickled by the smell of something spicy on the stove and the sour stench of beer seeping in from the Front Rooms.

Janine stood with her hands on her hips. 'The wee'n's your responsibility, Ishmael. Nae money's worth the trouble she brings tae my door. Fightin', settin' up cheek to all an' sundry, causin' havoc. She'll not keep a pair of shoes on her feet, nor wash her face. Eatin' me out of house and home on top of all that. Ah'll be in the workhouse before long.' She folded her arms and glowered at him.

Ishmael looked down at Kitty's defiant face, her ragged clothes and her bare feet, one arched too high and turned slightly inward. He stroked his beard then frowned at Janine. 'I'd have thought the shop's doing all right now, Janine Druce. All right enough to put shoes on this child's feet.' His voice was soft, its articulation very distinct. 'These are prosperous times. Those cotton workers may be laid off

39

in Lancashire but the collieries and ironworks are going full pelt across here. There's a fair deal of money around for fancy cloth.'

'All right for some. Ma suppliers won't supply me. Ah've got nae stock tae sell. Ah need to get new suppliers, ones that dinnat dun yer for payment every five minutes.'

'I wonder why that is, Mrs Druce? Why do they dun you for payment so hard? Are you a bad payer?' His tone was harder and his use of her title made her blink. His glance dropped to the child. 'Come here, Kitty Rainbow, so that I can see you properly.'

He turned Kitty to the gauzy light coming through the window. The hand on her shoulder was as light as a feather, as big as a frying pan. He peered into her battered face and his knobbly fingers grasped her more tightly. 'Have you been doing this, Janine? Good God, woman . . .'

'Not me. Ah told yer. She gets into fights.'

Kitty put up her chin. 'Antijan didn't do it. A lad did. One I was fightin' with.' She had to crick her neck to stare defiantly at this giant of a man.

He nodded and looked towards Janine, one eyebrow raised.

She shrugged. 'Ah told yer. Ah can dae nothin' wi' the lassie. Somethin' in the blood.'

Kitty cocked her ear. What was the matter with her blood?

'Yeh'll have ter take her back, Ishmael,' Janine sniffed.

Kitty frowned. Back where? Where had she come from? Who did she belong to?

'Back where?' The words came out of Kitty's mouth. They both looked at her. 'Back where, Antijan?' She fixed Janine with a stony gaze.

'He brought you to me, Kitty.' Janine's tone was softer now as she remembered the little scrap, growing brighter by the day, more responsive from the first than her own

Thomas had ever been. 'Yer were verra small. A wee thing. Ishmael brought yer to me to take care of.'

Kitty turned her gaze to Ishmael. 'Where from?' she demanded.

He stroked his beard. 'You came to me, wrapped in a shawl, at the end of the rainbow, one wet afternoon,' he said.

She scowled at him. 'That's a story, just a story.' She threw a punch at him which he easily caught.

'Steady now, child,' he said.

'See?' said Janine, spiteful again. 'There's no holdin' the lassie. Ah've tried the belt, an' me slipper, but she just pops up like a cork in a barrel. Ye'll have ter have her wi' you.'

An image surged before Ishmael of the dead kittens bobbing about in the rusty tin bath. He shook his head. 'It's not appropriate, Janine. Mrs Gullett ... she would not permit it.'

Kitty closed her lids and spiky red and silver stars shot across her inside eye. She could hear her own heart beating, boom boom boom. The stars dissolved, to be replaced by what looked like a solid mop-head beating a round silver disc. Boom boom boom. She put her hands on her ears to shut out the sound, then twisted out of Ishmael's grasp, to look behind her and see if she could see the drummer.

She opened her eyes. There was no drummer here in this vast cluttered kitchen.

Her eye lit on Thomas, who had eventually arrived and was reaching for a squeezebox which was lying on top of other debris in a barrel in the corner of the kitchen. He picked it up, and it swung free in his hand, wheezing a little. He caught the other end and squeezed the thing between his large smooth hands, making the hard green tiles on the wall reverberate with a reedy, whistling sound.

'Put that thing down, Thomas,' said Janine automatically, but he took no notice, vigorously squeezing it in and out, his face expressionless.

The scullery door clashed and Mirella Gullet bustled in with Esme in tow. 'Ishmael, I thought you might come and collect me from the station. We did agree . . .' She paused.

Thomas stopped playing and his eye fixed on the wall beside him, the squeezebox swinging again from one hand.

'Ah, Ishmael. I see you've got visitors.' Mirella smiled at Janine, but her eyes under her beetle brows were cold. She remembered this woman. Never forgot a good customer, did Mirella, though this one had gone downhill; she was unkempt and dishevelled.

Even so, Mirella could scent competition. Slowly she peeled off her gloves, slipped out of her velvet cape, then smoothed it over her arm. 'It's Mrs Druce, isn't it? You travelled in cloth and stayed at the Royal George a few times, if I remember rightly. That must be a few years back now. And then didn't you work for Mr Long, on the corner of the market?'

She didn't miss much, the old trout, thought Janine. Sound memory's a good thing in her trade, I suppose. That time at Long's Emporium had been a disaster. The old boot was so prim and proper when he was acting the boss. Not so with his braces down in Janine's back room, though. That came to an end, of course. Jack Long'd been frightened as a tender cat when his wife caught wind of his fancy for the Scotch draper widow . . .

Mirella's heavy voice was driving on. 'Haven't you got that little shop now, Mrs Druce, under the arches on Back Lane? Myself, of course, I go to Darlington these days for all my stuff. Grenadine, French merino, you just can't get it here in Priorton. And curtain damask. There's no choice at all. And the train's so convenient, don't you think?' Her eye dropped to the scruffy child standing just before Ishmael: spiky black hair which looked just as though it'd been cut with a knife and fork, and impudent silvery eyes daring to meet hers before they slid to Esme, standing frozen at her side. 'And who might this be?'

Kitty felt Janine's hand pulling at her so she was backed right on to Janine's hard chest, and felt a scrawny protective arm around her. 'Ah know for a fact, Mrs Gullet, that yer kin get grenadine and silk merino at Mr Long's. Yer could save yerself the ticket money.' Then she could not resist the lie. 'An' if you took a walk down Back Lane to mine, you'd find that I've got the best stock in County Durham, of maroons and damasks, as well as calicos, flannels, linens, ticks, counterpanes, towellings, sheetings and oilcloths . . .' Her voice faded at Mirella's smirking face. 'Anyway, this is ma niece Kitty Rainbow. Ah'd say, Mrs Gullet, there's naething you could get in Darlington you couldnae get at my shop, like. Or even down at Jack Long's. All front, he is, though. Ah've the same suppliers as them big stores.' She was gabbling. The rage was building up in her again and she needed a drink to calm it down.

Mirella smiled at her. 'Can you get shoes, Mrs Druce, in Priorton? There are several fine shoe shops in Darlington.' She looked pointedly at Kitty's dirty bare feet. 'Perhaps we could look out some of our Esme's old ones. A shame for any child to go barefoot.'

Kitty's eyes were fixed on Esme standing like a frozen rabbit beside her mother. The rag-set curls now in disarray, the streaming white ribbons, the fragile arms and legs – this was the spindly girl who had been tormented by the boys, the one whose cries had brought her running.

Esme returned Kitty's look with an agonised glance and shook her head very slightly. Kitty's eyes narrowed but she said nothing. While the sparring talk went on over their heads she surveyed Esme's fancy clothes with a clinical eye: the white gloves, the shiny buttoned boots fashioned in soft black leather, and the bushy, ringleted hair which made her look even more scrawny.

The scullery door clashed again. Kitty blinked. Before her stood the heavy boy, Gabe, ringleader of the boys who had tormented Esme and beat herself.

Mirella turned towards him, her frozen face melting into a genuinely fond smile. 'Gabriel, this is—'

Gabriel Gullet marched straight across and snatched at the squeezebox, knocking the passive Thomas against the wall as he did so. Thomas stayed where he was thrust and very gently started to knock his forehead on the wall.

Kitty wrestled away from Janine and launched herself at Gabriel, screaming, 'Leave him alone, leave him alone!'

The women set about disentangling the wrestling boy and girl, Mirella crying with dismay and Janine uttering little squeaking noises of annoyance. Ishmael, standing with his great arms folded, left them to it, his face impassive.

Esme ignored all this, her fascinated attention on Thomas, who had stopped banging his head on the wall and, quietly smiling, picked up the squeezebox again.

'Out!' Mirella clasped Gabriel to her heaving bosom. 'Out! Get that guttersnipe and her so-called aunt and her idiot son out of my kitchen, Ishmael!'

Esme clasped her mother's elbow. 'No, Mamma. No!'

They all looked at the girl in surprise.

'What is it, Esme?' said Mirella, furious at being distracted from her righteous anger.

'She saved me. That little girl saved me. Gabriel and those boys from school were ragging me, calling me spindleshanks, and . . .' She was sobbing and gulping at the same time. 'The little girl came in and stopped them.' She raised her head to Gabriel and took a deep, hiccoughing breath. 'She knocked him down, flat,' she said scornfully.

'Esme, how can you say such a thing?' Mirella clasped Gabriel even closer to her and he wriggled against her throttling embrace.

Ishmael whistled.

Janine smirked. 'Ah know Kitty isn't yer own child, but she should be, Ishmael. She's a scrapper if ever Ah saw one.'

Free of his mother, Gabriel curled his fists, standing

44

before his sister in a fighter's stance. 'She did not knock me down.'

'She did so.'

'Course I did,' said Kitty, shrugging off Janine's restraining hand. 'The lad fell flat on his face. Flat as a pancake.'

The silence that followed was broken by a great wheezing squeezebox chord, struck by Thomas's fumbling fingers.

Mirella now assumed a great calm. She stroked her hands down her embroidered skirt, 'Well, Ishmael, I've my shopping to see to. Gabriel! Esme!' She paused. 'I can see you would have trouble getting the girl shoes, Mrs Druce, her being a cripple an' all.' Then she sailed out of the kitchen, pushing a protesting Gabriel before her.

Esme trailed after her, casting one last look at Kitty, who raised a hand to give her a discreet waist-high wave as she departed, to what they both knew would be some kind of reckoning. Whether the reckoning would be with Mirella or Gabriel, Kitty was unsure.

Ishmael turned to Janine. 'You're right, Janine, she's quite a scrapper, the child.'

Kitty stood squarely before him. 'Will you stop talkin' about me like I'm a dog or something, mister? I'm here, you know. I'm here.'

He chuckled. 'Oh yes, Kitty Rainbow, I know that you're here. We all know that. Young Gabriel certainly knows it!'

'It's no laughing matter, Ishmael. Ye can see what she's like. A little wildcat,' said Janine, grim again. 'Ye've got tae do something about her.'

'Is it more money you want, Janine?'

'Money?' said Kitty.

'No.' Wearily Janine pushed her hair back into her cap. 'I canna keep up with her. She takes things in the house an' hides them...' She didn't mention that it was gin that the child hid. 'An' Thomas was with her this afternoon. He gets hit in these scraps.'

'It seems to me that she was protecting him, Janine.'

Janine shook her head stubbornly. 'I'm at the end of me tether, Ishmael. Stuck in that hole of a shop. I'll dae better on the road. Get some new suppliers.'

'What of the boy?'

'I'll take him with me. He can lift things if he's pushed.'

'Take the girl with you.'

'What? I'll be chasing her all over the Northern Counties, following a trail of broken heads.'

Kitty was on Janine then, pummelling away at her. 'No, Antijan! What're you saying? I can't...'

Janine held her off, then thrust her towards Ishmael. 'Here. She's yours.'

She grabbed Thomas by the hand and pulled him through the back door. Kitty made to go after them but was hauled back by Ishmael. The door clashed and he turned her to face him.

She shivered, taking very deep breaths to stop the tears coming to her eyes.

He pushed the straggling hair from her scowling face. 'Now then, little Kitty. Just what are we going to do about you?'

5

A Pair of Green Slippers

'Leave?' Mirella stood up violently, upscuttling her small desk and dispersing her neat piles of money all across the 'turkey' carpet. Ishmael put the desk to rights and joined her in the scramble on the floor to retrieve her pennies and ha'pennies, her florins and guineas.

Sitting back on his heels, he piled the coins back on to the desk.

Mirella's stays creaked as she sat back herself and looked up at him. 'You want to leave the Royal George?'

'Well, I'll have Kitty Rainbow with me now...' He paused. He could hardly say he thought Mirella would drown the child in a rusty tin bath. 'There's not room for her here.'

Mirella shrugged. 'You're quite right there, Ishmael. There is no room for that child here. But surely ... there's plenty widder-women in Priorton as'll 'ave 'er for a few pence a week?' Her accent, which she had polished assiduously in recent years, reverted under stress. She hitched her bottom on to the chair again and, her steel-rimmed spectacles perched on her nose, concentrated on putting the coins back in their neat piles.

47

This done, she looked across at Ishmael. 'What's she to you, Ishmael, this child?' The words came out easily enough. Mirella had been in public houses, as daughter, then wife, of mine host all of her life. Despite the contrived modesty of her appearance, she was much bolder and more open in her talk and allusion than any of the Priorton women whom she called her friends. This broadness and lack of simpering modesty was just one reason why she would never be taken to the simpering heart of the burgeoning middle classes of Priorton. It was also one reason why Ishmael retained a soft spot for her.

Now he chuckled openly. 'Kitty's not my own, Mirella, in anything except my sense of how things ought to be. She's a kind of . . . foundling. It has been my commitment to care for her. I have taken her for my own.' His words were courtly, alien, in this workaday parlour.

'Like I say, get some other widder-woman to take her on,' said Mirella, pushing out her full bottom lip.

They were interrupted by a scratching at the door. Mirella glanced across just as it flew open, sending Kitty Rainbow sprawling across the parlour floor.

Mirella leaped up and grabbed Kitty by the arm, hauling her to her feet. 'Esme!' she shrieked.

Kitty stood passive in the woman's grip, smiling faintly at the drama she had caused.

A scrambling clatter at the top of the stairs heralded Esme, tall, bony and immaculate now, new wide blue ribbons perching like butterflies in her hair.

Mirella thrust the compliant Kitty into her daughter's arms. 'Take this child away, will you?'

Esme put out her hand and Kitty smiled up at her, curling her fingers round the smooth palm, enjoying the feel of the long fingers of the taller girl.

'What do I do with her, Mama?' said Esme, rather disconcerted by the instant intimacy assumed by the smaller girl.

'Do what you like ... try some of your old shoes on her. It's a disgrace the child going barefoot.' Mirella pushed them out of the room, shut the door behind them and wiped her hands on the small black apron she used to protect her fine dress from the dirt and grease on the coins.

She rubbed her fingers hard, scouring from them any residual contamination of Kitty Rainbow.

'No, Ishmael, you're right,' she said firmly. 'There's no question of having that child here. You wouldn't know what she'd bring in: cockroaches, vagabonds, the Lord knows what else.' Her voice was getting more *refained* by the second.

'I'm not saying she should come here, Mirella,' he said evenly. 'I don't want that myself. I'm going to move out of here and have her with me. Take care of her myself.'

Her eyes gleamed 'Hmmph! How could you do that?'

'Well, I've watched out for you, and Esme and young Gabriel, for long enough. I did all that for Jossy as well, when he was with us. But now the child needs me more.'

Mirella bridled. 'Well, don't you think if you move out of the George you can still work here. I can get plenty of paid help, you know!'

Ishmael blinked slightly; he hadn't reckoned on this. Then he shrugged his shoulders. 'I'll make money, Mirella. Mend shoes, make shoes. Work as a mate for the carriers. Perhaps I will get a cart and be a carrier myself.'

Mirella pouted. 'You'll need money for premises.'

'I have a bit of money. Anyway, a bit of cobbling I can do from home.' He pulled his fingers through his beard, a new thought striking him. 'And that Mr Philip Crane was in the billiard room just now, saying he wants someone to live in one of his houses in Forgan Buildings, no rent to pay. To collect his rents. Keep a bit of order. Never considered it, but perhaps I could give that kind of thing a try.'

Mirella laughed unpleasantly. 'Those Forgan Buildings're a rabbit warren, Ishmael. Teaming with ragamuffins.

Fighting Saturday till Tuesday. Loose women. It was in the paper last week that they never empty the privies down there. Mrs Peacock, that has the woodland joining alongside there, had a man up before the magistrates, for . . . well, using her piece of woodland for . . . well, you know what. The *Priorton Gazette* said that was common practice, as the privies were never emptied.' She shuddered, and he had to smile at her uncharacteristic show of delicacy.

'Then there'll be plenty of order to keep, plenty of boots to mend in a place like that, won't there?' said Ishmael firmly. 'Now, Mirella, Mr Crane's in the billiard room. I'll just go in there and make him an offer.'

Upstairs Esme was looking down at Kitty's feet with some bewilderment. 'They're very small,' she said doubtfully.

'Aye, an' they're different shapes, see?' Obligingly Kitty turned one foot over to demonstrate its curiously high arch and the slight twist to one side. 'That makes me limp. Shoes hurt, so I don't wear'm.' One by one she fingered the line of buttoned boots and neat laced shoes in Esme's closet. 'None of these things'd fit my feet. You'd be better off sailing in'm.'

'They're not that big,' objected Esme. 'Those green slippers're tiny. Anyway, you can't go without shoes, it's not decent. It makes you funny. Only poor children go without shoes.'

'Oh, that's all right,' said Kitty reassuringly. 'I'm poor as well. You see, my Antijan takes all the money from the till at the shop and buys gin at the Talbot Hotel. It was whisky before but gin's cheaper.' She cocked her head. 'But you know that 'cos you sell it here, don't you? So, anyway, there's only money left for food and for Thomas's shoes. An' he needs them, 'cos half the time he's so daft he'd be walking in mud an' water if you're not alongside him.'

Esme sat down on the bed, her wide skirts fluttering around her. 'Thomas? The boy with the squeezebox? He looks like one of those angels you see in the colour pages in the Bible. What's wrong with him?'

Kitty shrugged. 'He's kind of daft. He won't talk to you. Not even look at you. But there's sommat ... kind of ... nice about Thomas. He bliddy loves that squeezebox. I was hoping maybe he could keep it.'

'Kitty!' said Esme. 'You mustn't swear. That's rude.'

Kitty grinned. 'Deary me!' she said. She started to pick her way through the fancy, frilled dresses in the closet, holding them against her: first one, then another. 'These are bliddy awful frocks, Esme. Like lardy cakes with extra icing.'

Esme nodded. 'Yes. If the dressmaker puts on two frills, Mama insists on one more. If she sews three frills, Mama still insists on yet another.'

'Which one's your favourite?'

Esme stared at her for a second, then bounced off the bed. 'Wait here!' she said, then vanished through the door.

Kitty had just run her fingers over the last piece of crystal on the top of the dressing table when Esme was back. 'Deary me!' said Kitty, chuckling at the sight of her.

Esme was standing there in boy's black knee breeches and a white shirt with a black high-buttoned waistcoat with narrow revers. Around her neck was a blue tartan handkerchief and on her head a large boy's cap which hid her blue ribbons and only allowed random curls to escape down her back.

Kitty clapped her hands, 'Tha' makes a very handsome lad, Esme.'

Esme grinned with delight and went across to the mirror and peered at herself. 'I do, don't I? Too big and bony for a girl. Not even as pretty as our Gabriel, but...'

'Does he know you borrow his clothes?'

Esme shook her head soberly. 'He'd belt me if he did.'

'Did he get wrong this afternoon, for hitting you, like? For hitting me?'

It was Esme's turn to chuckle. 'What, him? Holy Gabriel who c'n do no wrong at the moment for our dear Mama? His turn to be the golden child. Why d'you think I'm up here? Sent to sit in my room for aggravating him and causing trouble. Now he's had his tea and is off out to play with that lot again. Probably tormenting some other poor lass.' She stood with arms akimbo, turning this way and that, preening herself before the glass. 'There's one way I can stop him doing that to me. Though I don't care for what I have to do, I don't care for it at all.'

'What—'

Kitty's voice was interrupted by Mirella's bellowing from below and she jumped. 'Esme, bring that child down!'

'Where are we going, Mister?'

Kitty was swaying on top of a handcart, perched on disassembled beds, bundles of bedclothes and groceries: surrounded by odd chairs, cupboards, cabinets and bags of coal. She had watched Ishmael haggle with the furniture man and the coal man, and question the grocer closely as to what a man should stock up with in setting up a new household. So now he was stocked up, right down to scouring stones and candlewax.

Kitty hugged a small parcel to her chest. This was packed with clothes sorted out for her by Esme. From the parcel dangled the pair of soft green leather slippers, the left one of which fitted Kitty exactly.

The streets were getting narrower.

'There's a little house in Forgan Buildings, Kitty. I thought you and I could live there. The houses there are owned by a customer of Mrs Gullet. His agent's ... gone away.' No need to tell the child about the prison sentence for fraud. 'This man, Mr Crane, says I ... we, can stay there for free if I collect the rents for him.'

Forgan Buildings was in one of the poorest parts of Priorton, out on the edge of the town, away from its prosperous flourishing centre. Despite looking dilapidated and ancient, the ramshackle collection of buildings was only twenty years old, having been thrown up for pitmen when the short-lived seam called Ivy Lea had been sunk. Through two prosperous years coal was won from the Ivy Lea, making a fortune for its London owners. But then more money was needed to sink a deeper seam and the owners abandoned it, hunting for cheaper profit elsewhere.

The houses in Forgan Buildings, sold off to Mr Philip Crane for a song, had been left to decay, and were among the cheapest places to rent in Priorton. Consequently there was no shortage of takers from families with only one tiny wage coming in, or from those eking out their final years on the last scraps of a miserable life's savings. Or those who came to occupy the cottages in the middle of the night, people who were known to brazen it out when the rent man came.

That first night Ishmael started out by clearing the fireplace of its long-cold ashes and lighting a fire to warm the dank room. Then he erected a bed for Kitty in the small loft room, and one for himself in the living kitchen. He put up the table, with a chair at either side, and placed the bread and potatoes on its surface. He put the tin bowl on the stone slab by the window and told Kitty that she could come out later and hold the big jug, while he pumped the water from the pump at the end of the street, beyond the arch.

Kitty relished Ishmael's calm efficiency as he set about all these tasks. This was a revelation, used as she was to her Antijan's random, scattered style of organisation where things more or less stayed where they fell and were hunted for beneath the piles when they were required.

When he had finished, Ishmael sat on the chair on one end of the table and began to cut at the loaf with a large knife. She climbed on to the chair opposite and put her hands on her chin. 'Is that your real name, mister? Ishmael Slaughter?'

He smiled slightly. 'No. My name is Levinson. I had the name of Slaughter for the boxing ring. A *nom de guerre*. Slaughter was appropriate. I once saw a man killed in the ring. Killed by a deaf man. Slaughtered.'

She didn't quite understand all he said but loved the gentle tones of his voice. She noticed the way he spoke: softly but very precisely. The intonation was foreign to her: but as she had only ever heard Priorton voices in all their variety, she did not realise that this was not an English accent at all.

'The ring, Mr Slaughter?'

'The boxing ring. I used to fight in the boxing ring. And other places. For money.'

Her eyes brightened. 'You can get money with fighting? I could do that. I'm a good fighter.'

'I noticed that. Now, you can spread that butter on the bread. Right to the edges, please. Nice and even.'

She completed the task neatly. 'I can do this. I often do it for Antijan. Can I go home now? After tea? To Antijan?'

He shook his head. 'This is your home now. I asked Janine Druce to take care of you. And she did. Now you are home with me.'

She scowled at him. 'An' can't I see her? She wasn't bad, you know. An' she can't manage Thomas without me.'

He took the jug from the windowsill. 'Come and hold the jug for me at the pump.'

They were silent as they waited their turn behind two haggling women. Finally, 'Hold that straight now, Kitty, so the water doesn't spill.'

When he had finished pumping he took the jug from her and they walked together in the gathering gloom back to the house with its flickering fire. 'And if we're to live together, Kitty, I think you should call me Ishmael. We have to be as family together. You will see Janine Druce again. Have no fear.'

She thought for a second, put away the last confused thought about the woman who had guided her in the world so far, and slipped her hand into his. His hand felt right, in hers. She had always known Janine was not her mother although the two of them had lived together in a kind of barbed equanimity. So who was this man? Not her father, she felt sure of that. But his hand holding hers felt right, and for the moment she was satisfied.

Kitty loved Forgan Buildings from the first. She savoured the kindness among these people who spent more time in the street than in their houses. The fact that the newcomer went barefoot and limped did not draw much attention here. Forgan Buildings teemed with people suffering from much greater disabilities: rickety children, old soldiers with limbs missing, men rendered disabled by pitfalls or gas in any one of ten mines in the district, women old before their time with the yearly calvary of childbirth.

On their third day together Ishmael asked Kitty about her limp, and she told him of a time before her real memory when she had flown through the air, from a window or some high space and landed in pain. And she remembered some sweetmeats and a half eaten iced bun from Antijan, guilty at what she had done.

'I think she threw me. She has this temper, has Antijan. After that the foot grew funny,' she said. 'I can wear neither clogs nor boots. So now me feet are as hard as any shoe.' She hitched herself up on to the table and lifted her feet into his hands. 'Feel.'

He turned them this way and that, seeing the difference between them, her hard soles rasping his hand. 'They're good feet,' he said. 'Aside from that turn on the right one.'

She nodded seriously. 'They've done well by me, those feet. I like them.'

'Would you not wear boots?'

She took her feet from his hands. 'Like I said, they hurt

when I wear boots or clogs. Antijan tried to make me and I bit her.'

'I could make you some that didn't hurt. Wouldn't you like that?'

She put her head on one side, then went across to her bundle, which was in the little cupboard to the left of the fireplace. She took out Esme Gullet's green slippers. 'Some like this?' she said.

He smiled. 'They're very light. Wouldn't take the knocks around Forgan Buildings.'

She started to shove the slippers back in her bundle, but Ishmael took them from her. 'I could take that right one to pieces, and rebuild it for you, Kitty. That will be easy enough. You could use them for high days and holidays. But you'll need some other sturdy shoes, perhaps boots, to play about in.'

'And they won't hurt?'

He shook his head. 'They'll be light as swansdown, tough as old boots.' He laughed. 'Now that's something. Tough as old boots. Like you.'

Kitty did not laugh. 'And I don't have to wear them all the time?'

He hesitated then nodded.

'All right then, I'll have them.' She jumped down from the table. 'Now, can I go out to play, Ishmael?'

It took some days for Ishmael to find the materials to alter the green shoe. Then he set to and worked on it, holding it up against the left one a hundred times to check the match.

Finally the shoes were ready. Ishmael made Kitty put on blue cotton stockings from Esme's bundle, then handed her the shoes and sat watching while she put them on and buttoned them up.

She slipped on the left one first, then the right. Then she stood up before him. He put his hands to her shoulders and straightened them slightly. 'There, Kitty, you can hardly tell at all. Now let us see you walk down the lane.' He led her to the door.

Walking along, she felt constrained, tottering. Pushing her in front of him he urged her to run, to run hard.

She ran without limping. It was much better. 'It's horrible,' she said, hurtling back towards him, gasping. 'Like wearing rocks on your feet.'

He looked down at them. 'Do they hurt? Where do they hurt? I will fix it.'

She shook her head. 'Not hurt exactly. It's just I don't like them, shoes. Never have.'

'Can you do something for me?'

She shrugged.

'Can you just leave them on for a whole day, and then tell me? If they hurt, I mean?'

'Don't see why not.'

'Well, go off with you. I've got your new boots to cut, and a rent round to do.'

She grinned at him then.

He watched her skip away, then went into the house to collect the leather purse he had fashioned for his rent-collecting. He set about going from house to house, collecting pennies from some, excuses from others. At some houses the doors were bolted and the only sign of life was twitching rags of curtain.

When he returned he stacked the money on the table and counted it. Then he made a mental list of defaulters, so he would remember next week. His inability to read or write, which had driven him to the cobbler's last and then to the the boxing ring as a young man, had developed his memory to the point of total recall. He could remember blow by blow every fight he had ever seen or fought. He could remember, word by word, conversations from years ago. He could remember, and make note of, every money trans-action he had ever had on his own or on behalf of the Royal George. All this had proved useful in his life.

Later that day he took the money to the smoky billiard room at the Royal George where he knew Mr Crane would be nattering with his cronies.

Mirella, holding court in the bar parlour, heard Ishmael's measured tones and made her stately way through to the larger lounge bar. She smiled at him with surprising warmth. 'Ishmael, you're here on business, I see. Are you well settled out there in that dark place?'

'Comfortable enough, Mirella. The child seems very settled.'

She shook her head. 'It might be right for her but it isn't for you.' She fiddled with her bonnet strings. 'Now, Ishmael, I'll have the teapot on the hearth in the bar parlour when you've finished your business with Mr Crane. You will join me?'

He smiled faintly, then nodded and turned back to Mr Crane, who was counting out the money on the small table.

Crane replaced his cigar in his mouth. 'More than usual, but there's still two guineas short here, Mr Slaughter.'

Ishmael reeled off the numbers of the houses who wouldn't or couldn't pay up. 'Just leave all that with me, Mr Crane. Those who can pay, I'll get it out of them.' He looked the small man in the eye. 'Those who honestly can't, we might as well bide our time. They might get some work sometime. And it's better to have people in the houses than let the rats take over. You have five empty there in a terrible state.'

'Aye, they'll be in no fit state to let even if folks do come back,' said Crane gloomily. 'Would you take a gill, Mr Slaughter?'

Ishmael stood up and shook his head. 'Never touch it, sir.' Ned Lumb had the custom of thrusting at him a gill of brandy before a fight, just to set his rage away. It had been only too effective.

'If you like, Mr Crane, those men that really can't pay I can get them to clean and sort the empty houses, kill the rats, plaster the walls, fill in the holes in the roof, all that sort of thing. In fact they can work on all the houses, the ones with people in too, keep them in some decent state. Protect your investment, I say. And the bits of rent you lose'd be much less than if you paid them a wage for doing it.'

Crane stroked his chin. 'It has virtue, this idea. Enhance the value of the whole Buildings.' He clapped Ishmael on the shoulder. 'You're a true son of your race, Mr Slaughter. You'll make my fortune yet.'

A shadow crossed Ishmael's face at this, but he said nothing as he rose to his feet and shook hands with Mr Crane. Then he went through to the bar parlour for a cup of tea with Mirella, who spent the time asking weedling questions about the terrible happenings at Forgan Buildings and complaining about her new cellarman and the cost of retaining a book-keeper. He stirred his tea uneasily, anxious to be back to Kitty, hoping the child had not returned to Janine Druce. He was beginning to enjoy himself in his role of – what was it? Parent? Guardian? Whatever it was he was glad.

6
The Sun, the Rain and a Good Right Fist

Esme stepped carefully in the dust, her mind quivering from one topic to another as it usually did on these flights from the noisy bustle of the George, and from the repetitious whining reproach in her mother's voice. And the discreet savagery of her brother's attentions.

Her mind finally settled on the topic of her mother's practice in bestowing favours. Even as a very small child Esme had noted a certain routine of preference between her and her brother; one of them might be in favour for as long as six months, then it would be the other. There would be little rhyme or reason to Mirella's preferences; perhaps it would be an impending birthday or some other event, which promised the import of some glamour or excitement into the rough routines of the George.

Just after Jossy's funeral Mirella had drawn Gabriel to her and told him, in Esme's presence, that he was now the most important person in this family, that he was her 'little man', the only light in her life. She had even, on occasions, taken him into her bed when she was revisited by childhood night terrors of the armies of Napoleon breaking down the doors of the Royal George.

But this habit of intimacy had faded as her beloved son began to grunt, snore and fling his arms about in bed. The custom stopped altogether when his feet started to smell like rotting cabbage; this was too much for the fastidious Mirella.

After that Esme had had to battle to stop him creeping into her bed at nights. At this point too, it seemed that it was Esme's turn to move back into Mirella's good books. Her delighting eye had moved from Gabriel to Esme, and she started to dress her daughter up, to insist on frills and furbelows which emphasised her girlishness. Plain and gawky as she was, Esme's raw virginal state still caught the attention of the hotel customers: her chin was chucked, her hand held, and more than once her bottom patted by men old enough to know better.

Mirella interpreted this attention as a compliment, and told her customers that as a young girl herself she had always been an asset to her father's hotel. Customers liked a young face around the place.

In these months as she watched Esme, Mirella had been feeling a strange combination of disturbance and excitement. There was something tugging away at her mind, the edge of a memory elbowing its way to the front.

One day she came upon a customer talking away to Esme in the side-alley which led out to the stables at the back of the hotel. The man was looming over the girl, leaning against the wall with his hands over Esme's head. Mirella had spoken to the customer sharply and hustled Esme indoors.

Her own fugitive memory had returned.

Two men, most valued customers of Mirella's father, had come upon her in this same alleyway late one night, and embarked on their usual avuncular teasing. Then they had pulled her, struggling, into the stable, thrown her down beside the snorting horses and played a game with her which involved, by a blustering, chuckling process, the destruction of her maidenhead.

For two days and nights Mirella hid her blood and her shame by barricading herself in her room. When she eventually emerged, she told no one of the incident, and the two men continued to be honoured customers.

For many years Mirella would have nothing to do with any man, and was all set to be an old maid. Then Jossy Gullet turned up, to make her smile with his rough boxer's ways and his amazing, reassuring innocence, and she married him.

Paradoxically this recovered memory did not make Mirella more protective of Esme, rather it made her turn away from her daughter, blaming the girl for being 'forward', for causing trouble for Gabriel, who now came back yet again into his mother's favour.

Walking along the dusty back streets, Esme reflected on the fact that her own recent reign of favour with Mama seemed to have faded altogether.

These days she could do no right with her mother. And Gabriel, if he was at home, would hunt her down in the furthest corners of the hotel. So Esme was always seeking ways of escaping, offering to run messages or visit people, or saying she was going for a walk with a schoolfriend. Sometimes she just crept away, hoping that her mother, holding court in the bar parlour, would not notice her absence.

It was on one of her wanders that she had fallen foul of Gabriel and his cronies, and had been rescued by Kitty Rainbow.

Now she stepped through the dust, retracing those steps, and finally turned the corner to find Kitty herself sitting on a stone which jutted out on the edge of The Green behind Salvin Row.

Esme grinned. 'Hello, Kitty Rainbow.'

Kitty grinned back up at her. 'I knew you'd come. I

wished you here. I've got your shoes on,' she said, holding her feet out straight, her heels at right angles. The green leather shoes shone in the pale sun.

'I thought you said they wouldn't fit you,' said Esme.

'I thought they wouldn't, but see here! Ishmael fixed them so they'd fit – this right one, that is. See where he's cut it and put a bit of extra in?' She jumped to her feet. 'At first it was like walking with rocks on me feet. But now I can walk without limping. Watch!'

She ran twenty yards, dodging the washing lines, and walked back.

'That's good!' said Esme. 'Steady as a bell.'

There was a silence. 'Can you read?' said Kitty.

'Course I can. Best reader in my class.'

'Well, what does this say?' Kitty squatted down in the dirt beside the standing stone and fingered the squiggly lines on its uneven surface.

Esme squatted beside her. 'Dunno. All the letters aren't there, are they? And there's worn bits. It doesn't say anything. Not in English anyway.'

'Oh.' Kitty was disappointed. The letters had been on her mind for some days.

'It might be Latin,' said Esme reassuringly. 'I'll bring some paper tomorrow and copy it down. My teacher at school might know.'

Kitty sat back on the stone. 'Which school d'you go to?'

'I go to Miss Petty's. My mama thinks it'll make a lady of me.'

'Do they beat you with a stick in that school?'

'Hardly ever,' said Esme.

'Can I go there?'

Esme shook her head. 'It costs a lot of money. My mama says she has to work her fingers to the bone to pay for me.'

'Oh.'

Kitty looked so crestfallen that Esme laughed. 'You're keen to go to school?'

Kitty looked at her. 'I want to go to school if you do. I like you.'

Esme went red. 'Well, you can still go to school if you want. You can go to the Prior's School. My Mama says it's for the children of the poor. The prior pays for them.'

Kitty brightened. 'I'll tell Ishmael. He'll take me there.' She looked up at Esme. 'I was wonderin' what was it that stops your brother ... fussin' you.'

Esme pursed her lips and went red.

Kitty pulled her down to sit beside her on the stone. 'Tell us!' she commanded. 'What is it you have to do to keep him sweet?'

Esme played with her bonnet ribbons. 'Did you see the bedspread on my bed?'

Kitty frowned. It had been white and heavily sculpted. 'A big thing with fringes?' she said.

Esme put her head down. 'Those bobbles on the fringe?'

'There must be thousands of them.'

'Some days he gets me cornered and says he'll leave me alone if he can put one in me.'

'In you? Where?'

Esme pulled her wide skirts tightly over her lap, then drew her finger between her thighs to her crotch. 'In there.'

Kitty fell off the stone. 'In there? Inside?' She clambered back. 'There's no space.'

'There is now,' said Esme sadly.

The silence stretched to minutes, then Kitty jumped up. 'Now I tell you what we're going to do, Esme.' She took hold of the other girl's hand. 'We're gunna stalk that brother of yours, and his cronies, to find where they go. I saw them at the end of Gulson Street half an hour ago. Heading for the woods. Let's go and stalk'm. You know, Esme, my Antijan had this cat. You should a' seen it stalk the mice in her back yard!'

Ishmael was amused by Kitty's demand to go to school. He

shook his head when she mentioned the Prior's School. 'You'll have to read and write properly before you can go there, Kitty.'

In the end he took her to a Mrs Coulthard, who ran a little school in her front room and charged threepence a week, a penny if you were very hard up.

Mrs Coulthard was the fat shuffling widow of a flourmill clerk who had married above him. She was limited and thorough and had a very hard hand for children who tried to skylark around, or did not catch on straight away to her laborious explanations.

At first Kitty sat on a bench with three other children, all younger than herself, struggling with her letters and numbers. However, as the weeks went by the blows from Mrs Coulthard got fewer, as sheer temper and doggedness helped Kitty to a breakthrough. Then she raced ahead. In no time she was Mrs Coulthard's best pupil.

Kitty met Esme most days now at the stone. Esme had discovered from Miss Petty that the words on the stone were in Latin, but even so they did not make much sense as there was so much missing. There was one word, which was 'celebrate' and 'branch', but apart from that, it was all hieroglyphics.

'Hieroglyphics?' said Kitty. 'That sounds just lovely.'

'It's Egyptian,' said Esme grandly.

To Kitty's delight, Esme was impressed with the speed of her new friend's learning. 'You'll be ready for the Prior's School in no time,' she said.

Their regular game now was to stalk the boys without the boys seeing them. They had found the boys' hideout in the woods and messed it up, throwing broken cups around and upscuttling the makeshift bench. They walked the High Plains, a craggy cliff by the woods, as the boys walked in the valleys below, and hooted and hallooed at them from a safe distance. Once Gabriel had given chase, and they had escaped, they thought, without being seen.

Esme started to spend a good deal of time with Kitty and Ishmael at Forgan Buildings, toasting bread on the great fire, and listening while Kitty teased more and more out of Ishmael about the old times when he moved around the country with the circus, challenging allcomers to a fight. She made him tell her again and again about the bears and jugglers and two-headed lambs.

Esme reflected on the amount of time Ishmael had lived with them at the George, going quietly about his tasks, talking only to her mother and to certain privileged customers. Sometimes she had even heard the rumble of his voice in her mother's bedroom late at night. But she herself had never known anything about him; he had been a mystery to her.

Now he seemed a different person, answering Kitty's burrowing questions in his slow courtly voice as he tapped away at some boot on his last.

Esme's wandering mind was brought back by Kitty's latest question.

'Ishmael?'

He took the tacks out of his mouth. 'What now?'

'Will you learn me and Esme to box? Properly, like. Like that man taught you when you were young.'

He looked at the two girls: one tall and gangly, the other smaller, so much younger. 'Why?'

'If we were two boys you'd teach us, wouldn't you?'

Ishmael glanced at Esme. 'They'll say it isn't what a lady would do.'

'All the better,' said Esme fiercely, fired by Kitty's idea. 'Ladylike is horrible – mincing-pincing-cooking-serving.'

'Your mama wouldn't like it.'

'She doesn't need to know, does she, Mr Slaughter?'

'Call him Ishmael,' instructed Kitty. 'If he's gunna show you about boxing you can call him Ishmael.'

Esme looked at Ishmael, who shrugged, then laughed. 'Yes, call me Ishmael, and I will show you things about boxing. How to build up your energy and stamina, how to face down your opponent. But not to box. It is not for girls to box. But I'll show you the rest. But only if you do as I say. Exactly!'

They nodded, very seriously. 'Exactly,' said Kitty. 'Isn't that right, Esme?'

That night Kitty crept into the Royal George with Esme. They got up to the bedroom. She picked up the fringe and saw the frightening number of places where the bobble was missing.

'Right!' she said. She started to haul the heavy bedspread off the bed. 'Help me!' she said. Esme looked hard at her and then set to with a will. Between them they heaved the great fringed counterpane through the door and dragged it along till it was in a coiled hump outside Gabriel's bedroom. At the centre of the coil Kitty planted a new candle, stolen from the storeroom beside the kitchen. She went back and got Esme's own lit candle from her bedroom. She thrust it at Esme.

'Go on. Light it,' she said fiercely. 'When he sees this he'll know he can't do that horrible thing again or he'll burn in hell.'

Esme took a breath and ignited the candle. They stood and watched it flare for a while, then crept back into Esme's bedroom where they curled together on the naked bed, waiting for tumult.

It was Mabella, the maid of all work, who noticed the blaze and sent a boy running for the new cellarman, who doused it with three stout buckets of water. There was some speculation as to the cause, but Mabella took the blame, saying she had a pile of washing on that floor ready to come downstairs. She told Mirella bluntly that she should get gaslights upstairs too. Candles were a menace.

Later, Mabella caught Esme in the corridor. She held her shoulder and peered at her, a shrewd light in her narrow eyes. 'That'll get that brother of yours off your back, hinney.

Me own brother was no better. Trouble is, there was only one bedroom there for seven of us.'

In the months following the fire at the George Ishmael trained the girls in running and stamina, taught them to shadow box, showed them little tricks of finding weak spots in their opponents. Always he stressed the importance of not, in your heart, being afraid of your opponent.

Mirella began to notice how subdued Gabriel was these days. She told her cronies that Gabriel had been so affected by that fire, he'd been distracted for days – weeks. Even when his bedroom was rebuilt exactly as it had been before that dreadful fire. Really she felt she should have given that Mabella her notice, but she was such a hard worker and no one else would work for the coppers she earned.

Mirella noticed also that Esme seemed always to be missing. She knew that her daughter spent most of the time with Ishmael now. Mirella made a show of objection but did not stop Esme going across to Forgan Buildings. In fact she reluctantly allowed that she was pleased, as Jossy would have been, that Ishmael was keeping an eye on her Esme.

One Market Day in autumn Ishmael returned to Forgan Buildings from Priorton, pushing a cackbarrow loaded with a tall wardrobe. People from the neighbouring houses in the court watched with interest as he unloaded it.

Kitty laughed at him. 'It'll be a long day before we'll have enough clothes to fill that cupboard, Ishmael.'

'It's not for that,' he said shortly.

He pushed the wardrobe against a wall in the kitchen and unscrewed its great mirrored door. Then he took this outside and leaned it against the back wall where its glitter reflected the dark houses opposite, glowing in the flat afternoon light.

The two girls stood in front of it and stared at themselves, side by side. Kitty put her hand to her head. 'My hair's like a bliddy spuggy's nest.'

'Kitty, don't swear!' chided Esme, patting her own rag-curled hair approvingly.

Kitty peered in. 'Yer can see the back wall, and Mr Kelly's, and look! There's the wheel for White Leas Pit.'

People drifted over from the other houses, stopping six feet away, wary of coming too near to the big man who was collecting their rents now, and organising the maintenance work of those with no jobs who couldn't pay. He was genial enough, but they said if you crossed him he could 'come it'.

But some of them had never even seen such a large mirror and were genuinely curious about what Mr Slaughter was to do with it.

Ishmael was standing behind the girls. They could see his reflection looming over theirs. He put his hands on their shoulders and straightened them. 'Now see! That is what people see! Those boys who hit you. That is what they see. Would you be frightened of such timorous fidgeting girls? Get your shoulders down. Get your chin in. Now then, scowl! That's better.'

Kitty started to splutter with laughter and Esme joined in.

'Stop!' he roared. The crowd fell back a pace. The girls hiccoughed to a halt. 'Who asked to train for boxing? Do you mean it?'

They nodded uncertainly.

'Then you will take me seriously. Now,' he said sternly, 'chin in, set your shoulders, hands up. That's better. If you get good enough at this you will never need to fight. They'll run away scared before you've laid a finger on them.'

As the weeks went on Kitty became envious of Esme's long, capable hands. Her own were small and neat, not much use for a boxer. But as they sparred together, their hands protected by gloves which Ishmael called mufflers, Kitty knew that in terms of courage, bobbing and weaving, feinting and getting in the unexpected jab, she herself was superior.

Late in the evenings Ishmael would sit by the dying fire

70

and tell Kitty of great fights he had seen, his favourite boxer being the great black fighter Richmond, who fought under the patronage of the Duke of Northumberland. 'Came here from America and beat men twice his weight. Skill, not weight. That's what counts, Kitty.'

One day, after they had completed their prescribed daily return race to Lewis's farm, the two girls turned into the corner of the court and bumped into Thomas Druce, squeezebox in hand, leaning against a wall playing a distinct but unrecognisable tune.

The door to number six was shut, and as Kitty opened it Ishmael and Janine Druce looked up almost guiltily. Kitty noted Janine was wearing quite a respectable bonnet, and her shawl was more or less clean.

'Ha! Kitty!' said Ishmael with a forced geniality. 'Here's Janine Druce come to see us.'

'I'm not goin' back there. Not with you,' said Kitty, folding her lip.

Janine folded her arms. 'I brought you up from a baby,' she said grimly. 'You owe me something, lass.'

Kitty glared at her. 'Owe you? Ishmael paid you. I didn't know that before. I thought you did what you did because somehow I was in your family. Now I don't even have you. No mother. No father. Not even you. Owe you? I'm laughing at you!' She gulped to stop any tears betraying how bereft she really felt.

'Mrs Druce says she misses your help, Kitty,' said Ishmael quietly. 'That she was surprised how much it seems you did. That you were a good stitcher.'

Kitty shrugged. 'I'll come and stitch a few aprons, Antijan.' She looked around the clean kitchen, sparse except for the grand wardrobe and its glittering mirror, now fixed back in place. 'I'll bring some here an' do them while Ishmael's at the shoes.'

Janine's tension left her. 'Well, that'll be a—'

'A penny apiece,' pursued Kitty. 'You sell them for

71

sixpence an' make them out of odd pieces, so there's plenty money for you there.'

Janine Druce glared at her for a second, then started to laugh. 'Well, Ishmael, this one's been here before. Seven going on seventy, I'd say.'

Ishmael rubbed his hands and put them towards the fire. 'Well, that settles that. You two seem to have some kind of business arrangement.' His head swung towards the door. 'What in heaven is that?'

Sweet forceful music was floating through the door. They went outside to watch. Esme was already there, with a small crowd of Forgan Buildings residents, listening intently to the music. Thomas had started to play tunes on the squeezebox – hymns from the chapels, popular songs, and tunes they didn't recognise.

'Where'd he learn that?' asked Kitty, intrigued.

Janine shrugged. 'Never stopped tinkerin' wi' the blessed thing since he picked it up. Hanging round the pubs and chapels earwiggin' like the ghost at the feast.' She didn't add that this was while she left him on his own for many hours, while she herself went wider and wider afield to find places which would give her credit. 'Ah'm threatenin' all the time tae tek it back to the Gullet woman, but Ah dinnet seem tae get around to it, wi' everythin' tae dae mahsel now.'

'He can have it,' said Ishmael absently. 'It's mine. A fellow gave it to me in payment of a debt.'

'Anyway, never mind him. Ah've gotta get on.' Janine looked at Kitty. 'I'll parcel them aprons up for you straight away.'

Kitty nodded, not taking her eye off Thomas. Janine tottered away but Thomas stayed and, staring at a spot on the wall behind Esme's head, played tune after tune. Esme swayed and hummed as he played.

Later Kitty walked part of the way home with Thomas and Esme, leaving them at the standing stone. As she wandered back, she was brought up short as a stone hit her on one shoulder, and another raised dust at her feet. She looked up to see Gabriel Gullet peeping at her from behind a wall.

'Stop that,' she yelled, clambering up the wall. When she reached the top he was twenty yards away. She glared at him. 'Stop that, you pig!' she said. 'We burned the counterpane to stop you bein' a pig. You know that. I know what you do to poor Esme. Do it again and I'll set fire to you next.'

He put his hands in his pockets. 'Bastard.' He spat the word out. 'Dirty little cripple.'

She dropped from the wall as though he had hit her with another stone, a shudder going through her, tears forcing themselves into her unwilling eyes.

She raced back to Forgan Buildings, running faster than ever she had in her training races with Esme. Seeing her face, Ishmael dropped his hammer. 'What is it?' he said. 'What's wrong?'

She told him of Gabriel's words and he pulled her towards him and sat her up on the table so that she could look him in the eye. 'Kitty, don't you know you're the child of three rainbows? A person with three parents cannot be a bastard, can she? Her parents are the sun, the rain and a good right fist.' He held his own great fist up in front of Kitty and told the tale of how she fell into his arms out of the sky. 'Here!' he rummaged in the box he had brought from the Royal George. He pulled out the rag of blue cloth. 'You were wrapped in this.'

She shook it out and held it up to the light. It was hard with age, the edges of the creases bleached to a pale blue. She ran her fingers over the creases and along the embroidered band on the edge. Turning this over she peered at the design, very finely embroidered, blue on blue: an interlocking design of acorns and oak leaves.

She looked down at him. 'I want to see where, Ishmael, where I fell from the sky.'

Hand in hand they walked through the town, then down the bank to the viaduct. Ishmael watched quietly as Kitty stood in its shadow and tried with all her strength to know the heart and the hands which threw her into the flooding waters: the hands which stitched the acorn design. For a split second she thought she could hear a drum, but it was only the rattle of a railtruck from overhead. She beat her fist on the stone, not very old but grimy already with coal dust larded into the cracks.

Ishmael watched silently as the child beat the stone with her fists until her knuckles bled.

7

Lessons in Life

Miss Philomena Adams, spinster and daughter of a colour sergeant who fought with Wellington at Waterloo, knew a fighter when she saw one. She looked down over her beaked nose into the bright rebellious face of her new pupil. 'Did you speak, Kitty Rainbow?' she said grimly.

'I don't wanter sit in the back row, miss.'

'And why not, pray?'

The other fifty-three children looked on with interest. Miss Adams was not slow with the old stick, which was always good sport, if you were a watcher rather than a sufferer.

''Cos my friend Esme Gullet says only dunces and dullards sit in the back row an' you never hear any good lessons there.'

Miss Adams leaned across her desk and grasped her stick, a thin willow wand well suited to her small hard hand. An indrawn breath, half satisfaction half fear, went around the class. Many of the pupils sitting on the tiered benches had felt the bite of that switch on their first day at the Prior's School. Miss Adams had her own way of pre-empting trouble and settling potential troublemakers.

75

'Put out your hand, Kitty Rainbow.'

Kitty glanced round the tiers of eager faces, then back at the ugly, bird-like face of Miss Adams. The teacher lifted her chin and glared into the silver eyes of this strange child. Kitty's gaze faltered and she raised both hands to chest height. Miss Adams reached out to measure her length, turning the small hands over. It was not her custom to beat children on the palms, as the effect on their writing was deleterious.

Miss Adams's glance faltered as she saw the lacerations and bloody scabs on the back of the child's hands, the last scars from Kitty's vain beating of the great stone viaduct. 'What's this? How did this happen?'

Kitty looked down at the scabs then back up into her teacher's eyes. 'From fightin', miss.'

'Fighting?'

'My father is the great fighter Ishmael Slaughter, who fought the great champion Richmond, a black man who was a brilliant fighter from America. A thinkin' fighter.' She glared belligerently at the teacher in the way that Ishmael had showed her. 'He's teachin' me to box, an' I'm goin' to be the first girl champion in England.'

A low mutter of appreciation flickered around the class and Miss Adams's wand fell down to her side, the barest flicker of relaxation to one side of her mouth. 'Well, whatever the reason,' she said grimly, 'I cannot cane a hand covered with sores. Go to your seat.' She paused. 'At the very back, mind you.'

Kitty mounted the shallow steps, knowing that all eyes were on her. Halfway up, a curly-haired boy winked at her and shot his foot out to trip her.

'Freddie Longstaffe. Come out here!'

By the time Kitty had got to her seat Freddie was out at the front patiently enduring the six strokes Kitty herself would have had, and three more. As he mounted the steps clutching his sore hands under his arms he looked up at

Kitty and winked again before sitting down to listen meekly to Miss Adams, whose deep powerful voice was now resonating through the room recounting the drama of Moses being found in the bulrushes by the daughter of the Pharaoh.

At dinnertime on the patch of land beside the Prior's School, the children clustered around Kitty, pulling at her, demanding that she show them her hands. Freddie Longstaffe pushed his way through the crowd and stood before her. 'Gissa look!' He grabbed her hands and turned them over, then whistled. 'Yeh gave them a good batterin'. Are yeh really a boxer? Did they get like this with yeh boxin'?'

She laughed and shook her head. 'I got'm like this with battering them on a wall in one of my paddies. I've got a very bad temper.'

He looked at her with some respect. 'So all that about boxing was a lie?'

She shook her head. 'No. It was all true about Ishmael, only he's not really me father. An' it's true he's learnin' us boxin'.'

Freddie put up his fists in the fashion of the years-old battered circus posters still to be seen on some walls in Priorton. 'Show us, then. Show us some of this boxin', if that Ishmael of yours is so good.'

The other children had formed a circle around them by now and were looking on with interest. She put up her fists and said, 'Hit me.'

He jabbed at her, his fist hitting the air as she ducked away to one side. He jabbed again and she danced back out of his reach.

'That's not fair. You gotta stand and take it,' he said, dropping his hands.

'Who says?' She poked a neat blow at his unguarded chin, landing a crack on his jawbone. At that point he gave up any pretence of boxing and jumped at her, grabbing her hair. The other children cheered.

Suddenly Miss Adams was breaking through the circle and hauling them apart. 'Cease! Cease this battling. Go and stand by my desk, now!'

Freddie Longstaffe got the cane again and Kitty was told to wait behind after school as Miss Adams would accompany her to her home to discuss with her parent whether or not such a termagant could come to the Prior's School at all.

At home Ishmael handled the little teacher very smoothly, assuring her that Kitty would not – *ever* – fight at school again. He would see to it. And for her information the injury to the child's hands came from an accidental clash with a wall, and was nothing to do with boxing. He would not have permitted that, he said slowly, fingering his own twisted and battered hands.

Miss Adams, impressed by the gentle demeanour of this man, went away mollified, and Kitty had to stand in the kitchen for a very long time while Ishmael talked to her endlessly about self-discipline and self-control and if she wanted to go to school like Esme she must not, must not, be wild. He went on until she was swaying with tiredness and he told her to sit down and eat her broth.

Miss Adams was very hard with all the children she taught, but was particularly hard with Kitty, seeing the child's combative spirit as a lively challenge. At the beginning Kitty hated her teacher but bit by bit this feeling wore off. She came to be fascinated at the way Miss Adams could make the things of nature live in the narrow enclosed classroom: make trees blossom and butterflies and birds flitter before you; the way that when she told stories it seemed that princes rode before your very eyes; the way she would make numbers work with a neat magic and the way she could make even the chore of copying copperplate writing from the blackboard seem to have a fine purpose. Beside all this, the hard sting of Miss Adams's swishing stick was but a fleeting pain, and her hard words were of the moment and had no lasting sting.

78

In this brisk, brilliant atmosphere Kitty Rainbow continued to be very quick to learn and in no time was in the front row with all the cleverest children in the class. She discovered that Freddie Longstaffe, who was the best at learning poems off by heart, often made it to the front row, but equally often was sent to the back for some prank or other which generated Miss Adams's energetic and peculiarly physical disapproval.

Kitty did well in all the lessons but she shone particularly at sewing. Miss Adams, an expert embroiderer herself, started to set Kitty increasingly hard tasks and her skills multiplied.

As the years went on, Esme and Kitty's friendship grew closer and closer. Kitty, though younger, was the leader and protectress of the duo. In time their fitness training, and the play-boxing they did under Ishmael's strict supervision, began to make a difference to each of them. It brought Kitty's temper under control, and gave Esme confidence, filling her out physically and making her surprisingly attractive.

When Mirella caught Ishmael in the Royal George she talked long and hard about the great changes in Esme, ascribing it all to the benefits of the only slightly pretentious Princess May School run by the Misses Petty, who charged a modest fee from the tradespeople in the town to educate their daughters to a standard level of gentility, if not literacy. Mirella confided that at this school Esme would learn to become even more of a lady than she herself was.

The silent grimacing Thomas was often in the girls' company, so that they made up a strange trio in the streets and lanes of Priorton. He played his tunes to them on his squeezebox and Esme sang, often making up the words. She taught Kitty to dance, the hopping and skipping movements disguising altogether Kitty's slight limp.

As they danced together Esme would sing, and her low throaty voice would send shivers down Kitty's spine. Then

Kitty would laugh and thump her friend on the shoulder and tell her to stop codding on.

Thomas, always dumbly attentive to Kitty, began to attach himself to Esme like a limpet, sometimes staring at her with shining eyes as though she were a winged angel. Janine noticed this, telling Ishmael it was the first time she had seen her son look directly at anybody.

One day in the summer after Kitty's eleventh birthday, Esme and Kitty announced that they and Thomas would create a little concert for the children in Forgan Buildings. Ishmael could look on from his cobbler's stool in the doorway.

After much shuffling and giggling, Esme appeared, from behind a screen which was made from a threadbare blanket suspended on a string, She was wearing a feather boa filched from her mother's wardrobe and a long underskirt in panne velvet. She strutted and pranced around in a guying version of the music-hall singer Nellie Wakes, whom she had once observed in a song-and-supper room at a hotel in Darlington.

The supposedly shy Esme was entirely transformed in this coquettish and powerful performance. Kitty clapped her hands till they were sore and then put her fingers to her mouth and whistled in appreciation. The barefoot children sitting in rows in the dirt, and the Forgan women hanging out of their doors, applauded and whistled too.

Esme took great sweeping curtsies, looking around with pleasure, her bony face beautiful with satisfaction. She ducked back past Ishmael into Kitty's house, then re-emerged in an old sailor suit of Gabriel's and embarked on a set of sailor songs, the final one accompanied by a clumping, jumping dance performed by herself and Kitty.

They took their bows together, only ceasing when they caught sight of the strangers who had silently appeared in the archway which gave access to Forgan Buildings.

The applause petered out and the children in the audience peered round, following the wary gaze of the two performers.

The women drew closer together and the children nudged each other, giggling.

Kitty frowned, wondering just how long they had been lurking there, those men. They must be something to do with the landlord.

'Ned Lumb!' Ishmael got to his feet and made his way through the children.

He shook the hand of a small sharp-faced man of perhaps sixty years. The man wore gloves, carried a cane. His long coat parted slightly to reveal an unlikely yellow checked waistcoat.

'Ishmael! Good to see you old man.' Ned Lumb's smallness was accentuated by his tall hat. 'I've brought my friend Jarrold Pommeroy to meet you. We were up for Sedgefield races and I was telling Jarrold what a very fine fighter you were. So I decided to dig you out. We're staying at the Royal George and the delightful widow of the late lamented Jossy Gullet told us where we might find you.' He smiled and nodded towards his companion, showing large yellow teeth with gaps between. 'Jarrold and I have a little proposition for you.'

Kitty kicked at the dust under her feet as she watched Ishmael proffer his hand to Jarrold Pommeroy. This younger man was taller, heavier, hairier and darker than Ned Lumb. He switched on a big smile and his clasp was too close as he shook Ishmael's hand. 'It seems you have quite a show going here, Mr Slaughter, in your own backyard.' He nodded towards Esme, who, still wearing her sailor's clothes, was watching the newcomers closely. 'Diamonds in the dust. Diamonds in the dust. There's talent there, Mr Slaughter. Talent there.'

Kitty shivered, grabbed Esme's hand and pulled her into the house. 'Come on, Esme, come on in and get yer own clothes on.'

Ned looked round the grey stone court. The children melted into the shadows and the women went back into their doorways. 'So this is where you live, Ishmael? Among the poor and dispossessed? Bit of a comedown I'd say, old chap.'

Ishmael, pulling on his heavy jacket, said grimly, 'I'll walk back to the George with you, Ned. This is not a peepshow.'

At the George a fluttering Mirella gave them the best table. Ned urged Ishmael to have a brandy, a double, to celebrate old times.

'I don't touch the stuff. Never since the last fight.' An image of the battered face and winded, wounded body of his last opponent flashed into his mind. 'Never.'

Ned smiled thinly. 'All it ever did for you, Ishmael, was put a bit of heart in you.'

Ishmael shook his head. 'The heart of a savage, a *berserk*. Not my heart.'

They sat quietly at the table, their noses twitching at the heavy mixture of sweat and camellias as Mirella served two glasses of her oldest brandy. They watched the door shut behind her.

'So what is it that you want of me, Ned?' said Ishmael.

Ned glanced at Jarrold Pommeroy. 'We're following the racing up here, and alongside that putting up a series of matches outside the tracks before the races. A bit of sport to set the mood. Jarrold here has some acrobats and jugglers lined up, dancers and so on. We catch the people in a gambling humour, money burning a hole in their pockets, and we'll fleece some sovereigns off them before the horse men get at them.'

'Matches?'

'You know what I mean. Up-and-coming hopefuls. Local bruisers, favourites. Strong men.'

'And me?'

'The dark horse. The unexpected.' Ned took out his

handkerchief and blew his nose. 'You take 'em on. Rout 'em. And we all fill our pockets.'

'I'm fifty-five years old, Ned. You're talking nonsense.'

Ned shook his head. 'Think about Richmond, the black fighter, and the great Tom Spring, both fighting at the top of the game in their fifties. The darlings of the fancy, those boys. Strength, skill and endurance, that's what it takes and that's what you had, you have, I'm sure. And your grey hairs are an advantage. Lulls the boys down, don't it? The dark horse, like I said. They think you're an easy mark then, wham!' He slapped his own fist into his palm with a resounding crack. 'And wham! Money into our pockets.'

Mirella whipped too quickly round the door at this. 'Was there something you needed, gentlemen?'

Ned lifted his glass and said with yellow-toothed geniality, 'Perhaps a single before we complete our business, dear Mrs Gullet.' As the door closed behind her, his voice switched in an instant to the icy tones of business. 'I can't think what you're doing there, Ishmael, down in that slum, hammering at boots like some rustic. There's money to be made.'

'Well, you can make it out of some other fool.'

'We lost our other fool,' murmured Jarrold.

'What was that?' Ishmael turned to him.

'The man had an ... accident,' said Ned smoothly, 'and is no longer with us.'

'Accident? In the ring?'

Jarrold laughed. 'No, out of it. He'd made a private arrangement with some fellows – horse men as it happens – to lose a bout we'd set up. Seems he got carried away by the desire to win, so they got carried away behind the tent.' He touched his moustache. 'Won't walk again.'

Ishmael stood up. 'It made me sick then and it makes me sick now. Gentlemen, you can keep your ring and your blood and your sovereigns.'

Ned shrugged and stood up, putting out his hand. 'We

could have done each other a favour, Ishmael. We'll find someone to do it for us. Ten a penny, fighters.'

Ishmael looked at the outstretched hand, then touched it very briefly.

Jarrold Pommeroy stood up. 'Mr Slaughter, those children dancing at your door, are they yours?'

Ishmael looked at him evenly. 'One of them is.'

'The taller one? The one who sings?'

Ishmael shook his head, and turned as Mirella came in with a tray with two glasses on. 'No. That young lady is the daughter of Mrs Gullet, the landlady here at the Royal George. Esme's her name.'

Mirella's head went up. 'Esme?'

Jarrold Pommeroy ducked his head towards Mirella. 'Your daughter is a gifted performer, Mrs Gullet. Does she perform here at the George?'

'Performer?' said Mirella, bewildered. 'Our Esme a performer?'

'A very promising one,' said Jarrold. 'I know talent when I see it.'

They all turned their heads as the kitchen door clashed in the back regions. Mirella bellowed, 'Esme! Is that you? Come right in here and tell me just what you have been playing at. This minute!'

8

The Unicorn

The day after the performance, Freddie Longstaffe cornered Kitty in the school yard. 'Hey, lass, gerra look at this!' Cradled in his dirt-engrained palm were two small eggs no larger than a man's thumbnail. Kitty touched them with her little finger. She and Freddie had become firm friends since their first battling encounter. It was not the first time he had brought in some treasure to show her.

In the four years she had known him she had been shown 'black gold' and intricate fossil creatures brought up by his miner brothers from the pit; white mice, brown rabbits, and potatoes so grotesque they took on the form of man or animal; and fancy buttons made by Freddie himself with clay burned in bonfires on The Green behind his house.

And many, many birds' eggs.

These eggs were a milky blue, their surfaces scattered with splotches of brown. 'They're lovely,' she said. 'What are they?'

'Yeller'ammer.'

'Where d'you get'm?'

'Our Tucker'n Mikey showed us where to get'm in White

Leas Woods. An' we saw a unicorn there. Remember like Miss Adams told us last year?'

Miss Adams had let them stay back after school so that they could pore over the fine engraving of a unicorn in a book. They had been thrilled at the image of the strange creature.

'But that was magic,' said Kitty.

He shrugged. 'We only caught a peep. Our Mikey said it was a roe deer. Only white. But he never saw the picture we saw, like.'

Later, after school, Kitty decided it would be a good idea for her and Esme to go across to White Leas Woods looking for birds' eggs and maybe even see a unicorn. The day was held in a brassy fist of heavy stormy light, but the rain was still holding off. If they looked sharp they might get an hour's play before the rain came.

When Kitty arrived at the Royal George, Gabriel Gullet was sitting on the high pub wall, long-trousered now, and quite the young man.

Esme, who had been watching for Kitty, ran out and dragged her into the side-alley, further away from Gabriel's gaze. 'I can't come out, Kitty,' she whispered. 'Mama bawled at me like a banshee about us putting on our concert. Said I was making a show of myself down at Forgan Buildings. An exhibition, she said. And she wasn't paying all that money for me at Princess May's for me to go prancing in the dust in our Gabriel's clothes, singing for paupers. She says you're a bad influence. That I'm to be a young lady...'

Kitty put a hand on her arm. 'Just come, Es. Tek no notice of her. I'm gunna show you a unicorn and these lovely eggs...'

Esme glanced up at Gabriel. 'She's put him to guard me, Kitty. I've to stay and help Mabella with the dusting.' She wrenched her arm out of Kitty's grasp. 'Sorry, Kit. Maybe she'll loosen up tomorrow.' Her face was thin and drawn.

The radiance which had shone from her after her performance, endowing her with disconcerting beauty, was now extinguished. 'Maybe tomorrow we can see the unicorn.'

Kitty stepped back. 'Aye, maybe.' She watched as Esme walked away, shoulders hunched, head down. Then she set out along the street, not knowing quite where to go or what to do.

'Kitty Rainbow!' a voice called softly behind her.

She looked around and a clod of earth exploded at her feet. She raised her eyes into Gabriel Gullet's smirking face. He put out his tongue. 'So what does it feel like to be a pauper, a cripple, and a bastard too, Kitty Rainbow?'

'Shut yer gob!' She leaned down and picked up a stone, took aim and threw it at him. He ducked and looked her hard in the eyes. At this moment, to her dismay, her eyes began to fill of tears.

Gabriel, sensing her fragility, leaped down before her. He removed his long scarf and wound one end in his right hand, letting the other trail to the ground. Then he moved towards her.

Kitty bolted, pushing through crowds of busy shoppers in the Market Square, jumping over walls and down alleyways to get right out of his way, her eyes streaming.

She glanced back and saw she was managing to keep a good distance between herself and the dodging Gabriel. The running training meant she was in much better shape than he was. But still, at that moment, the long scarf, ribboning up into the air from his hand, was to her more menacing than any sword or cannon, any rifle or sabre.

Finally, gasping for breath, Gabriel Gullet stopped at the bottom of Viaduct Street and watched her run on. He grinned, slung his scarf around his neck, put both hands to his mouth and yelled, 'Ba-astard! Ba-astard!'

She reached the broad stretch of lush grass which led to the river and finally slowed down. She looked back and Gabriel Gullet was nowhere to be seen. She bit some deep breaths from the air, wiped her eyes with the back of her hand and sat in the grass. But the tears continued to come, developing into sobs of anger as she cursed herself for not turning and facing Gabriel Gullet as Ishmael had taught her; she blamed herself for not putting on the glowering face which had always stood her in good stead in times of threat, and had fended off many an adversary.

Something to do with Esme, it was. Something to do with the birds' eggs and the unicorn. Something to do with Esme's narrow worried face, with the feel of her arm wrenching away, her back turning and vanishing though the greasy door of the George Hotel.

Kitty wiped her face again with her hand, from her chin up through her hair. Her hand stilled. Her hair was wet as well as her face. She put her face up to the sky and soft rain joined the tears on her face, washing them down her neck and into the collar of her dress, right through to her thick shift.

She stood up and started to skip round and round in circles, slowly at first, then faster and faster. One of Esme's songs came into her mind and she started to sing.

> 'Are you going to Scarborough Fair?
> Parsley, sage, rosemary and thyme.
> Remember me to one who lives there.
> He once was a true love of mine . . .'

She stopped, swaying, and looked towards the viaduct, where the sun was still struggling to penetrate the rain from behind a sulphurous cloud. Then she smiled through her tears as she saw the rainbow arched like a protective hand over the viaduct. And under the viaduct, ghostly against the grey stone, stood a white roe deer, its head on one side, its round bland eyes in her direction. She peered more closely and saw that it had no horn. She would inform Freddie Longstaffe about that. Definitely not a unicorn.

Walking slowly back home she knew that Ishmael was right. The sun, the rain, and a strong right fist – they were her parents. She was no bastard. No bastard at all. But she did wonder who her real parents were.

Later, as she turned in through the arch into Forgan Buildings, she caught sight of the comforting, familiar figure of Ishmael in the doorway, hammer in hand. Janine Druce was sitting beside him on a cracket and her voice carried the length of the yard.

'Ah'd tek her back altogether, Ishmael. Never mind the money. Keep yer money. She's a miss, that bairn. All these years! She's been a miss. Ah've got our Thomas, but all yeh ever hear is that blessed squeezebox o' his, an' half the time he's chasin' after that Esme Gullet. Kitty Rainbow was company for me at least.'

Kitty started to smile. There was no doubt she loved living with Ishmael but in some ways she had missed her foster mother. Antijan was abrupt and sometimes violent; sometimes she hooked herself to a bottle and you had to risk injury to loosen her grip. But the most damage she did seemed to be to herself. And she was loyal to Thomas, who lots of people said should be in a lunatic asylum. Janine had befriended Ishmael and Kitty all those years ago, and she would defend Thomas with her last breath. There was something good about Janine.

How different Janine was to Mrs Gullet. A different kettle of fish altogether. And yet Ishmael had time for Mrs Gullet too.

Janine looked up and saw Kitty threading herself through the junk that littered the Forgan yard. 'And what're yer furrowin' that brow over now, Kitty Rainbow?'

Kitty grinned and dropped to sit on the ground beside her. Janine raised an eyebrow at Ishmael. 'She's been here before, that bairn, Ishmael. I've said that to yeh a thousand times.' She tapped Kitty on the shoulder. 'Yon Mrs Gullet's been in the shop complainin' o' the goin's on down here,

Kitty. Even warning our Thomas off. As if he had the wit to do any harm. Ah'm sayin' ter Ishmael yer should come back an' stay with me in the town now. No decent girl should live out here.'

Kitty shook her head. 'No thanks, Antijan,' she said firmly. 'I'm staying here with Ishmael. We belong together. Him an' me an' the rain an' the sun.'

It was Janine Druce's turn to shake her head. 'The Gullet woman's right. Bein' down here's turned yer head. Made you a lunatic.'

Ishmael laughed his deep laugh. 'Kitty is fine, Janine. Less a lunatic than me, you or even that very sane lady Mrs Mirella Gullet.

'Are you sure you won't have brandy, Mr Pommeroy?' Mirella smiled encouragingly at her visitor.

His curly hair and fine whiskers trembled on the air as he shook his dark head. His white teeth gleamed in response to her smile. 'I thank you, Mrs Gullet. Tea will be fine.' He took a sip. 'This is very fine tea.' His deep voice was threaded through with a reassuring sleepy tone, reminding her of a jockey friend of Jossy's who'd come from Devon. Or was it Dorset?

Mirella smiled her satisfaction. 'Assam, Mr Pommeroy, Assam! Mr Clintock gets it specially for me. I've to keep it under lock and key, or that Mabella, who calls herself my maid, would have it in a screw paper and off to her mother up in Wolsingham in a trice. Caught her at it once, you know.'

Jarrold Pommeroy shook his head in sympathy. 'Thieves everywhere, Mrs Gullet. You have to be so careful. So, like I was saying, Mrs Gullet, your little girl has some talent, seems to me.'

Mirella scowled. 'But she doesn't sing, our Esme. And the only dance she does is what she learns at Miss Petty's Academy. Ladies' dancing, you understand. What you saw was children's play. A make-believe. I had to punish her for it. And warn off that idiot Thomas Druce.'

He shook his head. 'What I saw, Mrs Gullet, was a young woman who with a bit of pushing and a bit of placing, dear lady, could be entertaining hundreds. Thousands.'

The beaded fringes on Mirella's dress trembled as she wriggled her shoulders, kneading her plump back into the plump chair. 'And is it you who could do that pushing and placing, Mr Pommeroy?' she said, her eyes narrowing.

He pursed his lips and took another delicate sip of his tea. 'Well, as you know, I'm working in travelling shows at this moment but I've an interest in one of the new music halls in Leeds, and very good friends in other places who'd show an interest in her.'

Mirella laughed. 'Mr Pommeroy! You have me intrigued and yet I can't think you're right about Esme. But...' He caught a whiff of her sweat as she leaned across and turned the bell lever at the fireplace.

Seconds later Mabella bustled in, wiping her hands on a none-too-white apron. 'Aye?' she said, wondering why the missis hadn't bellowed her command from the door as usual.

'Will you call Miss Esme, Mabella?'

'*Miss* Esme?' said Mabella. 'Ah'll gerr 'er for yeh.'

She stumped out and Mirella flushed, vowing to give the woman her notice and no reference. It was true Mabella did the work of four women, and between her and the three men in the bar, they kept the whole place going. But she showed you up, and that wouldn't do.

Esme sidled into the room, finally lurching forward as Gabriel pushed her in front of him, curious to know who this dark visitor was, sporting a velvet collar, deep lapels and velvet stripe down his pants. Quite the swell, he was, standing up now in a mannerly fashion on Esme's entering the room.

'Ah, Esme! You'll remember Mr Jarrold Pommeroy?' said Mirella sweetly. 'I believe he saw you dance and . . .' she coughed, as though the word was a huge pebble in her throat, '. . . sing.'

Esme bobbed a quick curtsy in Jarrold Pommeroy's direction without raising her eyes, and whispered, 'We were only playing, Mama.'

'. . . only playing,' echoed Gabriel in a sneering echo of her trembling voice. Esme jumped forward as he poked her on the bottom.

Mirella laughed. 'That is what I said, Esme. Children's play. But Mr Pommeroy thinks you're a charming singer. So perhaps you could sing now. For me.'

The ticks of the heavy mantelpiece clock sounded like the beating of a drum in the ensuing silence.

'Well, go on!' said Mirella crossly. 'Sing.'

'"A-are you going to Scarborough Fair? Parsley, sage . . ."' Esme's voice petered out.

Gabriel giggled. '"Are you going to Scarboro' . . ."' he whined in cruel parody.

Esme turned and faced him, her chin up. 'It's not the same here, without Kitty and without Thomas's music. How can I sing here?'

Jarrold Pommeroy came, put a soft hand on her shoulder and looked her in the eye. She noticed that his eyes were a bright grey-blue and thought in passing that his thick lashes would be the envy of many of the girls in her class. 'How would it be, Esme, if we went across there, to that place? If we took your musician? I've my gig outside.'

'Nice horse. I took a look,' said Gabriel appreciatively.

'Oh, I know my horses, my boy,' said Pommeroy. 'I know my horses. Now, Esme,' he continued briskly. 'Shall we do this? Show your dear mother just how good you are?'

The people of Forgan Buildings were agog at the procession of Pommeroy's gig and Mirella's chaise as they squeezed their way through the arch and stopped just by the middens, ten yards from Ishmael's door. Pommeroy handed Esme down from his carriage as though she were a fragile ornament. Gabriel leaped down from his mother's chaise and came across, very willing to hold the head of the restive, finely bred horse.

They had called at the draper's shop but Thomas Druce was nowhere to be found, so when Esme saw Thomas leaning with his back to Ishmael's wall, she breathed a sigh of relief.

Janine Druce hauled herself to her feet and walked across to Mirella's carriage. 'Evenin', Mrs Gullet. Now this is a surprise!'

'Hmmph!' Mirella stayed where she was. She rolled back the top of her chaise so she could see properly, and then pressed a purple frilled handkerchief to her nose at the smell which hovered all around her. The springs of the carriage creaked as Janine sat down on the steps. 'Och, Ah'll just take ma weight off ma feet an' watch the fun. Sommat's up here. Anyone can see that.'

Mirella, resisting the desire to poke her with her parasol and tell her to get off the chaise, glared helplessly at the back of her bonnet. Ishmael and Kitty watched all this for a second, then Kitty, her face splitting into a big grin, ran across to put her arm through Esme's. 'What's this? It's like Miss Adams says in her story, the mountain coming to Muhammad.'

'She,' Esme nodded wearily in her mother's direction, 'says she wants to hear me sing. I couldn't sing at home so they said I had to sing here. He,' she nodded at the figure of Jarrold Pommeroy, 'wants to hear as well. His name's Mr Pommeroy.'

'Pommeroy?' said Kitty. 'That's a bliddy silly name.'

'Nothing wrong with it.' Esme, smiling for the first time, poked Kitty in the ribs. 'No worse than Rainbow.'

Kitty laughed. 'Right!' she said. 'Let's get the curtain up

and do it properly.' She bustled Esme into the house past a stern-faced Ishmael, and reappeared with the blanket to drape over the washing line. From behind the blanket she peered across at Pommeroy and Mirella Gullet, sitting in their carriages, and the crowd of Forgan people who had gathered to witness the drama.

Kitty stepped out. 'I'll sing a song with Esme first 'cos she's nervóus,' she called in her loudest voice. 'Then she'll sing herself. The lad playing the squeezebox is called Thomas Druce.'

Thomas looked blandly over the heads of the crowd and continued to fiddle with his buttons.

Esme and Kitty sang 'Scarborough Fair' together, then Esme continued on her own, her songs wound round and punctuated by the fluid, spritely tones of Thomas's squeezebox. With every round of wild Forgan applause Esme seemed to stand up straighter, and her sparkle increased. When the people shouted for her to sing the sailor songs she raced in and threw on Gabriel's sailor suit and performed them with gusto.

The last applause died down and both she and Jarrold Pommeroy looked across at Mirella. 'As I said, Mrs Gullet, with a bit of primping and placing, that is a talent which could fill your pockets with golden guineas.'

After a second's silence Mirella's tones rang across the yard. 'Of course, Mr Pommeroy, I was always known for my singing voice when I was a girl.'

'She's wearing my clothes, Mama,' complained Gabriel. 'She looks a rare cut.'

But now all their gazes moved to Ishmael, who had put down his hammer and was striding across to Mirella Gullet's chaise. Then he was shaking it.

'No, you stupid woman, you can't do this. Not to that little girl. Not even you can do such a wicked thing, putting the children on show like some little pierrots. You know what happens to such girls,' he roared.

Kitty drew closer to Esme and realised they were both trembling. 'Stop it, Ishmael,' she shouted. 'You're frightening Esme. You're frightening her.'

9

Making the Deal

Esme turned over in bed, disturbed by the scrape of curtain rings which preceded the flood of white winter light into her narrow bedroom. She peered through her tumbled hair into Mabella's open leathery face.

'If yer sit up, hinney – sorry, *Miss* Esme – I'll put yer tray on yer knee.' The maid was watching her with the smallest of smiles.

Esme struggled into a sitting position. 'What's this, Mabella? *Miss* Esme? A tray?'

Mabella settled the tray, with its dish of eggs and fine china cup of tea, on Esme's knee. She plumped up the pillow behind Esme's narrow back. '*Her ladyship* – sorry, yer ma, Mrs Gullet – telt us to bring it up for tha. Said thoo'd be *fatigued* with thee efforts yesterday.' Mabella plonked herself down on the embroidered stool beside Esme's bed. 'So what's tha been up to, hinney?'

Esme giggled.

'Mabella, can you believe it? Seems Mama and Mr Pommeroy want to put me on the stage. I'm to go to Leeds and take singing lessons with a woman Mr Pommeroy knows. Then maybe I'll sing in music halls.'

Mabella shook her head doubtfully. 'I'd watch that Pommeroy feller, Esme. Snake eyes, that's what he's got.'

'No,' protested Esme. 'He has these really silvery blue eyes, and thick lashes...'

'Like Ah said, snake eyes,' said Mabella succinctly. She creaked herself to her feet. 'Now Ah'd better get on, hinney. Sittin' round here winnet get the bairn a bonnet, will it?'

She stumped off and Esme sipped her tea, contemplating the delights of being in her fickle mother's favour once more.

A few minutes later the latch clicked and Kitty's head popped round the door. 'What's this? Breakfast in bed?'

'How d'you get in?' grinned Esme. Kitty was not normally allowed over the Gullet threshold. Since the burning of the bedspread there had been other small decisive incidents which had put Kitty firmly out of favour at the Royal George. The one thing these incidents ensured was that Gabriel never again came after his sister. Instead Kitty had became the deliberate focus of his malevolent, though not lascivious attention.

'Mabella let me in the back door. So what's all this royal treatment?'

'Seems, Kitty Rainbow, that Esme Gullet – *Miss* Esme Gullet, the great singer, mind you – *Miss* Esme Gullet, can do no wrong!' Esme held out her fork, 'Here, have some egg. I think Mama's fattening me up for the pot.'

Kitty climbed into bed with her and they set about polishing off the remnants of the breakfast together.

'So what's it that feller wants you to do?' Kitty said, spitting bits of egg as she talked.

'Wants me to go and get singin' lessons in Leeds where he comes from, and sing for my supper. He knows this woman who was very successful on the stage. She would teach me the tricks.'

'Where'd you sing?' asked Kitty, wiping her mouth with the corner of her apron.

'In halls I think at first. Song and supper places. He seems especially interested in me singing in boy's clothes. Natural. Unaffected, he said I was. Mama was shivering with delight at all the compliments.'

Kitty cleared out the last of the eggs. 'Unaffected. What's that mean?' she said.

'I don't know. Maybe he thinks I'd make a bonnier boy than girl.'

Kitty kneeled up in bed and turned Esme to face her, pushing the tangled hair away from her friend's face. 'But you're a bonny lass, Esme. You've a fine face and a lovely long straight nose.'

'But what about these horrible cheeks,' said Esme, inflating the maligned flesh with air to emphasise the effect. 'Our Gabriel says they're like bags of tripe. I'm like some old alderman.'

Kitty put her head on one side and half closed her eyes. 'Well, now you come to say it, you are pretty ugly.'

Esme shrieked, picked up a pillow and started to batter Kitty, who picked up the other pillow and took a whack at her. The fabric broke over Esme's head, exploding like blown dandelion seed; the air shimmered with a foam of white goosefeathers.

The door burst open and they stopped mid-blow to see Esme's mother, red-faced, standing in the bedroom doorway. In the second's silence which followed, the white feathers fell softly, a particularly curly one settling on Mirella's padded, elaborately coiffed head.

Then the girls started to laugh again and Mirella caught Kitty by the elbow, yanked her off the bed, pushed her through the door and banged it behind her.

She advanced on her daughter. 'Now, lady . . .' she said.

Making her way back to Forgan Buildings Kitty came across Freddie Longstaffe and two much older boys sitting on the long wall outside the Methodist Chapel. They must be his brothers – taller, broader, versions of Freddie himself; their features, like his, large and well-chiselled. In addition, they had the powerful sinewy hands and corded muscles of the coal hewer, the most senior member of the mining brotherhood.

''Lo, Freddie.' Kitty cocked her head in greeting.

He grinned. 'Now, Kitty Rainbow,' he said, jumping down to walk beside her. 'How goes it?'

'Mrs Gullet's just chucked us out of the George for funfightin'.'

Freddie looked up at his brothers. 'Kitty Rainbow was in my class at school. She's a scrapper,' he said proudly. 'Her dad was a boxer. Boxed the big fellers. Kitty, this is our Albert an' our Hughie.'

The older boys exchanged glances and winked at Kitty. 'Watcher, Kitty Rainbow,' said the one called Albert.

'He's not my dad,' she said.

'Who is he, then?' said Freddie.

'He's my ... we belong together.' She walked on with Freddie prancing alongside her. 'What's it you want?' she said crossly.

'I'm going in the pit,' he said. 'Starting Monday.'

'I thought you were working at the chemist's?'

Freddie shrugged. He'd won a rare scholarship to the Grammar School but had been unable to take it up. The Prior's School had been established in the time of King James as a school for poor scholars, the costs and remaining fees to the Grammar School were too high for his father and brothers to contemplate. Work was good at present but they had no confidence in its permanence. Fees were a five-year commitment. His headmaster, frustrated at the waste of talent, had obtained a job for him in Mr Mackie's, the chemist's, recommending him as a very good scholar, quick to learn whatever he was set.

'Only stuck that smelly shop for a week,' said Freddie. 'Expected yer to bow an' scrape to the customers, an' to him an' all. Wanted more'n a day's work for a day's pay. Like our Albert says, more'n yer dignity's worth. Better off down the pit with the proper men. Anyway, Albert got me set on at White Leas Pit. Not on the traps, I'm too big for that. But he says I can help his putter an' he'll give us money off his wage.'

Kitty winced. 'Down there in the dark! Aren't you frightened?'

He put back his shoulders. 'Me da's down there, Kitty. An' all our lads. They'll show us. Nowt to be frightened of.'

They were at the corner of the High Street. 'Can I walk yer down to yer house?' he said.

'Why?'

He shrugged. 'For company? Last wish of the condemned man?'

'It's a free country,' she said, walking just a bit more quickly.

He lengthened his stride. As they walked along his hand bumped hers and he tried to grasp it. She pulled her hand away and put it in her apron pocket, talking, pretending nothing had happened. She was relieved when they parted at the big archway into Forgan Buildings. Freddie nodded briefly to her, turned away and started to run.

She called him back.

He walked slowly towards her. 'What is it?' he said.

'Just, I hope it's all right Monday. In the pit.'

'Bound to be,' he said. 'The pit and me was made for each other.' Then he leaned over and kissed her cheek and was off with a bound, giving her no chance to reprimand him for taking her on the wrong foot; no chance to respond with a sound left hook, which she had been known to do in their four-year half-friendly, half-combative relationship.

She rubbed her burning cheek and wondered about the world, which seemed to be performing somersaults around her. First Esme being swept on to some stage or other and

101

now Freddie Longstaffe doing this. She rubbed her cheek and was surprised how soft it felt under her own hand.

Jarrold Pommeroy rubbed the dry palms of his hands together with frustration. He should have been on the train now, sharing a pipe with Ned Lumb, instead of sitting here in this dingy bar parlour arguing the toss over a slip of a girl, with a greedy-eyed woman who was upholstered like a sofa.

This trip north, with Ned Lumb and a group of other followers of the turf, had been by way of a neat break from a little tangle he'd got into in Leeds about a horse which had lost a race when it shouldn't.

Then, when Ned had taken him on the visit to the old boxer in that sewer across the town, he had seen that child singing and he was hooked. He was annoyed at his own obsessive reaction to this feline girl child strutting round the stage with bold sailor's steps. In his mind's eye he could see her lit by flaring lamps on a low stage. In his inner ear he could hear men's voices roaring with approval at the blunt quality of her innocence. He had seen fillies in the horsebreeders' yards with that same nervous star quality.

Jarrold had been certain the vulgar Gullet woman would be putty in his hands. He had always, even when he was young, had a way with older women. But here was this pretentious old trout turning down an excellent chance for her daughter.

His even teeth gleamed when he smiled. 'It's an excellent chance for her, Mrs Gullet.'

Mirella nodded sagely. 'I do appreciate that, Mr Pommeroy. And had you not been so kind as to drawn my attention to it, I'd've been quite unaware of my Esme's very special talent. Quite unaware.'

'Then put that talent in my hands, my dear lady.' His drawling tones sharpened somewhat. 'I keep trying to tell you, Mrs Gullet, it's more than just talent. Esme has a strong sweet voice, but so have many young women, standing at their father's piano singing "Greensleeves". What she has is something more. A kind of presence; a shining self that, when she's up there on the platform, makes people want to look at her, to share with her . . .'

Mirella was staring at him, baffled.

He breathed very deeply. 'I guarantee to you, Mrs Gullet, if you let me take care of her, your daughter will be singing for the Prince of Wales in five years. Three years!' He sipped his tea, slurping only very slightly.

Mirella's eyes gleamed. 'This seems very beneficial to Esme, Mr Pommeroy. Even beneficial to me. I wonder how all this will benefit you, Mr Pommeroy?'

'It'd be an honour to be the manager of such talent.'

She put her head on one side, her eyes narrowing.

'Well, I can see what you're thinking,' he said. 'You're a businesswoman, Mrs Gullet, first and foremost. If Esme comes up to scratch, benefits will accrue to the man who makes the arrangements. That much is obvious. I will make a fair profit from it. But so will you and so will she. Don't you see that?'

'I see well enough. And what I say to you, Mr Pommeroy, is that I will think about all this. Perhaps she could become such an entertainer under my guidance alone.'

He shook his head. 'You know nothing of the world about which you speak, Mrs Gullet. That would be disaster. It has its own rules.'

Corset creaking, she sat inches taller in her overstuffed chair and glared at him, her eyes bulging.

He could have eaten the words almost before they were out. 'I don't mean . . . a genteel lady such as yourself . . .' Pommeroy leapt to his feet as Mirella stood up.

She walked towards the door and opened it, standing back. 'Well, as I say I have my doubts, Mr Pommeroy. My Esme is barely sixteen. She's not even put her hair up yet.'

Jarrold Pommeroy thought again of that pure voice and the slender deceptive figure, and scrambled to regain grace with this formidable woman. 'Well, perhaps you're right. Perhaps I could be of some limited service in advising you and Esme...'

'Perhaps.' She smiled blandly at him.

He grasped at a straw. 'There's another matter, Mrs Gullet. About your son...'

'Gabriel? He's no singer.'

'No. No. He tells me he's leaving the Grammar School and'll be looking for a place soon. I've a friend, an acquaintance really. A lawyer who's looking for a clerk. Tobias Hunter, of Hunter, Brewster and Co.' His acquaintance Tobias Hunter was a cold creature, as many gamblers are, but he owed Jarrold Pommeroy more than one favour.

Mirella beamed at him, her earlier reservations forgotten. She could not turn down what might prove to be a good chance for Gabriel. 'That firm's very well known in Priorton, Mr Pommeroy. It'd be a good start for him. Jossy would've liked that, his son a solicitor. He was a man of humble origins himself.'

You too, thought Jarrold Pommeroy sourly. You're no lady and never were. However, he was satisfied. The connection of obligation was made. He was good at making tenuous connections of obligation. He would get his way about young Esme eventually, he knew that now. He shook her hand heartily. 'I'll talk to Mr Hunter about Gabriel.' He paused. 'And we can keep in touch about young Esme?'

She nodded. 'Oh yes, Mr Pommeroy. You seem to have shown a genuine interest in the child. I can't deny you that, my dear sir. I can't deny it at all.' Her eyes narrowed as, unbidden, into her mind came an image of the men in the entry all those years ago: the sound of joshing voices, the change of tone, and the pain as they despoiled her.

She stood up. 'Now if you please, sir, I've an extremely busy afternoon ahead of me. A public... a hotel doesn't run itself, you know.'

He touched rather than shook her hand, and half-backed

from the room. Outside, he shook out his hat and perched it on his head. He smiled. It had been touch and go, but he felt that this round had been down to him. Even despite the woman's brusque dismissal. Even despite that.

10

Apprentices

The following morning, when Kitty returned with the milk, Ishmael told her to put on her best dress and give that wild hair of hers a good brush. Make it smooth and tidy.

'Why?' she asked.

'We have business to do. First with Mrs Druce, then I want you to come with me to the George. I have the rent money to pay over to Mr Crane and I want to speak with Mirella Gullet about you.'

'About me? You're gunna talk me over like I was a pound of fish?' Sparks crackled in the little kitchen as she brushed her hair with furious energy.

Her funny tale about being thrown out of the George yet again yesterday, for pillow fighting, had been greeted by scowls on Ishmael's part. 'She has no reason to treat you so,' he had said crossly. He was feeling badly about losing his temper with Mirella over Esme. Paradoxically, his guilt made him blame her even more, though Kitty shared the blame.

'It seems you're not trained to a proper house. You're trained to fight, to face up, to be at the ready, to enjoy hard fun. But go on like this you'll be outcast from . . . you won't

107

be able to spend time with girls like Esme . . .' His voice had trailed off then; he was not quite sure what he wanted to say.

Now he was even telling her to put on her bonnet.

'My bonnet? That's only for every second Sunday for chapel!'

But he insisted. So far in their life together Ishmael had been a very tolerant parent, had been insistent on very few matters. On the rare occasions he did express himself with force Kitty obeyed him with alacrity.

Janine Druce seemed to be expecting them. She was wearing a fine lace cap and the chenille-covered table was clear, except for a large sheet of paper, a pen and an inkwell. Thomas was sitting in the corner by the fire polishing his squeezebox with spit and hard rubs.

Kitty leaned over the sheet of paper in the dim inside light and made out the word 'INDENTURE' printed out in an elaborate hand.

Ishmael sat down in the big chair by the table and pushed the paper towards Kitty. 'This is to apprentice you to Mrs Janine Druce for seven years, Kitty; a binding agreement so that then you will be a proper draper. Then you will always make for yourself a living. Even when I am nowhere around to cobble shoes to buy our bread.' The foreignness in his accent always intensified when he was moved or upset by something.

Kitty pushed the paper back towards him. 'I'm not signing anything for seven years of my life.'

'You already do apprentice's work with me, Kitty,' said Janine, pushing the paper back towards her. 'Sewing's in yer blood. Dinna forget that embroidery yer came wrapped in. Ah'd wager yer mother made that. You've been sewin' yerself since you were seven years old.'

'But I never signed anything,' Kitty said uneasily, suddenly invaded by the seriousness of all this, a sense of destiny. Her lip trembled. Perhaps if her mother had kept her *she* would have been teaching her to sew.

Ishmael pulled her towards him so that she stood in the warm leathery circle of his arm. 'It's time to grow up a little, Kitty. There's a time to put to one side the wild joys of the small child. We do you no favour if we allow you to grow into a misfit.'

'Ha! Can't have a misfit as well a cripple, can we?' Unshed tears were standing in her eyes.

His beard bristled her cheeks as he kissed each one. 'No, little one, we can't. Not if we want those there in the outside world to treat you well. Here.' He dipped the pen in the ink and handed it to her.

She signed.

Janine peered at her signature. 'She writes with a fine hand,' she said.

'The Prior's School has done very well for Kitty,' said Ishmael. He reached into an inner pocket and brought out a clinking leather pouch which he laid carefully on the chenille cloth by the document.

Then Thomas struck up with 'What Shall We Do with the Drunken Sailor?' and they all laughed. Janine poured them each a glass of lemon cordial without a single glance at the sticky bottle of whisky on the top of the dresser.

'Do you know what she wants me to do now?' said Esme later, as Kitty let Ishmael go on inside the Royal George and perched herself beside Esme on the short wall which faced the hotel stables.

'What?' said Kitty, still subdued by the awful finality of signing the indentures.

'Sing in the billiard room.'

'You mean standing on a billiard table?'

'No. They're taking the billiard tables out, putting dainty little tables in. She's bought a grand piano from Mr Maxted the grocer. She's going to have what she calls a *very superior* song-and-supper room.'

'Who'll play the piano?'

Esme shrugged. 'Don't know and don't care. I've told her twenty times I would only ever sing with Thomas playing...'

Thomas, sitting six feet away, braced against a stall, lifted his head as his name was spoken, but did not look in their direction.

'...and with you there.'

'Me?'

'We started it together.' Esme blinked and looked harder at Kitty, her thoughts finally penetrating the world outside her own dramas. 'So what's this, Kit? Best frock? Is it Sunday?'

Kitty folded her arms. 'I've changed, Es. I'm now an indenture...'

'I read about that in the paper. Isn't that where they make you china teeth instead of your own?'

'No, no. I signed an indenture paper and am 'prenticed properly to Janine Druce. A draper's apprentice. A proper one.'

'You probably know more'n her anyway. You've been doing her work for years.'

'Only aprons and petticoats for her to sell in the shop; dressmakering, not drapering. She has to show me drapering. Being a draper's about buying cloth from travellers and factories, supplying dressmakers more than being a dressmaker yourself.'

'I can't imagine it,' said Esme, giggling. 'You!'

'Neither can I,' said Kitty gloomily. 'And there's another thing.'

'What?'

'Freddie Longstaffe kissed us an' I don't know what to do about it.'

Esme was intrigued. 'But that's not fair, Kitty. I've not been kissed yet and I'm four years older than you.' She paused. The pushing mouth of Gabriel in the dark, stopped now, did not count. 'What was it like?'

'Toffee fudge,' said Kitty. 'Sweet and soft.'

Inside the George, Ishmael's tone with Mirella was both reprimanding and pleading. 'You must not keep her away from Esme, Mirella. They are sisters, those two, and Esme stops her from being completely wild. Kitty is young, Mirella. And, but for me, alone in the world. Isn't she bound to be wild? I am trying my best. I have had her sign proper apprentice papers this morning with Mrs Druce, so there's a grown-up obligation now to tie her down. And I will keep her tidy.'

'I must say she was tidier when she came today. A decent dress and a bonnet.'

'She made them herself,' said Ishmael eagerly. 'She has patience and skill when she needs it.'

Mirella bowed her head. 'I concede this, Ishmael, but I can't understand why you're pressing me so.'

'You've thrown Kitty out of the George three times in a week.'

Mirella fiddled with her gold watch chain. 'But she's a reprobate, Ishmael. And she sets free the same wildness in my Esme, who's uncontrollable when Kitty's around. It all started with that matter of the fire years ago. I'm sure it was something to do with Kitty. And there's been some incident every week since.'

He nodded his head. 'Yes. I know that. But I've given her stern warnings now, so none of that will happen again . . .' He met Mirella's frosty stare. '. . . Well, only very rarely.' He paused. 'But you must not take their comradeship away from her, Mirella. The child has neither kith nor kin, even though she and I are closer than any father and daughter. And she made Esme her sister almost from the start. Esme has blossomed in the friendship they share. You cannot deprive her of her sister.'

Mirella sighed, then tossed her heavily coiffured head. 'My dear Ishmael, who said anything about taking her away? Perhaps she has learned her lesson now, with the two of us bearing down on her from both sides. There is no question of their not remaining ... connected.' Mirella looked across at Ishmael with involuntary and uncharacteristic softness. He was one of the few men who did not arouse a well-stifled fear in her. Jossy had been like that: strong, powerful but with nothing to prove. And Ishmael had been so good in bed. Powerful, directive, comforting. When she could get him there. It seemed such a long time ago.

'Now.' Her jet beads swung as she leaned towards him. 'Let us old friends have a drop of brandy to celebrate our taming of the shrew ... sorry! ... our bringing the lamb into the fold of good behaviour.'

Ishmael shook his head. 'You know I never touch it now, Mirella, never. But a strong cup of tea would not come amiss.'

'And then perhaps you'll stay awhile with me?' With her head on one side she looked for all the world like a sharp-eyed parrot.

There was genuine, if reluctant sympathy and admiration in his smile. If there was to be a price for Kitty's reinstatement, so be it. 'Indeed I will, Mrs Gullet. Indeed I will.'

Esme was at first a modest, then an increasingly popular success, performing in Mirella's new 'superior song-and-supper room' at the George. Kitty spent some time helping her to sort out her music, choosing songs which generated waves of approval from the audience, mostly men, in the brightly lit room. These successful songs were fixed in the programme. The girls took no advice from Mirella, who wanted Esme to sing only her personal sentimental favourites, but soon learned to include in their programme a fast song and a slow song, a comic song and a sentimental song.

Mirella did make one contribution. One day she travelled to Darlington and returned with two heavy books: *Songs for the*

Parlour and *Songs from the French Stage*. From these books the girls chose songs for their sentiments, for their drama, and one or two for their sauciness. Kitty knew instinctively what was right for Esme. Her choices drew roars of approval from the crowd.

Esme sight-read the chosen pieces and sang them to Thomas, who instantly transformed them on his squeeze-box to tunes which, in their jauntiness and tone, fitted Esme like a glove.

The success was reflected in more money in Mirella's till. Encouraged by this success, she employed another singer, an Irish baritone, and a string quartet who played obscure scraps of fine music which were not understood, but, like the other acts, were cheered to the well-oiled echo.

Reverberations of this fine music wove their way through Thomas's skilful fingers into Esme's performances, giving them a style and polish unusual in such *ad hoc* presentations, which were being made at this time in small hotels, public houses and improvised halls right across the country.

Jarrold Pommeroy was a regular customer at the music evenings at the George. From time to time Esme found herself looking across the brilliantly lit room into his bright dark face. Each time this happened it made her falter in her song.

In the end, noticing this same incident three nights running, Kitty worked her way across to Jarrold and asked him to go into the smoking room, as he was putting Esme off, stopping her from doing her songs properly. His hands tightened round his cane as he looked angrily down at this large-eyed, bushy-haired girl, neat and tidy now but radiating the residual aggression of the street child.

'Like I said,' insisted Kitty determinedly, 'there's comfortable seats in the smoking room.'

He stayed put. 'So what are you, Miss Pushy? Her guard? Her dresser? Her manager?' His voice coarsened. It had lost the affectation, the oiliness he reserved for Mirella. His glance dropped to her foot, clad in its finely made, neatly stacked right shoe. 'Not her dancer, I imagine.'

A patter of applause clicked through the room for Esme's less than perfect rendition of 'I'm the Dark Girl Dressed in Blue'.

Kitty curled her hands into fists. 'I'm Esme's friend, Pommeroy. An' if it wouldn't upset her more I'd punch you on the nose here an' now.'

He stood up, so near her she could smell his pomade, then he clicked his teeth, pushed past her and made for the smoking room.

As the months went by Kitty started to spend spare minutes altering and making Esme's performing clothes, cutting Gabriel's clothes to a tighter and smoother fit, creating masculine-style shirts, cut and tucked to a fine fit, which emphasised Esme's slender feminine figure. This was in strangely attractive contrast with her long heavy face, which lit up as she sang her earnest songs of a sailor longing for his distant sweetheart, or relishing the robust sailor's life with its opportunity for colourful travel and fine ladies.

All this fuss over Esme was observed with sour resentment by Gabriel. Here was his weedy, whiny sister luxuriating in all this attention and he had to go out six days a week, sombre-suited and high-hatted, to Tobias Hunter's office in the Market Square. Once there he had to spend endless hours standing at a tall desk laboriously copying long, extremely boring documents.

His only highlight was when Jarrold Pommeroy called on his friend Tobias Hunter. Pommeroy always had a cheery word for Gabriel, slapping him on the back and saying he hoped Mr Hunter was not too much of a slave-driver, ho-ho! Only by the shiver of a cheek muscle did Hunter show his distaste of such *bonhomie*.

One Saturday Gabriel was informed by a sour-faced Hunter that he was free for the afternoon, and he left the office with a spring in his step. Round the corner he bumped into Jarrold Pommeroy, who was lounging nearby with his tall hat tipped to shade his eyes. He stood up and shook Gabriel heartily by the hand. 'Ha! Just the boy! Now then, how would you like to taste the pleasures of the turf, Gabriel Gullet? I need someone to run errands for me today at the track. I understand from your mother that your father was a keen racing man.'

Gabriel glanced at the massive door which had just swung to behind him. 'Is it because of you that Mr Hunter...?'

Mr Pommeroy pushed his hat to the back of his head, took off his yellow suede glove and cupped his hand under Gabriel's nose. 'There, my boy. I have that lawyer there in the palm of my hand.' He smirked. 'So are the mighty fallen.'

Gabriel frowned at Pommeroy. 'How so?'

Pommeroy put a finger to his nose. 'The weaknesses of men, my boy.'

'So what about me in all this?'

'Well,' said Pommeroy, his face smooth, 'I had a thought you could be a kind of ... apprentice. Learn the tricks of the trade.'

It was Gabriel's turn to look innocent. 'And what trade would that be, Mr Pommeroy?'

'Well, dear boy, the trade of robbing Peter to pay Paul, of gulling fools for their money, of painting horses and shaving odds, of warming marks and pleasing women. What say you, dear boy? Are you on?'

11

Performance

Kitty took to her apprentice work with gusto. For a time Janine enjoyed playing the role of master-draper with her new apprentice in tow. She started to wash her face properly again. She wore her hat at a jaunty angle and there was a bounce in her step. In the leather sack in an inner pocket of her petticoat jingled the sovereigns given by Ishmael, part of their bargain. This sum, almost his total savings, was to secure Kitty's future in the trade.

Janine relished this more optimistic turn of events and drank less, to demonstrate her goodwill. She decided that here, finally, was the new start of which she had dreamed.

She made Kitty dress in sober clothes, pin her wild hair back with a dark blue ribbon and sit beside her in her trap. Together they called on her former customers: dressmakers in the villages and small towns of South Durham. She explained to these good ladies that she was now in the process of restocking her shop and had a new apprentice, a highly skilled girl who would make all the difference to the service she would offer. Kitty's ears burned to hear herself described in this way. Janine rehearsed the litany of bombazine, calico, flannels and worsted, which were all due now for delivery, as were the cottons just imported from India. Would they like to see samples next time?

Janine bought Kitty a small ledger of her own and made her write down the details of each customer: what garments she usually made, who were her clients, what special item she might be interested in if it were obtainable. In addition she made her note there the personal information about the woman's family and her life generally: knowledge which might, in some esoteric fashion, be useful. Kitty added notes of her own which she kept private from Janine.

Janine's optimism, and the demure promise implicit in the person of the neat new apprentice, infected even the most taciturn and reserved of the village dressmakers. These were successful outings. In each cluttered parlour there were nods all round when Janine said they would call again.

After that, the pair processed around the warehouses and mills where Janine owed money, so that she could flourish the leather bag of sovereigns, pay her bills and inform her creditors that from now on her new apprentice, Miss Kitty Rainbow, might be collecting stock.

One day they called at Scree Hall Mill, a small old-fashioned woollen mill three miles outside of Priorton, in a hamlet called Swanby. Here, wool collected from cottage spinners in Weardale and Swaledale was made into very basic flannel for working clothes. Unlike more advanced mills, the work here was still done on handlooms which clanked and rattled at the behest of brawny hands and feet.

The overman was Tom Vart, a muscular man who worked a loom himself. Catching sight of Janine in her frills and flounces, he wiped his hand on a dirty rag and came across to greet them. Like many men, he had a soft spot for the engaging Scotch draper who knew just how to talk to a man: hard and businesslike with her rasping

Scottish voice, but somehow resonating with availability. More than once in their acquaintance she had settled an outstanding bill with 'services rendered', until Tom Vart's wife, an Irishwoman with the instincts of a hare, had got wind of the nature of the transactions and had put a stop to it.

Today Tom Vart's voice was unctuous as he informed Mrs Druce with regret that once again he would have to refuse to supply her stock, what with her owing so much still. Then his face split into a grin when, after introducing her apprentice, she called over the clack of the looms that she was here to pay off her dues.

'Now that's nice to hear, Mrs Druce,' he shouted back. He moved down through the looms to the far end of the shed to his 'office': a battered high desk in a dusty corner. He rubbed his hand again on his smock and opened the ledger that was sitting on its greasy surface.

While the two of them completed their business Kitty wandered around the shed, counting the looms and making notes in her book; she fingered the pile of finished cloth and made more notes. The six weavers, men aged between twenty and sixty, flicked glances in her direction but never stopped once in their actions. Tom Vart took special pleasure in punishing and fining for any breach of the rules. In her book Kitty wrote down, 'Six looms, all worked by men.'

Finally she climbed on to the stool behind Tom Vart's deserted loom by the door, and sat, extending her toes to touch the pedals, and rolling the bobbins to and fro on the tight weft. A bobbin rolled off and she bent to peer at where it had gone.

'Well, miss, does it meet your approval?'

Her head shot up into the severe face of a very tall man, heavy-nosed and full-lipped. He must have crept into the loomshed. She tipped up her chin. 'I was thinking, sir, with blocks on, a woman could work this, easy.'

'Were you now? Easy, you say?'

She met his eyes, which were large like his other features. And they were so dark it was hard to tell pupil from iris. They gleamed like those of Ishmael's old cat when it had a mouse between its paws.

Her hands, lying in her lap, curled into fists. 'No law against thinking, mister,' she said.

'Gerroff that loom, lass,' boomed Tom Vart, bustling up from the other end of the shed. 'Yeh'll be doin' damage.' He removed his cap and clutched it between his hands. 'Ah didn't see yeh come in, Mr Scorton, sir.'

'Evidently,' said the man called Scorton. 'And whom have we here, Vart?' He planted his ebony cane before him, placed one hand over the other on the silver top and looked from Janine Druce to Kitty.

Tom Vart coughed, cursing his luck at being caught out. 'This is Mrs Druce, sir, the Scotch draper what buys flannel from us . . .'

Janine bobbed a curtsy.

'. . . an' her apprentice, whose name—'

'My name's Kitty Rainbow.' Kitty slid off the bench and waited a fraction too long before sketching her own curtsy.

Scorton nodded, not raising his hat as he would have with a perceived equal. His mouth stayed straight and grim, but the almost black eyes flickered with something that just might have been amusement.

'This is Mr Scorton, Mrs Druce, what just bought the mill from the old gaffer.'

The silence ticked on as the woman and girl were caught in Scorton's gaze like flies in amber. William Scorton completed his close examination of what he perceived as a very odd pair, then he put his stick under his arm, pulled off his gloves and turned to Vart. 'Now, Mr Vart, I want your purchasing and your sales ledgers for the past two years; I wish to have them at home. You may lift them into my trap . . .'

Tom Vart breathed a sigh of relief. The women were dismissed.

Janine curtsied again before dragging Kitty away. As they climbed into their trap, Janine bubbled on about Scorton. 'Now there's a fine man,' she said appreciatively. 'A fine man, Kitty. A handsome man.'

'Fine,' spluttered Kitty. 'Fine? He's an old man . . .'

Janine cackled. 'Old? Can't be a day over thirty.'

'. . . looking us over like he was at a cattlemart, more like. Who does he think he is, I'd like to know. Who the hell does he think he is?'

One Saturday afternoon Freddie Longstaffe called on Ishmael to have his best boots mended. The boots were newly inherited from his brother Albert, but, as Albert insisted, in no bad condition for all that.

Freddie said to Ishmael that he would wait for the boots, if that were all right with Mr Slaughter. It seemed he needed to wear them on that very night, as Albert had promised to take him to the Eagle for his first time 'in men's company'.

Ishmael chuckled at this and said that he would have to make a good job of it, if the men were going to look Freddie over in the Eagle. Kitty was in the yard outside, beating a mat with the back of a broom. On the line were three other mats waiting their turn.

'By, you've got better muscles than a coal hewer, Kitty Rainbow,' said Freddie appreciatively.

Kitty rolled up her sleeve and flexed her muscle. 'So I do,' she said proudly.

'I bet you're dyin' ter see mine,' he said.

'No I'm not.'

He grinned and rolled up his own sleeve and put his white, well-muscled arm alongside hers. 'There,' he said. 'Three times the size they were when I went down the pit. Even so you've got decent enough muscles for a girl, I'll give you that. Yours is half as big as mine and there's not many lasses in Priorton you could say that about.' He turned his hand and caught hers tight in his. 'What say we go for a walk in White Leas Woods, Kitty?'

'No fears,' she said, wrestling his hand away with her other hand. Her cheeks were bright red with the thoughts of that toffee-sweet kiss on the cheek, bestowed after their last walk together.

She could feel the warmth emanating from him: a tension in his whole body. 'Ah, gan on,' he said. 'A nice walk on a nice afternoon. I only get one Sat'day afternoon in two. Gan on!'

She picked up her broom again. 'No fears.'

'Doesn't Kitty need a nice walk, Mr Slaughter? Put roses in her cheeks, won'it?'

Ishmael, sitting in the doorway at his last, took the tacks from his mouth. 'The mats will wait, Kitty. You also have been working hard at your apprenticing this week. You should walk. You can bring back bluebells. I will have Freddie's boots ready when he gets back.'

She shrugged, took off her apron and put on her bonnet. Ishmael was right. It had been a hard week. There had been all the work at night on the aprons which were still a staple item in Janine's little shop, as well as the calling on customers and suppliers. It was a real pleasure to be pulled out of routine, whatever the reason.

Walking along with Freddie, she was conscious of other people's glances and, looking sideways at him, she tried and failed to bring into her mind the image of the cheeky, clever boy who had been her schoolmate. Here was a man. He, who had been a big, good-looking boy, was being pushed too early to manhood by doing a man's work. Suddenly she was pleased to be walking with Freddie Longstaffe; she relished the covetous glances of other girls as they walked by.

They picked bluebells and poked around birds' nests. He told her tales of the pit; of the heat and the wet and the heavy-laden tubs it was his job to push. He told her of his brother Albert and Albert's marrah, his workmate; how they gossiped on and abused each other and talked in a kind of code that was hard to crack. Freddy talked proudly of his brother's strength and endurance, and how that, above all, was admired underground.

They strolled slowly back to Forgan Buildings and as Kitty massed the bluebells into an old stoneware jar she was annoyed at herself for the disappointment she felt. This time, when he walked back with her, he had not attempted to kiss her.

Freddie collected the boots from Ishmael, strung them together and looped them round his neck. Then he pushed his cap to the back of his head, winked at Kitty and grinned. 'Canny walk, Kitty Rainbow,' he said, then strode off through the arch, whistling 'Scarborough Fair'.

Kitty removed her bonnet, put on her apron and picked up her broom.

'That young man seems to have taken a fancy to you, Kitty,' said Ishmael thoughtfully.

'That's rubbish, Ishmael,' said Kitty severely. 'You should know better than to say that. He was just waiting for his boots to be mended. That's all.'

There were now several song-and-supper rooms and music halls in Priorton, which operated with varying degrees of fame and notoriety. The room at the Royal George was both popular and well respected, with the intriguing Esme Gullet performing there nightly, and a changing bill of other artistes week by week. The most eminent venue in Priorton was the Windlass Theatre, a new, much-curlicued edifice prominent on Priorton High Street, which alternated popular melodramas with a music-hall bill.

One day the manager of the Windlass came to Mirella with a request that Esme should do a turn for him on a variety bill, between the acrobats and the magician. Urged on by her mother, Esme agreed to this, on condition that Thomas played for her and Kitty stayed close.

The following week, on stage at the Windlass, Esme played to more people in an evening than she played in a week at the George. She relished the experience, her voice deepening and strengthening in the larger auditorium. At first her accompanist, the glamorous, blankly silent Thomas Druce, was an object of some amusement to the musicians in the orchestra pit. But when they heard him play their amusement was cut short. Soon they were encouraging him to play alongside them for the other acts, the perky tension of the squeezebox adding a crisp counterpoint to their wheezing strings. Mr Molyneux, the conductor, said that Thomas's squeezebox 'gave a bit of beef to their rather thin ensemble.'

Freddie Longstaffe would sometimes come to the theatre to watch Esme, sitting with Kitty in the front row. He always stayed after the final curtain, while Kitty went backstage to reassure Esme that yes, yes, she had been all right, she was better every time. This was nothing less than the truth, so it was easy to say. Later Freddie would walk back to Forgan Buildings with Kitty. Often he would catch her hand and their arms would swing together as they walked and she would enjoy the rough texture of his work-worn skin against her softer palm.

Some of the 'theatricals' started to come into Janine's shop to talk to Kitty about the costumes she made for Esme, and order costumes for themselves. For the first time since Janine set up the shop, it started to flourish.

One night Esme's teachers, Miss Emily Petty and her sister, Miss Edina, attended the theatre, especially to see the drama of Mary Ann Cotton, recently hanged in Durham Gaol for murdering her children. Esme's turn closed the first half, before the presentation of this heart-rending drama. Seeing their quietest top-class girl cavorting on the stage in boys' clothes, which outlined the shape of her legs so very distinctly, the teachers leaped up in their seats and, whispering fiercely to each other, walked out.

The next day the teachers invited Mrs Mirella Gullet to school, there to discuss Esme's education, which they felt was suffering from this – er – *other activity*. They had not – er – *quite realised* that Esme, such a quiet girl in school, had such other calls made on her time. Miss Emily touched delicately on the propriety of exposing the young lady to the doubtful influences of the theatre and theatrical people.

The interview ended with a mortified Mirella storming from the school, having told them that, as *spinster ladies*, they were out of touch with real people and real life and her Esme had quite outgrown the limitations of the education they had to offer, thank you very much. She was nearly eighteen anyway, too old for school now. It had only been a matter of weeks anyway before she ceased to benefit from their guidance.

Another regular attender at Esme's performances, when he was in Priorton, was Jarrold Pommeroy. He was careful to keep away from Esme's eye-line during her turn, but sought her out afterwards and heaped her with oleaginous praise, picking out in endless detail the aspects of her performance deserving of high acclaim. He never forgot to praise himself for discovering such talent. He brought Esme flowers and wonderful chocolates which he said came all the way from Belgium. Esme fell on these with delight, insisting that Thomas and Kitty ate them with her, one for one, until they were gone.

Esme blushed at Jarrold's flattery and in time ceased to join in with Kitty in her wholesale dismissal of Pommeroy as a rogue. Before long, Esme was protesting at Kitty's critical comments about Jarrold, saying that, really, Jarrold was very nice. He only wanted the best for her, after all. He was so kind, so generous.

The two girls came close to quarrelling for the first time in all the years they had known each other. In the end Kitty refused to mention Jarrold to Esme, or even acknowledge his presence when he was there.

More often than not on his visits to the theatre Jarrold was accompanied by Gabriel, who now not only dressed like Pommeroy but walked with the same swagger. Gabriel had grown beefy-faced and heavy with the self-indulgences of drink and company learned alongside his older companion.

One night, after the two of them had shared a free bottle of brandy in the back parlour of the George, Jarrold joked with Gabriel about that stray Kitty Rainbow being his sister's guard dog, and an irritating little bitch at that. 'Needs bringing to heel, that one, dear boy. Bringing to heel. A good seeing to, if you know what I mean. She needs teaching what's what.'

Later, Kitty was threading her way through the back streets, making her way across to Forgan Buildings, when Gabriel jumped down in front of her from a wall. Swaying slightly, he stood with his hands on his hips, glaring at her with glittering eyes.

Kitty waited for the spoken insults but they did not come.

She took a step, trying to pass him one way and he blocked her. She tried to pass him another way and he blocked her again. Icy sweat started to trickle from her nape to the backs of her knees as she suddenly knew for certain his intention was worse than ordinary harm.

She took a deep breath and feinted a movement to one side, then caught Gabriel off balance as he bent the wrong way. She drew back her fist and felt it explode with agony as it smashed into his cheek. He crashed to the ground and was still. Trembling and nursing her sore hand, she kneeled down beside him, sighing with relief when she heard his stentorian breathing. Then, drawing painful ragged breaths, she made her way very unsteadily towards the arch and into the safety of Forgan Buildings.

12

Entering the Doors

Mirella gasped at the sight of Gabriel's bruised face. Fending off the fuss, Gabriel told his mother he had been set on by footpads on a track by the river. As he splashed his painful bruise at the kitchen sink, Mirella steamed off for a good ten minutes about the lawlessness which seemed to be around these days. Then, having other things on her mind, she let the matter lie there.

In the office, the following morning, Tobias Hunter viewed Gabriel's swollen eye and bruised cheek with distaste and sent him up to one of the high attics with instructions to sort and catalogue boxes of papers which had mouldered there for at least twenty-five years. Hunter observed sourly that the stigmata of a bruiser were hardly an appropriate sight for the respectable clients of Hunter, Brewster and Co.

Two hours later a jocular Jarrold Pommeroy came upon Gabriel crouched under the eaves, his scowling face covered with dust.

Jarrold leaned against the doorjamb, his arms folded. 'Well, well, the little cat scratched back, did she?' he drawled, the slightest of smiles on his face.

129

Gabriel stood up, cracked his head on a beam and groaned. 'She caught me off balance. I didn't get any chance to...'

'To what, dear boy?'

'You know. What you told me to do.'

'Told you?' Jarrold raised an innocent brow. 'I told you nothing. What you do, dear boy, is up to you.'

Gabriel rubbed his head and shook it like a dog shaking out a worrying bee. 'Anyway, old Hunter says I've to stay out of sight until my face is back to normal.'

'Ha! And I come with a solution, dear boy, to this very problem! I've just requested a week of your invaluable time from *old Hunter*, as you so sweetly describe him. I've to go to Leeds to do some business for Ned Lumb. I am to buy, or frighten, someone off a fight. And you must come with me. You can do some fetching and carrying.' Pommeroy laughed, showing his fine white teeth. 'Apart from anything else just a sight of that face of yours'll frighten the living daylights out of some poor punters. You look like a genuine bruiser now, which could just come in very useful, dear boy. They're not to know you were knocked down by a little lame girl, are they?'

'Leave off!' said Gabriel bitterly. 'Leave off, will you?'

When Kitty returned to Forgan Buildings with her broken hand, Ishmael was all for going and giving Gabriel Gullet a thrashing there and then but Kitty stopped him. 'I broke my hand myself, by my own will did I smash it in his face, Ishmael. You should see his face. That's why my hand's like this. If you cause a rumpus at the George, Esme might blame me, and she's the wrong way out with me already these days.'

It was true. Esme seemed to care less now whether Kitty was or wasn't at her performance, and did not seem too disturbed when Kitty was too late at her own work, or too tired, to make the trek either down to the

Windlass Theatre or the song-and-supper room of the George.

Ishmael turned Kitty's injured hand this way and that in his great paw. 'Now why would that be, Kitty? What is it between you? You two have always been the best of friends. Sisters, in fact.'

Kitty winced at his touch and drew back her hand. 'We *are* the best of friends, but that Jarrold Pommeroy's always lurking round now and Esme doesn't seem to mind. Me and Esme shouted at each other about it at first but now we don't talk about it at all. Maybe that's even worse.'

Ishmael shook his head. 'Things should not be unsaid between true friends, Kitty.'

Kitty nodded. 'I know. It spoils it all.' She held up her sore hand. 'Now can you bandage this, Ishmael? It's really that sore.'

'I know how sore it is. I've broken my hands many times in my life, Kitty.' He held out his own knobbly, arthritic hands and put them beside hers. 'Now this is another thing we share.'

He reached on top of the mirrored wardrobe and pulled down a small leather jar which contained the very last six sovereigns of his savings. 'We will go to Dr McBride. It will take a surgeon to fix it so it is straight. There are bones broken here.'

Kitty pulled on her bonnet, fastening it awkwardly with one hand. 'An' I can't go through life with a crippled hand as well as a crippled foot, can I?'

'Oh, dear Kitty,' he said, shaking his head as, carefully and clumsily, he took her bonnet ribbons from her and tied them himself.

In the months which followed it looked as though Kitty might just have to go through life with a crippled hand. Twice, an infection flared up in it and the doctor talked ominously about gangrene. He had seen that as a volunteer doctor in the Crimea and it was 'not a pretty sight, my dear.'

131

Ishmael's leather jar was soon empty, but Dr McBride kept coming, surprising himself with his own commitment to see the cure through for this earnest child and her great Atlas of a grandfather. Or was it father? Dr McBride sometimes talked around his dinner table of the tortuous relationships in some of the families he met in this benighted community at Forgan Buildings. But this pair were not typical, he assured his wife. There was something different about them.

In the months it took her hand to heal, Kitty could do no sewing and could not drive Janine's trap to deliver the goods to their customers. One-handed she dusted, sorted and served in the shop, listening to Janine grumbling from the chair about lost business, and their luck turning to the bad again. Once the pleasure in paying her bills and flaunting her new apprentice had died away Janine became bored. Now there was no income from the theatrical folks for Kitty's sewing, and the stock of aprons and sleeves which she had made dwindled to nothing. So Janine's original good intentions started to slip. One day she came back from her round of suppliers with less material and a comforting quart of whisky under the seat of the trap. Kitty watched as her Antijan became secretive again. She quickly noticed the smell of whisky when she arrived at the shop at eight o'clock in the morning. She stood by as Janine's rages came more frequently, wresting the broom from her as she tried again to berate the unprotesting Thomas. She watched helplessly as Janine started to sell the stock off at less than cost, just to get her hands on more cash.

By the time Kitty's hand was properly healed, the shop shelves were virtually empty and the business was again at a standstill. There was no work for Kitty.

In the end Janine was reduced once more to the crudest of gin, and could not pay the rent for the shop. She gave up the premises and had to take two rooms over a grocer's shop in a street off the Market Square for herself and Thomas. There they lived off the few shillings of Thomas's squeezebox earnings, half of which Janine spent on gin. Kitty's apprenticeship was at an end.

Ishmael paid Janine a visit, enraged at her squandering of his life's savings and of Kitty's future in such a fashion. Then he was standing with her sobbing head on his shoulder and feeling sad for them all, hollow with defeat at the turn of events.

Despite these setbacks, his patient cobbling of shoes and his rent-collecting for Philip Crane kept a roof over his and Kitty's heads and food on their table. Because of his management, Forgan Buildings was now one of the best maintained districts in Priorton. This measure of success had its difficulties. It led to many battles with Crane, who wanted to put up the rents of his tenants. The tenants were offended at this, as they themselves, with Ishmael's encouragement, had made the houses sound. Why should they be punished for their own endeavour?

Closeted together in their little house, Ishmael and Kitty became even closer. In the evenings, she would read to him from the newspaper. One night she read a piece about a famous opera singer who had died of consumption. This brought his gaze from the fire.

'My little Jayne-Anne, she went to her Maker like that, Kitty. I was with her every day, right to the end.'

Kitty put the newspaper down. 'What was she like, Ishmael? Jayne-Anne?'

'She was small, like you.' He laughed. 'Very fiery. Hair the colour of a robin's wing and skin as white as milk. Oh, she had a temper! She had a great temper about my fighting. But she was funny. She could make stone statues laugh.'

Bit by bit Kitty wheedled the story from him about the wedding in the church in London, for which he had had to renounce the religion of his fathers. And their life in their little house in Spitalfields, and their walks by the great teeming river not so far away.

'I wish I'd known her.'

'You'd have loved her, Kitty. And you would have been dear to her.' He paused, his eyes blank with pain.

'I wonder about my own mother, Ishmael. If she was like that,' Kitty ventured, to pull him away from his dark thoughts. 'Was she tall, d'you think, Ishmael? And pretty like your Jayne-Anne? With hair like a robin's wing?'

He shook his head. 'I would think she would be short, if you're anything to go by,' he said cautiously. 'And dark. But if she had your sparkle, people would call her pretty.'

Kitty went across and stood before the long wardrobe mirror once used by her and Esme for their shadow-boxing. That seemed such a long time ago now, such a childish thing. She turned this way and that, staring at herself. 'Why d'she do it, Ishmael? Why did my mother do that to me?'

He shook his head. 'What can a person say about that? The world treats women harshly. Perhaps it was so with her.' He put a hand on her shoulder. 'Don't be sad, little one. Is it so bad here with old Ishmael? Your mother presented you to me and gave me a life where there was none. Is it so bad?'

She shook her head. 'It's good with you, and I feel like my proper self here. But this talking about Jayne-Anne made me want her for my mother.'

He hugged her hard. 'Then you have her. Wherever she is she is yours, watching over you, just as I think your own mother will be. Believe me, Kitty.'

She left it then, not displeased with the thought of the robin-haired Jayne-Anne as her guardian angel.

Wearily, Freddie Longstaffe kicked off his boots, dumped them in the corner of the scullery and washed his hands and face in the tin bowl already silted up with the black slime of his brothers' washing. He pulled on a new shirt, put on his best cap and made for the door.

'Woah, marrah!' Albert's large hand yanked him back. 'Thou needs tha dinner before thou ventures out.'

It was pay Saturday; their one afternoon off in a fortnight.

Freddie glanced at the cauldron of glutinous stew on the fire, left by Mary Kelly who, in a rough and ready fashion, took care of this house of men for a small wage. He shook off the restraining hand. 'I'll have my dinner at Kitty Rainbow's. I'll buy some pies an' bread from one of them Forgan women an' take it with me.'

Albert cuffed him on the chin in a friendly fashion. 'Kitty Rainbow! Seems thou'rt there all the time now.'

Freddie pushed past his brother and strode off. Albert was right. The little house at Forgan had become almost second home to him. It was a haven, compared to the crowded house in Sinker's Row where he lived with his father and his four brothers.

He loved to go to Ishmael's house. These days he was in the habit of walking through the door as of right. He was blithely unaware that his attitude of affection, even casual possession, was sometimes too pressing, too possessive for Kitty's peace of mind.

As a matter of practical fact these days Kitty was compelled to welcome the bounty Freddie brought into the house. Things were increasingly difficult for her and Ishmael. For the first time since they had been together, Ishmael had started to get tetchy. Then in one week he dropped his hammer ten times and had had to redo a sole he was mending. Spasmodic arthritis was attacking his hands and it seemed that fine cobbling work was getting beyond him. He had insisted that the last pair of Kitty's special shoes should be made by the best shoemaker in Priorton, and he made an arrangement to pay for them weekly.

This Saturday when Freddie called after work, Kitty was on her own. Ishmael was out gathering rents – always a long process as some payments, part-payments and payments in kind had to be closely negotiated. When Freddie burst through the door she looked up with a small smile from her mending. 'Freddie! Straight from work again.'

He grinned. 'Our Albert was just on about it to me. Says I'm never off your doorstep. I just telt him that at least here you could get a place by the fire and spread your legs out without kicking some other feller's.' He flung himself on the mat before the fire, then reached and took her bare feet in his hands. 'I never saw your feet before, Kitty.'

She struggled as he turned her feet this way and that. He held on to them, and she could feel his rough palm as he stroked them.

'They're fine feet, Kitty. Soft.' He examined the one which was slightly turned, its arch too high. 'You can hardly tell . . .'

She pulled it away and he retrieved it again, raising himself so that he was kneeling in front of her. 'I expect you'll marry me, Kitty Rainbow, because I'll marry no other.' His face was unsmiling, set and earnest.

She wrenched her foot away and scrambled to put on her shoes. 'Then you expect wrong,' she said. 'We're only sixteen, you and me. You know what people—'

But he had stopped her words with his mouth, pressing harder and harder, his hands going behind her to pull her to him. And she felt his sweetness, his earnest goodwill on his lips, in the press of his hands. An involuntary curiosity made her soften and respond to him, her hands going behind his head, her lips parting slightly under his.

He pulled away and groaned, took a breath, then said lightly; 'Is that kettle boiling? You make some tea, love, and we'll make a feast of these meat pasties from Mrs Cloggans. I reckon Ishmael'll be back any second.'

She went red. It was the first time he had called her 'love', and it sounded sentimental, strange. She could never, never call him that.

As he was laying out the pasties and the bread he started to talk about the miners across in Wales, who were being forced back to work now after a long fight. He said there was talk of some action at White Leas Pit where he and his brothers worked, due to a proposed reduction in rate and the lack of safety in one of the workings.

'So would you go on strike, like those lads in Wales?'

He shrugged. 'Not so bad for us in our house with six wages coming in, Kitty, even if the pit does get a lot of work for the money that comes in the door. But for fellers keepin' six or more bairns on one wage it must be well-nigh impossible. Worse than the workhouse. We'd probably strike for them if hell pushed. The Government don't like it, like, miners getting together. They've bankrupted our Association. They dinnet like us associating at all, that lot. All those big fellers'll be chuntering on about it, happy soaking up their port and going on about the "dreadful miners".'

That night Kitty and Freddie went together to the Windlass Theatre to see Esme, now a regular turn. Her performance was perter and funnier than ever. Kitty never tired of the magical change which came over Esme in the smoky light of the theatre lamps. She seemed even taller, more graceful. Her face lost its heaviness, took on a bright glow as the songs ebbed and flowed with humour, sentiment and salty spite.

Thomas was in the orchestra pit, resplendent in red velvet waistcoat, and a cravat which Kitty had made him from some curtain material. She waved at him and called his name and he nodded in her direction although he did not look at her directly.

These days Thomas played along with the orchestra for all the acts. Tonight he extended the interval with an individual virtuoso performance which had the taciturn men in the orchestra on their feet. Kitty too was on her feet, clapping her hands till they hurt, full of sisterly pride for her strange foster brother.

As she sat down again in the darkness Freddie's hand

grasped hers and kept it. The jugglers came on then, and they settled back to enjoy them.

Her concentration was broken by a tap on her shoulder, and a voice in her ear. 'So nice to see the young lovers enjoying themselves.'

She turned round to see Jarrold Pommeroy and a smirking Gabriel Gullet. Her pleasure fled. Turning back towards the stage, she snatched her hand away from Freddie and slid down in her seat. She hardly saw the following acts and had to bring all her concentration to watch Esme's second turn, in girlish attire now: a dress which Kitty had never seen, had had no hand in the sewing.

Afterwards Kitty left Freddie talking to the unresponsive Thomas over the edge of the orchestra pit and went round behind the stage to the capsule of a room where Esme changed.

Esme seemed pleased to see her and talked away excitedly as she poured water from a jug and splashed her face to get rid of the rouge.

Then someone pushed open the door without knocking and Jarrold Pommeroy bowled in. He ignored Kitty and blandly surveyed Esme's state of undress, saying, 'Not dressed yet? You must hurry, my dear girl. I've a table booked at the Gaunt Valley Hotel, and your mother and brother are waiting.'

Esme clapped her hands. 'Kitty should come too.'

His glance dropped to Kitty as though she had just materialised out of the air. He smiled and drawled, 'Oh, I don't think Miss Rainbow will have time for us tonight, Esme. She is very preoccupied with her beau.'

Kitty stood up. 'Don't listen to him, Esme. He has a snake's tongue. It's not a beau, it's just old Freddie Longstaffe. But I've to get back home anyway, thank you, Esme. Ishmael will be waiting up.'

She looked for some proper response from Esme, but Esme was fastening her skirt and pulling on her very neat

jacket with its bustle effect at the back, smiling engagingly at
Jarrold who was reflected in the scratched mirror.

Kitty was stomping with temper as she dragged Freddie
from the theatre and down the back streets towards Forgan
Buildings, gabbling away about Jarrold Pommeroy and
what she would do with him one of these days. Freddie
finally pulled her to a stop by the round wall of the church of
St Brigid. 'Stop, stop, Kitty. You're like a wild storm wind.'

The road was deserted. He turned her so that her back
was against the high wall and stood before her, his hands
resting on the stones either side of her head. 'Now what is it?
What is it that has really got your goat?'

'That horrible Pommeroy! And can you believe it,
Freddie? I think she likes him.' Her voice was trembling.
'She doesn't even mind if he sees her in her petticoat.
And...'

He put a finger on her lips. 'Ssh, Kitty. Leave it. Esme's
twenty now. She knows what she's doin'. Here! Let me
show you somethin'.'

He pulled her into the churchyard, down along pathways
until they came to a gravestone set in the ground like a great
box. 'Do you know what this says?' He made her sit down
beside it and guided her fingers to some indented lettering.

She shook her head. 'Daft thing. It's too dark.'

'It says, "Amelia and Joseph Durkin. Born 1789, died
1860. Lifelong in love, they enter the doors of heaven hand
in hand."'

His hand came up and he removed the little felt hat which
she had perched on top of her wild curls. He took out her
pins and ran his fingers through her hair, combing it round
her shoulders. 'It's like wire,' he said. 'Warm wire.'

She put out a hand and ran it through his hair and he
trembled, waiting. 'Soft silk,' she said, and pulled him close
to her.

They half fell, half sat down on Amelia and Joseph's last
resting place. Then they were pressing together, kissing and

touching each other. Then they were stretched full length, seeking more flesh to touch, her skirt coming up, his buttons undone. She cried out once and he put his hand softly on her mouth.

'I love you, I love you. Can you bear this?' he whispered, sweating.

She nodded and then started to laugh softly as the pain was replaced by an excess of feeling that filled her with strange delight.

Half an hour later they were walking demurely down the lane away from the church, her hand close in his. Her hair was neatly pinned up and he had smoothed his hair back from his brow.

She started to chuckle.

'What is it, what is it, Kitty?' he said.

'What a funny thing that is for human beings to do. Don't you think it's funny?'

He frowned, then laughed himself. 'That? Aye, I think you're right there, Kitty. People've been being funny like that since the human race began. An' we'll have some laughs before we're finished, I can tell yer. Just like those two beneath the stone. Seventy years of laughter. That'll do me.'

13

New Lives

Janine Druce turned up at the house in Forgan Buildings comparatively steady on her feet. Her face was flushed and shiny but her eyes were clear. She accepted Kitty's offer of a dish of tea, saying she would take the weight off her feet. 'Yer ferget just how long a walk that is down here frae the town,' she gasped.

Ishmael nodded at her from his place by the hearth. 'Are you well, Janine?'

Janine pulled her shawl around her. 'Ah'm feeling the cold more than Ah used to. An' Ah'm missin' our Thomas, who's alluss down the Windlass with that Esme Gullet. He plays in the band every night.' A certain reluctant pride threaded itself through the rancour in her voice.

'He's good at his music.' Kitty was pouring the tea. 'An' he'll be keeping out of the way of your broomshank, Antijan.'

'Aye, poor bugger. He gets a hard time from me.' Janine put up a half-mittened hand and tucked some hair under her hat. 'It was you Ah came to see, Kit. Ah was talking to Tom Vart in the Blue Bell last night.'

Kitty frowned.

'Och! Yeh know the feller! He's overman at Scree Hall Mill in Swanby.'

Kitty remembered the heavy, swarthy man. 'The place that'd just got a new master?'

Janine nodded. 'Well, he says they've more looms now an' are taking on lassies. He said he'll train yer up. Thought you had some gumption.'

'She's got that all right,' said Ishmael almost too eagerly. Something was rankling him about an urgent message he'd received that morning that Mr Crane wanted specially to see him. It wasn't a rent day so it sounded like trouble. Still he frowned. 'But I don't know about a mill. They're dark places. Bad women...'

Kitty shook her head. 'Don't worry about me, Ishmael. You above all know I can take care of myself.' She turned to Janine and nodded. 'I'll try anything, Antijan.' She thought of Ishmael's leather purse, now empty of its hard-earned gold. 'All Ishmael's money's gone now.'

'Aye,' said Janine wearily. 'I ken that fine well.' She thought of the rather uncomfortable and undignified episode in the ginnel by the stockyard which had bought this favour for Kitty from the rough and ready Tom Vart. Truly she was repaying Ishmael's generosity, in her own fashion, with her own coin. 'Ye're to go down there right away. I said you would be there for twelve o'clock.'

Later that morning, in the weaving shed, while Kitty was waiting to catch Tom Vart's eye, she counted two more looms than last time. They were operated by brawny women, rather than men. Apart from the clicking and rattling of the machines, and the whoosh of the bobbin, there was no other sound. The women had their heads down over their work. On the partition beside Kitty, where the desk was now screened to make a tiny office, was a newly printed notice warning of fines and dismissal for talking, singing, whistling or other such indicators of slackness. Kitty noted that blocks had been attached to the pedals of the loom to make it possible for the women to work them. So someone had acted on her suggestion.

Vart finally noticed her and came across. He looked her up and down, stroking his chin. 'I'd forgot tha' was such a titchy thing. Can't see you managing these looms.' He knew it'd put Janine Druce's back up, but there was no way he could do what she wanted and take this girl. He smirked to himself. At least now, though, she couldn't take back what she'd given him for the favour.

'I'm stronger than I look,' said Kitty fiercely. She glanced around and went across to a finished bale of grey flannel that he himself had problems lifting. She braced herself and lifted it over her head. 'There,' she said, lowering it carefully to the floor.

He whistled, then rubbed his chin. 'Well, tha't strong, but ist tha big enough?'

'I see you've put blocks on the pedals, like I said.'

He nodded. 'Mr Scorton's notion. His too that we get the women in. All right. Come across here.' He led her to a dark corner where a pale-faced woman with shadows under her eyes and her hair tied back in a kerchief, was leaning backwards and forwards, working the loom in a steady rhythm.

'Sarah, you're ter show this lass how ter work the loom.'

The woman kept up her steady rhythm. 'There's no spare loom, Mr Vart, we need no new girl.'

'I said show the lass how ter work the loom! Dee as yer telt. Yer'll get sent off whether yer show her or not. But if yer do show her the job yer'll get paid for the next hour.' He turned on his heel then and walked back to his own loom.

The woman scowled at Kitty. 'Ah'm ter show yer me job so he can get rid of us. D'yer know that? Liftin' yer skirt, is he?' she sneered. She stopped the machine and clambered off. 'Now yer sit here and yer dee this.'

Kitty's skin prickled as she realised that the women at the other looms were watching closely as the doomed Sarah showed Kitty how to work her machine. There was both malevolence and relief in their looks. It could so easily have been them.

True to his word, one hour later Tom Vart shooed Sarah off the premises with some pennies in her hand, and Kitty was on her own. Her fingers, made deft with sewing, her natural quickness and strength, all stood her in good stead with this task and her length of flannel grew on the loom at a satisfying speed. At four o'clock Tom Vart came across to pat her on the shoulder and tell her with oily approval that she was a good exchange for Sarah, who was slow and clumsy and whom he should never have taken on anyway.

Ishmael took out his watch and peered at the time. Two thirty. Crane was late. That was unusual. He was usually at the George drinking his gill of whisky when Ishmael arrived.

He had almost given him up when Crane came into the bar parlour at two forty-five. He was accompanied by a broad muscular man of about forty, and Gabriel Gullet, who went behind the bar and served them himself, neglecting to put any money in Mirella's till.

Crane rubbed his hands and held them before the fire. 'This is Mr Rutherford, Mr Slaughter, a friend of Mr Gullet, across here from Leeds.' Rutherford lifted his brown hard hat and grinned. Crane went on smoothly. 'I've decided that Mr Gullet will collect my rents at Forgan Buildings from now on. He's a lawyer, after all, and will, if necessary use the services of Mr Rutherford to press his point.'

Ishmael stood up. 'I collect the rents at Forgan,' he said. 'I have for years now.'

Crane shook his head in gentle despair. 'As you know, Mr Slaughter, I've been dissatisfied for some time with the slackness and lassitude at Forgan. In that time my growing feeling has been that your loyalty is to those indigents in the houses rather than to myself and obtaining the proper charges for what is first-class property. We're opening a new seam at White Leas Pit and have fifty men coming in, from Flint in North Wales. Good workers, prudent – they will need houses for which a fair rent will be paid. I have discussed the matter . . .' he raised his eyes to Gabriel, who was sitting on the settle by the fire, a brandy clasped between both hands, '. . . with people who are informed and have decided that a change of rent-collector would be the thing to do.' He smiled benignly. 'You do not need to be concerned, Mr Slaughter. Your own cottage is safe with you for a whole month. As you know, I am a generous man.'

Ishmael picked up his hat and marched out, brushing past Mirella Gullet who was coming in. She looked around the parlour suspiciously. 'What is the matter with Ishmael, Gabriel?' she said. 'He nearly knocked me over.'

As she made her way wearily through the loomshed at the end of her shift, Kitty was ignored by the other women, except one, who spat at her as she passed.

Tom Vart nodded at her. 'Good work done, lass. I'll tell yer auntie when I see her.'

Kitty heard the word '*Hooer*' behind her but when she turned round the faces were blank.

She hurried home, her bones weary, her mind racing with the growing determination to return tomorrow and tell Tom Vart to get Sarah back, as she couldn't take another woman's place that way. She wouldn't.

When she let herself in the cottage she found Ishmael sitting at the table, his head in his hands. She put her hand on his shoulder. 'What is it, Ishmael? What is it?'

He pulled his head up to face her. 'Dismissed by Mr Crane, Kitty. He'll put in Gabriel Gullet to collect the rents and a bully boy to turf the people out. It seems they have

Welsh rentpayers coming in. There'll be no roof over our own heads after the end of the month either. Mr Crane will kindly let us stay till then.' He laid his knobbly hands on the table. 'And these are no use, no use to either of us. Can't even knock a nail in straight.'

When Freddie came to the house that night he was shocked by the exhaustion and worry on Kitty's face, angry that she was working in a place that had such a bad reputation in the town. When he protested she pulled him out of the house, through the arch and into the lane. She told him of Ishmael's news. He took her hand. 'You mustn't work in that place, Kitty.'

She shook her head. 'We have to eat,' she said.

'There's only one answer,' he said seriously.

'And what's that?'

'We'll get married and I'll get a White Leas Pit house. You and me and Ishmael'll live here. Mebbe even the house you're in now. Good enough for a Welshman, it's good enough for me.'

She shook her head. 'They won't like it, Ishmael and your dad.'

'Dad won't mind. Our house is too full even now. And Ishmael? Well, he hasn't a lot of choice, has he?'

'Of course he can choose. Just 'cos he's down now wouldn't stop him objecting. He's his own man,' she said stoutly. 'And anyway I'm not marrying you, because I'm not ready to. I don't know whether I really want to anyway.'

'Well, we ... you let me ...'

She flushed. 'That was just that once. I was curious ...' She had been careful not to be alone with Freddie since that time in the churchyard. The strength of her feelings, positive though they were, had been a shock and she didn't feel ready to risk that again.

Freddie was silent for a while. 'But we're still, well, we're still *courting*, are we?' he said uncertainly.

She laughed and punched him playfully on the arm.

146

'Courting? If that's what you call all this, of course we are. Just not all *that* stuff, that's all. Not now. And not married. I'll work on at the mill and Ishmael an' me'll find some rooms in Priorton. An' if you're very good you can bring us beef pies there.'

He relaxed a little and they strolled on. Then he stopped again and he pulled a piece of paper out of his pocket. 'Here, Kitty. This is for you.'

She took the paper from him and, recognising his immaculate looping handwriting, she started to read.

> Love lives beyond
> The tomb, the earth which fades like dew!
> I love the fond,
> The faithful, and the true.
>
> Love lies in sleep
> The happiness of healthy dreams:
> Eve's dews may weep,
> But love delightful seems.

There were more verses. She looked up at him. 'Where d'you get this, Freddie?' she said softly.

'A feller at the pit showed us a book with it in. Said it was written by a workin' man, not some velvet-collared fancy cove. It made us think of you an' I asked him if I could copy it. The feller said the man who wrote it's dead himself now, like.'

'It's lovely, Freddie.'

'It's just for you,' he said gruffly. 'Now put it in your pocket and forget about it.'

The rain drove into Ishmael's face as he opened the door to two men, rivulets of water running from their hats. He stood back as they pushed past him, eager for his dry hearth.

Ned Lumb removed his hat and knocked it against his

forearm, drops hissing as they hit the flames. Jarrold Pommeroy, less flamboyant in his movements, dripped on to the floor in silence, removing his gloves and holding them, steaming, before the flames.

'A feller couldn't tell it was June,' said Ned glumly. 'Is it always wet up here?'

'You'll sit down, gentlemen?' Ishmael indicated the two chairs by the table. They sat down and watched as he settled himself on the fireside chair. 'Now what's your business?'

Ned arranged his damp coat away from his dry knees. 'Same old business, Ishmael.'

'Fighting?' Ishmael thrust his gnarled hands deep into his pocket.

'Like I told you before, Jarrold, wiliest, cleverest fighter I ever saw was Ishmael.' Ned nodded at Pommeroy and turned back to Ishmael. 'It seems Jarrold saw you a long time ago, one time when on the drum, didn't you, Pommeroy?'

Jarrold nodded, his sharp face set to be sympathetic and appealing.

Ned went on. 'So why not fight for me again, Ishmael? There're purses to be won, even in these godforsaken climes. More so, with this black gold under our feet pouring guineas into men's pockets at a high old rate. You'll get your reward. They won't expect—'

'An old man to beat a younger man?'

'Not old, Ishmael. Not old! A man in your prime. A clever wily fighter. But your grey hairs may deceive a few. It's the element of surprise which'll suck the money in.'

Jarrold cleared his throat. 'I did hear from Philip Crane – or was it Gabriel Gullet? – that he has other boys on his rent-collecting here at Forgan. Perhaps the purse'll be extra welcome, Mr Slaughter.'

Ishmael cocked an eye at the younger man. 'Ah! Now we have it.'

'Yes,' said Ned eagerly. 'A fair purse, win or lose,

Ishmael. The money'll come off the wagers. Good purses from these fairs in the North. But we need good contenders! Men who can stand their ground and take the pace. It would set you up. Don't you have this daughter to keep? Jarrold here tells me she's a cripple and you have to send her off to some wretched mill to earn a crust. Such a child needs some care, Ishmael.'

Ishmael stood up, his hands clenched in his pockets. 'My daughter is no burden, sir. I will not keep you gentlemen any longer. I need no weasel words to push me to the edge. I will fight for you if the purse is right. Just tell me where and when.'

Kitty worked on at the mill, keeping her head down and ignoring the whispered comments of the other women. Unpleasant things had been happening to her. The warp on her loom was mysteriously loosened and a length of cloth was ruined, causing Tom Vart to cuff her painfully around the head. And she found blood, which she knew in her heart to be someone else's menstrual blood, on her bench seat by her loom.

One night Tom Vart asked her to stay behind and complete a length. When the others were gone he jumped on her in a clumsy attempt at a kiss. She remembered the sacked Sarah, and contained the desire to punch him. Instead she ducked out from under his arm and fled.

Trudging home in the wet, her mind whirled constantly with thoughts of other ways to make a few shillings. But there seemed no other way. Many girls went into service, cleaning, cooking and washing for those in the town with more money coming in. But Kitty knew she was not cut out for that. She was not gentle or submissive enough for service in one of the new villas they were building, in the streets stretching out from the ancient centre of Priorton.

Tom Vart had her benumbed. She did not want to flinch before people, to run away. But she did from him. All the years of training with Ishmael, the running, the lifting of stones, the facing up to one's opponent, had come to nothing in that dark shed with the hard defeated women and the sly foreman.

It came home to her very early that if she did set up her cheek with Tom Vart, if she did spoil a length of cloth in a temper, there would be no more work for her, no more pay at the end of a weary week. And without her money she and Ishmael could not manage; there was no money coming in now from cobbling. Soon they would have to pay rent for new rooms. Her few shillings would keep them out of the workhouse. If they were to have a roof over their heads she would have to endure the miserable mill a bit longer.

Her shoes became worn right to their uppers with the long walk to and from work. Her leg started to hurt. She found herself limping properly for the first time since she had come to Ishmael as a little girl.

In spite of all this, as the days passed by Kitty found that the actual work at the mill was not intolerable. It was hard, but there was some satisfaction in seeing the stretch of cloth on the clacking loom grow under her fingers. Her deftness ensured that the only faults in the cloth were those not under her control, mostly caused by the snapping of the rough, poorly spun yarn. Even so, such faults would still earn her a shove in the back or a slap on the head from the heavy-handed Tom Vart.

There was no respite in the atmosphere in the shed. When she asked a woman where the privy was, she was told to cross her legs, hang on till bait time, and shut up, or Tom Vart would fine her sixpence. Another thing to be endured was the stink in the shed, a combination of wool not far separated from the sheep, and women in clothes unchanged for a week, who wet themselves where they sat.

This reeking atmosphere started to make Kitty feel sick and she found herself forced to take deep gulps to keep the vomit down. Bending over her loom she thought Tom Vart probably had some fine up his sleeve for being sick, as well as all the other rules.

Tom Vart was a hard enough worker. He kept one loom going himself, and also mended stopped looms and adjusted warps for the women. He moved around in the clacking space like some dark wizard: a very small man relishing the pleasure during these hours of being lord of all he surveyed.

Kitty watched as, at least once every day, he would leave his loom and tap one of the younger women on the shoulder, then stride off, leaving the woman to follow him out of the shed. As the high door scraped shut behind them there would be hooting and whistling and the women would call lewd words across to each other, alluding to Tom Vart's priapic powers, to the poor woman's virtue, and speculating on the views of the cuckolded husband. Some of the women joined enthusiastically in this hysterical condemnation, knowing that another day it might be they who were tapped on the shoulder, they who were castigated behind their backs.

One day Tom Vart tapped Kitty on the shoulder. 'Hey, lass, yer can come an' see ter these bobbins for us.'

She stood up and the rattle of her own machine ceased, making a pool of ominous silence in the middle of the clamour. The woman at the corner loom cackled out loud and was treated to a thunderous look from Tom Vart.

'Is there sommat wrong with the bobbins, like?' said Kitty.

'Yer'll see.' He led the way out of the loomshed round the side of the bobbin shed to a low door set in a clapboard wall. This he opened and stood to one side.

She peered into the dark space. 'What am I to do in here, then?'

'Sort the big'ns from the little'ns.' He pushed her shoulder, breathing heavily. 'Gan on in, lass.'

She could smell damp and moss and the spicy sour scent of dark human activity. Her stomach heaved. She wrenched her shoulder away from him and stood up to face him, her fists curling. 'There's not any bobbins in there, Mr Vart. It's not sorting bobbins you want.' She paused. 'Did Janine Druce tell you that my father was Ishmael Slaughter, the fighter?'

He looked hard at her, then shrugged. 'So she did.' He paused. 'It's on'y a bit of a kiss and cuddle I'm after, lass. I like to keep the women happy, see? They get a bit extra for sorting the bobbins.'

She pushed past his shoulder and strode away, stumbling over her skirt as she did so.

Back at the loomshed she looked at the glistening expectant faces of the women. 'An' if you think I did anything I didn't. How can any of you go in that filthy hole with him? How can you?'

The woman at the nearest loom wrinkled her nose at her. 'Dist tha' think tha's too good for the gaffer, then? Too good for us? We've bairns ter feed an' men ter keep—'

Another woman interrupted her. 'No cause fer you ter be high an' mighty, lass. Tha's up the stick thesel' an' no band on your finger, far as I can see.'

Tom Vart bustled in. 'Shut that, Mabel, or tha'll have nee pay left fer them bairns.' He pushed Kitty in the back. 'And, thoo, Rainbow, get back ter that loom or I'll report thee ter Mr Scorton an' he'll have yer out in no time.'

Kitty sat at her loom, her brain wrestling with Mabel's words. *Up the stick*. Wasn't that . . . ? She put her hand on her waist.

'Gerron, Rainbow!' bellowed Tom Vart.

She picked up her shuttle.

That night, lingering over aromatic broth made by Ishmael, Kitty finally confided in him about the hustling, the catcalling, the bullying and the enmity of the other women. She didn't mention the bobbin shed, but did say, 'An' that Tom Vart he . . . kind of presses the women. He's too . . . much for them.'

152

Ishmael raised a brow. 'Does he bother you?'

She shook her head. 'He tried. But got short shrift. I faced him out.'

'Good girl.'

'I resisted hitting him, even though I could have knocked him down in one. He'd sack me as soon as look at me an' we need the money.'

Ishmael put his hand on hers. 'Good girl. Good girl. This won't go on for long, I can tell you that. Something will turn up. I know it.' He stirred uneasily at the thought of his unwritten contract with Ned Lumb.

Kitty blushed, thinking again about Mabel's mocking words about being pregnant. If Mabel was right then it wouldn't have to be long before she herself stopped at the mill. Tom Vart had sacked one pregnant woman just last week, saying she was such a fat cow there was no space behind the loom. She wondered if Freddie would call that night. She wondered what she would say to him if he did.

So they sat there close together in the dusk, each holding a secret they would not tell the other.

Freddie Longstaffe had been relishing the game of catch-as-catch-can that he was playing with Kitty Rainbow. Depending on his shift he was now spending every spare moment at Forgan. Sometimes only Ishmael was at the house, and the two men would sit together watching the fire fall, each busy with his own thoughts. Sometimes Freddie read to Ishmael one of his battered collection of poems, copied from his friend's book. Ishmael listened with graceful respect and told Freddie of his own grandfather who had memorised whole sections of the Jewish book of law called the Torah and would speak them as poetry at family gatherings.

Freddie himself now knew many of his poems by heart and liked to chant them in the ear of his pony, Dart, as they shared the responsibility for hauling the grinding, rocking tubs of coal through the workings. It was hot work. Sweat would pour off Freddie's shoulders and down his back, making rivers through the gathering coal dust clinging to his skin and tracking a passageway right into his pit hoggers. These cotton drawers were all he wore in the pit, apart from a kerchief to gather the sweat from his face.

It was a normal enough shift and Freddie had finished the litany of his poems, spouted for Dart's benefit. He kissed the air near the pony's feathery ear. 'Come on, old lad, keep on. Keep on! Or our Albert'll have me guts fried for tea if I don't get this lot *in-bye*.' He pulled the tubs by him to take some of the weight off Dart and started to shout to the pony from further down the black tunnel. 'Pay Saturday today, Dart. An' yer know what? I'm gunna go right down Priorton an' buy that Kitty Rainbow some yellow ribbon with white stripes. She's not a bad'n, Kitty, you knaa. She's sparky, has a temper, like. An' a scrapper. Put two fists up to any man, she would. I like that, me. Puts a whole ten inches on her height.'

Dart was struggling now up an incline.

Freddie came back and put his weight on Dart's collar to help the forward impetus. 'Keep on, Dart,' shouted Freddie. 'I'll get down the back. Sommat's caught there. Jammed on the curve, shouldn't wonder.' He squeezed his way along the narrowing wall, his candle a dour flicker against the makeshift jumble of wood, coal and stone which was a seam being worked. 'Keep pullin', Dart. Keep pullin', marrah!' he called behind him.

Then a draft of hot dry air blew out his candle. He had to feel his way around the problem at the third tub, whose axle had twisted, and whose wheel was jutting off the track at an angle. He made a vain effort to lift the tub and kick the axle straight, but the sheer weight defeated him. Then he squeezed himself in right beside the tub, braced himself against the wet tunnel wall and forced his heavy clogged feet on the side of the tub. Then he heaved, to try to rock it straight. The tub righted itself and at the front of the line

Dart lurched forward, reverting to a swift plod, relieved that his burden was suddenly lighter. The line of tubs whipped across the curve, reducing the space for a human body to nil.

Freddie's scream echoed through the galleries and men came running, Freddie's brother Albert forcing his way to the very front.

Kitty looked blankly at Esme, every inch a lady, dressed in deep green with velvet bands and white undersleeves of very fine lace. Beside her stood a smirking Jarrold, resplendent in yellow tweed, leaning on his silver-topped cane.

Kitty removed the heavy serge apron she wore for her Saturday afternoon chores. 'Come in, Esme, me in my dirt and you in your finery. We make a right pair.'

Esme grinned and reached across and hugged her. 'Don't play the poor working girl with me, Kitty Rainbow. I know better.'

They sat on either side of the flickering fire for a moment, just looking at each other. Jarrold pulled out a chair and sat by the table.

'I've missed you, Kitty Rainbow,' said Esme.

'I've been out earning our daily bread,' said Kitty, without any rancour.

'I should have come to see you,' wailed Esme, 'but what with the George and the theatre, I'm singing my tonsils out.'

Kitty held up a hand. 'We'll only ever meet with no backwards glances, Esme, you and me. It's the only way.'

Esme's smile broadened. 'I told Jarrold that. Told him.'

'Jarrold?' said Kitty.

'He was saying you'd be jealous of him. Miffed at me for neglecting you. You'd think I thought myself too good for you, you being a mill girl now. He said you'd have changed.'

Kitty's shot a hard look at Jarrold and folded her arms. 'Did he now? Well, he's wrong, isn't he?'

Esme shook her head. 'Not about everything. There is something I think he's right about.' She refastened the strings on her bonnet and fiddled with the clasp on her lizardskin bag. 'Kit ... I've agreed with him that I should go to Leeds to try my luck in a new music hall there. He knows some men ...'

Kitty closed her eyes for a moment. Jarrold was right, of course. She was jealous of him. She hated the fact that Esme was drawing away from her. She opened her eyes and said brightly, 'Well! If there's fame and fortune away in Leeds for you, Es, why should you wait here in Priorton? There's nothing to keep you here, nothing.'

Esme breathed out and smiled. 'I told Jarrold so. That I'd go to Leeds with your goodwill. Sure to, I said. And one day you can come there and see me sing?'

Kitty nodded gravely. 'Oh yes, Es, I'll take a week off the mill any time I like to travel halfway across the land to see you sing.' She paused. 'What about Thomas? He'll be heartbroken to see you go.'

Esme shook her head. 'Oh no. He's to come with me. Janine Druce is off on her wanders again. Down in Yorkshire, last we heard. So Thomas is on his own. Jarrold here thought perhaps he wouldn't manage all the strange places, him being a little simple an' all that. But you know I couldn't sing without him. He and me will help each other in that strange place. So Jarrold was persuaded!' She smiled proudly at her mentor, who was sitting stiff-necked at the table. Then her eyes went down over her purse again. 'Oh, and there's one other thing, Kit. I have this problem with my name. Whoever heard of a famous singer called Esme Gullet? Could you see that comic name on a bill-poster? They would laugh so.'

'But your name *is* Esme Gullet. That's who you are!'

'But I don't *have* to be Esme Gullet, Kit. Lots of people in the halls choose another name. Jarrold and me wondered if I could borrow your name? He thought Esther Rainbow would be a cracking name. Could just see it on a bill-poster. Can't you see it?' She leaned over and put a hand on Kitty's. 'And then at least we can be proper sisters. Can't we, Kitty? Kitty and Esther Rainbow.'

Kitty finally exchanged glances with Jarrold. He returned her look blandly enough but she could feel his triumph bleeding from every pore. Not satisfied with taking her friend, he had now taken her name. She put her hand to her throat, feeling sick again. She reminded herself that really she had no name. Her name was just something dreamed up by Ishmael.

She stood up and they followed suit. She moved closer to Esme. 'It's not my name anyway, Es. Nothing to stop you using it. It's anybody's name. So you're welcome to it.'

She stood by the door and watched them as they made their dainty way through the mud to the arch where the gig was standing. Children stopped their play to give due attention to the gaudy couple as they passed by.

The gig had just drawn away when a giant figure bolted through the arch and raced towards her. It was Albert, Freddie's brother.

She knew why he had come, the minute she saw his face. 'The bliddy tubs,' he moaned. 'The bliddy tubs.' And he caught her as she fell to the stone slabs which Ishmael had laid so carefully, to stop the mud walking into their nice clean kitchen.

14

Fairground

'Father, look! There's a man on stilts by the Priory gates.'

'And there is a great bear, Papa. See him dance!'

William Scorton looked down at his sons, pleased at his inspiration to bring them to Priorton Fair. For two days his house had rattled unbearably with their almost palpable misery. In the end he had told them angrily to get on their coats and into the gig and he would take them somewhere to see something interesting.

Well, he supposed a man on stilts and a bear in chains must be very interesting to a six- and an eight-year-old. Even interesting enough to take their mind off their dead mother and the drama of being torn away from doting grandparents in the tall London house in the busy street, to be planted in a house in a forest where even the nearest miserable miners' rows were three miles away.

The boys raced ahead and William watched them with pleasure. Their grandparents had obviously nurtured them, body and soul. He wondered whether they truly believed, as their raving daughter had told them, that he plotted against her life and theirs. They had been remarkably civil when he went to collect the boys after the funeral.

The boys had grown so much in the two years when he had been denied a sight of them. They were tall for their years: Michael finer made and more girlish in demeanour, but by far the more intelligent of the two; Samuel younger, sturdier and sunnier.

Priorton Market Square was surging with people, the whole town crowded for the autumn fair: animals, poultry, fruit and vegetables, goods exotic and mundane for sale; roundabouts and mechanicals to engage the children; jugglers, musicians and stiltwalkers to entertain all. And for those amused by the sight of misery there was the great, brown, sorry-looking bear, which was tramping and jumping at the behest of a thickset man with a whip and a boy with a penny whistle. And there was even a boxing booth with a boy, as dark as shining mulberries, playing a drum on one side to draw the custom.

He was indeed drawing a curious crowd.

'Does the black come off, Papa?' said Samuel, his eyes wide with interest.

William shook his head, watching the boy with the drum, who met his gaze with a calm and almost ironic dignity. 'No, Sam. When I was in Africa, most people were of that hue, and only odd people were pink like you and me.' Michael was racing on ahead.

'Come on, Papa. I want to see the bear!' Sam's small hand was thrust into his and for the second time he blessed the inspiration which brought him to this place. As he was dragged forward towards the bear, he had a guilty image of the face of his wife, also chained by the foot, staring at him with vindictive glee as she had raked his face from temple to jaw with a secreted nail.

William's thoughts were dragged to the present as he was almost tripped to a halt as Samuel stopped by the makeshift stall of a young woman who was sitting on the cobbles on a low stool. She had black bushy hair under her bonnet and a bleached curtain on the ground beside her. Lying on the curtain, in neat piles, were folded aprons and children's clothes. The curtain was held down at one corner with a stoneware jar. Stuck into this jar, like so many lollipops, were cunningly made rod puppets.

Samuel bent down and picked up one of these: a figure of a harlequin, it was skilfully constructed in tiny squares of light and dark leather stitched neatly together. He held up the puppet to his father. 'Can I have one of these, Papa?'

William took the toy in his hand and turned it over. 'It is very finely made. Did you make it yourself?' He addressed the stallholder, who was steadily looking at him.

'Yes,' she said. He noticed the absence of the customary *sir*. 'I did make it myself.'

He reached into his pocket and counted out three coins, paying the girl and pushing the toy into his son's hand. 'There, Sam. Go and join your brother. He is with the bear now.'

He turned back to the woman, frowning. 'I think that we've met, miss. Did we meet somewhere? I feel I know you.'

'So you have ... sir. I am the foster daughter of Janine Druce, the Scotch draper who buys – who *bought* your cloth. And I've worked not long ago at your mill at Scree Hall.'

He slapped his gloves against his hand. 'The child! You are the child who told me to put women at those looms.'

She stood up and looked him unflinchingly in the eye. 'Did I do that? I never should have. That place, that Scree Hall Mill is a sink. And that Tom Vart, who has it in his sway, is a terrible man. He preys on the women like a vulture. He doesn't let them talk and sing and he makes them sour with each other...' Her voice was high now; angry.

William Scorton looked at the virago before him, perplexed. Scree Hall Mill was just one of a score of almost fanciful enterprises he had picked up in the North-East since he had settled here, a restless refugee from the

161

pursuing demands of a manically resentful wife, now mercifully dead. He formed the last thought guiltily. Scree Hall was a very old-fashioned mill, but he had had thoughts of modernising it, putting in steam looms and even bringing the spinning into the mill. Cloth made there and finished in Leeds might bring in some profit. The foreman Vart had seemed competent enough, an obliging fellow.

'You worked there, at the mill?'

'Yes. For a short time, then I was dismissed as he had dismissed others in my . . . dilemma.'

William kept his eyes on her face, but his peripheral vision was suddenly, hotly, uncomfortably aware of her bulky shape, so ungainly and alien beneath the bright, very youthful face. 'The conditions are bad at the mill, miss?'

She looked him in the eye. 'I've seen pigs better kept than people who worked at Scree Hall . . . it's Mr Scorton, isn't it? I've seen pigs better kept, even down in Forgan Buildings where I live.' She sat down heavily on her stool again. 'I'd be ashamed to have a mill like that, if I were you.'

Her gaze went past him and he felt himself dismissed. He walked on, to find his sons feeding the resting bear with apples they had bought at a nearby stall.

Without rancour Kitty watched the man lope away. Abstractedly she noted that William Scorton's smooth coat sat very elegantly on his broad shoulders and the thick curls escaping the back of his tall hat gleamed in the slanting afternoon sun.

She put her hand to her waist, pressed in a certain way and felt the baby roll and stretch beneath her touch. She shifted a bit on the stool. She was getting very heavy now. The discomfort was new. Wriggling to get comfortable on her low stool, her mind cast back over the last few months.

When she had told him about Freddie's death, Ishmael had held her close for many hours, joining her grief to his. In the end she had sat away from him and told him about her condition, her suspicion about the baby. He nodded slowly then put his hand on her shoulder. 'This baby is a blessing, Kitty, just as you were to me.'

'You should be castigating me, Ishmael. Throwing me off as a sinner.' She had glimmered a smile at him then.

'Freddie was such a *boy*, Kitty, such a source of light which will not now be dimmed. If he were here now, you would have a ring on your finger and naught would be said. It is common enough. We would be celebrating and, as I say, naught would be said about . . . the timing of this event.'

Kitty was not so understanding when she eventually made *her* discovery about Ishmael's agreement with Ned Lumb. She cried and raged; she pulled at his arthritic hands and laid them before him on the kitchen table. 'See! You can't fight with those. Ned Lumb won't let you.'

He shook his head. 'Ned will care naught for anything, save his spectacle of blood and I will give him that. And if Freddie's daughter is to fare well, we will need this purse, you and I.'

'A daughter?'

'That's for sure, Kitty.'

That very day Ishmael had set about a training regime of walking and running. He lifted his stones and great logs. He shadow-boxed before the great wardrobe mirror. He borrowed money, which was lent without demur, from Mirella Gullet, for the rent to keep on their home, and for proper food, to give him strength and to sustain Kitty, now dismissed from the mill.

Kitty, determined to play her part, went to Janine's old rooms, closed down now that Thomas was off playing his squeezebox for Esme. She raked in a cupboard and found bales of linen and cloth and heaved them back to Forgan to sew into small items which she could sell. She got hold of Ishmael's sharp needles and scraps of off-cut leather and made the puppets. In this way they had both prepared for the event which looked as though it would change their lives forever.

163

These puppets were a good seller and had brought her to this fair where, to her great regret, Ishmael was fighting again.

'Ah! Kitty Rainbow! A marketeer, no less. Esme will be entranced!'

She came back to the present to see the bland face of Jarrold Pommeroy. Alongside him stood Gabriel Gullet, even bulkier now, his face red and half wrecked with drink.

'Evening, Jarrold,' she said, with every appearance of jauntiness. 'Gabriel?'

Gabriel tipped his hat.

'And dear Mirella said that . . .' Jarrold surveyed her bulk with insulting closeness, '. . . you were not too well. Esme'll be so sad to hear.'

'You can tell Esme I am very well.' She glanced around. 'Is Esme here?'

He shook his head. 'She is very busy in Leeds. They love her winsome grace there. They are having special songs written for her now. And there are engagements in halls in Manchester and Liverpool.'

'She was always her best on the stage, was Esme,' she said evenly. 'Tell her I asked after her.'

Jarrold tipped his hat. 'An honour, Miss Kitty.'

She watched the two men stroll away and her anger made her restless. She stood up clumsily and asked the woman on the next pitch, a fortune-teller called Leonora Lee, to take care of her patch. Then she made her way through the crowds towards the boxing booth.

It seemed that every citizen of Priorton and people from much further afield were crowded around the booth. The crowd was imbued with a nervous, almost hungry anticipation. Men of all kinds of appearance, from the very high to the very low, moved through the crowd talking, whispering into ears as money was changing hands. Women were there too alongside their menfolk, relishing the fairground drama.

'Excuse me, sir, excuse me!' Kitty squeezed her way through, being finally allowed into the front row by William Scorton, who pulled one of his small sons to one side to let her in.

The black drummer boy vanished through a greasy makeshift curtain hung with bedraggled red flags, and two men emerged. It was some minutes before she recognised Ishmael. He seemed to have grown a foot in height and six inches in breadth. His mane of grey hair was pulled back into a queue, and his great scarred chest was bare. His glittering eyes passed over her, unseeing. He walked around the ring raising a hand to the crowd.

The people roared and shouted. A man with a neckerchief called to the crowd that this was the great fighter from London, well known to have downed champions, Mr Ishmael Slaughter.

Kitty clutched the arm beside her. 'My father,' she shouted proudly. 'That is my father.'

'Is it now?' William Scorton was looking down at her with amusement. She reddened, taking her hand away from his arm as though it were burned. Then she turned away, the mill-owner forgotten, as Ishmael set himself, standing toe to toe with his opponent – a much younger man with huge muscled shoulders, a great belly and massive legs. The neckerchiefed man shouted that this was Jim 'Butcher Boy' Perrington who had swept all before him in the Northern Counties.

There were more roars, and another flurry of betting, as the punters weighed the virtues of Ishmael's experience against this strong young bull of a man.

Butcher Boy came at Ishmael from the beginning, but Ishmael's skill at moving and ducking kept him at a distance. The crowd roared with increasing disappointment as no blood was spilled, despite the five knockdowns which constituted five rounds. Then there was a roar of approval as Ishmael finally landed a blow to Butcher Boy's right ear making blood pour over his massive shoulder. There was a sigh from the crowd as though from the mouth of one man, and they settled down to the festival of bloodletting which was the true lip-smacking attraction of these crude country bouts.

There were fifteen more rounds, with Ishmael down in only five of them. Butcher Boy's bull-like weight, his only asset, became a disadvantage, his strength worn down by Ishmael's swerves and his quickness on his feet. In the end Ishmael had him placed, feinted with the left, then landed a right on the same ear he had injured in the sixth round.

Butcher Boy went down like a stone. The crowd roared.

Kitty saw Ishmael's face as he landed the blow and was riven with the agony she saw there. She sagged. An arm went round her. 'You should not be here, miss,' said William Scorton in her ear.

She straightened up, away from his grasp. 'This is my place,' she said. 'This fighter is my father.'

The black drummer boy came on with sand and brushes to wipe up the worst of the blood. Abstractedly Kitty wondered if Ishmael had told him of the great black fighter Richmond who had beaten the best in Britain. The ring was finally being cleared of blood and more sawdust was being spread.

The neckerchiefed man was coming around the crowd with a hat. Ned Lumb was up in the ring calling out that, for a consideration, the great Ishmael Slaughter would fight any man here. Of course Mr Slaughter was a man of mature years, but a wily fighter. Surely there was some upstanding man here who could give him a decent round?

A gaggle of men, powerful miners and beefy farmers from up the dale, were clustering at the corner of the ring. Ishmael emerged again from behind the curtain, his eyes glittering. He was wiping what Kitty knew to be brandy from his lips. A cheer went up from the crowd as he squared up to his first opponent. There was another cheer as he squared up to his second, then his third challenger: all men drawn from the crowd eager to demonstrate their worth over this reeling Atlas of an old man.

It was the fourth opponent, a great blacksmith from Gibsley foundries, who finally sent Ishmael flying, scraping on his belly across the ring until he was just two feet from Kitty. He lay awkwardly on his side, very still, his face twisted in agony.

'Ishmael!' Kitty tried to clamber into the ring, but was cast back herself by the greatest pain she had ever known in her life. Then she felt nothing, only saw blackness.

Kitty struggled to make her eyes open but they wouldn't. She struggled to lift her hand but it too disobeyed her brain's command.

Her brain did recognise Mirella's voice. 'Of course the child has been a virtual daughter to me. My own daughter's bosom friend. Did I tell you my daughter is prominent in the theatre? Here, see this piece in the newspaper about her. This child? Of course their ways diverged, my own daughter on the high road to eminence and this child on the narrow and thorny path to – I am afraid to say this – wickedness.'

Kitty struggled to say something but her mouth seemed full of cotton wool.

A deeper voice was murmuring something which she didn't catch, the door clicked and she knew she was alone. She started to take deeper and deeper breaths and finally forced her eyes open. She saw what she knew to be the pink painted ceiling of Esme's bedroom at the George. Her breasts were sore. She felt another dull soreness. She put her hand on her flat stomach and flinched. Now she could remember a numbing ride behind horses which, as she screamed very loudly, were finally brought to a stop. She could hear the chuffling sound of a train. She could feel a wild pain. A man telling children to run, run! Then a hard firm hand on her brow and even wilder pain.

Then the blackness.

Now she pulled herself up on to her elbows and looked around the room. There was no crib. No sign of any baby. She remembered hearing the train and was visited by an image of a child thrown from the viaduct, flung into the air in an arc, falling into the waters. And this time there was no Ishmael to catch and cradle the baby in his arms.

She shrieked. 'Ishma-el!'

There was the drum of footsteps on the stairs outside and the door flew open.

'Well, yer've woken up, hinney,' said Mabella, hooking Kitty's arm and pulling her up to a more comfortable position. 'I must say yer've tekken yer time.'

Kitty pulled up the neck of what must be Esme's nightdress and pushed back her hair. She looked round again. 'What happened? Where's my—'

'Ha'd on!' said Mabella, swishing the curtains back, letting sun stream into the room. Then she went to the door and bellowed down the stairs, 'Ruby! Bring up that bairn.' She turned back to Kitty. 'Our Ruby took the bairn. She's just had one of her own an' she's had one on each titty for more'n a day.'

Kitty felt the flood of relief and a charging pain in her breasts. Ruby, a gaunt young woman whose bonnet was too large, placed the swaddled bundle in her arms. The pink face rested like a tight rosebud inside the close folds. A single black eye opened, seemed to survey her, then closed. 'Oh Ruby!' Kitty said. 'Oh Ruby.'

'Her name's Leonora!' said Mabella helpfully.

'Leonora?'

'Feller what delivered her in his gig thought he'd lose her to Heaven, so he baptised her. Quite the gent, that one. Yer should'a seen Her Ladyship, dancin' and curtseyin' around 'im! Anyway he said yer said she was to be called Leonora.'

Kitty shook her head, puzzled. The baby had come in a carriage. She recalled a voice shouting in her ear for a name!

A name! Then she remembered the gypsy who had taken care of her patch. A woman called Leonora something.

The baby started to stir and squeak.

'A gypsy. It was a gypsy's name.'

Mabella cackled and leaned over to loosen the strings on Kitty's nightdress. 'That's all as might be, hinny. But in the meantime let's see if yer can give this bairn some suck.'

The pain was almost unbearable at first but then her body seemed to click into proper shape; she felt a deep thrill of feeling travel from her breast almost to her heels and she settled down to feed her daughter. She looked over Leonora's head into Mabella's eyes. 'What about Ishmael? How is he?'

Mabella shook her head. 'Like a squashed fly, poor old sod. *Her Majesty*'s had the surgeon to him four times.'

The baby unhooked herself and whimpered. Kitty, with Mabella's help, set her close again.

'The old boy's in Mrs Gullet's own room and, to do her justice, like, she's caring for him tender, like he was that bairn in your own arms.'

Kitty hugged Leonora even closer, wondering just what they would all have to do now. It seemed that she and Ishmael had both been beaten, beaten to the floor.

They had been through hard times, she and Ishmael. The towel, now, was truly in the ring.

Or was it? Kitty pressed her chin gently on the baby's soft head. 'But maybe not, Leonora, maybe not,' she whispered. 'There's me and Ishmael, both fighters. And there's you to fight for now. I'll fight for you like no mother ever fought for me. I promise.'

PART TWO

Janine

15

Summer Cushions

1879

Apart from the times when Thomas Druce was creating musical fireworks with his glittering accordion, he made the other musicians at the Princess' Palace Theatre in Leeds rather uneasy. There was so much contradiction in him. Here was a tall, handsome, very normal-looking man, muscular and apparently powerful. But he never spoke, did not seem to hear, and did not even look at a person directly. However he could not be deaf, could he? His music showed you that. All this, as well as his occasional dumb headbanging rages, made his fellow musicians treat Thomas rather carefully. Then there was his slavish devotion to Miss Esther Rainbow, that pert and saucy singer, which made them snigger derisively and made more than one of them, who had a fancy for Miss Esther, want to punch him on the nose.

One or two of the musicians had tried their own luck with 'Miss Esther', only to be treated with a show of either innocent incomprehension – about which they were sceptical, given the content of her saucy songs – or the gracious reply that yes she would love a walk in the park. Thomas would too, wouldn't you, Thomas? Hadn't they been stuck inside this stuffy theatre for so long? Didn't they need a bit of fresh air, the air in Leeds being so smoky and dense compared with the fresh country air of County Durham, where both she and Thomas came from?

Then, of course, there was that *flash* cove Pommeroy, the feller with his fine velvet jackets, who came to see Miss Esther once every week, spending half the time buttering up Mr Van Diemen, the burly manager, and half the time holed up in Miss Esther's little dressing room getting up to the Lord knew just what. But, the musicians would say to each other with some satisfaction, even Pommeroy couldn't get rid of the lunatic squeezebox player.

In the end the musicians left Esme – the said 'Miss Esther' – strictly alone, apart from batting their bows and stamping their feet in reluctant professional admiration, as her performances brought the house down yet again.

Thomas, unlike Pommeroy, did not approve of Esme wearing the boy's clothes which were a well-established part of her performance. If Thomas came into the dressing room after her performance and she was lounging in velvet breeches, with one leg over the other, a buckled shoe in the air, he would bustle her behind her screen, sling her day dress over it and push her dainty leather slippers underneath its gilded frame. 'Clothes on! Clothes on!' he would say in his rusty, seldom-used voice.

These activities had lost her more than one dresser, who considered such actions and attitudes their territory. Anyway, dressing was not the business of some squeezebox player – a man, to boot – who was only a shilling in the guinea, anyway. Look at the musicians! They liked his music well enough, but even they were scared of him. What was a poor dresser to do?

For the most part, all this amused Esme and she would patiently comply with Thomas's silent, dogged bullying. However, at other times she would shriek, throw shoes and hairbrushes at him and tell him to get out. He took no notice whatsoever of her temper, his bland gaze flickering round the room and only occasionally settling on her angry bright red face.

Jarrold Pommeroy never bullied her. He applauded her performances, brought her new songs, and delivered her performance money from Mr Van Diemen in a series of little red purses with silk drawstring tops, which he'd had specially made.

For a while her life seemed both glamorous and steady, if completely exhausting. One performance would be followed by another, followed by rehearsals for new songs, followed by early evening performances in smaller, more intimate venues kindly fixed up for her by Jarrold. And then there were the painstaking singing lessons two mornings a week with Miss Elvira Smith, who smoked cigars and had the makings of a very good moustache. In all this rush, her spot at the Palace of Varieties was her greatest pleasure: the unambiguous approval of the halloo-ing crowd reassuring her that it wasn't all a dream.

One day Jarrold brought her Belgian chocolates and on top of them, wrapped in tissue paper, a small figure of an accordion player rendered cunningly in chocolate. Esme clapped her hands in delight at this and called out to Thomas, who as usual was sitting on his haunches outside her door.

'Look, Thomas, see what Jarrold has brought for you.'

He loped in and took a sidelong glance at the object, his eyes gleaming when he saw what it depicted. She thrust it into his hands. 'There now. Isn't that kind of Jarrold? He found it specially for you. Now say thank you.'

Thomas held it slackly. 'Go on, man, take a bite,' said Jarrold, with uncharacteristic joviality.

Thomas thrust the tissue bundle into his trousers pocket and turned to the door.

'Thomas! Say thank you!' Esme called to the swinging

door. She turned, smiled at Jarrold, shrugged, selected a chocolate from her own box and popped it into her mouth. 'Lovely, Jarrold. These are truly lovely.'

Kitty pulled the curtain right back to catch the last of the daylight, then held up her needle to receive the fine silk thread. Leonora, lying asleep on the counter like a stretching kitten, stirred and muttered. Kitty put the edge of her hand on the broad brow, and looked at the face. Even with its childish contours, it was so very like Freddie's. Leonora was only three now, but by the time she was six that face would have fined down to show the same handsome broad, well-cut planes as Freddie. And she was very quick and bright, just as he had been.

Freddie's brother Albert came to see Leonora from time to time. He would sit on a chair watching baby Leonora in clumsy amazement, putting out a large calloused finger for her to clasp. He always left behind money: a florin, sometimes even a guinea, to help with his brother's child.

Kitty told Leonora stories about Freddie: all the naughty things he had done as a child (making Leonora hiccough with laughter); how very clever her Daddy Freddie had been about the world; how brave he was, going down that black hole every day. She read Leonora the poems from the battered sheets brought to her by Albert, along with twenty guineas' death insurance money, soon after Freddie's funeral. Albert had handed the items over gravely, saying the money was due to her and if she didn't want the poems they would 'just go to the back of the fire, like.'

She smoothed the fine collar on the white protective cloth she had laid on the counter beside Leonora's sleeping form. She looked with satisfaction at the way she had worked the fine fabric with the subtlest shades reflecting all the colours of the rainbow. She picked up the collar again, and started to put in the fine stitches which would justify the high charges she could now make for this work, so much in demand for the wives and daughters of Priorton tradesmen. Many of these customers came to her from Mirella, who had been unexpectedly kind when Leonora was born. Her clients now included Miss Philomena Adams, her former teacher, who first came to investigate whether the embroiderer of whom she had heard such praise was the Kitty Rainbow she had taught.

As she stitched, Kitty surveyed with satisfaction the broad polished counter stretching away to the shadowy corners of the shop, and the patterns made by the colourful bolts of textured cloth against the wall. Freddie's twenty guineas and Ishmael's purse from that last punishing series of fights had done all this: allowed her to set up on her own behalf, without the bleeding ulcer of Janine's need for drink to destroy all her efforts.

But she'd had to work very hard to achieve this virtually on her own. It was true that Ishmael tidied the shop and the rooms above, and made their food, but his hands were no good at all for cobbler work. And he was absent-minded and distant sometimes, suffering raging headaches, which she tried to cure with every patent medicine advertised in the newspaper, and with visits from the doctor for which she had to pay.

Janine Druce had come and gone, and come and gone again, in the three years of Leonora's life. She usually came back derelict, too distressed and unkempt even to use her body as currency for another bottle of liquor. Kitty welcomed her home at these times, cleaned her up, and let her help in the shop with some sewing, or minding Leonora when Kitty herself was off collecting cloth, or was very busy with a rush order. This second-fiddle position with no responsibilities at all seemed to calm Janine down, and her desire to flee had finally begun to recede. Her occasional excesses were ignored by both Ishmael and Kitty as though they had never happened.

Kitty looked up now as Janine herself entered the shop with a packet from the carrier whom she had encountered on the pavement outside. She put the packet on the counter, fished another one out of her pocket and put it beside it.

'Here, give me that bairn,' she said, picking up Leonora from the counter. Leonora clambered about her like a somnolent monkey before she settled down to sleep again as Janine sat in the chair at the customers' side of the counter. 'Aye, she'd sleep through the second coming, this one. Not like you. Twenty hours a day on the go, you were.'

Kitty cocked her head. 'Was I?' Tales of her own childhood were more interesting to her now she was watching Leonora going through the same process.

'Aye. You were a greet handful.'

Kitty stuck her needle carefully in the back of the collar. 'Did you really know nothing about my mother, Antijan? Where I came from?'

Janine shook her head slowly. 'Nothing, hen. There were no stories afterwards, no whispers in the town like yer'd've expected. Yer might just as well have been hoyed down by that rainbow Ishmael's always talking about.' She nodded at the packets on the desk. 'One of them is the silks you ordered from the carrier. The other's from our Thomas. It says it's to me on the top.' She pushed it along the counter. 'You open it.'

Kitty sighed and folded the collar in the white cloth. 'Light's going anyway, so we'll go upstairs to take a proper look at it. Ishmael'll have our suppers ready. We can lock up now, I suppose.' Kitty shot the bolt and pulled down the blind.

She would come down later and light the gas, and open the shop again. She tried to keep the shop open as long as possible, until very late in the evening. It was surprising how many people would want a spool of thread then, or how some men, meandering home from the public house, would fix their sentimental eyes on one of the cloth dolls made by Kitty and buy it with their last pennies, 'Foh the bairns, like, dis tha knaa? Not much in their lives is tha?'

She opened Janine's package, pulled out and unfolded a big poster from the Palace Theatre, Leeds, which proclaimed, alongside a dog show and other star attractions, Miss Esther Rainbow, the golden songstress of the North, to be presenting her finest songs. There was a colour sketch of a woman with a high pluming feather coming out of her head which looked nothing at all like Esme.

'Look at this, Antijan!' Kitty thrust the poster under her nose. Underneath Esme's billing in smaller letters was stated: 'At the concertina, Mr Thomas Druce.' 'Look, he's famous. Our Thomas!'

Janine put her head on one side. 'Who'd a' thought it, Kitty. Our Thomas! No use to man nor beast. Now there he is with his name on a poster.' She allowed a grim smile to visit her countenance. 'There's a letter there from yon Esme as well, Ah see.'

The summer evening light was now masked entirely by the blinds. 'I'll read it when I get my supper, Janine. Can you put Leonora to bed for me?'

Leonora shared the big bed in the back bedroom with Kitty. Ishmael had the bigger front room and Janine, when she was there, had the pull-down bed in the cluttered back kitchen of the shop. Kitty offered to share her bed but, to her shamed relief, Janine always turned her down: 'Yer want nothin' sleepin with a drunken old woman, hen!' waving away Kitty's protests about how good Janine was now.

Ishmael, much gaunter and slower-moving these days, was putting the finishing touches to a cold supper of fat bacon, potatoes and pease pudding. The fact that the meal was cold was a relief on such a stifling evening. They ate with the silent efficiency common to hard-working people.

Then, as Ishmael poured them all a dish of tea, Kitty reached into the packet for Esme's letter. Ishmael cocked his head with interest as she read.

'Dear Mrs Druce,
   I write on behalf of Thomas to say he is very well. He is eating well and keeps himself clean and presentable. He is learning new tunes all the time and is very well respected for his music. We went to an orchestral ensemble the other night to listen to the music of Mr Beethoven and Mr Tchaikovsky. When we came back to our lodgings he roused the house with an exact rendition of what he had heard. The landlady...'

'There he is! He'll get himself thrown out,' said Janine glumly.

Kitty continued.

'...the landlady is a music lover and I must say he has tickled her fancy, so there is no problem there, thank goodness. I thought you would like to see the poster with Thomas's name on and also a portrait of me and Thomas in our theatre costume. You would be surprised. They will sell these pictures in hundreds. People buy them at the ticket office. Thousands, according to Jarrold who takes care of these things.
   Yours sincerely Esme Gullet (now *Esther Rainbow* of course!)
   'Postscript. Will you give my warmest felicitations to my friend Kitty Rainbow and inform her of my high regard? Tell her I was thinking about the unicorn she once promised to show me but never did. E. G.'

'Warmest felicitations?' said Janine. '*Warmest felicitations*, bigod.'

Kitty peered again into the heavy packet, shook it, and

two rectangular cards fell out. She held them towards the lamp.

'She's no beauty, ye couldna' say that,' said Janine thoughtfully, peering over Kitty's shoulder. 'But she's got something.'

Esme was leaning across a gilded table, looking boldly out of the photograph. She was posed against a painted background of hills, woodland and trickling streams. Her luxuriant hair was loose and tumbling over her shoulders. Her pale face was supported on her beautiful long-fingered hands, which in turn were resting on a pile of books. The detail on the lace cuffs stood out sharply against the sleeves of her dress, sensuous folds of taffeta seeming to swirl and engulf the lower part of the photograph like living water.

Kitty caught her breath. 'You're wrong there, Antijan. She is beautiful. It's her to the life. These photographs are so clever, don't you think? A miracle, really.'

Janine grabbed the other card. 'And here's our Thomas. Large as life.'

So he was, standing handsome and glassy-eyed clutching his accordion, standing behind Esme who, sword in hand, was striking a fencing pose. She was dressed in the garb of a cavalier, her long shapely legs clearly revealed in close-cut hose, her jewelled doublet tightly clinched by a figured belt from which dangled a tiny dagger.

'I don't know that it's decent. The lassie's half-naked,' said Janine, handing the cards to Ishmael.

He smiled slightly. 'She cuts a fine figure indeed. I would not think bad things about it, Janine. It is theatre. She plays a part. I think that your Thomas cuts a fine figure also,' he said encouragingly.

Janine peered closer. 'So he does. He always was fine-looking, wasn't he, hen? That was why the rest of his ways were such ... such...'

Ishmael touched the back of Janine's hand. 'I know,' he said. He raised his glance to Kitty, who was looking closely

181

again at the pictures, her lips folded in a hard straight line. 'Does this trouble you, Kitty?'

Kitty shook her head. 'I was thinking of the unicorn and Freddie. And Esme when we were little. It's just that she's there looking like that and she was my friend, and . . .' She looked around at the bright crowded kitchen. She was no longer satisfied with it, nor with the long wooden counter and the bolts of cloth downstairs, nor with the fine embroidery which she did into the night. 'I miss seeing her. You would think that in three years she would make her way home, wouldn't you?'

He shook his head. 'Time passes so quickly, little one. So quickly.' He stood up and started to gather the dishes. 'I think Mirella misses her too.'

Janine looked from one to the other, her face sharp. Then she pushed the photographs back into the envelope. 'An' will yer make a summer cushion, this year, Kitty? For Midsummer Day? Only a few weeks to go.'

Momentarily distracted from her gloomy thoughts, Kitty frowned. 'I hadn't thought . . .' She knew that Priorton women made these fancy cushions for Midsummer Day. She'd seen them sitting in the streets on that day, their embroidered cushion beside them on a low stool covered with a white cloth, a china saucer alongside for the expected collection of pennies. 'I used to think they were a waste of time . . .'

'Yer should do one, hen! A better hand with the 'broidery than any of those sausage-fingered hags. A way to get some pennies and to show off your wares.' Her eyes narrowed shrewdly. 'Yer should do sommat special, Kit. Different. Mark yerself out. It's not just yon singer that can do things. Here, I know . . .'

She vanished into the bedroom and they could hear her rooting about. Kitty and Ishmael smiled faintly at each other, used to Janine's erratic behaviour, her strange impulses.

She returned carrying a small scrap of material and thrust it into Kitty's hands. Kitty looked down at the faded fabric with its intricate design of acorns and oak leaves, blue on blue: the corner of fabric which had wrapped her as a baby. A thrill shot through her as she thought of the woman who was her mother and the nagging question that scratched her mind now and then, of just who she was, this woman who had sewn the acorn design. 'Make a cushion of that, Kit,' said Janine. 'Sew it like your ma did. That'll make a summer cushion. Yer've got three weeks ter do it. Can yer do it in three weeks, do yer think? With all the work in the shop?'

'Janine!' warned Ishmael.

Kitty stood up. 'Of course I can do it in three weeks, Antijan. I'll do it.' She went to her workbasket and started to pull out blue silks. 'What a lovely idea, Antijan. What a thing to do!' She took up the lamp to go down into the shop to find a piece of material which would do justice to such a task.

Esme looked up at Thomas's gaunt face. 'What is it, Thomas? Tell me!'

He had just been massively and wrenchingly sick.

Esme shook his hand to get him to focus on her, and then put one palm on his cheek to make him look at her but he twisted his face to one side. Her hand came down and she stood quietly beside him.

He looked almost dreamily through the window and then gracefully turned further away to allow another fountain of vomit to spew from his mouth on to the dark reds and blues of their landlady's carpet.

Esme finally got him to sit down, so that she could reach his face properly to pat his mouth with her handtowel. She put her fingers on his brow, which was cold and clammy. 'Oh Thomas, my dear, you're as sick as an old pig.' She rang for the landlady. 'Did you eat something?'

Mrs Montague, a Londoner of uncertain age with an improbably young husband, had an arch confidence which had helped her deal with theatricals for thirty years. She frequently told her Eric that after so long, nothing could surprise her.

Esme smiled engagingly at Mrs Montague, pressing a half-guinea into the woman's hand before she was a yard into the room. 'I'm afraid my friend Mr Druce's in a very bad way, Mrs Montague, and will be unable to go to the theatre tonight. He must have eaten something that didn't suit.' She took out her silver fob watch (a wonderful surprise present from Jarrold), and peered at its face. 'Would you and your husband be so kind as to see Mr Druce to his bed? If I don't rush now I'll miss my curtain.'

'Well, Miss Rainbow, I know all about curtains.' Mrs Montague thrust the coin into her apron pocket, her eyes on the white seepage on the carpet. 'There will be extra cost to clean that carpet,' she said, not too grimly.

Esme nodded.

Mrs Montague smiled then, and put her hand under Thomas's arm. 'Now come on, sir. I've a bottle of Dr Khan's Patent Mixture in my kitchen cupboard as'll put you right in no time.' Thomas stood up obediently and allowed himself to be led to the door, not acknowledging Esme at all. The landlady shook her head at Esme. 'One of the innocents, this one, miss. Funny that he plays that concertina thing like an angel.'

It was only when she was rattling and jolting along in the cab at a fine pace, that Esme started to wonder how she would cope on stage without the curling and bouncing rhythms of Thomas's squeezebox to support her. She smiled to herself. Of course she would manage. She wasn't a child any more; the days when she needed Kitty out front and Thomas at her elbow were long gone. How many hundreds of times had she done this now? How much had she learned just standing there and doing it? And the orchestra knew her programme backwards. There was nothing to worry about, nothing at all.

Her concerns melted further when Jarrold met her at the stage door. He looked behind her. 'Where's Thomas?' he said.

Esme shook her head. 'He's got a bad bellyache. Some of Mrs Montague's pickles must have been off, I reckon. Or the ham. Perhaps that chocolate thing? Anyway she's put him to bed, jingling the silver in her fancy apron pocket.'

Jarrold's brow wrinkled with concern. 'Poor fellow,' he said, shaking his head. 'Couldn't possibly have been the chocolate, Es. That was best Belgian. Must have been the pickles. Poor old fellow.'

She frowned slightly, surprised by his unexpected unctuous concern. 'He'll be a big miss, tonight.'

He pulled her arm through his and hugged it to her side. 'Nonsense, Es. You're a professional. This is the time to show it. Some of the best musicians in the North in that orchestra pit! And you're a trouper now. You can do it with your eyes closed.'

She did feel comforted and, after a few minutes' conversation, shooed Jarrold away while she changed into her neatly fitting sailor suit and teased a few curls fetchingly below the rim of the cap.

Later, as she waited in the wings for Marvo the Marvellous Juggler to acknowledge the shouts and whistles and applause after his act, Esme's eye fell on Thomas's empty chair in the orchestra pit. Her stomach churned and she started to shake.

She was still shaking as the orchestra struck up with the jolly version of the 'Sailor's Hornpipe' which they always played for her as she rolled on with a nautical swagger. Tonight she tripped nervously on to the stage, then stood just above the central flickering footlight while the orchestra played her introduction. Once. Twice. Three times over.

Each time she opened her mouth, but no sound emerged. She coughed and tried one more time but failed to produce more than a squeak.

The audience started to mutter. Someone called out from the back, asking whether she had a frog in her throat. Then there were more shouts and catcalls. A half-eaten apple landed on the stage. Tears came to Esme's eyes.

Then she saw Jarrold standing up, moving purposefully towards the stage.

Suddenly from the very back of the auditorium came a few reedy chords, a chirpy phrase from the 'Sailor's Hornpipe'. The orchestra stopped. People in the front row turned round in their seats, straining to see what it was about. Esme peered through the swirling smoke and darkness to see Thomas walking down the central aisle, elbows out, playing on his concertina the opening phrases of her sailor's song.

There was a scattering of applause.

Esme took a deep breath, opened her mouth and her voice joined that of the concertina, gaining strength with every phrase. The orchestra started up again. As she sang she started to clap in time. By the time Thomas had leaped over the barrier and taken his place in the orchestra pit the audience was laughing and clapping with her.

She looked down at Thomas as he played with that usual intense look on his averted face, which still had a sick pallor. As they moved into the second song she noticed too that he was wearing his jacket inside out and that his tie was only half tied.

What she did not notice was Jarrold Pommeroy's grim face as he retrieved his usual seat in the third row, bitterly regretting that his chocolate gift had not had its desired effect.

Kitty placed the tissue parcel on the table in the bar parlour at the Royal George. Mirella Gullet opened it up with care, then turned the embroidered sleeves this way and that in the bright light from the window.

'This is really wonderful work, Kitty. I never saw such handiwork, even in Darlington. Now ... how much do I owe you?' Mirella was much fatter and stiffer now, feeling her age, but she still liked her pretty things.

'One and threepence each sleeve. Two and six all told.'

Mirella doled out the shillings from her purse. 'I have to say that you're very reasonable, Kitty Rainbow.'

'It's half what I'd charge anyone else.'

Mirella raised her brows. 'Very obliging, I'm sure.' She was still a little reserved with this girl. Kitty might be a woman now, mother to a child, but she'd been a hoyden in her youth, and the source of so much conflict at the George. But Esme was never home now, and despite herself Mirella quite enjoyed these little business dealings with Kitty Rainbow, who, reluctant though Mirella was to say it, was making quite a go of the little drapery. Mirella had watched with interest the metamorphosis of the little barefoot guttersnipe into the shrewd young businesswoman. She chose to believe that all this was something to do with her. After all, were not she and Ishmael old friends? Had she not given Ishmael yards of advice through the years about his 'daughter'?

Kitty met her gaze steadily. 'I am very obliged to you, Mrs Gullet. I've many customers now, on your recommendation.'

Mirella ran a finger over her immaculate cuffs decorated with drawn threadwork, also perfectly executed by Kitty. 'It's always hard to find good craftswomen – or men. Jossy used to say when you find one, hang on to him. Or her, as is the present case.' She paused, then said almost to herself, 'I do miss Jossy, you know. You miss someone of your own.' She coughed. 'Are you sure you won't join me in a dish of tea, Kitty? Or a glass of port?'

Kitty shook her head and stood up, smoothing down her

skirts. She never took Mirella up on any of these invitations. She could never get used to her change of status with Esme's mother. It felt too strange sitting here, nose to nose in a social situation, in a place where she had been thrown out more than a score of times.

Mirella followed her to the door. 'And how is Ishmael this week?' she said meekly.

Kitty shrugged. 'He's up and down. He has these awful headaches, and gets miserable because he can't do what he used to. He's very nice with little Leonora but I think he's impatient with the world and himself.'

Then Mirella did an extraordinary thing. She put a hand on Kitty's arm. 'Don't forget I'm here, Kitty. Ishmael's an old friend of myself and my dear old Jossy. Send him here some afternoons and we'll sit and talk about old times. Perhaps that'll give him some cheer.'

Threaded into her voice were the strands of her own loneliness and her increasing isolation. The Royal George had not been the same since last year, when Gabriel had persuaded her he should come out of the lawyer's office and had, in fact, left very promptly to take over the hotel himself. So, when he proceeded to fill it with his racing cronies, he drove away all her old chums, who preferred a quiet drink to a wild time.

Kitty put her hand on to Mirella's and was struck by the dry, papery quality of the skin under hers. 'Certainly I'll do that, Mrs Gullet. I'm sure Ishmael'll be pleased to come.'

Kitty went out the back way and was stopped in the entry by Gabriel himself. His stained black coat strained across his large stomach; he had lost some hair and two side teeth.

He put up a hand to stop her progress. 'Ah, Miss Kitty! Been in to see my mama, I imagine?' His tone was benevolent, oiled by an early brandy.

She folded her arms. 'So I have. I delivered some sleeves she ordered.'

'She's always much cheered when she's seen you, I'll say that.'

'I think she misses Esme.'

He scowled. 'Esme has no consideration. Though she's going great guns on the stage, according to Pommeroy.'

She put her head on one side. 'You've seen Jarrold?'

'Up here for all the northern race meetings and regularly at the big fights in Newcastle.'

'And Esme's never with him?'

He shook his head. 'Too busy singing for his supper.' He opened his mouth and cackled at that. 'Got my darling sister on a short tether, has that old devil. Says she's earning money hand over fist. Must be, the money he's losing on the four-legged angels of the track and the two-legged devils in the ring.'

Kitty's hands came down to her side, her knuckles curling. 'He's losing her money?'

He shrugged. 'Who's to know, Miss Kitty? Who's to know?'

'Does that not concern you?'

He shrugged again, his casual air not betraying the enjoyment he was getting out of this uppity little orphan. 'That mincing sister of mine deserves everything she gets, if it were down to me.'

She strode on by him now, down the entry into the brightly lit square. He stumbled after her, catching her elbow. 'Hey, miss, can't you enjoy a little jest? I'm sure old Pommeroy's on the level with my sister. I'm just a bit mad at her for not coming home to see my old ma, so I'm sounding off for that reason. Don't mind me.'

She relaxed a little at this. 'Well. That's fair enough. I think she could have made it back home myself. Just now and then, like.'

'We get these letters. About pantomimes at Christmas, about summer varieties, about working six days and nights in the week, but...' He left it delicately in the air, knowing he had got his little fish hooked. 'Anyway, Miss Kitty! Enough about the sister. My ma tells me your little business is enjoying exemplary success, and you are becoming *known*.'

It was her turn to shrug. 'It should be, the work I put into it.'

'And does it leave you time to dally a little, to spend time with friends?'

It dawned on her that he was making a play for her particular attention and she almost chuckled out loud. Controlling this desire she shook her head gravely. 'To be honest, Gabriel, it leaves me with no time at all except that which I spend with my daughter, Leonora, and with Ishmael. And I'll not steal time from them. Now I must get on. I've lost time here already.'

And she bustled on, leaving him standing, arms akimbo, watching her as she made her way through the crowds in the Market Square.

Janine continued to make a great fuss about their 'summer cushions', stitching away at her own effort and peering at Kitty's work, giving her gratuitous advice at every turn. Janine's cushion was a rather stiff design of red tulips in a green vase. She held the half-done cushion up for Kitty's inspection, telling her how it was an exact copy of one which she made when she was fourteen, for her own marriage chest.

She laughed merrily at that. 'Marriage chest! Ma benighted husband took the lot – linen, cushions, petticoats and teacloths, everything – and sold them for sovereigns within ten days of getting a ring on ma finger. And the ring followed, ten days later. Ah took a curtain ring out o' stock an' put it on me own finger just for decency.'

It took Kitty some time to work out the intricacies of her own design: making sure of the symmetry between the pale blue acorns and the dark blue oak leaves, so that the balance was not lost. In the end she had to incorporate some clear spring green into the density of all the blue. This made the whole pattern leap to the eye. All the time, as she puzzled with the design, in her mind's eye she could see the oaks in White Leas Woods and the little deer flickering beneath the branches of the old trees: the unicorn that Esme had never managed to see.

One morning she woke up very early and, while the kettle was boiling on the fire, picked up the half-done cushion. In a minute she found herself looking for white silk and threading her needle and then stitching a chainstitch outline of a white animal in one corner of the cushion. The kettle had boiled dry and Leonora was banging her spoon for her breakfast by the time Kitty had finished, having embroidered in satin stitch the small figure of a unicorn, which now seemed to be dancing on a field of acorns.

'Now that's a verra nice touch,' said Janine. 'A craftswoman's touch. What made yer think o' that?'

Kitty shrugged. 'I don't know. I dreamed last night of a time I was with Freddie. We once saw a white roe deer and he swore it was a unicorn, like one we once saw in our schoolbook.'

Leonora got very excited when she saw the unicorn, pointing and chattering about the 'nice horsey'; so Kitty rose even earlier the next morning and fashioned Leonora a toy unicorn from an offcut of white linen. The next afternoon, while Kitty embroidered during a lull in the shop, Leonora played with the unicorn, pushing rough stitches into it with a bodkin threaded with blue wool.

The week leading up to Midsummer Day was stormy, but the day itself, once the sun had burned off the mist, was fine and bright. Down below in the town of Priorton, cautious citizens took off their thicker bonnets and shawls and mopped their brows. The narrow streets just off the Market Square, where lay Kitty's shop, were cooler, being thrown into shadow by the height of the buildings and the very narrow space in between. This was good for business, as people retreated into the shaded lanes from the blazing arena of the Market Square.

Kitty's shop was well placed at the head of one of the narrow alleys, just beside Goldstein the jewellers. Latterly Ishmael had made friends with Isak Goldstein and he spoke with him in stumbling half-remembered Yiddish, which was a treat for Mr Goldstein, whose English, even after twenty years, was strictly confined to business transactions.

The drapery now was doing good business on all fronts and Kitty and Janine had to squeeze time to complete their cushions, working far into the night. By ten o'clock in the morning of Midsummer Day they were sitting outside the shop on chairs, their summer cushions laid carefully beside them on stools which had been covered with white teacloths; their saucers chinked with pennies and farthings dropped by passers-by. Kitty had to empty hers several times to stop it overflowing.

Passing women leaned down and commented on the quality of the needlework, and the fine work on the collar which Kitty was stitching as she sat. Men passing by were more interested in Kitty herself and she was treated to several winks and told many times she was 'a bonny lass'.

She turned to Janine. 'Does this happen every time then?'

Janine grinned conspiratorially. 'Only if yer a bonny lass, hen. Ah dinnet notice any lad a-sayin' that to me.' She sat back complacently. 'It's been said o' me, like, times gone by. To be truthful, that's what it's all about. All this.'

'That's what what's all about?'

'It's a way of seein' the wares. Young lads like. Seein' more than some embroidered cushion.'

Kitty stood up, almost tipping over her summer cushion. 'Like cattle down the cattle mart, you mean? I'm not doin' any of that.'

Janine pulled her down again. 'It's a jest, lassie. It can't be just that, can it, or why am I sittin' here with me frozen

192

tulips? It's old, doin' things like this. Old as time. Once they used to make the cushions of real flowers. It's about the summer, lass. Summer delight. Now sit down, will you, and dinnet be such a soursides!'

Kitty had just sat down again when two men in tall hats turned into the alleyway from the Market Square, large black shapes against the slash of sunlight forcing itself down the narrow street. She blinked, and screwed up her eyes, finally descrying that one was quite elderly, the other forty years old or thereabouts. The younger one was clean-shaven and wore a coat of fine cloth, a stray strand of sunlight gleaming on his heavy watch chain in the shadowy gloom.

Tension rippled through her as she recognised William Scorton, owner of Scree Hall Mill: the man who had stood beside her that day of Ishmael's last fight; who had carried her with his own hands back to the Royal George with Leonora whom he had just seen born. She had not set eyes on him since then, or even thought of him. Now she was blushing at the enforced intimacy of their last meeting.

She sat stiffly while they lingered beside Mr Goldstein's small circular window, deep in discussion about a pair of fine Georgian wine decanters displayed there. They moved on and paused beside the summer cushions. She kept her head down over the collar, stitching furiously away, her face shaded by her bonnet.

She had recognised the older man also: he was the solicitor whom Gabriel Gullet had started work for, Tobias Hunter. She wriggled a little as he took out his pince-nez to take a closer look at her cushion. He placed a finger on it and said brusquely, 'May I?'

Kitty nodded, lifting her gaze now to William Scorton, who was looking closely at her. She looked quickly away.

Mr Hunter brought the cushion closer to his eyes then looked at her. 'Where d'you get this cushion, madam?'

'I made it myself . . . sir.' She stuck her needle in her collar and paid him her full attention, her skin crawling now with extra awareness, a sense of the importance of the moment.

'And, pray where did you get the notion for this design?' His tone was keen, interrogative.

'I have a ... sir! In my own head. I always think up my own designs. See here? These little fishes?' She held up the collar she had just been working on. 'This cushion here I made very special because it was for Midsummer Festival.'

Janine broke in now, unable to hold back. 'Yer ken the custom, sirs? Maids make these an' show'm on Midsummer Day.' Her smile, designed to be appealing, came out as a leer. She rattled the saucer. 'And with the pennies we make tansy cake, a spicy cake which goes well with fine sherry wine. We'll be making our tansy cake this afternoon. You're welcome to join us for—'

'Antijan!' warned Kitty.

The man dropped the cushion as though it were a cinder and stepped back almost on to his companion's toes. Then he caught William Scorton's arm and pulled him away without a backward glance.

Kitty straightened the cushion, her face burning. 'What was that all about? Why did you say such a thing? They will think...'

Janine shrugged. 'What should they think? They were showing close attention. The younger one was staring at you as though yer were some exotic creature from the deep. Yer could do worse than look for a ... gentleman, Kit. It's hard on yer own.'

'Gentleman? Those two spiders? They're old enough to be my father. Or Freddie's. Anyway, I know them. The old man is Tobias Hunter, that Gabriel worked for. The other is called Scorton. I worked for him once. He has sons, great big boys. He was ... there the night that Leonora was born.'

'Still, lassie. Arrangements can be made. You can be taken care of...'

Janine was looking so earnest that Kitty started to laugh.

'You're a funny one, Antijan, engining away to get me a position of mistress to the gentry.'

Janine threw up her hands. 'Well, Ah see nae chance of yer linkin' up with a collier lad or a butcher boy.'

'Freddie was a collier lad.'

'Well, he was different.' She paused, smoothing the fringe of her cushion. 'Don't you find yourself kind of . . . wanting something?'

'Wanting to be married?'

'No. Yes. Ah mean being in a bedspace, close wi' a man. Yeh musta been that close wi' Freddie. There's the bairn.' Her voice was weedling, inviting confidence.

Kitty giggled. 'I was only . . . *close* . . . as you put it, the once.' She grinned widely. 'In a graveyard.'

Janine yelped.

'And as far as I can remember, bein' *close* was lovely. But I've almost forgotten it now. Anyway that was all about Freddie. We were children together. No one else has drawn my glance since. And no one's been drawn to me. Who'd want a lame girl with a child out of wedlock and an old man to support?'

'As well as a drunken old Scotch draper woman?'

'I didn't say that,' said Kitty. She leaned over and gathered up her cushion to look at it more closely. 'This certainly made an impression on the old man.' She examined the interlocking acorns and oak leaves, the silvery white unicorn in the corner. Then she leaned down and from the bottom of her workbasket, took out the scrap of material she had so assiduously copied. 'Do you think he would know something about this, Antijan? Do you think he might know something about her? My mother?'

16

The Torn Coat

Esme paid off the driver of the hansom cab and told him to return in an hour. She looked up at the tall house. It stood in the middle of a row of ten, and its grand proportions were in conflict with its drab curtains and its stone, stained and spotted by the dozens of industrial chimneys belching forth nearby. She wrinkled her nose at the acrid smell, put up her parasol against the floating soot and mounted the steps, then pulled the bell pull and waited.

Jarrold's note had been quite mysterious. About 'opportunities not to be missed and fortunes to be made'. She must come to his lodgings and for heavens' sake she must not bring the unfortunate Thomas Druce. It was important that the right impression be made.

The door squeaked open to reveal a plump woman in middle years in her outdoor clothes. Esme's hand was grasped in a vice-like grip and pumped up and down. 'Miss Rainbow? I'm Alice Corton Smith. *Miss*, that is. I've seen you many times on the stage, Miss Rainbow. Mr Pommeroy is kind enough to furnish me with free tickets from time to time.'

Her voice sounded like Miss Petty, Esme's old teacher,

but the rouge on her cheeks, like the dirt on her house, told a different story.

She peered short-sightedly at Esme. 'But you are so different off the stage, so ... more... not so theatrical.'

Esme knew perfectly well what she meant. Others had commented indirectly on how plain she was, this side of the footlights. Jarrold, in his surly moods had told her more than once she was ugly. She was used to it.

'Now I'm to put you in the drawing room, as Mr Pommeroy just stepped out to collect his other guest from the hotel. He says to sit tight and he'll be here in a wink.' She laughed in grotesque merriment. 'Oh he has a turn of phrase, has Mr Pommeroy.'

She led the way upstairs along a landing and through large double doors into a large drawing room, in which it was impossible to move in a straight line: it was so crowded with chairs, tables, and footstools, glass cabinets of dead flowers and animals, trinkets and objects of indiscriminate value and quality scattered on every surface. Despite the heat of the day a great fire was burning in the hearth.

Miss Corton Smith settled Esme in a battered armchair close to the fire, thrust into her hand a sticky glass of sherry, which had been already poured, and pulled on her own gloves. 'And now you must forgive me but I regret I must leave you. I have a very pressing appointment with Madame Corsiksky. Have you heard of her? No? Well, my dear, she is the most wonderful *seer*. She tells the Tarot with the most miraculous vision. And she is *very* strict about her appointments. More than my life's worth to miss her. *Au revoir*, Miss Rainbow, I'm sure we will meet again.'

Esme was relieved when she left, more relieved when she heard the downstairs door bang. She stood up, already sweating, tried and failed to open a window, then settled herself to sit on a hard chair furthest away from the fire.

It was a good ten minutes before she heard the rumble of men's voices in the hall and the clatter of heavy feet coming up the stairs The two men entered the drawing room in veils of tobacco smoke. Jarrold's companion was a bulky, much-caped figure of a man, built like a bull with an extra layer of fat on his clean-shaven cheeks and wild hair controlled by pomade as dense as lard.

Esme coughed as the wreathing smoke reached her. Jarrold took her hand. 'Dear Esme, you're looking well. Very handsome, very handsome today. Don't you think so, Mr Cullen? May I present Miss Esther Rainbow, who gave you so much pleasure with her performance last night?'

She smiled politely and her hand was shaken by his hand which felt like a fistful of cold sausages.

'Mr Cullen has halls in London, Es. Is building up a great empire of entertainment.'

'You have been in the newspapers, Mr Cullen,' she said. 'I read about you bringing some dancers from India.'

The great man removed his cape, threw it on one of the many tables, sat on the fireside chair and mopped his brow before he lit another cigar. He looked at her over the flame; his small eyes were dark purple, almost all pupil.

'Yes, Miss Rainbow. Fine performance. Immaculate. Immaculate. Enticing. Enticing.' He repeated the word in a voice which seemed much too light for such a big man. 'A consummate performance. Consummate.' He drew deeply on his cigar, allowing a silence to grow.

'And he thought...' prompted Jarrold.

'And I thought, I wondered, Miss Rainbow, if I could persuade you to honour the metropolis, the great city of London with your presence. I have in mind a spot for you at the Crystal Theatre in North London. The good people would consume you with delight. Consume you, indeed. And I have a further six venues where you will be consumed ... with delight.'

The hair on the back of Esme's neck prickled at his choice of words. She looked across at Jarrold.

'It'd be the making of you, Es,' he drawled. 'The finest and the best in Europe pass through Mr Cullen's portals.'

Cullen waved his cigar in deprecation and Esme coughed as her lungs filled with acrid smoke.

Jarrold clapped his hands together. 'Well, if you'll excuse me, Mr Cullen ... Esme. I've some fight papers in the drawing rooms which Ned has asked me to complete. I'll be five minutes, no longer.' He smiled blandly from one to the other. 'Five minutes.'

'Jarrold!' squeaked Esme.

But the door had closed already behind him with a distinctive click.

Cullen patted his broad, tartan-clad knee. 'Now then, Miss Rainbow, why not come and tell old Uncle Cullen what new costumes you may need for your London appearances.' His sausage-like fingers came up to remove a fat wallet from an inside pocket and place it on the low table beside him. 'You'll find I spend generously to kit my performers in the best. You can go to the finest men's tailors in London. Men's clothes are your preference, I think? The gentlemen are every keen on that. Very popular. Very popular indeed.'

'I-I- don't think ...' Whirling through Esme's head was the feeling she'd had when Gabriel and his friends were buffeting her from one to the other, before Kitty Rainbow came to her rescue. 'I-I can't, won't ...'

With surprising speed he had heaved himself to his feet and his sausage fingers were fingering her silk-clad forearm. 'Now, my dear Miss Rainbow, a little kiss is not so much to pay for the favours which are about to be heaped on you, is it? In London you'll drink champagne each night: I'll bring the great men of London to your door. They do like a bit of *clean-and-neat*. I can assure you of that, my dear.'

She was frozen to the floor. His rubbery lips were on her cheek. His hand was on her breasts over her frogged jacket. 'And the poor little heart is fluttering so.' Then the lips were against her ear. 'Strange, this *touch-me-not* in one who sings in such a teasing fashion in tight boy's gear. But then there is currency in this. Currency! I know this,' he whispered. Then he went across to the door and rattled it. It was unlocked from the outside to reveal Jarrold.

Cullen threw on his cloak and gathered up his cane. 'She'll do, Pommeroy. She'll do.' He swept out.

Jarrold came in and closed the door behind him. 'What is it, Es? You're shaking.'

'He's mad. He tried ... He tried ... You locked the door.'

'That? Nonsense! The lock clicked of its own accord. Of course I didn't lock it, my dear.' He pulled her into his arms. 'Now what did he do?'

'He kissed me.' She put one hand on her cheek. 'And he touched me.' She put the other hand on her breast.

'The snake! Here, let me take that horrible touch away for you.' He kissed her on her cheek and his lips were warm and dry. Then he unfastened the frogging on her jacket and touched the bare skin on her breast. She shivered. 'There! Isn't that better, my dear child? The touch of the nasty man is gone.'

Then his lips were running across her cheek, up across her brow into her hair. The whole of her body seemed to be tightening up like a bowstring. Then his lips touched her and she was on fire, kissing him with an energy and gauche earnestness which he obviously relished.

He murmured into her ear, 'You mustn't mind old Cullen, pigeon. Or any of the other Cullens. Just a means to an end for us to go up in the world. A bit of slap and tickle. I'll always make it better, never fear. Always.'

Now he was unfastening her jacket properly. He pulled away at her stays and kissed her throat and breasts till she was swooning on the sofa, her mind tumbling about like a balloon in the wind, her body on fire.

Then just as quickly he sat away from her. She felt suddenly wretched and utterly and terrifyingly alone. She put one hand over her breast.

'Now is the time,' he said, his voice thick. 'Now is the time, my little pigeon.' He stood up and went across and she heard the door click again. Then he moved to the window to pull across the thick curtain, casting the room into gloom. She could hear him feeling his way back to her, cursing as he kicked over a table. Then she could sense him kneeling before her.

He kissed her, and again she grasped him as though she were drowning, 'Don't worry, pigeon. I will make it all so nice for you. So nice.'

Then he set about his work with an artist's satisfaction. Long practice had led him to know just how to make this first time work. And if you made the first time work, they were yours for ever.

Or as long as they were useful.

When they had finished and she was crying and stroking his face with grateful fingers, he was suddenly visited by the memory of another time, another one who was grateful, and felt an unfamiliar faint twinge of regret, wondering just where that one might be after all these years.

Janine made a great business of buying the ingredients for the tansy cake from the pennies that had gathered, and contrived a ceremony of serving it that night, after the lamb stew which Ishmael had made for their supper.

Ishmael listened patiently as Kitty told her tale of the man who had shown such an interest in her summer cushion, in the acorn and oak leaf design. 'He seems to know it, Ishmael. Do you think...?'

The old man shook his head. 'Do not think anything about it, Kitty. It will be of no matter. A coincidence only. No more. Please, please do not go off chasing hares.'

Leonora crumbled the tansy cake on her plate and asked for more. Kitty watched her daughter and thought of her own mother who had never had the pleasure of watching her child eating with a child's uncomplicated greed. She wanted to ask Ishmael more questions but could think of none. Ishmael knew no more than herself.

Esme returned from Jarrold's lodgings in a daze. She was tired, aching, but felt new-made all over. Her mind was performing somersaults, remembering resentfully how Jarrold had deliberately left her to be pawed by Cullen, then recalling how tender and intricate he had been as he showed her how to make love, how to enjoy it.

There had been surprises: the surprise of the explosion of her own feeling; the surprise of the strangeness of the body of a man, forceful and almost laughably different; the surprise at the sense of personal power she'd felt at the end of it all, his body drained and sleepily relaxed in her arms.

Ishmael had taught her and Kitty about power. About standing your ground and handling your fear. So where did this activity stand in his pantheon of power? Perhaps it was the power of knowing your opponent's weak spot. That desire to overwhelm, the desire to dominate was in itself Jarrold's weak spot. This was where she had him. This would make him marry her one day, for sure.

On her landing she was brought up short by the sight of Thomas Druce, curled up like some gigantic baby on the threshold of her room. His eyes were wide open and he was silent, but tears were streaming down his face.

'What is it, Thomas? What's the matter? What's happened?' She threw aside her reticule and her parasol, and dropped to her knees beside him. She wiped his tears with her organza scarf and put her arms around him, resisting his efforts to squirm away from her. 'What was it, Thomas? I can hear your heart crying out to me. What is it?'

He stumbled to his feet, dragging her with him to his little room at the end of the corridor. The door was wide open. On the bed was his concertina, broken into a hundred pieces, arranged in neat rows of matching components.

She was puzzled. 'Who did this? Who did this, Thomas? Did you do it in one of your tempers?'

He shook his head like a dog. Then he went and crouched in the corner, his hands together before him. Then he leaped out of the corner, looked at the little rug by his bed and clutched his head, moaning. Then he kneeled down and mimed the tender picking up of pieces and placing them on the bed, where they now were. She touched the tiny screws, the broken leather bellows.

'But who did this, Thomas?'

He stood up straight and strolled across the room in eerie mimicry of Jarrold's slightly rolling walk which reflected his time as a sailor.

'No. No. Not Jarrold! He—'

Thomas shook her shoulders then and made her watch as he mimicked again the unmistakable movement. Then very gently he touched her eyes and closed them.

'It was Jarrold,' she said dully, the fleeting joy of the afternoon finally draining from her body. 'You say I'm blind to his badness. Oh no, Thomas. I know about that.'

He went back to the corner and picked up some lengths of bailing rope and trailed them over his wrists which were still red, showing where they had been tied earlier. Then Thomas opened his mouth and emitted an eerie giggle: an exact replica of Jarrold when he thought he had been particularly clever.

'It was Jarrold,' she repeated dully. 'I know that. Don't worry, Thomas. We'll get it mended. I'm sure someone will mend it.'

He looked her in the eye then. Straight in the eye. Then he rolled up the clinking metal and the rustling leather of the concertina in the bedspread, strode across to the window and threw the great bundle outside. It clanked and clattered, and they could hear shouts of protest which they both ignored.

She took his hand and he actually let her retain it. 'Now,' she said, 'you come with me.'

Jarrold affected great surprise when he opened his door to them. His face folded into attitudes of deep concern as she told him of the broken instrument. 'Poor old fellow,' he said.

She put up a hand to stop the torrent of sympathy. 'You did it.'

He laughed. 'Nonsense, my dear girl. Some thief broke in.'

'He told me. You tied him and made him watch while you broke it to little pieces.'

'He couldn't tell you. Feller's dumb.'

'He told me, Jarrold,' she said steadily. 'He told me and I know.'

Thomas groaned and started to rock backwards and forwards where he stood.

'See? He couldn't say a thing. Feller's an idiot. Can't talk. Can't think. Can't do anything except play that blasted instrument and hang around you.'

'Is that why you broke it?'

He stared at her, then shrugged. 'So what? Just a little game to show him his place. I'll buy him a new toy.'

'So you will. And not just a concertina. A piano accordion. He'll like that.' She pulled on her gloves. 'And I'll go to Mr Van Diemen and get my own wages now. I know you've been taking a slice for your own pocket but I didn't mind because I was just learning and you . . . seemed to be taking care of me. Well, Jarrold, I can manage on my own now.'

Jarrold scowled and his hands curled into fists. 'Well, you go on your own, you little cat. And see if you can find someone to marry you. It was marriage you were babbling about there on that couch, wasn't it? See if you can find someone to take care of you like I have. A woman so ugly she looks better as a man than as a woman.'

Her face crumpled at this and he reached out and pulled her to him, smoothing her hair back from her face. 'But don't let's quarrel, pigeon! Jarrold loves Esme in spite of all that, in spite of you getting into this silly pet. As long as Esme is a good girl and sings for our supper. That'll be champagne soon. Then afterwards we can creep into our nice bed with silken sheets and play our little games. You liked those little games, didn't you? I can tell.' He tapped her not so lightly on the cheek. 'But no more talk of wedding rings. Makes you sound like some little village girl. There're much better things in store for you. Much better.'

She pulled away, pushing his hands from her as though they were particularly troublesome flies.

His face now settled into its pleading mode. 'Look, Es, I know I've been a naughty boy. We'll get the feller a piano accordion. The cheapest money can buy. And we'll talk to Cullen about London.'

She stared at him steadily. 'Did you hear what I said? I am going on my own now. You can come along if you want but I'll give you your pay, not the other way round. But first, we buy Thomas the *finest* accordion in Leeds. Then *we* can talk if you wish about London. But you're not shipping me there like a parcel of fish. And, most important, Thomas is coming too. And you're not to try any of your nasty tricks on him.' She took a step towards him. 'If you do, I'll kill you. I think I do love you, Jarrold. More, I know, than you love me. But Thomas is closer to me than my fingernail, as essential to me as my tongue. Without him I can't . . . *won't* sing.' She put her hands up and shook his shoulders. 'Do you hear?'

'I hear.' He smiled faintly. Here was a worm turning indeed. This was going to be a close call.

Her decisiveness grew as she spoke. 'I think I – me and Thomas – will go to London, so long as Cullen keeps his hands to himself.' She let out a long breath. 'But first I'm going home. I want to see Kitty. Every time someone calls me Miss Rainbow I look round for her. And me and Thomas are sick of the fog and stench in this town. We want some real fresh air.'

Thomas stood up straight then and lumbered across to the door.

Jarrold sneered. 'Fresh air? You mean among all those coalheaps and the cokeworks?'

She pulled back from him and adjusted her sleeves. 'At least there, there's a green field at the end of every street. At least there, there are no fat tigers like Cullen. And no snakes like you.'

He caught hold of her then and pulled her to him. 'Yes, yes, yes, dearest Esme. You win! Anything you say. Now let's just go and get this beggar his piano accordion, shall we?'

A week after Midsummer's Day the two men in tall hats came again into the shop. Kitty was on her own. Janine was sewing in the back room, and Ishmael had taken Leonora down to Bart's Farm to collect vegetables, potatoes and milk.

The elderly lawyer coughed and introduced himself properly and his companion, Mr William Scorton.

She looked from one to the other. 'I know of you, Mr Hunter. The brother of a friend of mine worked for you once. Gabriel Gullet.'

His brow darkened. 'Feller holds court at the Royal George now, I hear. He was a scallywag. A reprobate.'

She smiled slightly. 'I can only agree with you on that, sir.' She turned to the other man. 'And we also've met, sir. I worked for you once at Scree Hall Mill. And you assisted me once ... when ...' Her voice faded, unwilling to recall the time with this cold-faced stranger. Yet he was the one, they said, who had carried her in his own arms, tender as a babe, from the ringside to the Royal George.

William Scorton bowed. 'I did have an inkling. But it was a time ago.' His glance moved around the trim shop. 'And much has changed since you ... suffered so at my loom, and by my side at the boxing ring and in my carriage. You appear to be prospering, if this is not too bold a thing to say.'

'I've a daughter and a father to keep, sir. It takes hard work and—'

Impatiently Hunter slapped his gloves into his palm and coughed. 'We're here about a certain matter. The cushion. I wish to buy it.' He peered round the shop like a bloodhound on the scent.

Slowly, she shook her head. 'No, sir. It's a special thing. Special to me. It's not for sale.'

The shop clock ticked in the silence. 'May I see it, then?' he burst out impatiently.

She reached underneath the counter and placed the cushion on the polished surface. Hunter grabbed it and took it to the window to peer at it more closely. 'And where, madam, did you obtain that design?' he rapped out, his voice harsh.

'Hunter!' admonished the other man.

Tobias Hunter breathed more evenly. 'It is a very unique design. I have only seen it in one other place. I am merely interested in the source, the inspiration for this design.'

She reached into her workbasket and brought out the scrap of material. 'I copied it from this.'

He grabbed the piece from her. 'And where does this come from?'

She looked him in the eye and said evenly, 'That's a matter of confidence, sir. A very personal thing.'

'Confidence? Confidence? You must tell me where you got this. Did you steal it? And how did you know about the unicorn? There is no unicorn on this rag.' He threw the scrap violently down on the counter.

She flushed. 'The unicorn? I didn't—'

'You have other things, other pieces! Secreted! I know about this.' He reached over and grabbed her forearm.

She shook him off and raced round the counter, advancing on him. 'Get out! Get out of my shop!'

'Madam, I—'

'Out! You too!' She was pushing them both with her not inconsiderable strength. William Scorton caught his coat on a nail on the window partition, and Kitty's heart fell as she heard the ominous ripping sound.

They all stopped and William Scorton looked down at the torn broadcloth with annoyance. 'Drat it!'

Kitty met his annoyance with a flinty gaze. 'Now you're pulling down my shop. Get out, the pair of you!'

She stood leaning against the doorjamb, watching their trap as it made its wobbly way around the potholes in the lane. Hard though it was to admit it, there might indeed be some truth in his words, impertinent as they were; some truth about just who she was, and the ownership of the precious scrap of cloth.

She was still there ten minutes later, pondering the significance of Tobias Hunter's words, when a smart woman in furs, followed by a handsome well-dressed man, came tripping down the street. They were almost on her before she recognised them.

'Esme, of all the people!' She put out her hands and Esme held on to her, engulfing her with feathers, furs and scent. She struggled free. 'You're very elegant, Es. Quite the lady.'

'And you're quite beautiful, Kitty Rainbow. Mothering and shopkeepering must suit you. Our Gabriel's been talking about you all afternoon, snake that he is. You want to keep away from him.'

Kitty turned her gaze to Esme's companion. 'And can this be Thomas? I can't believe it. What a gent!'

Thomas smiled faintly at the window behind her head.

Kitty smiled ruefully at Esme. 'But I see he doesn't really change.'

Esme shook her head. 'We wondered if Janine Druce was here.'

Kitty grinned. 'Come on through.' She pulled back the curtain and called, 'Antijan, you've a visitor come to see you!'

17

Visitors

For a while Kitty's little house and shop seemed to spill over with bodies. However, Esme stayed only a short time, hugging Kitty and proclaiming her delight at being home, before taking her hired chaise back to the Royal George. She left Thomas at the shop, saying airily she knew he was dying to be with his mother.

Thomas ignored Janine's fluttering attention and sat silently in the little sitting room surrounded by his cases. Later, he slept on the floor in Ishmael's room, his choice of that space a rejection of Ishmael's offer of a share of his bed.

Janine was visibly excited at the return of her son, but frustrated at his lack of reaction to her. Still, she talked excitedly to Kitty about how Thomas had made his way despite his . . . difficulty . . . with his smart, well-cut suits and bright neckties.

The ability to feel, and even express, affection had been raised a minute fraction in Thomas's soul during his time with Esme. But whatever minimal affection he managed to feel was all now focused on Esme herself. He seemed not to know Janine. It was as though he had never spent those troublesome, exasperated, perversely fond years with his mother. After they had all gone to bed Kitty could hear Janine crashing about downstairs – sounds from the past when Antijan had cast around in vain for a missing bottle of spirit.

On his first morning at home, Thomas ate a huge breakfast made by Janine, then went straight across to the Royal George, only to be sent straight back by Esme, who was in the middle of a big row with Gabriel over the state of the hotel.

Not visibly moved by his rejection, Thomas went to sit out in the yard behind the shop to pick out notes and runs on his glittering new piano accordion. Leonora sat beside him, her big eyes never leaving his long slender fingers as he made music on the air. He played 'Scarborough Fair' and 'I Had a Little Nut Tree', and she joined in, lisping the words in her child's voice. Then he played some of Esme's more saucy songs and she beat time with a stick on her fat knee.

Janine peered through the window at them. She soon stopped talking about how well Thomas was doing and became glum and morose. The next day she went missing all morning. At one o'clock the constable came into the shop and asked Kitty if she would come to get Mrs Druce, as the draper woman was dead drunk on the floor of the police station. Kitty went there with Ishmael, who carried Janine home in his arms, like a baby. They put her to sleep in Kitty's bed.

Later, Esme came into the shop. She plonked herself on the customer's seat, and talked with Kitty as she worked. She started by telling Kitty how good her life was, how the audiences loved her performances. 'A long way from concerts in your back yard across at Forgan Buildings, Kit.'

'You were good even then, Es,' said Kitty.

'Yes, but how would I've known it if you'd not gone on at

me, made me do it? Even gave me your name. I think of you every time someone calls me Miss Rainbow. I carry you with me.'

Kitty smiled a little at that. 'What about Jarrold? He's not with you here.'

'He's doing deals for Ned Lumb up in Newcastle.'

Kitty frowned. 'Your Gabriel says Jarrold was gambling your money, taking from you.'

'He's a nice one to talk. We've just had a big argument 'cos he tried to get money out of me to pay some gambling debt or other. Such a sob story.' Esme stood up and started to twist and turn, looking at herself in Kitty's long shop mirror. 'I know about Jarrold anyway, Kit. I went to Mr Van Diemen, the manager, and when he told me what he's been paying me all this time, you could have knocked me over with a feather. Jarrold had been robbing me of three-quarters of my wage. So I'm gunna look after myself from now on.' She paused. 'Jarrold's all right, you know. He's his own worst enemy. To tell the truth, Kit, I think I . . . kind of . . . feel a lot about him. But he's a naughty boy and needs to be kept in his place.'

'Boy? He's old enough to be your father!'

Esme smirked. 'I think not. Yours, perhaps, seeing as you're such a babe!'

They gulped back their laughter as a customer came in, enquiring about some materials she had ordered. Then Ishmael followed, from where he'd been cleaning the shop window outside, and started to attack the inside of it with hot water.

When the customer had gone, Esme's mood had changed. 'Really though, Kit, have you seen what a mess our Gabriel's cooked up down at the Royal George?'

Kitty shook her head. 'Only get there an odd time, when I'm taking a bit of work for your mother. I never linger.'

'How d'you find her, my mother?'

'Well, to be truthful, she seems a bit, like, on her own. Lonely.'

'Lonely? She seems to me to've shrunk. Lost inches. She's shorter than me now. And when we talk it's like I'm the mother and she's the child. And Gabriel's up to his ears in debt to bookmakers and is drunk by ten o'clock in the morning. He's pledged mountains of money he hasn't on some fistfight, and is dunning me for money now, having sold everything moveable at the George. My ma's retired to her bedroom and indulges in screaming fits every hour on the hour. She won't come out. Won't even wash. The Royal George itself's the haunt of thieves and vagabonds, all drinking my mother's profits. This *hoi polloi* now even inhabit the Front Rooms of the hotel. Nobody respectable would cross the doors.'

'Is that so?' Ishmael's deep voice came to them from the window. He bent down to lay his washleather carefully across his bucket and then rose like some ruined colossus. 'I will see to it for you, Esme. The Royal George and Mirella. And Gabriel.' His voice was tight with anger. It was a long time since Kitty had heard that tone.

'Ishmael, there's no need—'

'I have neglected them, Esme. Jossy Gullet, your father, who saved me once, who gave me a roof over my head, would be turning in his grave at the thought that such things have come about.' He tied his neckerchief, which had been loose around his neck, and made for the door, waves of his old rage shimmering about in the room.

'Oh dear. We'll have to go with him.' Hurriedly, Kitty went and told Thomas to watch Leonora, put up the 'CLOSED' sign, then she and Esme followed the old man, impressed by his rage and at the same time afraid of what he might do. He flung open the wide front doors of the Royal George and strode in, his great boots slapping the tiles. They hurried after him and stood coolly side by side and watched equally coolly as he, full of his old strength, threw

214

Gabriel out and cleared the Front Rooms of the overdressed spongers who had been drinking with him in the faded plush seats. Then he stormed upstairs and routed Mirella out of her bedroom, demanding that she take up again her role as mistress of the house, as Jossy would have wanted.

'But how can I? They walk all over me. Gabriel—'

'Nobody will walk over anyone. I will come here. I will stay here. I will sleep again in the attic,' he said grimly. 'Anyone of that ilk venturing in, I'll box their ears.'

Mirella, calming down by the second, started to nod. 'Just the sight of you, that was always enough, Ishmael.' She wiped her tears. 'Jossy always said that.'

'But the boy goes!' he said.

She looked at him uncertainly.

'Goes!' he repeated.

Mirella shrugged. 'He must have a bed. Jossy would want that.'

'Only that, a bed only,' he conceded. 'And now I want you to walk through the hotel. You will tell me how you want things done and we will set about doing them.'

She nodded, then put her hand to her falling hair. 'But first, if you'll excuse me for just five minutes, Ishmael, I need to ... change. I've this new cap which young Kitty made. So pretty...'

The next day Jarrold turned up at Kitty's shop, looking for Esme, who was there again, talking to Kitty as she worked. Through the plate-glass window they could see Gabriel lurking on the pavement outside. Oddly enough, Gabriel had accepted his expulsion from all parts of the George except his own bedroom with relief. Now he didn't have to go through the motions of all that work. Anyway, being in the George made him all the more available for his savage creditors.

He had welcomed Jarrold with open arms and accepted

an invitation to the races with alacrity but did not feel quite up to facing both Kitty and Esme in the same room.

Jarrold was all smiling charm, kissing Esme on the cheek, asking after Kitty's health, and chucking Leonora under her chin.

'Gabriel and I are off to the races, Es. Will you come? Wear that pretty pink bonnet with the strawberries on? Enjoy a little wager on the horses in swell company? Topped up by a cracking bout between Hammer Molloy and old Terry McBain.' His head was on one side, his eyes shone into hers. The air suddenly hummed with the physical attraction between these two, as overt and palpable as honey on bread.

Esme looked at him for a moment, then nodded, smiling faintly. 'Very well.' Jarrold could be very entertaining when he wanted to be. She gathered up her skirts and leaned over to kiss Kitty, holding her too tightly, so that she too was infected by the physical excitement shooting through Esme. 'I'll just say hello to Thomas, Kitty. In the yard, is he? After that I'll go to the races and keep my eyes on these naughty boys.'

Sober-faced, Kitty watched them go, angry at Esme for flitting from one to another, and for leaving Ishmael to cope with the mess at the Royal George. She was also in a confusion of feeling she couldn't quite identify. She leaned down, picked up Leonora and called Janine down from upstairs. 'Will you watch the shop for an hour, Antijan?'

'Anything, hen. Anything.' Janine, shamefaced at her exhibition the previous day, was subdued.

Kitty passed through the yard on her way out. Thomas stopped playing his accordion. 'Thomas!' She pulled his face towards her. 'Go in and see your mam.' She put a hand on his piano accordion. 'Play a tune for her. Now! Go on!' He lumbered to his feet and she pushed him towards the door. 'Play for her!'

Outside the town Kitty set Leonora down to run and jump about in the river meadow. She herself sat down with her back to one of the rearing columns of the viaduct. Her mind tumbled with repeated images of herself and Freddie in the graveyard, turning and twisting in mutual enjoyment. Her body turned in on itself, excitement running right to her toes, to be replaced by an aching, urgent need for some kind of relief, for some bubble to burst. Her cheeks flamed at her thoughts and she pressed her fists to them as they were finally cooled by her own tears. 'Will it only ever be one time, Freddie? Am I to be an old widow before I've even started?'

She sighed and stood up, away from the rough comfort of the viaduct. She took off her bonnet and shook down her hair, calling out to her child, 'Come down by the water, Leonora. We can take off our stockings and plodge. That'll cool us down, won't it?'

It was an hour later when, hand in hand with Leonora, Kitty returned to the shop, her bonnet askew, her hair still half down, her apron damp where she had dried their feet. She was brought up short by the sight of Mr William Scorton standing outside the shop, a parcel in his hands, flanked by two young boys.

He bowed slightly. 'Good day, Miss Rainbow.'

She pulled Leonora in front of her damp skirts, a hand on each shoulder. 'Good day, Mr Scorton.'

'May I introduce my sons? This is Michael, he is eleven...' The boy shyly proffered his hand to be shaken. 'And this is Samuel, who's nine.' The younger boy grinned at her, showing his broken front tooth.

William Scorton gazed down at Leonora. 'And how old is this one? This must be the young lady who caused such a rout at the boxing match. She was lively from the first, if I remember rightly.'

Kitty's cheeks were hot. 'Yes. This is Leonora and she's three now.'

Samuel Scorton put out his tongue at Leonora and she returned the compliment, chuckling.

Kitty looked up at Scorton. 'Was there . . . ?'

He held up a parcel he had in his hand. 'I have a job for you. Can we go inside?'

In the shop he put the parcel on the counter and opened it. Inside was the broadcloth coat which he had ripped on her nail the other day. 'I wonder if you would mend this and deliver it for me tomorrow? It is my second-best coat and much in use.' He paused. 'Naturally I will pay you.'

She wanted to shout and rail at him. He was being very clever. Wasn't this just the way to put her in her place? But his money was as good as anyone's, and it was the kind of service she offered in the shop. There was a notice in the doorway to that effect. So she held her peace.

'Very well.' She put the coat back into the parcel. He placed a small pasteboard card in her hand.

'That is my address. I'd be grateful if you could deliver the coat personally before noon tomorrow. I'll need it in the afternoon.' He paused. 'If you would be kind enough to deliver it yourself I would be grateful. There is another business, a certain other matter, I wish to discuss with you.'

She watched him stroll away, a child on either side, and wondered what he was up to. Such a man must have five coats in his cupboard, at least. She fingered the torn coat and then put her fingers to her lips.

'Tekken a shine ter yer,' came a voice from behind her. 'Ah telt yer that the other day.'

Kitty leaned across the counter to find Janine's beady eyes staring back up at her from the floor. 'Antijan, what on earth are you doing down there?'

'Well, hen, Ah was down here sortin' the cotton bobbins when the pair o' yer came in, an' I thought it was more than my life's worth to interrupt.' She hauled herself to her feet.

218

'An' who were those two braw lads? Were they his own? Is there a wife in the closet somewhere?'

Kitty stared at her, wondering why that thought had not occurred to her. And it certainly hadn't.

The crowd at the racetrack parted like the red sea before Esme, a vision in bright green taffeta and high-plumed pink hat, and Jarrold in his tweeds and yellow waistcoat.

Esme, shiny-eyed and lightly rouged in the theatrical fashion, drew many comments, kind and unkind. She took them in her stride. She was careful never to lard on the facepaint like a clown, but was aware of the dramatic difference it made in contrast to the pale pasty faces of more 'respectable', even more attractive women.

This bringing of elements of her theatrical presence into normal life was Esme's way of making the best of herself, of countering Jarrold's not infrequent reminders that, in fact, she was ugly. If she had this impact, which she usually did, she could not be ugly. Could she?

At the track, Jarrold was pawed on all sides, by slick, well-heeled people as well as those who, to all intents and purposes, were paupers. The men were open in complimenting him on his striking companion and more than one acquaintance affected surprise that this was the little sister of Gabriel Gullet, well known in these chancing circles.

Gabriel himself hung back, hoping that the glamour of his companions would throw him into a convenient shade in which he could remain relatively invisible. His eyes darted around warily, hoping for a first warning sight of certain people who would do him no good if they got their hands on him: men with whom he had shared delightful times, who were now, damn them, turning on him like vipers.

But he was confident that the last fight this evening, between Hammer Molloy and Terry McBain – known as Rooster – would surely be the solution to all his problems.

He had waged a lump of money on Rooster: money culled from the sale of a little hoard of gold jewellery belonging to his mother, which he had just happened to come upon minutes before Ishmael Slaughter had slung him out of the Royal George. Rooster McBain was bound to win and then Gabriel would pay off all these people who had been treading on his heels for some months now. Then at least he could go out and about without looking behind him all the time.

Esme ignored her brother and watched the afternoon's racing with only passing interest, but after enjoying pies and ale provided by a pieman at the track, she settled down to watch the evening fights with relish. She was the only woman in the crowd, a fact duly noticed and commented on. Undaunted, she leaned forward on the figured silver head of her parasol and watched the fights, blow for bloody blow, her remarks so insightful and sharp that the sarcastic asides around her faded away.

Between each bout, as the ring was cleaned and cleared with sawdust and brushes, there was some entertainment. An acrobat, in greasy trousers and a bright red tunic, walked the ropes of the ring in tightrope fashion. A man with a long pole threw a pair of monkeys into the air and they clung to the pole, chattering with panic, while he swept and swung it around the ring like some great conductor's baton. Then each new fight was preceded by an elaborate drumroll performed by a young boy in pantaloons and a fez, a silk kerchief round his neck.

As the last but one fight ended, Jarrold leaped up into the ring, the cheers of his cronies echoing in his ears. He stripped to the waist and wrested the silk neckerchief and the drum from the drummer boy, then marched around the ring to even greater cheers, rattling out elaborate rolls and throwing the sticks high in the air and catching them. Finally he drummed Molloy and McBain into the ring, returned the scarf and the drum to the boy, and leaped lightly out of the ring. As the two fighters faced each other he buttoned up his shirt and jacket and retrieved his space beside Esme.

She leaned towards him, chuckling. 'You're mad, Jarrold. Mad as a March hare!' Then she turned to concentrate on the fight.

Jarrold settled down to enjoy the star spectacle of the night. He knew Esme was pleased, even impressed. She was on her way back to the palm of his hand. He had only to wait. He was certain of that, just as he was certain that Molloy would win this scrap. He had money on it. Esme's money.

Gabriel watched the fight from the back of the crowd. He watched Rooster McBain (who he'd heard on good authority was 'unbeatable'), get trounced almost to the point of death. The crowd erupted with delight.

Jarrold sat back happily and thought of the heap of money which was now due to him.

Gabriel started to sweat. He had no pity for the defeated broken man, all his pity was focused on himself. He looked around in fear, and caught the eye of two men as they in turn caught sight of him. He turned and started to run.

18

The Cornelian

Leonora raced ahead of Kitty through the stable yard of the George and leaped into the arms of Ishmael, who raised her above his head, then shook her like a floppy doll. She shrieked with laughter, then held on to his neck, the picture of contentment.

Kitty watched them with some pleasure. While he had been at the Royal George she had missed his quiet powerful presence in the house more than she dared admit. He was only minutes away, and, by all accounts, doing great work bringing Mirella and the pub back into the land of the living. And he looked well on it. There was a spring in his step.

'Can you have her for an hour or so, Ishmael? She's missing you so. She's been playing the mischief with Antijan who's so distracted by Thomas. Anyway, Antijan's watching the shop for me.'

'What is it?' Mirella was at the kitchen door, her hair loose-combed and pinned under her cap and – Kitty blinked at the sight of it – an apron round her waist.

'We're to mind the little one, Mirella,' said Ishmael, a quiet warning in his voice, 'while Kitty goes on an errand.'

Mirella paused for a split second before she smiled. 'That'll be fine.' She held out her arms. 'Well, little girl, you can help Mabella and me to bake. We're hard at it this morning. Our old customers are demanding the meat pies, the ones we always used to serve with the ale.'

Kitty was amused to see Leonora jump out of Ishmael's arms into Mirella's and sit there smiling. Mirella straightened the child's skirts and turned again to Kitty. 'And where does your errand take you this morning, Kitty?' she said, rather smug in her small conquest.

'I'm delivering something to Purley Hall. I'm not sure just where . . .'

Mirella raised her brows. 'Purley Hall? Sir Marcus Tipton's house? Well, well! Eeh, me and Jossy went to some racing parties there, years ago! Jockeys, actors, boxers. Fine times . . .'

'It's not Sir Marcus Tipton, Mrs Gullet. It's a man called Scorton.' Kitty was struck by the change in Mirella, now flushed with her old self-importance, with the keys of the Royal George swinging again from her waist.

'Ah, rented out, that'll be.' Mirella adjusted one of Leonora's curls. 'Or given to a friend, don't doubt. More business these days in Mayfair gambling saloons than Priorton for swells such as Sir Marcus.' She chucked Leonora under her chin, making her giggle. 'Just follow the river north for a mile, Kitty, then turn sharp right through Purley Woods and it's a mile along there.'

Kitty pulled on her gloves.

Mirella's glance dropped to Kitty's built-up boot. 'Will you walk there?'

Kitty shrugged. 'Shouldn't take too long.'

'Take the trap,' said Mirella, eager now to show her goodwill. 'It won't take a minute to harness Bonnie, will it, Ishmael?'

'Not a minute,' said Ishmael, his hand already on the half-door of Bonnie's stall.

Kitty looked up at the windows. 'Is Esme...?'

Mirella shook her head. 'Dead to the world, m'dear. Delivered to the door at the dead of night by *Mister* Jarrold Pommeroy. City ways, those two have, but there's no excusing it. But what say can a mere mother have these days? Mabella's tried to wake her three times and got a thrown jerry-pot for her pains. Do excuse the vulgarity, m'dear.'

A few minutes later, on the edge of Priorton, Kitty clicked her tongue once, sat back and allowed Bonnie her head. They had left the last mean streets of the town behind, and, barring the sight of one or two colliery wheels in the distance, all before her was open green countryside, with the busy gurgle of the river to her left. She breathed deeply. She was so rarely on her own. She'd had Ishmael at her back, Antijan at her side, and Leonora at her skirts, for three years now. Sometimes she didn't know where she ended and they began. The thought of Esme singing and frolicking the evening away, and still in bed at eleven o'clock in the morning, gave her a rare twinge of envy.

She laughed at her melancholy thoughts and rattled the reins. 'Come on, Bonnie. Mr William Scorton'll be pacing the floor, impatient for his blessed coat.'

She allowed the thought to blossom, of Scorton with his broad shoulders, his thick hair curling under his hat; the spark in his eyes as his coat ripped. She moved on, then, to thinking about his tense-faced companion, Tobias Hunter, who seemed so drawn to the summer cushion. Now there was a bad man, mean-hearted, mean-spirited, worse in his way than Gabriel or even Jarrold Pommeroy because he clenched his badness to him, like a miser hoarding his gold, rather than spraying it out over all and sundry as they did. Yet he it was who had been so startled by the summer cushion's design and who had asked about the unicorn. Against her inclination, Kitty would have to pursue that acquaintanceship to find the answers to the mystery that left the irritating hollow in her past.

Well, she felt certain Mr William Scorton would be satisfied with his coat. She'd sat late into the night sewing it with infinite care so that the mend was, indeed, as invisible as stated in her bold advertisements.

She nearly overshot the road up to the house and had to back Bonnie up and make her way up a narrow, well-made side road, which meandered through woodlands bursting with fresh summer leaf. Rabbits leaped away from the wheels of her trap and once she had to slow down to let a rusty brown squirrel scurry in front of her.

Then Bonnie whinnied and jumped a foot in the air as a shot cracked in the distance, the noise echoing and rippling through the trees and funnelling itself down the roadway towards them. The pony started again as another shot whined past her and thudded into a tree in an explosion of bark and fragments of wood.

Bonnie bolted, then, and the leather burned Kitty's hands as she clung on to the reins. She called to the pony that it was all right, all right! Finally, she hauled the trap to a stop and climbed down to hold Bonnie's trembling head. 'There, girl. Ssh, ssh. It's just some boss-eyed old game-keeper taking a potshot at some poor rabbit.'

She took some deep breaths to stop herself trembling.

She climbed up again and lingered several minutes, not wanting to draw a further shot, and when the woodland settled into silence, she felt safer. She clicked her teeth and they set off again, looking around all the time, no longer at ease in the tree-lined paradise.

But she forgot her fear altogether as the woodland opened up into a wide clearing, carpeted in dense feathery wild grasses. Set within it, at its centre, was a three-storey house so long that it looked low until you came close to it. Its large blocks of grey stone glowed silver in the white midday light. One side of the house was veiled by long hangings of

Virginia creeper and the upper-storey windows peeped through it like eyes peering through untidy hair. In the very centre of the front wall was a large double door which had been green but was now bleached to a peeling silver white.

A hoarse cry drew her attention to a pair of peacocks who were making their wandering pecking way across a path.

The hair stood up on Kitty's neck. She swallowed. She had been to most of the best houses in the district on one errand or the other for her business; never to this one, which, glinting silver in the sun and set so high in its ring of trees, on its carpet of grass, was by far the most beautiful. She alighted and found a large stone to hold down Bonnie's reins. She stood for a moment with her hands on her hips, surveying the house, then took her package out of the trap and set off towards a narrow side path which would lead towards the back regions of the house. She would leave her parcel at the kitchen door; that would suffice.

'Miss Rainbow! Miss Rainbow!'

Suddenly William Scorton was standing on the top step before the open double doors, his watch in his hand. He beckoned to her and she drew near. 'I had given you up,' he said gravely, 'resigned myself to wearing another coat.'

Her eyes settled on the fine broadcloth coat he was wearing, then she raised them to his. 'I beg your pardon, sir, but I can't imagine that a ... gentleman ... such as yourself would be put out by the absence of one of his many coats. That's very hard to believe.'

He smiled slightly, then stood to one side. 'You'll not be deceived, Miss Rainbow. This is indeed a ploy. Now will you do me the honour of entering my house?'

She passed him, leaving a good two feet of space between them, and entered the house.

They were in a wide hall dominated by a large fireplace in which flickered a fire, rather substantial for the time of year. The hall was bare, apart from a large couch draped with a

Chinese carpet. Coming towards her from under the stairs was an old man, his face as creased and brown as a walnut, dressed in some kind of white pantaloon suit.

'If you would give John your cloak, Miss Rainbow? Then we can go up to the drawing room and inspect this work you have executed for me.'

Unwillingly she gave up her cloak, embarrassed at the shower of bark and sawdust billowing out from it as the man called John shook it slightly, to fold it over his arm.

'I was driving along your road leading up here, Mr Scorton,' she said flushing, 'and someone shot a gun near me. Bits of tree came down all over the place, on to both of us. My pony bolted.'

He leaned towards her and she flinched back. 'Your patience, Miss Rainbow.' From the brim of her bonnet he withdrew a sizeable piece of bark. 'More debris, I fear.' He turned to the servant. 'When you've disposed of the cloak, John, perhaps you'd venture out and take the poor animal some sustenance.' His voice hardened. 'And then you may tell Tompkins to venture into the woods, find Mr Hunter and that reprobate Michael, and tell them to cease their gunfire. They're wreaking havoc. And now...' He turned to Kitty and opened his hand. 'Shall we go up, Miss Rainbow? John will have laid us a tray.'

For a second she wanted to run. Then, gathering her skirts in a dignified fashion, she preceded him up the shallow stairs and through yet more double doors into the drawing room. Here tall triple windows looked straight down the road by which she had come. And she knew William Scorton had been standing there looking out for her, watch in hand. Waiting impatiently.

'Would you care for coffee, Miss Rainbow?'

'That's very kind of you, Mr Scorton. Can I show you the coat?'

He poured coffee from a silver jug while she took the garment out of its tissue paper.

She held it up. 'You'll note, Mr Scorton, that the mend's invisible.'

He took it from her and put it on the back of a chair. 'Would you be so kind as to sit down, Miss Rainbow?'

She sat on the long hard sofa beside a small table covered with a white cloth, which held the fine coffee jug and fragile cups now shimmering and steaming with coffee.

Then he picked up his coat and examined it with elaborate care. 'Very fine work. As you say, invisible. Now what do I owe you for this fine work?'

She took a breath. 'There's no charge, Mr Scorton. It was my nail that ripped it, my push that caused it to rip. I was in error. I've a temper.' She had not intended this; she had intended to charge him her highest price.

He did not deny her self-description, merely bowed his head, replaced the coat and came to sit opposite her.

She took a sip of her coffee.

'Now, Miss Rainbow, let me tell you something about myself. I am a widower, with two sons, as you know. They are visiting me from their grandparents, with whom they have lived until now. I am afraid your recent adventure was caused by Michael, who is out in the woods shooting with Tobias Hunter, his godfather. I believe you know Mr Hunter?'

Kitty sat in puzzled silence as he took a thoughtful sip of his coffee.

'That puppet you sold me at the fair, it is still a favourite, if somewhat battered, toy of the boys to this day. Fine workmanship survives. My own father was a craftsman like yourself, Miss Rainbow: a clockmaker who invented mechanisms for the timing of processes in ironmaking and thereby flourished in that boom time thirty years ago. I now flourish because of him. I buy businesses like Scree Hall Mill, and play with them. I have a workshop where I work on mechanics and clockworks, to take my father's inventions further. And everything seems to flourish whether I do well or ill. It is as though he lit a touchpaper with his great craftsmanship.'

She put down her cup. 'What is this about, Mr Scorton? Why do you tell me this? All this is naught of my business.'

At that moment, as though she could bite it out of the air, she felt the palpable tension, giddying of the senses, which she had witnessed many times between Esme and Jarrold Pommeroy. She shook her head slightly against the thoughts and feelings which were surging through it: feelings which had never invaded her mind or senses since those first teasing times in White Leas Woods with Freddie.

He was looking at her, eyes narrowed. 'I am not quite sure, Miss Rainbow, how to answer that. Except that I have the great desire to do so. I feel we should know each other. That we have known each other in other times. Our paths have crossed several times now and somehow I want to fix our acquaintance in a proper way. I do not go in society. I would not come across you there.'

It was a relief to laugh heartily at this. 'You'd not meet me anyway, Mr Scorton. I am a draper woman, with good hands for fine sewing. I support my daughter who . . .' she lowered her voice '. . . was born out of wedlock, her father dying in the bowels of the earth beneath our feet. Her father, whose name was Freddie Longstaffe, knew my temper. He used to call me a "scrapper". My father trained me in boxing. He was a fighter himself. I support him now – and my foster mother, who is one of God's very fragile creatures. Go in society? You make me laugh. What do you want with me? In this house? I'm certain it is not a bit of sewing.'

He stood up and walked to the window. 'The house? I'm here by the courtesy of Sir Marcus Tipton, who has lent it to me for five years. He's also given me a workshop in Priorton. He wants me to develop a factory for clockwork artefacts, whose products will rival the Swiss and will sell all over the Empire and the world beyond it. It is an interest we share, Sir Marcus and I, the magic of mechanics.'

'You do not answer my question, sir.'

He swept on. 'And you, Miss Rainbow? Where do you come from? Your voice does not quite have the ... density of others in this district.'

Suddenly a river inside her was undammed and she started to talk. 'That's Ishmael, who brought me up and who I know as my father. He talks funny English, just about foreign, I think. His family were from Riga, somewhere near Russia. He sings in Russian. Talks English kind of precise, you know? Funnily enough, Ishmael can't read English, or write it. You might think it strange in a man so clever in other ways. He's brilliant at arithmetic and the wisest man I know in his talk. He came here, to London that is, from Russia when he was little.' To her consternation she found herself babbling on, telling him about Ishmael and her parentage of rainbows. '"The sun, the moon and a good right fist," he calls them,' she said too shrilly now.

Scorton listened respectfully, with close interest.

Kitty stopped, red-faced, then stood up. 'Well, if that is all, Mr Scorton, I can't stay here talking...'

He sat down again, opposite her. 'Please sit down, Miss Rainbow. We have not finished. Bear with me.' He poured more coffee. 'One reason I stay here, in this house, is because the land hereabouts holds such interest. I am in thrall to the ancient world, Miss Rainbow, the ancient civilisation of the Romans. I've travelled far in pursuit of that interest. My servant John, who took your coat, returned with me from Egypt. But here, here in this very place, there are riches of the ancient Empire beneath our feet. The land all round this house was, in ancient times, a Roman camp. This house itself is, I am certain, on the site of a Roman villa. The stones in which it was fashioned were chipped and shaped by Roman craftsmen. And the villa itself is on the site of a house even more ancient.'

She leaned forward, interested despite herself.

'I was shooting here ten years ago with Sir Marcus Tipton

and I acquired this interest. In earlier days I helped him with his collection. Then he insisted I stay here, take possession of this house. Come, come, I will show you.' His face was now alight with enthusiasm and, despite her determination to cool her senses down, Kitty warmed to him.

She followed him along the corridor and into a small room lined with shelves, some of which held books but many of which held a higgledy-piggledy collection of items. There were stones, large and small; whole pots and containers, and pottery fragments; one whole black pot depicting a hunting scene with fleeing white deer. There were coins, small figures and bits of fine carving. On its own in the middle of a shelf was a small shoe, a frail curling sole with fragments of leather attached to it.

Kitty trailed a lingering finger over its wrinkled surface. 'A little child wore this. See! It has the marks of his little foot. A child no older than my Leonora.'

'Yes, yes,' he breathed. 'Wherever you walk here, you kick against these things, the flotsam and jetsam of ancient times. Here! This will interest you.' Into her palm he put a cornelian. She could feel the ends of his fingers on her skin.

She smiled faintly down at the object. It was rough on one side but smooth, with an incised design, on the other. She fingered the pattern on its surface. Then, looking closer, she saw etched there a design of interlocking acorns and oak leaves, heartbreaking in its familiarity. She looked up, pleasure, excitement, delight breaking flickering across her face like moving light.

He came closer, pulled her face to his and attempted to kiss her. Kitty felt a great surge of anger. Her right hand closed into a fist, came up, and socked him in the eye. He fell back against a cabinet, as much in surprise as pain. Then he reddened, let out a roar of anger. 'Out! Out! Get out, you ... cat.'

She fled. Getting into the trap she realised that she had left her cape behind, and that she still had the cornelian in her hand. She also realised that she had lost the chance to ask about Tobias Hunter, the lawyer. He was the one who had been so affected by the cushion with its acorn and oak leaf design. And he knew something about the unicorn. There was so much she needed to know. She raised her eyes and saw William Scorton watching her from the tall central window of his drawing room. He raised his hand in some kind of salute. She pushed the cornelian up her sleeve, jumped up into the trap, then used the whip on an offended Bonnie to get away as fast as she could.

When Kitty got back to the Royal George, Esme was galloping around the stableyard with Leonora on her back. She whinnied to a halt beside Kitty, then lifted Leonora over her head and on to the ground. 'Well, what's been happening to you, Kit, to put such roses in your cheeks?' she said. Then she shouted for Rob, the stable boy, to let Leonora help him get Bonnie back into her stall. She tucked one arm through Kitty's and said, 'Tell Auntie Esme.'

'I don't know what you're talking about.'

'Something's happened,' insisted Esme.

Kitty stared at Esme. 'Well, I think I might be on my way to finding just who was the woman who threw me . . . into Ishmael's arms.'

'It's more than that! Come here!' She dragged her into the back hall of the hotel and across to a large mirror, none too clean, which graced a broad wall. 'Look!'

They stood side by side before the mirror. Kitty's eyes were crystal-bright, her cheeks were high-coloured, and the wind created by the careering trap had blown her hair into wild curls on her forehead.

'Look! You're beautiful, Kit. Look at me,' said Esme mournfully. 'I look ugly. I look ten years older than you and short of a good night's sleep.'

'No!' protested Kitty. But there was some truth in it. Esme's hair, in its undressed state was as straight as pumpwater. Her skin was a greyish white, her face was fuller than it used to be, her cheeks more pendulous. Her eyes were reddened with too much drink and too much tobacco-smoke. 'All you need is a week or two out of Jarrold Pommeroy's company, some good food and some good rest. Then you'll be your usual beautiful self.'

'Now that's a thing I could never do. Give up Jarrold. He's too good at ... well, the nice things in life.'

'Oh, Esme, you're a bad girl!'

'I try my best!' said Esme solemnly. They collapsed into laughter at this and when their laughter faded Esme leaned over and, in the mirror, ran a finger down the image of Kitty's face, making it squeak. 'But you're up to something, Kitty Rainbow. Or someone is! I'd put money on it!'

'I should be careful about that, Es. Gambling's a weakness in your family. Or so I hear.'

The buzz went out of Esme a little then. 'Talking of that, our Gabriel's gone missing. Had three different sets of bruiser-types looking for him here this morning. I don't know what'll come of him.'

Kitty sat down on the bench in the hallway. 'Never mind about him, Es, tell me about the races.'

'Oh, Kit, it was such a lark down there! Jarrold's quite the swell in that world, don't you know? Everybody likes him because he's winning at present. And they were all making up to me, telling him what a lucky feller he is. And the boxing was good. Fast. Hard. None of them as good as Ishmael. I'm sure of that. And Jarrold won such a packet! It was champagne for everyone afterwards. And you should have seen Jarrold before the last fight!' She giggled. 'Up on the stage, stripped to the buff, playing the drum. Seems he was a drummer boy once, and one of his first jobs was drumming the fighters in. That's why he knows so much about it all.' Her tone was fond, like someone talking of the talents of their favourite horse, or dog.

'Oh, Es! You do love the feller, don't you?'

'I don't know,' Esme sighed. 'Sometimes I do, but sometimes he makes me cringe with what he gets up to.'

There was a pause.

'Do you care about Gabriel and all his shenanigans?' ventured Kitty.

Esme hunched her shoulders. 'When I'm away I neither know nor care. But here? Well, look at the state it's got Mama into. As well as that look at the state it's got himself into! He cringes around the place. Not the bully-boy he was, not by any means.'

Janine was not quite coping with five customers in the shop when Kitty and Leonora got back, so Kitty started to serve without taking off her bonnet. The bell had just tinkled after her last customer when there was a crying wail from upstairs. Kitty bounded up. 'What is it, Leonora! What is it?'

'There's a man on my bed, Mammy. Like Goldilocks.'

Kitty opened the door to find Gabriel snoring on his back, a cudgel in his hand. She pulled Leonora back through the door and closed it firmly. Then she went downstairs, got a broom and returned to the room.

She tickled his face with the broom end and he snarled and sat up, his cudgel at the ready. 'Wha...! Wha...!'

'It's me, Kitty Rainbow, and you're in my bed. You can get out. You can get out now.' She held up the broom, ready to fend him off.

He swung his feet to the ground. 'Na, na, Kitty. I jus' came ter see if yer could len' us sommat. This shop's going great guns, I hear that. You could len' us—'

She pushed at him with her brush. 'Nothing. Not a groat. Now get out of here.'

He put the cudgel on the floor and his head in his hands. 'Aw, Kitty, I mean you no harm. We're old friends, you and I...'

She lowered the brush. Just behind her Leonora was crying. 'Well, Gabriel, I can see you're on hard times, but they're all of your making. Now go. You've frightened my little girl.'

He lumbered to his feet and stumbled past her. She pulled Leonora into her skirts and shouted after him, down the stairs, 'And don't you come here again. Do you hear?'

'I hear. I hear!' the grumbling voice came from down below.

She leaned against the doorjamb, breathing hard. That was a strange thing. She had been involved in two throwings out that day. In one she had been the one doing the throwing out. In the other she had been the person being thrown out.

'Mammy, Mammy!' A hiccoughing voice from below her elbow penetrated her thoughts. 'Why are you smiling?'

'Nothing, sweetheart. Nothing at all.'

19

Saved

''Ere 'e is!'

Gabriel Gullet flinched away from four heavy, purplish faces which veered up in front of him.

The tallest man, who had a fringe of golden red hair as fine as silk, fingered the heavy block of wood in his hand, ''Ere we 'ave, gen'lemen, your *man*. Your *man* who flashes the guineas in the chase after three-legged ponies, lends off his friends and flashes their guineas in a chase after *two*-legged ponies with big fists.'

Gabriel tried to make a run for it to the left and, tripped up by a great boot, crashed to the ground.

'Then, sirs . . .'

Gabriel screamed, as another boot crashed into the small of his back.

'. . . then, sirs, your *man* 'ere goes to ground like some slinking fox the minute payment is due!' Gabriel gazed in horror at the great cudgel held by a hand with black, split and ridged fingernails; then all he knew was blackness reaching out towards him from the horizon.

It seemed just a second later that he found himself

struggling up out of that blackness to the sound of another, lighter voice.

'And what is thy need, brother? Hast thou needs?' A sopping warm wet cloth was being applied to 'his brow. Water was dripping into his ears.

'Wha'? What?' He could smell a wood fire and feel the warmth of a flickering flame. He forced his eyes open and made out above him a narrow face dominated by blazing, unblinking eyes. 'Where is this? How long...?'

He was lying in a low room lit by one uncurtained window and the flickering light of the fire in the narrow hearth.

The wet cloth was replaced by a large hot hand, which pressed hard on his brow. 'Six, perhaps seven hours, sir. I came upon some ruffians laying about thee, threatened them with the constable, an' they fled. Mayhap they'd done their business by then. Thou war stone dead, it seems, on the pavement. Who art thou, sir? What might be thy name?'

'Gabriel Gullet.' He grasped the papery hand as he sat up groaning. He shook the hand heartily. 'And who are you, sir?'

'Name's Tom Vart. A poor soul, me, persecuted by the wicked ones in this life and then saved, at last, by the Lord.' He held a cup of warm tea to Gabriel's lips and he drank it eagerly. 'And thou also, sir? I'll wager it has a woman at the base of it?'

Gabriel rubbed his head and winced. 'Just so. My mother'll not let me have my dues, my sister laughs at my dilemma and her best friend, to whom I have been very kind, rejects my every cry for help.' Tears stood in his eyes at the thought of it.

Tom Vart placed a consoling hand on his shoulder. 'So with thou, so with me, sir. I'm a weaver, sir, a skilled man. A woman it was who laid me in, lost me my job an' with that went me wife, as run off wi' a coal hewer, and me house, for want of rent money.' His voice whispered in Gabriel's ear,

'But I found the Lord. I read of the serpent and the apple and came to the truth in the Lord. I have saved another who suffered so, and I shall save thee, Gabriel Gullet. I shall show thee the path to righteousness where demon women have no place. It is there in Revelations: "And the ten horns which thou sawest upon the beast, these will hate the whore, and will make her desolate..."'

Gabriel lay back on his pillow and decided that he would allow himself to be saved. He had tried all the other things and ended up with a sore head and a bruised backside. Perhaps the Lord would prove more fruitful. He daren't go home for fear his creditors would find him again there. He had nothing left but the clothes he stood up in, so had nothing to lose. The idea of raging at other people for their sins, the notion of leading from the front with promises of life everlasting – all this had a certain appeal.

'Yon feller's in the shop askin' after yer.' Janine came into the back, wiping her hands on her apron. 'Yellin' after yer, more like.'

Kitty took her time in checking and ticketing the last rolls of French merino cloth and grenadine before she made her way through to the front shop. She decided to be cool and businesslike with William Scorton: thank him for the return of her cloak and certainly not apologise for socking him.

She swept in. 'Mr Scorton, I...'

It was not he. This figure was taller: this face narrower, these eyes more ferocious.

'Ah, there you are, miss,' barked Tobias Hunter. 'I have been waiting a good five minutes. I informed your employer...'

'She does not employ me. It is more the reverse, Mr Hunter...'

'No matter, no matter.' He flickered his fingers dismissively in her face. 'I have come for the cornelian. You stole it from Mr Scorton.'

239

'Did he say I stole it?'

'Stole it ... took it, what odds? You have it.'

She put her hand in her apron pocket, crossed her fingers and slowly she shook her head. 'I certainly looked at a cornelian with a fine decoration, just like my summer cushion. The one which interested you so, Mr Hunter.'

'You have it, I am sure.' He took hold of her forearm and brought his face close to hers. 'It belongs to the house. It must not be removed.'

Her flesh crept at his touch and she was visited by a fear she had never felt before. Her usual instinct to strike out was paralysed. With anyone else she would have fought, but with this man ...

'Where is it, miss?' he rasped.

He pushed past her, flung her into a corner and made for the middle door. Finally galvanised into action, Kitty leaped in front of him and stood with her arms against the doorjambs, preventing him from entering the back area. 'Antijan,' she yelled at the top of her voice. 'Go for the constable this minute. This minute!'

He looked her up and down with a slow insulting gaze. 'You are a thief, madam, and most probably a harlot.'

She met his gaze. 'Go away,' she said slowly. 'Go away, sir, and calm down. You are slavering like a mad dog.'

'Let me at him,' came Janine's voice muffled from behind her. 'Ah've a yard broom here that'll dispatch the cur in a moment.'

He took a step back then, turned and swept out of the shop without another word.

That afternoon Esme came to the shop looking for Thomas. He stood up from the bench where he had been sitting beside his mother and came to stand quietly beside her. She touched his arm. 'Now then, Thomas, best bib and tucker tomorrow. We're on our way! Not Leeds. London this time.'

Kitty smiled across at her. 'Had enough fine country air, then?'

'Do you know, Kit, it could be the sight of your youthful glowing chops, but this place makes me feel like an old woman. Mayhap I need the bustle and the cheers to keep me young. And if I get to London there'll be even more of that. Jarrold says—'

'Ah, Jarrold!' said Kitty.

Esme pushed her arm. 'I can't think why you two don't like each other. I like you both so much and you two are there baring teeth like a pair of mongrels.'

'It's instinct, Es. Can't stand the sight of the man.'

'Ah, now, there's some balance. He can't stand the sight of you.'

Janine piped up from the bench. 'An' when is it yeh'll gerroff, the pair o' yeh?'

Kitty glanced at her. Janine's face was wooden. She appeared unmoved by the idea of Thomas's departure, but Kitty knew how much she had enjoyed her son's silent presence, how much unstated pride she now had in his entirely unexpected worldly success.

Esme pulled Thomas's face down so she could look in his eyes. 'Now get your gear ready, to be off for the train first thing tomorrow, Thomas. Don't forget!'

She had to be satisfied with a smile and a faint nod. He marched off, obviously to obey, and Janine trailed after him.

Esme looked across at Kitty. 'If your arch enemy Jarrold had his way, we'd be leaving that one behind. Jarrold can't stand him either.'

'Can't stand anybody else you have time for, that's his difficulty. One of his difficulties.'

Esme pulled on her gloves. There had been quite a row about Thomas. She'd had to insist again he was essential to her act, that he was even better now with the repertoire on the new piano accordion. A bigger sound. And he cost nothing but his keep, did he? Wouldn't know what to do with money, would he? Perhaps she could include that Russian song Ishmael had taught her in the new repertoire? How did it go? She had rambled on, singing snatches of songs under her breath.

Then Jarrold said if the idiot man came, he wasn't to travel with them. He could travel Third Class; they would travel First. She had objected then, even more strongly. And Jarrold had taken her wrist and twisted it until she thought it might break.

Then she gave in. Thomas could travel Third Class if it meant so much to Jarrold. It would not matter either way with Thomas.

Now she smoothed the embroidered gauntlet of her glove over her bruised wrist and smiled at Kitty. 'Still, it's been good to get home, Kitty, to see you. And to see Ma in better spirits, better by the day since I've been here, with Ishmael across there minding her like a baby. He has the measure of her like none of us ever had.' She put one arm round Kitty and hugged her. 'But the best joy's to see you, Kit. A real joy. The thing is, will you ever, ever, come and see me?'

Kitty put her head on one side. 'Well, maybe one day I'll surprise you. You never know.'

But she was paying lip service to her friend's eagerness. Her mind had already moved back again to Purley Hall and the connection between the scrap of cloth she had followed for the summer cushion design and Tobias Hunter. And William Scorton.

Outside the Royal George Esme was accosted by Gabriel washed and shaved; his suit was brushed, his linen clean.

'What've you been up to, Gabe? Mother's been worried about you.'

He shook her hand vigorously. 'I've been in retreat, sister, looking to the depths of my soul and perusing the hollow centre. Into that hollow centre is poured now the wisdom of the Lord, finer than any red wine. And the Lord has given me a mission to save thee from thyself, to teach thee right from wrong and to stop thee flaunting thyself before the populace.'

Esme put a gloved hand on his arm to stop the rant. 'What's all this "thee'ing" and "thou'ing", Gabe?'

'I am thine intimate. Thou art mine intimate. Repent and the Lord is thine. Or else He will hate thee and bring thee to ruin. I have repented and the Lord is mine.'

'Stop. Stop this! What do you want?'

'I want to save thy soul, and in return thou wilt give the wherewithal for my lodging.' He looked at the battered front of the Royal George and sighed. 'I can no longer live in this house of iniquity.'

She raked in her reticule and brought out some sovereigns. 'Here, Gabriel. Though how you can take such tainted bounty I don't know.'

'Ah, sister, only the virtue of the owner is invested in the goods.'

She shook her head. 'You're ready for the asylum, Gabe.'

He scowled at her. 'Thee and thy draper friend are snarling, superior. Thy day will come.'

She shrugged. 'Are you coming in?'

'I would see my mother. To tell her my good news.'

She led the way in, calling out, 'Mother! Mabella! Roll up! Roll up! Here is the prodigal son, here to save your souls and touch you for a guinea.'

She could hear him snorting behind her, but sailed on up the stairs to complete her packing.

With Esme and Thomas gone again, life at the draper's shop became much quieter. As Kitty had half expected, Janine went missing again. Apart from letting Ishmael know so he would keep an eye open for her, Kitty did nothing else. In a few days' time, as she had done before, she would pick Janine up off the floor, dust her down, and set her on her feet again. Till then she had the shop and the house to run, and Leonora to see to single-handed. During the day she had the empty peg by the door to remind her that her cloak still lay somewhere up at Purley Hall. Sometimes, when she had a quiet minute in the shop, she would get the cornelian from its hiding place behind the scissor tin, and stare at it. Then she would put it by the summer cushion and lay alongside them the fragment of cloth in which she had been wrapped as a baby. She remarked to herself how similar was her own design to that on the cornelian. It became clearer and clearer to her that there was a connection. She began to ache with the desire to talk boldly to William Scorton about this, to declare her right to know what the connection was. She knew that it was to do with the woman who had thrown her from the viaduct. And Tobias Hunter.

On the Tuesday morning following Esme's departure, the shop was very quiet. By eleven o'clock Kitty had not had a single customer. She drew the blind and put a little notice in the window saying she was on deliveries, and could any customer please call back, or put a note through the door with their requirements. Leonora jumped about with excitement at the thought that they were to get outside the confines of the shop for a promised walk in the woods.

It took the best part of an hour for them to walk to Purley Hall, with Leonora dawdling and crying for a carry. Kitty claimed for a long while that she had a bad leg and couldn't manage it, but in the end gave in and lifted Leonora on to her shoulders. Leonora finally leaped down to chase the peacocks, who were lurching around the lawn.

At the door of Purley Hall Kitty straightened her own and Leonora's bonnets and skirts before pulling at the large ornate bell. The double doors were opened by John, the little man in white pantaloons. He shook his head when Kitty asked for Mr Scorton.

'Mr Scorton at workshop, miss.'

Leonora looked up at him with wide eyes. Kitty turned to go, pulling her daughter with her.

The squeaky voice came from behind her. 'Stop, miss.

Stop!' A small hand dragged at her sleeve. John pulled her into the hall, went to the mantelpiece and reached up on tiptoes to grasp a white envelope which was lying there. He pattered over and thrust it in her hand. 'Here, miss.'

It was addressed to her. She tore it open.

Dear Miss Rainbow,

If you are reading this you have decided to return. I am pleased about this. I would have sought you out to apologise for my execrable behaviour, but, to be honest, I did not dare to risk another black eye. I am at the workshop each day. I would wish to see you there. If you have come to Purley on foot, John will bring you here in the trap.

I remain, yours cordially,

William Edmund Scorton.

John was advancing on her with her cape. He handed it to her and bowed. 'Miss will wait just five minutes and I get trap and horse.' Then he turned to Leonora and from the voluminous folds of his pantaloons he produced a small carved doll of dark oily wood. The doll was weighed down with necklaces and glittering beads. 'For little girl,' he said.

Leonora smiled broadly, took it from him and kissed the hand which had given the doll to her. He withdrew the hand as though it had been stung. 'Miss, no!' he protested. But as he walked away there was a glimmer of a smile on his narrow lips.

It took more than half an hour for them to reach the workshops, which were tucked away in the shadow of a flourmill on the far side of Priorton. The workroom was long, with about a dozen men crouched over long tables, their eyes strangely elongated by eyeglasses which helped them to handle the tiny tools of their trade.

Kitty stood in the doorway and watched as John made his way down one worktable, an incongruous figure, with his white pantaloons under his rather well-cut frock coat. He stopped and coughed beside one crouching figure which unfurled to reveal itself as William Scorton. He took out his distorting eyeglass and smiled when he saw them. Then he reached for his coat and pulled it over his waistcoat and naked sleeves. Kitty had to purse her lips to stop herself smiling broadly, gulping back her undeniable pleasure at seeing this man again.

He marched down the workroom and shook her by the hand. 'Miss Rainbow! Delightful to see you. I must tell you, every time we meet you leave me with something to do. I remember the first time we met in a loomshed, you were a mere child and you made me change the looms. I remember too how, later, your well-shot criticism made me race to dismiss the evil genius of that loomshed and set a more liberal man in his place. And then I had poor Tobias Hunter to soothe after the episode in your shop. And after our last meeting I had to tend to a black eye.' His gaze dropped to Leonora. 'And here we have the smaller Miss Rainbow. I see John has honoured you with a gift of one of his dolls.'

Gravely he shook her hand and she bobbed a curtsy. 'I called Leonora,' she said.

'Charming.'

Kitty, trembling slightly herself, was taken aback at his outburst, which had been delivered full-pelt as though, incredibly, he were the nervous one. 'I hope your eye has recovered, Mr Scorton,' she said quietly.

He fingered the last traces of yellow bruising on his cheekbone. 'Almost fully recovered, I'm pleased to say. I will have to remember in the future, Miss Rainbow, that you pack a powerful punch and I must mind my manners.'

She smiled faintly at this.

He looked round at the buzzing workshop. 'Little Miss Leonora Rainbow, would you like John to show you a little mechanical doll we have been making, while I talk with your mama? John?'

'Many toys to show, little girl.' John held out his hand and Leonora slipped hers into it. 'Many toys.'

'Miss Rainbow, there is no office, no private room here. Would you have an objection to a short ride in the trap? I would welcome the fresh air.'

She looked at him steadily. 'I've no objection to that.'

He set the horse's head away from the town. 'Now, Miss Rainbow, where to?'

'To the viaduct.'

'You wish to see the trains? The railyard?'

She laughed. 'That's where I wish to talk to you.'

He manoeuvred the trap so they were in a lane where they could see the viaduct, but where the steaming clattering cacophony of the railyards was merely a distant rattle.

He lay down the reins. 'Now, let me go first. I must apologise for my ... forwardness ... the last time. I have no excuse except that at that minute you were so ... alive ... my impulses got the better of me.'

'And I for landing out and giving you a black eye. I must learn to deliver the sharp word instead of the sharp uppercut.'

He sat back against the leather cushions then. 'I will not ask you to shake hands, as my impulse not to let it go might also be irresistible and I'll get another black eye. Now then, we can talk about other things.'

'I want to talk about this.' She spread her dark skirts wide and out of her satchel she brought the cushion, the scrap of material and the cornelian and lined them up on her lap, side by side. 'I want to know about the connection between these. I need to know because somewhere in here is the person I am. That is apart from the "scrapper" who is daughter to a boxer and a drunken draper woman.'

He picked up the cornelian and rubbed it between his palms. 'Well, this cornelian has always been some kind of treasure in the house which was on that site even before the Roman villa at Purley Hall. Some old Celtic artist carved

247

this stone to reflect, perhaps give power over, the oak trees that surrounded that hill then and were probably in this district as far as the eyes could see. Perhaps it was a magic tree. Did you know they ascribed magic and god-like characters to trees in those days? Then the Romans, who also had lesser gods of trees and streams, must have taken a fancy to the stone, as there are some notes somewhere to say that when it was found it was cunningly concealed in the back of a Roman stone of dedication. I suppose the Romans were invoking the power of the ancient gods alongside their own. That stone went missing, though. We don't have it.'

He handed the cornelian back to her and it was warm from his hand. He picked up the cushion. 'Old Toby Hunter has been in and out of Purley Hall all this time and knows the stone like the back of his hand. What amazed us, old Toby and me, was that, though your blues were brighter, you had invented a pattern for your cushion which was the exact twin of the pattern on the cornelian. We had seen that before, embroidered on cushions and curtains. The unicorn too, like the deer on the vase I showed you.'

He picked up the fragile scrap of fabric. 'And this is the link.' He held it close to his eye. 'It is faded but very familiar.'

'How familiar? Where is it from? Who sewed that?'

'Why do you wish to know?'

She sighed. 'You see that viaduct? When I was very small – we think about three months, so I count my birthday on Christmas Day three months before the date I was found. Anyway – when I was very small I was thrown from that viaduct when the river·was in full flood. A bit of excess baggage. Ishmael always says that it was the rainbow giving me to him, making him happy. He kept me happy for a long time with that tale. This bit of fabric is all that is left of the shawl in which I was wrapped when Ishmael caught me. I've always treasured it, as I suppose now it is the only connection between me and my mother – or my father – the one who threw me.' She put a hand on his arm. 'Tell me about this person. You must know who it is.'

He laid the scrap back in her lap and put his hand on hers.

'Her name was Maria Tipton. She seemed always there at Purley Hall twenty-five years ago when I was a lad, in and out of the house, helping Sir Marcus with archaeological digs, which were his great obsession at that time. Tobias Hunter too used to give him a hand. Maria was at least thirty-five then – maybe older – a very, very distant relative of Sir Marcus and as much part of the Tipton baggage train as the second-best crockery or the cook's favourite utensils.' He clung on to her hand as she tried to withdraw it. 'She was governess to the younger children, then lady's maid companion of the dowager. She did fine needlework, collars and sleeves – just like you make for your shop – for the girls and the young women in the family. She loved the cornelian design. She copied it on the collars, on the sleeves and shawls – on cushions. It was she who converted the deer on the pot to a unicorn for one of her cushions. There are still curtains at the house with her embroidery at the edge. So this is the last remnant of a shawl in which you were wrapped? There is no doubt that she was your embroiderer. She earned no wages, of course. Just her keep and the treat of being called cousin.'

'What was she like? What did she look like?'

He looked down at her. 'She was very tall, but aside from that she looked very like you. Pretty. Silver-grey eyes; neat nose. Hair much lighter but also . . . very lively. And she was angry but kept it in because of her situation. Her lips were not full like yours. They were folded, always composed, a hard line keeping such a lot of feeling in. Perhaps she was a "scrapper", but had not the courage to hand out a few black eyes. You could feel the pressure in her. Being in the room with her sometimes was like being with a ticking bomb.'

Kitty sat there for some minutes, letting all that information take possession of her, become part of her for all time. She took a deep breath. 'Does she live?'

He shook his head slowly. 'I think not. Apparently one day she went missing from Purley Hall, and that was it. Sir Marcus instituted searches, but nothing came of them.'

'Just find another skivvy,' said Kitty bitterly.

'Regrettably, it looks like that. But if, as it seems, we're saying that you are Maria Tipton's daughter, then that adds to our knowledge. I think there were rumours even then. A single lady in her late thirties ... of that class, however peripherally – a child would be unthinkable. There would be difficulties. How she—'

'You think she threw me in the river, then did away with herself?'

'I think not, Miss Rainbow. There were sightings.'

She drew her hand out of his and sat up straight. 'And where is Mr Tobias Hunter in all this?' She was dreading his answer.

'You think he may be your ... her...? I can see you would not...' He shook his head, smiling slightly. 'Not Hunter. They did not ... were not so closely acquainted because she would not permit it. He attended the Tipton household on some minor legal matters and helped Sir Marcus document his collection of archaeological artifacts, as I did. He was obsessed with the collection, and was also greatly drawn to Maria, following her around like a dumb ox. But she spurned him. I regret to say it was something of a laughing matter in those days – that, despite her situation, she was not so desperate ...' He coughed. 'On Midsummer Day, holding your needle up to the light to thread it, you were her double. I saw it, as did he. It was he who drew my attention to that fact. I had not thought of her in many years.'

'So you think she's dead, this Maria? Who was my father?'

'No one knows the answer to the second question. And as for the first, well, Maria went missing for the best part of a year, during which Tobias Hunter caught a glimpse, just a glimpse of her one May, at the Priorton Fair. Then nothing. Nothing at all.'

She sat back abruptly. 'I have to go. Leonora'll be restless and I had to close the shop to come on this errand. I can ill afford that.'

He nodded, then picked up the reins. He said very little as they made their way back to the workshop. Once there, he lifted Leonora back into the trap. 'John will take you home.'

Kitty said, 'Thank you for telling me all that. I've much to think about.' She slipped the cornelian into his hand.

'I understand that.' He raised his hat. 'Thank you, and good day, Miss Rainbow.'

She listened with half an ear to Leonora's excited babblings about the magic lady who danced when you wound her up, and the magic fountain that made music. Kitty's brain was bursting with thoughts of Maria Tipton, and her heart was bruising with heartache for the woman who must have been her mother.

The shop was busy all afternoon. Ishmael turned up at nine o'clock in the evening with a comatose Janine on his back. 'She's in a bad way this time, Kitty. Raving and ill. She coughs blood.'

They put her in Ishmael's old bed and Kitty changed her, washed her face and hands, forced some milk into her and let her sleep. She came down into the kitchen and washed her own hands and arms to get some of the stench of Janine off her.

'You're right, Ishmael. I've never seen her in such a bad way. She's missing Thomas so much.'

Ishmael sat with his hands out to the fire and they were silent for a moment. 'So what have you been up to today, Kitty Rainbow?' he said quietly.

She looked at him in surprise at his serious tone but told

him about her discoveries: about the scrap of cloth and Maria Tipton.

He nodded. 'She sounds like an interesting woman, this Maria Tipton. I knew she would be. So you know just a little more about yourself?'

'Yes. But nothing about who my ... well, who the man was who ...'

'Do you mean your father?'

She shook her head. 'No, Ishmael. I don't mean that. *You*'re my father.'

He stroked his beard. 'Seems like quite a sensible fellow, that Mr Scorton.'

Her head shot up. 'How do you know. Have you ... ?'

He smiled slightly. 'He came to see me. Six o'clock this evening. You know what he said, Kitty?'

'What?' She was red.

'He asked me if I had any objections if he called on you.'

'What did you say?'

'I said that I did not, but as you were a grown woman with a house, a shop and a child of your own, you could make up your own mind whether you had objections to him calling on you.'

She grinned and slapped a fist into the opposite palm. 'You didn't give him a black eye, did you, Ishmael? He'll start to think it's a family failing.'

20

The Christening

The next day at five o'clock William Scorton called on Kitty. He stood at the back of the shop, leaning on his cane, and watched as she dealt with five customers in sequence. She did not hurry. She dealt with each person with measured enthusiasm, proud as always to show the range of her stock and her ability to meet the needs of her customers. When the door clinked shut after the last one, he leaned his stick against the partition and applauded her. 'Bravo! The shopkeeper *par excellence*. Where did you learn that?'

She looked at him suspiciously but saw not a trace of mockery.

'Well, if you want to know, all the time I was working for Antijan – that's my foster mother who I was apprenticed to – all the time she made such a mess of things, I thought that if the business were mine I would do things this way or that way. Always different from her. And that's what I do now.'

He looked round at the immaculate shop with its gleaming mahogany and brass, then came to face her over the counter. 'And did she give this place to you?'

She laughed and shook her head. 'No, she was always stopping for a little glass of gin, was Antijan. So we lost shops and premises all the time. That was the main problem. It was Ishmael who got me started, just after Leonora was born, with money from his very last fight where he nearly crippled himself with the effort. So I've had to work to make it right. For his sake. For Leonora.'

'I met him. He's a fine gentleman.'

'So he is. He told me you'd called.' She stood quietly looking at him.

'He told me that you were your own mistress, and it was from yourself I had to seek permission to call.'

She rolled up her tape measure on the mahogany counter. 'And what would be the purpose of this "calling", Mr Scorton?'

'To deepen and strengthen our ... acquaintance. To put it on a formal, public footing. To see if we can be more than acquaintances.'

She smiled slightly. 'D'you really want an acquaintance who's an unbaptised foundling with a lame foot? And only a poor shopkeeper?'

He put out a hand on hers to stop her playing with the tape measure. 'Kitty Rainbow! You've more life, more go in you, than any ten women I have ever met.' He put a finger up to her cheek. 'And your face is so bright and beautiful it makes me want to weep. And I am only a watchmaker who happened to have a very clever father. And if you don't become my *acquaintance* I think I will shrivel up like a walnut.'

She laughed at that and turned her hand to grasp his. 'I think I will allow you to call on me ... William.'

'Ha!' He leaned towards her over the counter. The doorbell went ping! 'Damn!' he said, taking up his vigil again at the back of the shop.

It was not a customer. It was a young girl, carrying a heavy canvas bag which she placed carefully on the floor. She was

254

an emissary. 'I'm sent by Mr Slaughter, miss. Me name's Joan Wharton. Me Auntie Mabella works for Mrs Gullet at the Royal George. Me da was just killed at the pit an' our house's gone. There's three littler ones after me an' now no bed. Me, I'm a good sewer an' knitter. Mr Slaughter said he thought you needed an apprentice. An' I've brought me things. I can start straight off.'

An answer to a prayer. Kitty's face broke into a beam. 'Of course! He's right. I do need an apprentice.'

'An' my sister Kezia can come for any extra times. She is only twelve an' still at school but is very handy.'

'Wonderful. Having Mabella for an auntie is a sound reference for the pair of you. Put your bag round the back of the counter, Joan. Take your coat off and look through the stock, see around the shop. I'll just take Mr Scorton back to see Mrs Druce. Call me if any customers come.'

Janine was sitting, bundled in blankets, by the window in the back room. She was watching Leonora play with some children in the yard. Her tired eyes sparked when she saw William. 'Och, Ah know yer, sir! Yer had mills. She sewed yer coat an yer admired yon cushion of our Kitty's.'

'Indeed I did.'

'Mr Scorton is going to "call" on me, Antijan. It is arranged.'

Janine raised an eyebrow. 'Aren't yer gettin' posh now, young Kitty!' Janine held out her thin hand to William. 'Kitty's a fine gerrl, Mr Scorton. An' if she is, it has naught to do with me, as couldn't take her fiery spleen as a child an' abused her, an' threw her away from me. Although ye wouldn't think so now, sir, such a mother's kindness she has for me. No, if she's any virtues it's through her own common sense and through Mr Ishmael Slaughter, who's been mother and father to her: fightmaster, teacher and mentor all these years. A gentleman to his boots.'

'I have met him, Mrs Druce. He is all of those things.'

Joan Wharton called out from the shop and Kitty went

through, leaving William and Janine together. Kitty was still busy when William came back into the shop twenty minutes later. Kitty showed the last customer out and stood in the doorway with William. They stayed close; almost but not quite touching. She could feel the heat from his body; smell the crisp scent of fine machine oil on his hands.

She looked up at him. 'We must be proper acquaintances now. You've met my Antijan and still want my acquaintance.'

He smiled faintly. 'I remember that you called her one of the fragile ones. You have kindness, for a girl who hands out black eyes with such consummate ease.'

She shrugged. 'Will you do something for me?'

He glanced along the deserted street, then took her hand between both of his. 'Anything.'

'Do you know how I might get christened? And Leonora?'

He raised his eyebrows and nodded slowly. 'I know a clergyman in a parish three miles distant, a fine man with a liking for the unusual. I know he'd be happy to bring you into the fold.'

'I don't know about any folds,' she said doubtfully.

'I was speaking metaphorically.'

'You were speaking what?'

'Don't worry. I'll fix it.'

Gabriel was beginning to irritate Kitty. Almost every day he would stand outside her shop berating her customers for their sinfulness, so that for sheer peace she had to bring him in and give him some money from her moneybox to send him on his way. Once inside, he would harangue her for her greed, her sinfulness and her sloth, and accuse her of setting his mother against him, of poisoning his mother's mind.

One day she dragged him into the back room out of the way of customers. He raved on. 'You've poisoned her mind against me on the devil's ordering. She won't let me across the threshold of an establishment which is, by rights, my own.' He put his head in his hands and wept bitter tears of self-pity. 'My father would not've allowed it, never in this world. The Good Lord looks on and weeps.'

'But you nearly lost the place for her, Gabriel, with your drinking friends and your gambling! Now Mirella and Ishmael's getting it back to what it was, and you stand outside telling her customers that drink comes from the devil. She can't let you over the threshold, you know that. Just what is it you want?'

Gabriel rubbed his eye with a dirty fist and pouted. 'I want what's my own.'

She held out some coins in the flat of her hand as you would sugar for a horse. He reached out and grabbed them, stood up and pocketed them, and stumped out.

'What yon feller needs is a good drink,' piped up Janine from her place by the window.

Kitty pulled the blanket further round Janine, tucking it in tight. 'It's not the answer to everything, Antijan. Not quite.'

Two weeks later, Janine was witness to a far happier scene as Kitty stood in front of her, twisting and turning in a new grey silk grenadine dress with a small bustle. Janine touched the fabric with her thin fingers. 'Fine stuff, Kitty. Now, what about the hat?'

Kitty had smoothed her hair with sugar and water and it was drawn right back off her face with more or less orderly ringlets down her back. On top of this, well forward, she perched a hat with a small veil and a narrow brim and ribbons falling down her back following the line of the curls.

'Och, hen,' sighed Janine, 'who'd know you for that little scurryvaig who wouldn't put shoes on her feet?' They both looked at Kitty's feet, now encased in slippers of the finest morocco, the right one as always cunningly built up to make her walk straight.

'I wish you could come, Antijan.'

Janine shook her head. 'Och, I'll be happy here watching the birds. An' you can bring me back some sweetmeats from the tea.'

Janine never moved from the chair nowadays except to go to the privy or to the little bed she now had in Kitty's room. She ate very little. She drank less. Day by day she seemed to become more transparent.

Later that morning two traps went in procession from Priorton to St Matthew's Church, Brack's Hill. Kitty, Leonora and Ishmael rode in one. Mirella, Mabella and Joan Wharton, now a very keen draper's apprentice, rode in the second. William Scorton travelled in the Purley Hall maroon chaise driven by John. Kitty wore her new grey dress and Leonora wore a new white broderie anglaise frock with three petticoats. Mirella and William Scorton stood as godparents for Kitty; Mabella and Joan stood for Leonora. Ishmael, who for reasons of religion could not participate, watched with a quiet smile.

Kitty listened with quiet satisfaction to the vicar intone their new names. She had chosen them carefully: Catherine Maria Tipton Rainbow; Leonora Maria Tipton Rainbow. Now she would never be lost from sight – that woman who had been so desperate that night by the viaduct. Kitty stood up straighter in her new grey morocco slippers. Today she knew she had come of age.

Afterwards there was a large tea set out in the cavernous dining room of Purley Hall, served by John and his brother Matthew: a much taller man, equally brown, and wearing equally snowy white pantaloons.

When they had all had their fill, William announced that Matthew would take everyone on a guided tour of the museum room, the rose garden and the ornamental vegetable garden which Matthew himself supervised, and which was the source of much of the fine food at Purley. Perhaps Miss Kitty would stay behind? said William. He had a little surprise for her.

Kitty listened to the fading chirrup of voices as the rest of the christening party moved down the corridor. She looked up at him. William put a velvet-covered box on the table beside her. 'It's a christening present,' he said. 'Open it.'

There, nestling in black velvet, was the cornelian, now slotted into a silver setting on a silver chain. The setting itself was worked in a pattern of acorns. It weighed heavily in her hands.

'Mr Goldstein made it. Burned the midnight oil. Put it on!' he said eagerly.

She held it up to him. 'You put it on.'

He lifted it over her head and let his hands lie on her shoulders. Then he leaned down and kissed her. And she held on to his coat and kissed him back. In that kiss she paid homage to all the children's kisses she had shared with Freddie, and moved on, right on, into the present.

Reluctantly she pulled away. 'Thank you for the lovely pendant,' she said. 'It is truly beautiful. I'll wear it always.'

He took out his handkerchief and mopped his brow. 'What a relief!' he said.

'What?' she said.

'I thought I might get another black eye!'

She put her arm through his. 'Now!' she said. 'We'd better catch up the others on this tour. I so wish to see Matthew's ornamental vegetable garden.' She cocked her head. 'How do John and Matthew come to be here in County Durham?'

'They're from Egypt. They and a third brother, Luke, took care of our party once, when I was there assisting some archaeologists in their work. Then they wanted to come back with me and I was only too happy to bring them. The three of them take care of me here – the house, everything. John cooks and drives. Luke cleans. Matthew takes care of the house and the garden.'

'You've no women in the house?'

They could hear Mirella's clear voice declaiming ahead of them.

He hugged her arm to his side. 'My wife was very ill for a long time. What they call mad, I suppose. I never wished her to come here. So I've never wanted any woman here.' He put a hand over hers. 'Till now.'

Leonora came and dragged her away. 'Mammy! Come and see this!'

'This' was a silver boat set on a crystal sea. Leonora clicked a switch and the ship started to move and tip realistically on flickering crystal waves.

It was Mirella who noticed the cornelian pendant first. She leaned over and picked it up in her heavy hand. 'What a very pretty thing, Kitty dear.'

Kitty took it back from her. 'It's a christening present from Mr Scorton.'

'And there is one for Leonora,' said William, dipping into his pocket and pulling out a tiny silver locket, also worked with the acorn design. He slipped it over Leonora's head and she kissed it before she held it up for the others to see. 'See, Ishmael! My christening present from Willy-um.'

There were smiles all round at her first attempt at his name.

'No, Leonora! You must say "Mr Scorton",' scolded Mirella.

William put a hand on Leonora's head. 'I much prefer Willy-um,' he said.

There was no question that Gabriel's mentor, Tom Vart, felt himself to be a good man. He lived on the end of a row of houses at the edge of the river-meadows. Forty years before, some speculators had opened a small drift mine down there and thrown up some hutches for the workers. The drift mine was gone, most of the houses were empty now. Tom Vart had simply moved into one of them when he lost his other house. The place was spartan but very clean, furnished with a table, three chairs and two iron beds with rough blankets and palliasses. The only other item was a narrow dresser which was heaped with tracts, all packed in newspaper parcels and labelled with their contents. Vart spent three hours each day scrubbing and cleaning the house, and an hour scrubbing and cleaning his own person. He obliged Gabriel to do the same; Gabriel found all this mindless and not unpleasant, but he did have a problem with his hands. He never seemed quite able to keep them clean.

Vart did not allow eating or drinking inside the house as these activities involved the excrescences of appetite which he now abhorred. He and Gabriel ate in the back yard at separate times, as even outside Vart could not bear the sight of another's indulgence. This was fortunate for Gabriel, as his indulgences still secretly involved liberal portions of crude whisky, which he kept hidden behind a brick in the privy. To move the brick he had to get behind a large pot jar of 'boody' belonging to a child from one of the houses which shared the privy. 'Boody' were the glittering finds which children made as they wandered the streets and the fields. Gabriel sometimes sat on the privy with a bottle in one hand, turning over these stones and shards of pottery and glass, watching them gleam in the light which forced its way through a crack in the door.

In the afternoons he and Vart went off separately with their satchels of tracts, to preach the Lord's words in the streets and the Market Square, and to beg for money to sustain their mission. In the evenings they went with their satchels to the dark areas of Priorton, sometimes called 'Little London', to preach damnation and hellfire at the people who slunk there – drunkards and prostitutes, and people who enjoyed such low company and who should know better. Before his conversion, Gabriel had passed many a self-indulgent night there himself. Now he relished haranguing these people and painting lurid pictures of the road down which their habits were leading them. His knowledge of the detail of those habits added colourful details to his impromptu sermons.

The evil-doers thus castigated were surprisingly tolerant. Knots of them would stop to listen to the tirade, occasionally exchanging insults with the speakers. Some were sobered for an instant or two, uneasy at the revisitation of childhood terrors inculcated by Chapel or Church. The gamblers always made a small donation as a kind of good-luck token. The collection box soon filled with farthings representing conscience and superstition in equal parts.

Sometimes Gabriel came up against his former tormentors; even they treated him gingerly: he had found the word of God to be a remarkably effective shield.

One night as they walked home from their evening's labours through the streets still buzzing with midnight carousel, they bumped into another disciple of Vart's.

'Ah, Gabriel, you must meet another who goes about the Lord's quiet work.'

Gabriel stared up into the face of Tobias Hunter. Behind him was the shadowy figure of a woman, who dropped into deeper shadow when Hunter stopped.

'We are acquainted, Mr Vart. Mr Gullet was 'prenticed to me some years back,' he said drily. 'A rascal, as I remember.'

'And now you see a young man renewed in the Lord, Mr Hunter! Shriven for all time. We were all sinners, all sinners before the time of Light.'

Hunter bowed in silent agreement.

Vart glanced over Hunter's shoulder at the shadowy figure behind him. 'And have you another soul here on the way to salvation, Mr Hunter?'

'Indeed I have. A granddaughter of Eve, a cousin of Jezebel, a daughter of Oholibah the prostitute, who spills her evil into good men's souls and weaves her serpent coils about their brains. This fallen one has now some under-standing of the fires that await her if her soul stays in this tainted state. She knows her need for the Cleansing Light.'

Vart nodded sagely. 'And no finer man to bring her through to Light than yourself, Mr Hunter. No finer man. Come, Gabriel, we must not delay the Lord's work.'

As the woman swished by Gabriel, he caught sight of a face, whitened with lead, highlighted with rouge, topped by a fall of greasy ginger curls.

Hunter's voice made them turn. 'Oh, Mr Vart! I have need of more tracts. Can you provide them?'

'It will be my pleasure, Mr Hunter. My pleasure.'

'What will he do with the woman?' Gabriel asked Vart as they strode on.

'He'll pray with her, cleanse her spirit, inside and out. Then he'll dispatch her to Harrogate or to Newcastle where he has set up two agencies which set such women to hard God-fearing work.'

'What kind of work?'

Vart shrugged. 'They are lewd, foul-mouthed, unfit for the higher realms of domestic work, although they might be set to scrub. They say there are workshops now where women are permitted to do menial manufacturing things. But what odds what they do? They're better begging in the street than plying Oholibah's trade.'

Early the next day Gabriel was excused scrubbing duties at Vart's house so he could deliver the tracts to Tobias Hunter's home, a tall building in a row of like structures, on a quiet sideroad. The package was taken from him by an old woman in a widow's bonnet, who evidently could not hear a word he said. The door was banged in his face.

He had just turned to go when a chamber pot shattered in front of him. He looked up to see a face peering over the top sash of a narrow window.

'Hey, mister!' The face emerged further. He recognised the woman of the night before, disfigured now with bruises and signs of tears trekking through the deadly white powder. 'Hey, mister! Stop there an' catch us!'

To his astonishment she lifted her legs over the sill and, without hesitation, launched herself out of the window. Gabriel, rooted to the spot by the swiftness of the woman's desperate action, broke her fall, both of them ending up in a threshing mass on the pavement.

'Here, missis, you nearly killed me.'

'Nowt ter what that bugger's done ter me.' She hauled herself to her feet and pulled down a strange garment made from a sheet with a hole torn in for a neck-hole. Her head was bound in a strip torn from the same sheet. There was no evidence of the greasy ginger hair.

She glanced warily up at the house and caught his arm. 'Come on!' She dragged him along the deserted street and round the corner.

He grabbed her arm and pulled her into the shadow of a wall. 'Now! What is it?' he demanded.

'That feller's a lunatic. I took his guinea an' went with him. It takes all sorts, I know that.' She breathed hard. 'Then he had us tied, stripped off, cut all me hair.' She touched the white binding which covered the whole of her head. 'Ravin' on all night, every hour of the night, about bleedin' repentance an' serpents an' redemption. Had a ridin' crop.' She touched the small of her back, winced and shook her head. 'I've met some lunatics in my trade, but . . .'

In spite of himself, Gabriel was getting excited. Glancing up and down the street, he grabbed her and pulled her to him. She threw him off.

'Lawks. I forgot you was another Godwalloper.' Then her voice changed, becoming in turn whining, ingratiating and motherly. 'Now I know you're not like him, sir. I take yer for a genuine Godwalloper – sorry, a God-fearin' man. Too young to be in the deceptions an' delusions of that trade of *passion*.' She put her hand down the torn neck of her sheet-shift and pulled out a guinea. 'All I want is you ter get us somewhere where I can buy a coverin' of clothes. He burned me own clothes, that devil, along with me hair. Made me watch him,' she said bitterly.

Gabriel was sobered by her tale, ashamed of his earlier lascivious intent. Thankful that he was wearing a cloak against the chilly morning, he took it off and wrapped it round her. 'Can't do anything about the feet, madam. But you'll not be the only barefoot person in Priorton High Street,' he said, taking her by the hand.

She clutched the garment around her. 'Where are yer takin' us?' she said suspiciously.

'Don't worry,' he said soberly. 'I might be a gambler, drunkard and more recently a Godwalloper, but I'm not a lunatic.'

The shop had a new sign which swung above him: *C.M.T. Rainbow DRAPER*, picked out in gold on black glass.

Kitty was on her own in the shop, as Joan Wharton had taken Leonora to help her get the groceries. Kitty looked up at the ting of the bell, then stood up straight, ready to repel Gabriel, her eyes widening when she saw the strange apparition in the sheet beside him.

Gabriel put up one hand. 'No lectures today, Kitty Rainbow. Here's a woman needs some help and has the money to pay for it. I thought you'd need the business. I see there's a new shop sign. What's all those letters stand for on it?'

'I was christened last week. Catherine Maria Tipton Rainbow. C.M.T. I now know Miss Maria Tipton was my mother. Do you see?'

'I see you've got a great fancy for yourself and would tell you that pride is one of the Seven Deadly Sins and most certainly goes before a fall.' He bowed. The bell tinged again and he was gone.

'Well,' said Kitty. 'What can I do for you, miss?'

'Yer can get me a cheap frock an' petticoat an' bonnet so I

can get back ter me lodgin's without being hauled ter the cells.'

'We don't sell many made-up frocks but there's one or two that we made that didn't get collected.'

Looking her up and down to assess her size, Kitty bent down and produced a folded blue calico dress, a camisole and a chemise, thick blue stockings and a small blue cotton bonnet.

The woman looked at them. 'If they cost more than a guinea I can't pay for them.'

'Take them.'

The woman looked round. 'Can I have a wash?'

'Did he do that to your face? Gabriel Gullet?'

The woman exploded a dry laugh. 'No, he didn't do it. A babe in arms, that one, beside the devil I did meet. Gabriel? That his name? Well, he was a rescuin' angel all right today ter me, hinney, I can tell yer that. Now can I have a wash?'

The woman said nothing else as she washed and changed in Kitty's bedroom. When she came down again, with the filthy facepaint washed off her bruised face, and the bonnet on her shorn head, she looked a different woman.

'Who treated you like this? He should—' said Kitty.

The woman shook her head. 'Yer don't want ter know, hinney. Yer don't want ter know. I'm off now, ter me lodgin's an' on the train ter Darlington. Me sister's got a workman's lodgin' house there. An' I can scrub for her while me hair grows.' She barged past Kitty through to the shop. 'I'll say good day ter yer.'

Janine, who had watched this pantomime in silence, sighed loudly. 'The poor woman's a picture of fright. Yeh expect such things in her profession, sad to say. Men!' she said.

Men! thought Kitty as she went through to deal with a customer. Antijan knows all about that, I suppose.

But she herself had been thinking rather fondly of men lately. Ishmael was at present wreaking his magic at the

Royal George. And William Scorton, who called on her most days now, was making her feel like a princess. They were rarely alone, so their only contact was a lingering touch on the hand, a few snatched kisses. Even so, her liking for him was growing day by day. The days when he could not call were barren.

Today she'd had to make do with a note, delivered by John in the trap. 'Dear Kitty R., I am unable to call today, but would like to take this opportunity to ask you, and Leonora, to tea on Saturday (tomorrow). Michael and Samuel will be here from school and I thought a family tea would be the order of the day. Yours in utmost affection, William Scorton.'

She ran her finger over the words *utmost affection* and smiled. She was not quite sure of what she was going to do about William Scorton. Not sure at all.

21

The Room on the Third Floor

At first the tea at Purley Hall looked like being a restrained affair. The food could not be blamed: spread out on the dining-room table was an extended delight, a cornucopia, of English country cooking and Eastern sweetmeats, cunningly designed to tempt the very young appetite. John and his brother Luke darted around in their white pantaloons, replacing empty dishes or rearranging the table to maintain its picture-like appearance, smiling and nodding at the children like proud grandfathers.

Michael and Samuel Scorton stared at Leonora Rainbow as though she had just landed from the moon. She was dressed in her broderie anglaise christening dress with its three petticoats. Around her neck was her silver pendant, which now contained locks of her own and Kitty's hair in one side, and locks of Ishmael and Janine's in the other. Joan had done her goddaughter's hair in rags the previous night, so that she had long bouncy curls down her back and three little curls on her forehead.

The boys ate voraciously and efficiently. Their schools served food more praiseworthy for its quantity than its taste and, like camels, they stored up good food when they could.

After tea William told them to show little Leonora the tree-house which Matthew was building for them and they complied with grumbling unwillingness, trailing through the long windows on to the terrace with Leonora chasing after them. 'Take her hand!' called William. Samuel came back and took Leonora's hand in his. To his surprise it felt quite nice, warm and plump and dry. It made him feel old, able to protect this little creature.

Luke strolled after them at a distance, accustomed now to his protective nanny role.

William stood up and signalled John to clear. 'Come, Kitty, I have something to show you.' He led the way to his museum room, turned the key in the lock and pulled her to him to kiss him. 'The days're too long without seeing you.'

She laughed and pulled away. 'William! This was a trick. You've nothing to show me.'

'Indeed I have.' He went across to the worktable and turned over a section of carved stone. 'I found this when I was tramping the fields.'

It had a border of oak leaves. Kitty ran her fingers over the design, then down on to some fragments of words incised into it. She peered closer. 'I've seen something like this somewhere else.'

He put his head on one side, pleased at her interest. 'Where?'

She frowned. 'I think . . . I know! Down on The Green by Salvin Row, where Esme and I met each other as children, where we used to play. That had words like this, and the border. Though I hardly noticed the border then.'

'Can you take me there? Now?'

She looked out of the window. 'Leonora . . . ?'

'Matthew and Luke will watch her. Perfectly capable.' He rang for John and told him they would be out for forty minutes.

John bowed. 'I tell Luke. The child will be well.'

The Green behind Salvin Row had changed little in the years since Kitty had spent time there with Esme. Women were still hanging over their gates watching their children play on the grass. There were still lines of washing slung across between poles; pigs still snouted out any sustenance they could find in glorious freedom.

The stone was still there. 'I was walking backwards and I fell over it. Then I heard Gabriel Gullet and some other Grammar School lads tormenting Esme. Didn't know who they were then. Then I fought them and saved her. That's when we got to be friends, me and Esme.'

William stroked his chin. 'I bet you handed out a few black eyes that day.'

'Mebbe I did. But I got a good beating for me pains.' She kneeled down in the dust. 'See that writing? Esme got it translated in school. In celebration of . . .'

'Mmm. Perhaps it does match the other . . .' He went to the trap and brought out the pick and shovel he always kept in a box under the seat. He started to pick away at clumps of grass at the base of the stone.

Kitty put her hand on his. 'You can't do that. You can't just take the stone.'

He glanced round. 'What? It's only a stone to them. Means nothing.'

She started back to the trap, her limp evident as it was when she was angry. 'Typical of your sort, come, take what you want, no by-your-leave.'

He grabbed her elbow. 'Whoa! What's this? What do you mean?' He looked around at the women who were watching the drama with some interest, then marched towards them. 'Do you have any objection if I take this stone?' he asked crisply.

The women drew closer; eventually he had five of them clustered around him.

'Do any of you object if I take this old stone? Is it of any use to you?'

The oldest woman shook her head slowly. 'Only an old stone,' she said uncertainly.

The others nodded.

He put his hand in his pocket and gave them a florin each. 'This is for the disturbance. I will come tomorrow with a tree to replace the stone.'

'A tree?' said another woman. 'We've never had a tree, not behind Salvin Row.'

'If I can I'll make it an oak tree.'

'An oak tree? Ah dinnet knaa what wor Robert'll think of that.'

He came back to Kitty. 'There! Are you satisfied, Miss Kitty?'

She smiled faintly and handed him his shovel. 'The oak tree was a good idea. I'll keep you to that.'

The stone was much bigger than it looked, set quite deep in the ground. He needed her help to lift it on to the trap. 'You're stronger than I am,' he said admiringly as he handed her up into her seat.

'I'm hefting bolts of cloth all day, not fairy screwdrivers,' she said drily.

He squeezed her hand and picked up the reins.

Back at Purley Hall they placed the two pieces side by side. They fitted like two jigsaw pieces. William read out the complete inscription. '"In celebration of lifelong love and affection with thanks to the spirits of the great wood and to the god Sylvanus."' They could just make out a border of oak leaves and beneath the inscription a triangular lump with a single protuberance.

Kitty put her hand on it. 'It's a deer head,' she said. 'Here's our unicorn.'

He frowned. 'I can't see that.'

'I can. Wait!' Kitty lifted her pendant. 'Can you ease the cornelian out of its setting?'

Obediently he went to a drawer and brought out a tiny tool. The cornelian came easily out of the elaborate silver filigree. He put it into her hand. Tentatively she placed it in a neat space in the centre of the top of the stone. It almost clicked into place.

'There! The horn of the unicorn,' she said with satisfaction. 'It fits, with just one little chip out here. Do you see it?'

'Wonderful.' William reached out from behind her and stroked the stone as it sat above the letters. 'The cornelian was ancient even when these lovers found it. And they placed it in the stone as a signal of their lifelong affection. And then somehow it must have been split when the Roman camp was pillaged for its stone to build the farmhouses and churches round here. And it had to wait all this time to come together again. It had to wait for us.' His hands were on her waist and she leaned back comfortably against him. 'Kitty, you must marry me,' he murmured in her ear, 'I want to be with you always – a lifetime, like those two who set up the stone. I can't bear the hours we're apart. You must marry me.'

She turned in his arms and faced him. 'I must do nothing of the sort,' she said firmly.

He put her away from him and groaned. 'You are a torment. Why cannot you marry me?'

'Because I'm a lovebegot who is a mother of a lovebegot, and children borne in love are not seen to be quite whole. It'd not be proper for you. We would both be looked down on.' She held up a hand to his protest. 'As well because I'm a draper woman who loves her work and am turning business away, things are so good. I like that an'll not give it up.'

'But I wouldn't—'

She held up her hand again. 'Oh yes you would! But most of all because I've found something of my mother and I'm getting used to being a daughter in my head. And because of that I need to know about my blood father. Oh I know Ishmael is my father of the heart. But I want to know about the man who lay somewhere with my mother and made me.'

'Kitty!'

'See? You don't like me saying what I think. Don't your sort call it immodest?'

He nodded. 'Something like a black eye in words,' he said ruefully.

'But that's who I am, William Scorton. And that's who you'd have to take if you took me in marriage. I wouldn't change.'

'I don't want you, wouldn't want you to change. I want you as you are.' He started to replace the cornelian in her pendant.

'No,' she said. 'It must stay there. That's where it belongs.'

He continued with his task. '*This* is where it belongs. It stays here until I find someone who can copy it and then perhaps we'll return this one to the stone. I want you as you are,' he repeated.

She sat down in the chair by the fire and looked at him. 'Well, you can have me, but you can't marry me. At least not till I find who my father was, and feel a whole person. Then, if you want to, you can ask again.'

He took out his handkerchief and mopped his brow. 'Another black eye! You're saying you'd be my . . . mistress? In preference to marriage?'

She looked at him steadily. 'For this time, yes. But I'll not be kept. I'll be just as busy with the shop. I'm thinking of getting bigger premises. They say old Mr Long might be selling up.'

'So you're saying, if you can spare the time, you'll be my mistress?'

'Yes, that's about it.'

He reached out for her. 'Come here, you hussy!'

Then they were twined around each other, pressing together the numbing layers of cloth and button to get closer.

There was a knock on the door and John's quiet voice

outside. 'Excuse me, sir, the children, they are returning. It seems there has been a little accident.'

They disentangled themselves, opened the door for John and all three of them moved to the window. There, coming down the drive were the three children. Sam was dripping from head to toe, carrying his own shoes in one hand and Leonora's little slippers in the other.

Leonora was riding on Michael's shoulders. Her bare muddy feet hung down. Her frilly dress was sopping, streaked with mud, and her hair, unribboned now, was flopping over a grinning muddy face.

'Like a princess on her elephant,' murmured John at Kitty's side.

'Oh dear, oh dear,' said William, only barely containing his delight. 'We'll have to run baths, John, perhaps it would be better all round if Leonora and her mother stayed at Purley Hall tonight? We can't have the child catching a chill. Will that be in order, Miss Rainbow? John can ride down to Priorton with a note for Joan Wharton.'

Kitty nodded. 'I'd hate her to get a cold, you're right there. Children are dying of these chills. I wouldn't want to take the risk.'

'I know there is no chaperone. Perhaps John could bring Joan Wharton . . .' he offered.

'I am a draper, Mr Scorton. A grown woman. It is my business.'

That night, after all the children were asleep, Kitty and William dined together. John had made some kind of sweet chicken stew and they drank wine from fine crystal, and crumbled cheese as they talked. William told her finally of his wife, who had been sweet and fragile and then had an illness which turned her into a raging vengeful termagant. In the end she had died by her own hand.

She put her hand towards him on the table. 'Poor lady,' she said softly. 'Poor you.'

'I did love her, but the times between have been so

terrible that I have forgotten it. Now there are the boys, who are mostly at school, and my work. Up till now, nothing else.' He put his hand over hers. 'Now there is you. And Leonora, who by some glorious chance I helped into this world.'

The clock on the mantel struck ten.

Kitty folded her napkin. 'It's funny to think I'll be sleeping where Maria Tipton slept so many times.'

'Her room's on the third floor at the back.'

'You should have put me in there.'

He shook his head. 'Not good enough for you. Not good enough for her, in truth.'

'Is it made up, her bed?'

He nodded. 'John keeps the whole house as though we're to be invaded by an army.'

'Can you show me where it is?'

'We'll need a lamp. The gas only goes to the second floor.'

On their way up, they looked in on Leonora, who was fast asleep in the double bed she was to share with Kitty, one leg over the blanket in the hot room. John had banked up the fire. They looked in on the boys, who were asleep in iron bedsteads in the nursery. Incongruously both Samuel and the tall grave Michael clutched wooden soldiers, so old that their bright uniforms had faded to pale grey.

William led the way to the next landing, the lamp throwing up gigantic shadows on the great walls. There he stopped at the third door in the narrow corridor and pushed it. A fire was burning in the narrow grate.

'Are fires kept in all the rooms?' said Kitty incredulously.

'I thought you would wish to see the room. I had John air it. It would have been dusted and aired every time you came, even if you never saw it.'

The narrow iron bedstead was covered with a finely worked quilt which had the oak-leaf border. The curtains pulled across the small window were an exact match. They too had the oak-leaf border, and a row of galloping unicorns.

The floor was covered with quite a fine turkey carpet, worn to its threads just beside the bed. Across a corner stood a washstand with a dark blue washbowl and jug. Beneath that lay a fine mahogany workbox on the top of which the initials M.T., finely worked in brass, gleamed brightly in the firelight.

Kitty squatted down, opened the box, and gulped as the faintly musty smell of lavender drifted towards her. Inside, the silks were in apple-pie order and there was a half-finished collar with the needle stuck in it. It was faintly rusty and infecting the fine lawn with iron mould.

William was looking down at her. 'You take it, Kitty. Take the box back with you. It is yours. See! It has her initials on. Her mother's father was a cabinet-maker, a fine craftsman like my father, and me. But, of course, too lowly for the Tiptons.'

She fingered the letters and watched as her own tears fell on to them. He kneeled down, turned her round and took her in his arms.

'Sweetheart, sweetheart, don't cry. I am sure that wherever she is she is pleased that you've found her.' He kissed her then and she cried more. Then her arms came up round his neck and her tears dried as passion flooded through her body.

He sat back away from her and took off his jacket and necktie and threw them on the bed. She did not stop him as he started to undo the first of many buttons on the bodice of her best grey dress.

They made love there beside the flickering fire on the turkey carpet and as Kitty muttered and cried with pleasure she seemed to hear in chorus the shouts of joy of Maria Tipton, backed by the steady rhythmical beat of a drum.

22

Janine

The rescue of Leonora from the beck cast Michael, the rescuer, in the role of hero; it also cast Sam, who retrieved her shoes from the muddy water, in the role of assistant hero. In this rescue Leonora was transformed from a brat who deserved to be pushed off the branch where she was perched, into a damsel in distress. This made all the difference in the way they perceived the child. After all, as Michael explained to the enraptured Sam, Knights of the Round Table had to respect their damsel in distress.

The next morning Leonora cried when she had to leave the boys and Kitty had to drag her to the waiting trap.

'Stop blubbing, Leonora,' said Michael sternly. 'You can come and play again, can't she, Father?'

William tucked a rug closely round Leonora and Kitty and looked Kitty in the eyes. 'Would you like to come and play again?' he said.

She tucked an errant curl into her bonnet. 'I think so,' she said primly. 'I think that would be very nice.'

'Good. I'll call to see you in the shop tomorrow, on my way back from the workshop.' He stood back.

She smiled and waved, then settled back in the cushions,

ignoring the chattering Leonora, and savouring the thought of the rather tiring but very rewarding night she had spent in Maria Tipton's bedroom.

On her return she found Gabriel lounging against her shop front. He folded his arms and watched them alight. 'Early outing, Kitty Rainbow?'

Kitty unlocked the shop door and Leonora trotted ahead of her. She spoke over her shoulder. 'That's right, Gabriel. Early call.' She put her face through the curtain and shouted for Joan.

He followed her in. 'I came to ask about the woman I brought to you. To ask where to find her.'

She shook her head. 'I don't know. She was going to her sister's in Darlington. She didn't say much.' She scowled at him. 'Who did that terrible thing to her? She had bruises, and her hair was all cut off.'

He put a finger to his lips. 'None of your business. Private affairs. That unfortunate woman brought it on herself, plying her devilish trade. Many of those unfortunates end up with bruises and broken heads. Wasn't your Mrs Druce known for such activities in the old days? The Lord will visit His Wrath on such sinners.'

Kitty removed her bonnet and placed it on the counter. 'Get out of this shop, Gabriel Gullet. You're a vile hypocrite, talking about Janine Druce in that fashion. She's lying upstairs really poorly, and even like that she's worth ten of you. Go and wash your filthy mouth out. I wouldn't put it past you to've had a hand in what was done to that poor woman. The evil was done unto that poor woman, it was not of her doing,' she said through gritted teeth.

He placed a tract on the counter and, on top of it, a fragment of stone which glittered blue and turquoise in the morning light. 'One for you to read and save your soul. The other . . . I thought you'd like it – make a ring to go with the bauble round your neck.'

She fingered the stone. 'Why, Gabriel! This is off the same piece. There was a chip missing. Where did you get it?'

'From a child's jar of finds in the privy where I'm living. They call it *boody*. I thought it worth a guinea of anyone's money.'

'Have you stolen it from a child? Gabriel!'

'The money is for the child, for shoes for him and his brother. It is for him I ask it,' said Gabriel sanctimoniously.

She looked at him, her eyes narrowed. 'How do I know that?'

'If you will not trust a man about the Lord's work you are a weakling, less than the sod beneath my feet.'

She took a guinea from the drawer and gave it to him. 'See the child gets it!' she said. She went round and opened the door wide. 'Now out!'

He went off, whistling, to buy a bottle of whisky and to wait by the steps of Tobias Hunter's offices. Mr Tobias Hunter would be sad to know that the soul he had so assiduously tried to save was still at large. However, others might not understand the altruistic nature of his actions, and for the service of silence which Gabriel was offering, he should make a very generous contribution to the salvation funds. More than a guinea in this case, he thought.

Kitty turned to Joan and asked what kind of night Mrs Druce had had.

'Quiet enough, Miss Rainbow, though sometimes she talks in a right babble, on and on about her Thomas.'

As the season turned, Kitty's relationship with William steadily deepened and she and Leonora became close friends with William's sons. Sometimes it was days, even a week, between the times she and William saw each other, but Sunday tea and an overnight stay at Purley Hall began to be routine. In a town where gossip was the barbed pastime of the kept wives of the trading classes, this regular encounter went unnoticed. Mr Scorton's Egyptian servants were a much less satisfactory source of horrified genteel speculation than were the usual servants at the houses of the gentry. And Joan Wharton kept her mouth very firmly shut.

Then the boys went back to school and Leonora scoured the rooms and corridors of Purley Hall in search of them and returned in tears, finally and reluctantly accepting the elderly Luke as substitute playmate.

Janine did not need to be told what was going on between Kitty and William. But Kitty decided to have a long talk with Ishmael about how important William was to her; that he had proposed marriage and a formal betrothal but that she was not yet ready for that. Mirella, when told of this, veered between delight at such a superior connection between Ishmael's daughter and Mr Scorton of Purley Hall, and concern about the irregularity of the arrangement: the damage to Kitty's reputation would, most probably, prevent any marriage between Kitty and Mr Scorton. 'I'm surprised someone has not come running to me with this tale,' she said.

Ishmael shook his head. 'You in turn must say nothing, Mirella. Kitty has her own way, keeps her own counsel. Her sense of what is right for her, what will be appropriate, is very strong. What other people think is secondary to this.'

Mirella sighed. 'I know that that's your view, but rules do count. People notice . . .' She broke off, seeing the twinkle in Ishmael's eye. She changed tack. 'Mind you, I do wonder what my Esme's up to these days. It's months since we heard from her, not since she went to London. You'd think we'd get some kind of letter, a postcard even. It seems too she hasn't even written to your Kitty, who's supposed to be her best friend.'

Despite what may or may not be being said about Miss Kitty Rainbow over the teacups in Priorton, her draper's shop was flourishing. The extent of her stock and the quality of the work she offered brought more and more customers by word of mouth. She made special arrangements with dressmakers in the villages to channel work and customers in their direction, once the fabrics and patterns had been bought from her. The little section in her shop with puppets and toys brought children in, and with them their mothers, who lingered by the towering shelves of fine fabrics.

One day a previously silent regular customer, buying some dress-caps from her, complimented her on her range. 'I worked for Mr Long, the High Street draper, and he had nothing like the range you have here. I got dismissed 'cos he's losing customers hand over fist now. Pity, that, 'cos that used to be the best draper's in Priorton. But old man Long's lost interest since his wife died. Funny, that, seeing as he was anything but kind to her while she was here. An eye for the ladies, he had. Gone off his dip now, seems like. Wanders in half-dressed, smelling like a stoat. I sent customers by the dozen to you before I was dismissed.'

The next day Kitty herself wandered into Long's Emporium and bought some gloves from an unkempt woman who showed no interest at all in her purchase. She asked for Mr Long but was told sullenly that he was not yet there.

That night, when William called, she asked him how she could go about getting hold of Mr Long's premises.

'I'm sure it should be possible to rent it, to get the lease somehow. I'd make it flourish, William. There's so much space, and with those big windows, think of the display. I could go into ready-made mantles. I'm going to—'

He put a hand on her arm. 'Let me help. I'll get old Toby to look into it, check the lease. Have you some capital?'

She shrugged. 'Money? The shop's doing well, but I've no capital, having to replace stock all the time. That's why the customers keep coming. I might be able to get some money...' She frowned.

He held up a hand. 'Something'll turn up. Let us deal with first things.'

'Does it have to be Mr Hunter? He—'

'Not if you don't want him. It could be any of those partners. I'll ask old Brewster. I'll have something for you on Sunday. You are coming on Sunday, aren't you?' His eyes slid round the empty shop and he kissed her on the cheek.

That Sunday they were in the middle of tea when Tobias Hunter was shown in by John. He flinched, as though from a blow, at the informal domestic scene that greeted him, with Leonora playing with a row of faded wooden soldiers on the hearth rug, Kitty on a chair with the wooden workbox beside her, embroidering a collar, and William in his shirtsleeves at a table, mending a child's clockwork train.

William slipped into his jacket and stood up to shake Hunter's hand. Hunter's glance dropped to Leonora, who was watching him with interest. 'Not observing the Sabbath is a bad example to children, William,' he said sourly. 'No wonder the young fall on evil ways so that their hands soil everything they touch.' He looked directly at Kitty, then down to the workbox.

Kitty folded her collar, put it into the workbox and clicked the lid shut. She stood up with the box under her arm. 'Leonora!' she said sharply. 'I think Leonora and I will go, William.'

'No!' William took Hunter's arm and almost hustled him out of the room. The door clicked closed behind them but even through the thick mahogany Kitty could hear the angry voices rising and falling in vigorous interchange. She sat down, opened the box again and threaded her needle.

William was red in the face when he returned.

She looked at him. 'Am I an embarrassment to you?'

William thrust his hands into his pocket and stood with his back to the fire. 'The man's a maniac. He always was a dry old stick with a bitter streak, but now he's found the Lord he has a whole new lexicon in which to articulate his bitterness.'

'He hates the sight of me. From the first moment. It is an

offence to him that I look like Maria. You would think that
would please him. And now he sees something of us
together he has more cause for hatred. He thinks I'm lower
than a worm.'

William shook his head. 'No, it is more complicated. I
agree with you that from the moment he first saw you, he
saw Maria Tipton in you and I fear that stirred very muddy
waters.'

A cold shiver rippled down Kitty's back. 'Tell me about
Mr Hunter and Maria.'

'He was always here, doing little things for Sir Marcus.
And he followed Maria round the house like a dog. He
recognised the workbox, sitting there beside you. She was
often here in just such a pose. And he was apoplectic that I
gave you the cornelian, which I think was originally found
by her when they were both assisting Sir Marcus with a dig.'
He leaned down and picked the stone up from her neck,
then smoothed it down over her breast. 'Said I had no right
to give it to you.'

'And had you?'

'Every right. I bought the collection from Sir Marcus
when I leased the house. It paid a rather embarrassing
gambling debt for him.'

'And did she like him?' Kitty was tense. 'Did she like him
at all?'

He shook his head. 'Hated him, so far as I can remember.
I was always bumping into her going the other way. She was
always fleeing him.'

Kitty relaxed. 'Good.'

He looked at her and laughed. 'You're still thinking he
might be your father, aren't you?'

'Well . . .'

He leaned down and kissed her nose. 'Not in a thousand
years, my dear girl. He might not be your father, Kitty, but
he brought good news. Old Mr Brewster has taken steps to
acquire the lease for Long's Emporium. It seems it is very

available. It's just dawned on Toby that it was for you and that started him up all over again.'

Leonora was watching them both intently. 'Willy-um kiss the soldier, an' kiss Leonora,' she instructed, holding up the wooden doll.

William sat down on the sofa beside Kitty and patted his knee. 'Come here and we can all have kisses,' he said softly. 'All of us.'

When Kitty got home the following morning there was a chaise at the door and Joan Wharton was wringing her apron in her hands like a dishrag. 'Thank God ye're here, Miss Rainbow. It's Mrs Druce! I got the doctor . . .'

Kitty said quietly, 'You and Leonora go and get Ishmael.' Then she thrust Joan to one side and raced past her, through the shop and upstairs.

Dr O'Kane, who had been visiting Janine in the last month, was just coming out of the bedroom. He drew Kitty to the top of the stairs. 'She's in a very poor way, Miss Rainbow, holding on by a thread. I've made her easy but . . .' He shook his head.

She took off her cloak and bonnet, and dropped them to the floor. Then she breathed deeply, smoothed down her skirt and walked in. Janine was lying very still, a tiny bird-like shape under the green coverlet in the middle of Kitty's bed.

Kitty tiptoed across and Janine opened a single eye. 'So what're yer mincin' about for, hen?' she croaked.

Kitty took her hand. 'How're you feeling, Antijan?'

'Feelin' like I could do with a drop of decent malt, that's what Ah feel like. Nay, not a drop. A bucket!' She tried to laugh, then winced. She closed her eyes and seemed asleep for a few moments. Then she opened them. 'Where's yon Ishmael? He's never around these days. Too busy runnin' after that loud-mouthed pubwife.' Her painful laugh blossomed into a cackle.

'Joan's gone for him, Antijan.'

'I sent that lassie fer someone ter bless us.' She closed her eyes again. Then her mouth started to move. '"The Lord's my shepherd; I shall not want. He maketh me to lie down in ... still waters." Still waters. Still waters...' Then she laughed again. 'What about my Thomas, Kitty? He surprised me. Didn't he surprise them all?' She grasped Kitty's hand tightly. 'Take care of the little bugger, Kitty ... "Still waters ... still waters. He restoreth my soul... My cup runneth over." That Kitty, you know her? She used to hide the stuff, all the bottles. Hide it where I couldn't reach it ... "My cup runneth over... My cup runneth over..."'

The door opened and Ishmael came in on quiet feet. He kneeled beside the bed and took Janine's hand. 'Now, Janine Druce, dear old friend, what is it? What can I do?'

Stiffly she turned her head towards him. Then she smiled. 'Love...' she said. Then she coughed and gurgled in her throat. Then her eyes drained of light and became fixed.

'Oh, Janine Druce,' he said. 'Old friend.' Then he put his head down on the hand he held and wept.

Kitty kneeled beside him and put her arm round his great shoulders and she wept too. They clung together for many minutes like this and stayed wound together as they stood up.

Then Ishmael closed Janine's eyes. Kitty put her foster mother's hands under the green coverlet and pulled it up under her chin. She took a step back. 'She was the only mother I knew, Ishmael. Sometimes I hated her.'

Ishmael held her hand tight. 'She had a heart, Kitty. A tough old overworked Scottish heart.'

A light tap on the door heralded a clergyman whom neither of them recognised. 'Is this where the deceased is?' he said.

They stumbled out of the room and downstairs. Ishmael sat in a chair in the kitchen and put his head in his hands.

Kitty went through to the shop where Joan was sitting on the customers' chair with Leonora on her knee. She looked at Kitty.

Kitty shook her head. 'It's finished,' she said.

'Ye'll have ter shut the shop, Miss Rainbow. Pull the blinds.'

Kitty frowned in puzzlement for the moment, then nodded. 'You do it, Joan,' she said, taking Leonora into her arms and hugging her. 'You do it, if you please.'

The shop was plunged into darkness as Joan pulled the blinds, then bathed in light as she turned up the gas lamp. She pushed something across the counter towards Kitty. 'The postman brought this, Miss Rainbow. I'm sorry but I read it.' Then she started to cry, sobbing and snuffling uncontrollably.

It was a postcard, a view of the Thames bridges. Kitty turned it over and read the message. It was from Esme. 'Please come. Very bad accident. Thomas and Jarrold ill unto death.'

Leonora, unable to tolerate the baffling, unexplained tension and misery around her, started to scream.

PART THREE

The Missing Pieces

23

London Town

'Esme!' The rough, strangled voice emerged from the high bed in the corner of the room.

Esme swung round from the window and leaned over the bed. She took her handkerchief and wiped his brow, then sat down and took his hand. 'You said my name,' she whispered. 'You said my name.'

Three days he'd lain there like a stone. In between rushing backwards and forwards to the theatre she'd taken time to think back over the time they'd been together; how much he really meant to her.

The hand squeezed hers. The head rubbed restlessly on the pillow. The voice struggled out again through the thickened lips. 'Here.'

She lay her face close to his. The face on the infirmary pillow was almost unrecognisable. Every part of it was swollen and misshapen, greasy and glowing with salves. 'Yes, my dearest,' she murmured. 'I'm here. And you'll be all right. I'm certain of it now.'

'Stay here. Always stay.'

'Yes, yes. But just now I'll be away soon for a little while. I've to sing for our supper even more these days. Even more.' The bruised eyes closed and the hand gripping hers slackened. She lifted her head, then stood up, wriggling uncomfortably in the tight stays that squeezed her waist into its near-impossible twenty inches. What a relief it would be to change into her boys' trews and tunic to sing her soldier songs. They were very popular now; she had half the military hanging around her stage door.

The nurse, her angelic white garb contrasting strongly with her raw-meat face, was hovering outside. 'And will you wish to see Mr Pommeroy as well, Miss Rainbow?'

Esme hesitated, then nodded and followed her into the next room.

Jarrold was awake, his face pale, his bushy hair, blue-black, spread out against the white pillow, his bandaged arm and shoulder on top of the white sheet. Esme stood at the end of the bed, wondering briefly who he reminded her of. 'Hello, Jarrold,' she said. 'You'll be pleased to know Thomas has come to. He spoke to me.'

'Esme, dear,' he whispered, ignoring her reference to Thomas. 'I feel guilty lying here. This must all be costing a great deal of money.'

She shrugged. 'I asked where was a good place and they said this. I'm still working, and as you know, I have my savings.'

It had been the savings which had caused all the trouble. Since they had been in London, unlike when they'd been in Leeds, she had drawn her own pay, scrupulously paying Jarrold a shilling for every guinea she earned. For this money he did nothing except come and lounge in her dressing room, and, if she was not otherwise engaged, take her out for a late supper for which she paid.

Some of her money went to pay for her own and Thomas's lodging – which was in a much more modest place than Jarrold had first proposed. With some of the money she bought gowns and shoes, new parasols, and these awful new stays. The rest of the money she'd saved. She was not quite sure why she was so keen to save it.

Perhaps she knew she'd need it if she eventually did marry Jarrold, although the attraction of this idea seemed to be shrinking, now that Jarrold himself was so much keener. His lovemaking, when he was not drunk or in a bullying mood, could still be delightful. But there were horrible times when he seemed like a changed man and he forced her to do bad things. She had finally worked out that if they were married and he had total power over her, these horrible times would be the rule rather than the exception.

So, apart from when she was at the Crystal or one of Mr Cullen's other theatres, she would spend most of her time with Thomas. They would take a cab and walk in the parks. Or they would walk right from the East End into the West End: they would have luncheon in one of the new chophouses, then she would buy some pretty things and Thomas would carry them home for her.

There were hearty men of some wealth and standing who were besotted by her performances and hung around outside her door, even sometimes inside her dressing room, expecting her to be the same chirpy creature offstage as she was on. She would have supper with them and they would be entertained by her quaint Northern talk, her robust sense of humour and the stage-self, a good disguise, which was always to the fore in these encounters. She dined with some of them; she granted others (who entertained her particularly) further limited favours which kept them coming. Jarrold had never discouraged any of this; he saw it as part of the contract of entertainment which was her commitment, their fortune. In the early days he would rub his hands, saying they should both profit from it, one way or another.

Mr Cullen, pleased with her success in all his six halls, treated her with the greatest respect. He had made a single strong bid for personal favours from her but, if anything, her refusal enhanced her value in his eyes. He called her a great little performer, meaning a great little moneymaker, and left it at that.

Recently, Jarrold had uttered the surly complaint that she had spoiled it all by operating on her own behalf. The dole of a shilling in every guinea was not his idea of managing her, of being her patron. The idea that she had a little bag of money saved away somewhere had eaten away at him.

He was gambling again, in clubs where there were people much wilier than he. More than once he had implored her 'just to let me have your savings for a day!' He would double or treble them in no time. He knew of systems . . .

Her constant refusal would send him into a rage which did not turn directly against Esme – she was, after all, the golden goose – but against Thomas, who was always on hand and who was, it now seemed, Esme's chosen companion. Out of sight of Esme, Jarrold would push Thomas around and bully him. This was very unsatisfying, as Thomas would endure all the abuse with profound passivity, then stumble away, throwing off the attack as though Jarrold were an irritating fly.

All this had come to an end one night when Esme returned to their lodgings after a late supper with a rather pressing chap who claimed to be a distant relation of the Duke of Marlborough. She had cut the evening short when he fell off the chair in the supper club and failed to get up again.

As she climbed the steps to their rooms she could hear shouts and thumps from the inside. She flung open the door to find Jarrold and another man holding on to Thomas while a great bully with an unkempt beard was ramming into him with fists like hams.

'Jarrold!' she screamed, raising her umbrella over her head like a sword. When he saw her, Jarrold dropped Thomas, who slumped to the ground, unconscious. Jarrold shot a glance at the other men, who hustled past Esme, out into the foggy night.

'Look, Es! It's nothing. I was just trying to get out of him where your hoard is. I need it tonight or I'll be battered myself. I'd'a had it back for you, and more, by tomorrow.'

She came at him with her umbrella, which he struck out of her hand, letting it fall on the floor. 'Easy, Es, there's no need . . .' He backed away. She followed him. With the edge of her eye she noted the kettle bubbling away on the fire. Thomas always had the kettle bubbling when she came back, no matter how late. They would sit together drinking hot chocolate before they went to their respective beds.

Suddenly Jarrold stopped his retreat and started to come at her, his face transfigured with rage. Her mind darted back to Ishmael, telling her and the grave six-year-old Kitty Rainbow never, never to back down. Your opponent instantly had the upper hand when you backed down.

That was when she picked up the bubbling kettle and flung it at Jarrold. And he screamed. She had never in her life heard such screams.

Kitty leaned against the window of the hansom cab, breathing heavily, her eyes popping out at the heaving mass of people and animals, the tumble of buildings, the press of traffic. For half an hour the cab had been weaving its way through carts and carriages, carrier vans and omnibuses, smart chaises with high-bred horses, and single men riding horses of every size and quality.

Kitty's head buzzed with the noise and clatter.

Frequently the traffic was so gaggled up that the cab had to stop and she had the chance to focus on the pavements, and the openings where the narrow streets flushed into the broader ones. Here people swilled backwards and forwards like so much jetsam; people who by their dress, their every manner and attitude showed that they came from every station in life, from pauper to peer.

At one point she leaned right out of the window to get a clearer view of a whole line of shops which sported fine gold lettering and striped canopies against the sun. Kitty smiled to herself at the vanity of the sun canopies. How could sunlight penetrate the dense dark air of this beehive of a city – air which seemed to reach down with its grey insalubrious tongue to lick the very pavement?

She caught sight of two wasp-waisted high-hatted young women being assisted into a monogrammed cab by a white-gloved footman, outside a shop which stretched right round a corner and had ten cathedral-sized windows. Each window showed off some aspect of the goods for sale inside: mantles, costumes and dolmans in one window; prints, dress goods and heavy drapery in the next; bags and purse-bags, boots, gloves and umbrellas in another; then carpets, bedding, bedsteads; beautiful china vases, pedestal pots, figures and plaques... And so on. She caught her breath. This shop must sell everything. What it must be to own such a place.

Then she saw a woman with a tipsy hat and a shawl singing in a dark corner, a tin cup held out for pennies, and was reminded of Janine. She fingered the black mourning brooch: a thoughtful present from William. Her cornelian pendant hung unseen inside her black blouse. Janine's funeral had been strange: a brief service conducted in a distracted manner by the supercilious clergyman. This had been followed by a subdued gathering in a Back Room at the George. Kitty sat in a chair beside Ishmael and a surprising number of people came to pay their respects, from tradesmen and country dressmakers to odd people who staggered a little and wore clothes barely better than rags. Mr Goldstein came, as did Kitty's old teacher, Miss Philomena Adams.

Kitty thought how much she would miss Janine. What battles they'd had when she was small! And how strange and precious were these latter days with Janine sitting in the corner, her 'self' ground down almost to pure spirit before her body gave in.

Kitty's mind moved to Thomas. How would she tell him? Would he understand? Would he care? How was he? A letter had come from Esme on the heels of the card, saying that it wasn't after all 'unto death', although Thomas had had a very bad beating and Jarrold had had a very bad scalding. But please, please could she come as it was all too hard to bear?

The plea was irresistible. Kitty had started rescuing Esme when she was six and she was not stopping now. She smiled at her own childish thought. But it was true that, in the process of their lives, she and Esme had somehow become sisters, just as she and Ishmael had somehow become father and daughter. The same had not quite happened with Janine, who had spun her own distracted web in life which had Thomas at its centre and no space for a mere foundling. But in these recent months Kitty had felt almost like Janine's mother, as she helped her endure the pain that visited her daily, sitting with her in the corner by the window.

The shifts and movements in Kitty's life had locked a kind of family around her. She fingered her cornelian pendant. And now she had her real mother locked in her imagination, and William begging her to be his family. Patterns were forming and reforming all around. There were choices. She had chosen Ishmael and, in the end, Janine. She had chosen to embrace Maria Tipton and think of her as mother, and somehow Maria had reached from wherever she was and reciprocated her choice. William had chosen her, despite the social setup in Priorton which would frown on him.

The missing piece in the pattern was the man who had fathered her. She was just recovering from the shuddering possibility that it might be the slinking Tobias Hunter. But the act of resisting the image of that man as her father had roused her curiosity about the man who truly was her father. Where did she get her small stature and her dark colouring?

Maria Tipton was tall and willowy, her colouring non-descript, much fairer than Kitty's.

Kitty shook away these thoughts and knocked with her parasol for the cab-driver and asked him how long now to Merridew Court. He gabbled something in his impenetrable lingo, which had buried at its depths the notion of five minutes, *miliydy*.

The hansom finally came to a stop by an archway, behind which all was dark as ink. The smell reminded Kitty of Forgan Buildings. She'd thought Esme would live in a much grander place. The driver, a squat man with a keen face, pointed with his whip.

'Down *v*ere, yer *liydyship*. Number twenty-three'd be on the right. But ask some cove. Anyone'd tell yer. Can't get me 'ansom down there.' He tipped his tall cap. She heaved her valise to the ground and held out her hand with coins in it. His fingers hovered over it, then he took sixpence. He closed a heavy hand over hers and said, 'Aw cuuda tikin *v*e lot, yer *liydyship*. Git ter know *v*e fare afore ye git in, 'at's my advice. *V*ere's crimpin' coves all over *v*is benighted city.'

The area was like a rabbit warren. Kitty had to weave her way through two dark courts and down two dark alleys, before finally arriving at Merridew Court. She flinched at every out-jutting wall, more frightened here than at any time back in Priorton. Her nervous questions of passers-by finally led her to a dusty chandler's shop on a corner. Beside it was an outside staircase which led up to a heavy door. This must be it. She climbed the stone stairs and knocked tentatively. She jumped back as the door was opened immediately and the light streamed out into the darkness. Then she was engulfed in Esme's embrace, all silk and scent.

'Kitty, Kitty Rainbow. You came. I didn't believe that you would. You came.'

'You seemed so upset. Even in the second letter. And I've bad news to deliver myself.'

'But you're here now!' Esme dragged her inside. 'Look, Thomas, here's Kitty.'

The room was small but neat. There was a cheerful fire, a table with a crystal vase of chrysanthemums, still with a dedication card attached, a wooden bench and two chairs. On one of these sat Thomas, his piano-accordion upended on his knee, a small screwdriver in his hand. He looked up at Kitty and nodded slowly. 'Kitty,' he said gruffly. His face was bruised and his brow was bandaged. His head went back down over his work.

Kitty kneeled beside him and took the screwdriver from him. She put a hand on his heavily bruised face. 'Oh, Thomas, what have you been up to? Your beautiful face.'

'It was Jarrold,' said Esme. 'He got some bruisers to give him a pummelling.'

'Why? Why do this to poor Thomas?'

Esme shrugged. 'I think he wanted to get at my savings. And perhaps Jarrold's jealous that Thomas can make sweet music on that thing and he c'n do nothing useful.'

Kitty's eyes narrowed. 'And what happened to him? To Jarrold?'

'He was scalded. Quite badly. Very badly, as it happened.' Esme grimaced.

Kitty looked hard at her for a second. 'Thomas?'

Thomas was scrabbling at Kitty's hand to retrieve his screwdriver. Esme stood behind him and put a hand on his shoulder. 'Thomas? He wouldn't hurt a flea. You know that.'

'It was an accident?'

Esme shook her head. 'I did it.'

Kitty put her hand to her mouth. 'Esme!'

'I know.' Her eyes filled with tears. 'But I was so angry, Kit. So frightened.'

'Poor Esme.' Kitty stood up and put an arm round her shoulder.

Clumsily, Thomas put his piano accordion on the floor

and stood up. Then, his arms stiff as the branches of a tree, he put them around both women and his face beside Esme's, so that the tears fell down his cheeks as well as hers.

'Thomas!' said Kitty. 'Look at you. Actually crying. Janine would have been so pleased.'

Esme mopped her tears and his with a fine handkerchief. She eyed Kitty's black dress and cloak; her black bonnet. 'Would have been? You said you had bad news. I should have realised, Kitty.'

Kitty nodded and took Thomas's arm. 'Sit down, Thomas.'

Thomas listened to her stumbling words with his eyes averted. When she had finished he leaned down and picked up his instrument and the screwdriver, which lay beside it, and very carefully began to tighten the screws. 'Mam,' he said slowly.

Kitty glanced at Esme. 'Does he realise?' She sat down at the table.

Esme shrugged. 'Sometimes he catches on much more than we think. But I don't really know when he does and when he doesn't. Come, sit down, Kit. I'll pour you some sherry wine.' She placed it on the table beside Kitty, where it remained untouched.

Silence ticked away in the room, broken only by the clicking and scraping of Thomas's screwdriver.

Finally Kitty stirred and took a sip of the sherry wine. 'And Jarrold, Esme. How is he?'

'He's recovering quite well. It was mostly his shoulder and his arm. I enquire each day though I cannot bear to see him.'

'He must blame you . . .'

'Well, it was me that did it so he'd not be wrong to do that. He doesn't mention that, though. Goes on all the time about "the accident". Seems almost frightened of me. Didn't go to the constable. But the way I caught him looking at me – sometimes I think he hates me like poison. I know now he never thought anything of me. Just used me. Called me the goose.'

'The goose?'

'The goose which lays the golden eggs. Remember the fairy story?'

'Horrible man.'

'You'll be pleased to know I agree with you now. But Kit, I have to get ready to go to the theatre. You must come with me tonight. See Miss Esther Rainbow in action.'

'Miss Esther Rainbow? I'd forgotten all about that – you with my name.'

Esme shook her head frowning. 'What a thing I did to you, stealing your name. It was Jarrold, of course, pushing and pushing me. Now I'm stuck with it; it's on all the bills, and that's what I'm known as. People like it. Everybody calls me Miss Esther.'

Kitty laughed. 'Well, my name's not just Rainbow now. I was christened. It's Catherine Maria Tipton Rainbow.'

'And where did all that come from?'

She told Esme about Maria and showed her the cornelian pendant. Esme grabbed it. 'And who is this William who lives in this hall? William this and William that. His name's never off your lips.'

Kitty blushed. 'We're close . . . friends. He's asked me to marry him.'

Esme sat down opposite her, pins in her mouth, fixing her hat. 'And you will?'

Kitty shook her head. 'I've said no so far. I'm not sure why. Maybe, having found me real mother I want to find me real father first. There's something not quite right yet. Oh!' She raked around in her valise. 'I brought something for you. I forgot.' She handed Esme a white unicorn, the twin to that she had made for Leonora out of cloth. 'I started to make it when you first wrote that letter, then it got put away. You know you wrote and said you never saw the unicorn? I finished it on the train.'

Esme hugged it to her and smiled. 'Good of you to think about me in the middle of all this trouble.'

'I always think of you, Es.'

The clock struck six and Esme jumped out of her chair, still clutching her unicorn. 'Late! I'm so late. Kitty, come with me. I'm having to manage without Thomas, so you can be in the front row and be my inspiration. I've a cab waiting by the arch at six.'

Five minutes later they were making their way back through the courts. Gas lamps illuminated two corners and a couple of windows were lit, shedding a small glow in their immediate area, but intensifying the darkness beyond. Kitty was aware of people hovering just beyond the range of the light, women in dresses only, despite the cold night. Small ragged children played in a pool of light from a gas lamp, some game which involved throwing stones along the gutter. Esme dropped three pennies in their midst and forgetting their game, they scrambled to retrieve them.

'Hey, fanks, Miss Rainbow, fanks!' said the tallest one earnestly. 'Bless yer, ma'am!'

One woman called out, 'Evenin', Miss Rainbow!' Another called, 'Evenin', Miss Esther. Sing one for old Dolly, will yer, darlin'? Giv'm 'ell, those *cratures*. Giv'm 'ell.'

'How can you live here, Esme?' said Kitty crossly. 'This is as bad as Forgan Buildings.'

'Worse, dear heart. Worse. Things you would not think of. But you lived a decent enough life at Forgan and me and Thomas can here. Nobody bothers about us. Lovers, sister and brother – they don't ask those questions. You should have met some landladies we've had! Filthy minds; half the time terrified of Thomas, the other half terrifying him so that he hid under the beds. Here, we're invisible. There's much worse than him down here. No poking, prying eyes.'

Kitty did not quite know how to frame the question on her lips. It would have been so easy to sound like one of the prying landladies. They watched as a woman linked arms with a man and vanished down an alley. 'Do you know what they charge?' said Esme. 'Fourpence! The price of a night in the lodging house. Poor rags. What a life. In the paper they're called "unfortunates". Did you know that? Now that's an understatement.' She put her arm through Kitty's. 'We're lucky, you and me. We've other ways of making money and we can call our souls our own.'

'Hey! Miss Rainbow,' one of the women called across. 'Ain't yer forgot yer music man?'

They swung round to see Thomas limping behind them, in his cloak and hat, swinging his accordion in its leather case. They waited for him, then with Esme linking him, and Kitty linking her, the three of them made their way to the waiting hansom cab.

24

Showtime

'Drat it,' said Esme through the side of her mouth. 'Didn't think the old goat'd be here tonight.' Then she switched on a smile like a torch beam and put out her hand. 'Mr Cullen! How wonderful to see you!'

He brought her hand to his thick lips. 'Miss Esther, my ears ring with reports of the elegance, the charm of your performances. I can see we'll have to see about top of the bill. Top of the bill!' He waved a hand towards Thomas. 'And your accompanist. A wizard on the piano accordion, my musicians tell me. Perhaps a spot for himself?'

Esme shook her head. 'He will not perform without me, Mr Cullen. We are a pair.'

His eyes narrowed, almost vanishing into his head. 'I hear this also. Such remarkable loyalty, such possessive passion, my dear.' He put his cigar back in his mouth. 'And how *is* poor Jarrold? I heard that he was seriously ill.'

'Picking up by the day, Mr Cullen, picking up,' she said smoothly.

His heavy-lidded gaze moved to her companion. 'And who have we here?'

'May I present Miss Kitty Rainbow?'

'You must be Miss Esme's sister.' He took Kitty's hand and for one awful moment she thought he was about to kiss it. 'Although you do not look it, pretty as you are. Do you sing? Do you dance?'

She dragged her hand away from his. 'No, sir,' she said. 'I'm not her sister. Neither do I sing nor dance.'

Esme put an arm through hers. 'We are sisters by choice, Mr Cullen. Kitty's the daughter of the rainbow. Her father was the great boxer Ishmael Slaughter and he named her so. When I wanted a name to put on your bills, I borrowed hers, and it was she who put me on a stage and made me perform. So she started all this. She gave me courage.'

'Ah courage! We all need courage. So you put on shows, Miss Kitty? And is that what you do? There are fine halls up there. Sunderland, Newcastle, Gateshead . . .'

She shook her head. 'We were children then. I know nothing of all that. I am a draper by profession,' she said.

His eyes moved from her then and landed on the Italian tenor, top of the bill this week, a fat man whose cloak and hat were too large for him. 'Ah, Signor . . . a moment.' He turned back to Kitty. 'I will keep a seat for you beside me, Miss Rainbow. Left-hand side, front row.'

Esther pulled Kitty into the tiny cubicle which was her dressing room, pushed her on to a little stool, then leaned towards the mirror to take off her hat without disturbing too much of her high-piled hair. Then she pushed Thomas out of the door and told him to go and have a little play with Mr Coyne, the timpanist, who liked Thomas's accordion playing.

'How can you put up with all that flannel from that feller Cullen, Es?'

Esther shrugged. 'There's a lot of that, him and others: the manager of this theatre; mashers who hang around to slaver at the end of the performance – donkeys the lot of them. I'd rather have Thomas any day. No flannelling there. But you have to go along with them a bit, Kitty. All a kind of game, really.' As she talked she was stripping down to her corset. 'Now then, Kit. What about Janine Druce? Was she so desperately . . . ?'

'Well, Esme, she died.'

'You know what I mean.'

Kitty watched Esme through the mirror. 'She's been poorly with this consumptive thing for months. But lively and sharp. Then suddenly she seemed to shrivel, become almost transparent. If I'd known I'd've sent for Thomas, but she'd been frail for months. That's my biggest regret, that I didn't get him there. It was sudden, really.'

'I don't know that Thomas would have been much use . . . you saw his reaction.'

'Yes, but she'd've seen him. She needed him. She talked about him a lot at the end. Ishmael was very upset, really upset. I think he knew her better than anyone.'

Esme stood with her back to Kitty and took hold of the shelf on which her mirror stood. 'Can you loosen these strings on my corset and pull me in a bit more, Kit?'

Kitty put her knee on Esme's bottom and pulled hard at the strings, grunting as she did so. 'How you put up with this I don't know. It must be torture.'

'It's all right for you, Kit. You must have a sixteen-inch waist before you start. We bigger girls have got to make more sacrifices. It's not so bad in the second half; I get to wear the boy's clothes then, and they're so deliciously comfortable. So . . .' She pulled on a small sprung-wire crinoline, then two petticoats, then over these she slipped on a blue taffeta gown, which was low at the neck, and had dozens of deep frills at the hem. 'And what about you? How did you manage yourself with this happening to Janine Druce?'

'We were good friends at the end. She was always a puzzle to me, Antijan. Sometimes she was wonderful – funny and sharp. And a great draper, knew cloths, oh she knew cloths. But . . .'

'Then there was the drink.' Esme was leaning into the mirror and skillfully applying rouge to her cheeks and her lips.

'Yes. And then she was wild and pathetic in bouts. At those times, at worst I hated her, at best I was sorry for her. But I loved her at the end.' She blew her nose. 'That's a lovely frock, Es. Fine material.'

'I bought it from Monsieur Chanson, in the West End of the city.' Carefully, she placed a tiny hat, almost like an upside-down plant pot of flowers on her piled hair. 'I'll take you there . . .'

'Esme, that hat!' Kitty spluttered.

'Well, this, my dear, is for stage purposes only. Unlike the frock, I do not wear it off the stage.'

There was a knock on the door.

Esme took Kitty by the shoulders and steered her towards it. 'Now, my dear, you can go out there and sit beside the old goat. And if he gets an attack of the roaming hands, give him a slap. Don't worry, he likes it. They all do.'

Later, Kitty sat in the crowded hall, entranced. Up above the smoky lights Esme became even more of a different person than she had when Kitty had last seen her performance. Beautiful and commanding, she was dramatic, poignant, appealing, authoritative, funny and acerbic in turns. The crowd applauded for more, more! Mr Cullen, sitting beside Kitty, called the loudest of all.

When, as the curtains finally closed, the orchestra played the last strains of her encore tune and the chairman was taking up his gavel again, Mr Cullen whispered too close to Kitty's ear, 'Such talent, my dear. Your sister will be famous: a great star, you watch my words.'

Kitty leaned and whispered into his ear, 'I'm sure you're right, Mr Cullen, but if you don't take your hand off my knee I'll give you a black eye.'

The hand was removed instantly. He chuckled. 'You two

sisters chose each other well, my dear; twin souls, I would say.'

After the show, throwing off the attentions of various men, including Mr Cullen, Esme and Kitty, with Thomas in tow, took a cab straight back to Merridew Court. Inside, Esme poured them all tea in china cups and showed Kitty where she would sleep. It was a little room off the lobby which was bare of any sign of human habitation. 'It's Thomas's bedroom,' said Esme.

Kitty looked round. 'Where will he sleep?'

Esme looked her in the eye. 'With me,' she said simply. 'He has since he came out of the infirmary. He cried, so I took him in my bed.'

Kitty's cheeks were flaming. 'Esme, you can't ... he isn't ...'

'He's fine. He wants nothing from me other than an arm around him, a hand on his brow when he shivers. That's it.'

'Esme ...'

'I like it too,' she said defiantly. 'I think I love him, the great galoot – more than I've loved anyone, perhaps with the exception of yourself.'

'But what about the future, what if you meet someone?'

'Someone? Someone like my dear brother, Gabriel? Or Jarrold? Or that old goat Cullen? Or these dandies who want a nice little *gel* to warm their bed while they wait for some snooty lass with a fond daddy and a heap of gold?'

'What if, one day, Thomas wants ... what other men want?'

Esme shrugged. 'Then I'll probably give it to him with pleasure. And welcome him to the world of the grown-ups. I may even marry him.'

Kitty shook her head. 'You're serious, aren't you?'

Esme nodded. 'I told you. I think I love him. And it wouldn't be such a bad thing. He is a fine accordionist – you heard old Cullen. He's just a bit quiet, that's all. You know

309

the old nursery rhyme. "Rings on her fingers and bells on her toes, she shall have music wherever she goes." That's me. Anyway, you've got your William . . . whatever his name is.'

Kitty frowned. 'I haven't *got* him. I told you, I don't know whether I *want* him in the marriage way.' As she said the words they sounded true in her own ears.

Later, lying in Thomas's narrow bed, Kitty came to the conclusion that the relationship between Esme and Thomas, strange as it was, was profoundly necessary to Esme. Much more necessary than Esme's relationship with Jarrold Pommeroy had ever been.

Kitty pulled the blanket up under her chin. Esme's trials had changed her. She was harder, stronger, and something of a stranger to Kitty. Kitty turned over and rubbed her head into the hard pillow. Probably she herself had changed. A great deal had happened since they'd put on the show in front of the blanket curtain for the ragged children of Forgan Buildings. But as they had changed, so had their friendship, and it seemed to be surviving as strong as ever. She wondered if this was really what it was like, to be sisters.

The next day, with Thomas in tow, they went to the West End of the city and trawled the shops. Esme took Kitty to Monsieur Chanson's and bought her a suit in finest black broadcloth. 'I know you're in mourning but even in mourning you can be smart.' The jacket was closely fitted with frogging in velvet. And the skirt had the fashionable smaller bustle and immaculate tucking right round the hem.

Esme had the salesgirl parcel up Kitty's own clothes and handed the parcel to the waiting Thomas. Then they went to Mrs Fentimen, Esme's milliner, who produced a black narrow-brimmed hat with the smallest of veils and a sliver of silver-grey grosgrain ribbon round the crown.

Esme stood back and viewed her creation. 'My dear, you look a treat. A treat!'

Kitty looked at herself in the mirror and an elegant stranger looked out. She grinned. 'I like it!'

'Now, to Cartland and Cooper's. You must not miss this.'

Cartland and Cooper's was the great emporium Kitty had seen from her cab when she had first arrived. Thomas stood outside and the two of them made a grand progress through the departments, with Esme buying material here, a tablecloth there, and examining china and cutlery with dramatically close interest before telling them to wrap it up and to deliver it to her mother, Mrs Mirella Gullet, The Royal George, Priorton, County Durham.

When they got back out on to the pavement Kitty spluttered with laughter. 'You were very grand in there, Es. It's just like you were on the stage all the time.'

Esme handed her parcels to Thomas and tucked her arm in Kitty's. 'I've found, Kit, that in this city this is what works. They all do it. They're all performing on some stage or another, even the ones who never get near a music hall or theatre. And those salesgirls, they love you to be grand, to pat their head and give them little tasks, to smile sweetly and make their day.'

Kitty shook her head. This cynical side of Esme made her uneasy. 'It might be you serving behind those counters. Or me.'

'But it isn't you or me, Kitty. We're the ones doing the paying. That's why I live in Merridew Court and squirrel my money away. Don't you see? So I can be grand when I choose.'

Kitty shook her head slowly. 'But how do you know when it's you there, Es, not the elegant Miss Esther Rainbow, second top of the bill?'

'Well, Kit, sometimes I like it better to be Miss Esther. Esme was such a clot, wasn't she?'

'I liked her, that Esme. From the moment I saw her being tumbled about by Gabriel and those Grammar School boys. I liked her better than Miss Esther Rainbow lording it over a few little shopgirls.'

Kitty was suddenly tired with all the walking, and her leg was aching. Her right shoe, so carefully built· up on Ishmael's design, was becoming worn down with the hard city streets, and her limp was returning. 'Come on, Esme, let's go home, or whatever it is you call that rabbit warren in Whitechapel.'

Someone was bashing the privy door with great clouts. Gabriel jumped, hugging the whisky bottle to his chest. 'What is it?' he growled.

'Get thee into the open, sinner!' Tom Vart's voice came through the battered panel. 'Drinking the milk of Satan. Hypocrite! Blaming the good folk and gorging yourself. Are ye not more dissolute than any because of your deception?'

Gabriel looked at his whisky bottle and considered disposing of it down the hole. Then the thought of good whisky down there amongst all that filth made him shudder. He stood up, straightened his jacket and tucked the bottle inside it. Then he unbolted the door. 'What is it, Mr Vart?' he grumbled. 'What's all this row about?'

Tom Vart leaned towards him. 'I can smell it on you, that devil's brew.'

'I tell you you're mistaken, Mr Vart,' he mumbled, suddenly feeling very, very weary.

'There I am in the town, reminding men of their weakness and imploring them to turn from Satan's ways and I am buttonholed by the landlord of the Centurion, who tells me my companion, my soulmate, is his best customer for that devil's brew! And I stand here now, with its stench in my nostrils.' Vart's eyes were full of tears and he dropped into the dust in the back lane. 'Kneel with me, brother, kneel and ask forgiveness of Him who sees all, forgives all. Prostrate thyself. . .' He closed his eyes and started to mutter.

Gabriel looked down at Vart's bowed head and his scrubbed-clean neck, then left him there in the dust, muttering some bowdlerised act of shared contrition. It dawned on Gabriel that this man believed all this *bosh*; old Vart really did think he was going to Heaven on the backs of the souls he had saved. He must have had an experience, must have really 'seen the light' as it said in the hymn, to go on like that.

Gabriel shook his head to clear it of the whisky-fug. Of course, there was some kind of God. He knew that. It was unthinkable that there wouldn't be a God. Hadn't he sung hymns, read Bibles and seen pictures which told him so? But there was time enough to think of all that when he was old and grey and had no other preoccupations.

He crept back into the house and pushed his things into a battered velvet gownsack he had stolen, years before, from the lawyer's office. 'Time to go, Gabriel old boy,' he muttered. 'Time to go. You've been saved long enough.'

Later that day, on his way into his mother's kitchen, Gabriel tripped over a toy donkey and cart made from wood, leather and felt. His mother looked up from her chair by the fire, where she was nursing a lanky, mop-headed child who was fast asleep across her knee.

'Gabriel! Ssh!' She put her finger to her lips.

'What? What? So who're we grandmother to now, Mother dear?'

Mirella pushed a damp curl off Leonora's forehead. 'It's the child of Kitty Rainbow, who's in London now visiting your sister. Ishmael and I thought we could do no less than look after the babe.'

'Do you think that, Ishmael and you?' He sat on the edge of the kitchen table. 'So, how goes the affairs at the Royal George, Mother?'

'Well, seeing that you ask. Mabella and her Ruby have cleaned the place from top to bottom. Ishmael's sorted out the beer, and done deals with our suppliers. And he's got our old barmen back now our customers are returning. And the money is flowing into the till rather than out of it.'

'Good thing you got yourself on your feet again, Ma. This place needs your steady hand.'

She looked at him over her glasses. 'What is it you want, Gabriel?'

'Just a pillow for my weary head, just for a few nights.'

Ishmael, coming through from the bar parlour, stopped in the kitchen doorway and leaned on the doorjamb.

Mirella did not need his admonition. She was shaking her head already. 'No, Gabriel. You know what Ishmael said last time. And it's because of him that the George is not closed and shuttered now.'

'Just one night, Mama.'

'No. There's not room. Ishmael has Esme's room, and Mabella has the baby in with her in your room.'

His eye dropped to the sleeping head of Leonora. 'More room for a bastard child than for your own son,' he said bitterly.

Mirella raised her hand to stop Ishmael from picking up Gabriel by the scruff of his neck. She stared sadly at her son. 'Room in my heart, son, but not room in my house.' She reached into the purse which hung from her belt by a golden chain and put five guineas on to the palm of her hand. 'Here you are, son. There's more than a night's lodging there.'

He looked at it, then reached out and grabbed it and put it in his breeches pocket. 'By rights I should be here at your side, master of the George.'

Ishmael growled. 'You forfeited that right when you turned it into a bawdy house.'

Gabriel turned on his heel and stomped off, not unsatisfied with the plaintive note in his mother's voice as she called after him.

Ishmael came over and put a hand on Mirella's shoulder. 'You're a good woman, Mirella. In your own way.'

She touched his hand with hers. 'I'm learning much in my old age, Ishmael.'

Leonora stirred and reached up to bring Mirella's hand back down across her.

'The little one has taken to you,' Ishmael said.

'She could charm the birds off the trees. It'd be hard not to l . . . like her.'

'Do you know, long ago I thought if I brought Kitty here as a little one you would drown her?'

Mirella frowned. 'Drown her?'

'Just like you drowned my kittens. In a rusty tin bath.'

She laughed. 'Ishmael, I might then, as now, have been a bit of a silly woman, but even I know the difference between a child and a kitten.'

Tobias Hunter was not pleased when Gabriel pushed past his housekeeper to announce himself.

'Mr Gullet, I don't think . . .' Hunter stood up from his leather chair.

'I need a bed for the night, Mr Hunter. I felt sure that, in this great big house you would have space for a sinner like me.'

'Then you feel wrong, Mr Gullet.'

'Show some Christian charity, Mr Hunter. I cannot believe my ears here.' He paused. 'Do you know, I was thinking of writing a pamphlet about the fine work accomplished in the town, in the saving of fallen women? There are many hereabouts who would savour such a work, I feel sure . . .'

Hunter waved an impatient hand at the housekeeper, who stumped off.

'I forget,' said Gabriel smoothly, 'the lady's deaf as a post. Very convenient, shouldn't wonder.'

Hunter put his chin up. 'I resent your insolent tone, sir.' He coughed. 'However, if you are without a place to lay your head as you say, Christian charity demands—'

Gabriel threw himself into a chair beside the fire. 'Good man. Now is there such a thing as a decent glass of brandy in this God-fearing house?'

25

Sick Visiting

Kitty had never been into a hospital. Janine, in her final illness, had refused point-blank to go into one, saying that she was 'gannin' inter nae workuss, thank yer, doctor.'

The coolness and quietness of this London hospital unnerved Kitty. The polished corridors echoed her every step. She made an enquiry, and a man in some kind of uniform led her up a broad sweeping stairway. He pointed the way along a corridor and said she was to go to the room at the end.

Halfway down the corridor she was waylaid by a nurse, a strongly made woman with a red face. 'Yes?'

'I've come to see Mr Pommeroy.'

The nurse looked her up and down. 'You'll be his daughter, I suppose.'

'No.' Then she told a convenient lie. 'I'm ... sister to his friend Miss Rainbow. I'm Miss Kitty Rainbow.'

Esme had begged her to come, to see how Jarrold was. A combination of guilt at the terrible thing she had done, and loathing for what Jarrold had done to Thomas, made it hard for her to see Jarrold herself. But, she told Kitty that she was still concerned about him. 'Only for a split second did I really want him dead, Kit.'

Now the nurse was looking at her through narrowed eyes. 'Well, Miss Rainbow, Mr Pommeroy's asleep. It may not be my place to say it, miss, but I think the poor man has lacked the tender attention from loved ones which is the greatest medicine in the world.'

Kitty raised her eyebrows. It seemed that, even from his sickbed, Jarrold had practised his charm on the red-faced nurse. 'Well, nurse, I'm just down from the North myself, and his friend Miss G— ... Rainbow is very hard pressed with her performances in the theatre. She's resting this afternoon. She asked me to come in her stead.'

The nurse nodded sulkily and pushed open the narrow door. The room was drenched in a kind of daytime dusk because the curtains were fully closed. Kitty could just make out Jarrold's long shrouded shape on the bed.

The nurse opened the curtains very slightly. 'Sit quietly, if you please,' she instructed as she stumped out. 'Mr Pommeroy needs all the rest he can get.'

Kitty stood by the curtained window and gazed across at Jarrold. His bandaged arm was out on the coverlet. His face lay to one side, his mouth slack. He looked innocent, younger than his years.

Her mind moved to Leonora, and how much she was missing, aching for, her daughter. She would wake up in Merridew Court and look for the little hump in the bed beside her. Out in the endless city streets, she would glance down past her elbow, looking for Leonora's small trotting figure which had always been at her side.

This very morning she had received an elegantly scripted letter from Mirella, saying how grateful she was that Kitty had gone to Esme's aid. She proceeded to tell her what fine times she, Ishmael and Leonora were having, how good the child was, a pleasure to take care of. She was not to worry about her. Mirella had also reported that on her visits to

Rainbow's Drapery everything seemed in order. Could Kitty believe it? One day she had actually come across Mr William Scorton himself behind the counter, giving some assistance to Joan Wharton and her sister Kezia!

Kitty had had no word from William himself. Of course he had assured her before she came away that the shop would be fine, he would keep an eye on it. He would make sure Joan Wharton wanted for nothing. Kitty knew he would keep his word, but she had thought he would write.

'Esme? Is that you?' The whispering voice came from the bed.

Kitty came across and stood beside him. 'No, Jarrold. It's me. How are you?'

'Miss Kitty! How amazing.' He managed to inject a sarcastic tone into his sick man's whisper. 'This is a surprise. I wouldn't've thought you'd have any regard for my welfare.'

'Well, you're wrong there, Jarrold. I wish you no ill in the world and I hope you return to good health. If I'd found you beating our Thomas like that, mind, I'd have given you a black eye myself. But not...' She looked at the heavily bandaged arm and shoulder.

'It was an accident. I fell against the fireplace,' he said, blandly meeting her gaze.

She frowned at him, uncertain how to take this. Was he protecting Esme? Had the pain been so bad he had forgotten what happened? She looked at his eyes, which were both veiled and knowing, and realised that, even in his illness, this perpetual schemer had some ruse going. Perhaps he thought that Esme had put herself into his power by doing this dreadful thing: that he could use her guilty feelings to pull her back into his web.

Jarrold pulled himself up further on the pillows and winced. 'And how is my dear Esme?' he said, conjuring up an eerie heartiness.

319

'She's very busy, Jarrold. Two shows each evening and that Mr Whatshisname is talking about top of the bill for her now.'

'Good! Good! You must be proud of your friend, Miss Kitty.'

Kitty looked at him warily. 'So I am! What do you think of her?'

'I'm proud of her too, Kitty.' His voice hardened. 'And proud of the help I've given her to get her where she is. And I feel when we get over this little difficulty I'm sure we'll be back on our old footing.' He winced again. 'I can see you looking at me with a cold eye again. Never liked me, did you?'

She shook her head. 'No.'

'But think about it straight, Kitty, me and Esme've been part of each others' lives for years now. We enjoy each other's company. We're good for each other. Me, I've been on the loose, travelling, all my life. Esme is the first person I've stuck to in all that time. She's my only friend in the world. Oh! I know I went too far with the squeezebox player. But always, always, the feller's in the way. Made me lose my rag, you know?'

The words came far too easily. He was scheming again. Kitty folded her arms.

He frowned at her. 'You tell her to come and see me, d'you hear?' His voice was rising, more like the hectoring tone of the old Jarrold. 'Tell her she has to come to see me, or I'll come to see her, and she won't half know it!' He was shouting now.

The door swung open. 'Mr Pommeroy, Mr Pommeroy! Please, please calm down.' The nurse was patting his shoulder and adjusting his pillows, so he could lie down again. He took her hand. She turned angrily on Kitty. 'And you, miss, I advise you to go. Your presence is doing my patient no good at all.'

As she walked to the gates of the hospital and caught a

tram Kitty found to her surprise that she felt sorry for Jarrold Pommeroy. He was a sick man, and very desperate. He had lived a life where, apart from Esme, he had no close confidants, no friends, no family. Then, when, admittedly as a consequence of his own actions, the one person who had cared for him just a little turned on him and threw a kettle of water on him, he had been left alone in a dark little room at the end of a corridor.

He was frightened.

Kitty said as much to Esme when she got back to Merridew Court.

Esme looked at her in astonishment. 'Now there's a book turning a page! You can't, couldn't, stand the sight of him, Kitty! Hated me to be with him.'

Kitty nodded her head. 'That's true. I did. Do, even now. And, doing that thing to Thomas, he deserved nobody to bother about him ever again. But I do think he's truly frightened, Esme.'

Esme turned back to her mirror, and finished applying a final faint dab of rouge. 'There, what do you think, Kit? Will I do?'

Kitty tapped her shoulder with her gloves. 'Es, if I didn't know you better, I'd say you've grown entirely selfish.'

Esme shook her head. 'Me and Thomas have been out here among the ravening wolves on our own too long. We've decided now that we will only look out for ourselves, haven't we, Thomas?' She went and put her arm through Thomas's and he put one large hand over hers. She looked closely at Kitty. 'And we've decided Jarrold can look out for himself.'

'Then in that case. Es, it's time I got home to my Leonora. You don't need me. Any of you.'

Esme came across and took her hand. 'No, no! We don't want that. Stay a little bit longer, till Jarrold's out of hospital. Please, please, Kitty. To tell you the honest truth I'm frightened of him. He will hurt me. He's hurt me before.

Look what he did to Thomas. It could be my turn next. If
you go and see him you can ... tell him I'll manage on my
own now. That I can't see him any more. You're my
watchman, my guardian and my guide, Kit. I can't cope
without you – not yet.' She looked up at Thomas, who was
playing with the cuff of his jacket. 'Tell Kitty she must stay,
Thomas!' she commanded.

Thomas's glance fixed on Kitty's embroidered collar.
'Kitty ... stay,' he said mildly.

So Kitty stayed.

She tried tactfully to say something about the way things
were between Esme and Thomas, but Esme would have
nothing to do with tact.

'So you're worried about me and Thomas being – as close
as we are ... well, sleeping together?'

Kitty flushed again. 'It's not right, Es. He's our family but
he's a ... simpleton. It's not right for you to—'

'You're wrong, there, Kitty. He's not a simpleton. Look
at the music he plays. And he knows what's happening, I
swear to you. And he's told me he loves me.'

Kitty raised an eyebrow. 'Told you?'

'Told me. His talkbox might be a bit skewed but he has a
heart, Kit. I tell you he has a heart.'

Kitty shook her head.

'Listen! Do you know what's really the matter with him?'

'He's nearly dumb and a bit...' she said it uneasily,
'... daft.'

'That's not true. He knows everything that's happening
around him. He talks to me more and more – honest. I teach
him new words every week.'

'Like I love you?'

'Like that and many more. No, Kitty, what's the matter
with him is he's scared, terrified out of his life, of people,
faces, movements, everything. Why that should be, I don't
know. But if you look at the way Janine dragged him up
there could be reason there. And me, don't I know what it is

to be frightened of everybody and everything around me? I spent all my days like that till you and me met up. You rescued me from that. Can you remember when we went stalking those boys in the woods? Well, that was the first time I started not to be frightened.'

Kitty turned out her hands helplessly.

'Well, what you did for me, I'll do for Thomas. And do you know why I'll do it for him?'

Kitty shook her head.

'Why did you do all that for me, little and barefoot galoot that you was?'

'Because I liked ... loved you, probably.'

'Well, that's exactly why I'm doing this for Thomas,' said Esme victoriously. 'Because I love him and he loves me. Don't you, Thomas?'

He came across and put a hand on hers. 'Love Esme,' he said.

'I give up,' said Kitty with a half-smile.

'There now, that was easy, wasn't it?' said Esme smugly.

Esme and Thomas might now be a pair, but that did not stop Esme flirting with her patrons, occasionally going on to late suppers in private houses, to give private performances. Sometimes she took Thomas to play for her at these soirees, where, apart from the applause for his playing, he was ignored while the flirtatious chat proceeded to the point beyond which Esme did *not* allow it to go. Some nights Thomas was sent back to Merridew Court with Kitty; on these nights Esme kept her own counsel.

Kitty, 'Miss Rainbow's beautiful and enigmatic sister', was often included in these invitations, but Esme turned them down, telling Kitty afterwards, 'You want nothing to do with these people, Kit. They're mostly bad, and them's not bad is mad.'

Kitty never wanted to go, so was never troubled by Esme's refusal to include her. 'So why do you go?' she asked Esme one night.

Esme shrugged. 'Well, to be honest, sometimes I go for a bit of honest-to-goodness fun. When I've done a performance I'm sort of boiling up and if I come straight back here I'll explode. Sometimes I go along with them because Mr Cullen thinks it will be a good thing for all of us. Reputation. Business and all that. To keep'm coming.'

Kitty looked at her fingernails then. 'And do you . . . ?

Esme hooted with laughter. 'Just a little bit of flirtation, let them put their arm around you, or their hand on your knee when you're in the boy's gear, that's all. I'm not saying I wouldn't ever. If the price was right. Say someone wanted to make me a duchess . . .'

'And where would Thomas be if that happened?'

'Where he'll always be. By my side, playing my tunes.'

'You're a real odd one, a crackpot, Esme Gullet.'

Esme kissed her on the nose. 'Thank you, Kitty. I haven't had that good a compliment in weeks.'

Kitty was very relieved for her own sake on the nights Thomas came back with her. The streets of Whitechapel were dark; the people buzzed with a sharp wisecracking response to poverty and despair which was alien and unnerved her. Forgan Buildings had been dark and dingy, its people close to the hell's edge of total poverty. However Forgan Buildings had not heaved with the threat that these streets held. At least Thomas looked big and strong: any opportunist footpad might think twice before taking them on, not knowing that Thomas was as harmless as a fieldmouse.

The nights she had to come away from the theatre on her own she ran through the streets at her old training speeds in very unladylike haste. More than once she was jostled and stopped by carousing watermen or market men, on the lookout for a bit of fancy, and her ability to feint and twist away proved to be very useful; as did her 'good right hand' when a well-dressed young man caught hold of her arm and would not let go. She delivered a sharp right hook, he stumbled backwards into his friend's arms, and she fled to the sound of his bluster and his companion's laughter.

Deciding that now she must see this thing through for Esme, Kitty pushed away thoughts of Leonora and William.

She continued to visit Jarrold each day. One day she took him the day's papers and the sporting sheets, another it would be baskets of oranges and plums, the next a silk nightshirt, bought by Esme from a shop in Jermyn Street.

Jarrold was not to be placated with gifts. He grumbled at her and talked in a pathetic fashion about the way Esme had betrayed him. But all in all he was very polite to Kitty and she knew that *he* knew that she was his only connection now with Esme. As well as this it finally dawned on her that, in his strange way, he was genuinely fond of his little 'golden goose'.

One day the nurse met her in the corridor. It seemed that Mr Pommeroy was not so well today, Miss Rainbow. 'We had the dressings off and he has had a bad reaction to the pain. The doctor has given him strong doses of laudanum.'

They went into the room together and Jarrold was tossing and turning on the bed, muttering under his breath.

'I'll just sit down,' whispered Kitty.

The nurse went to the door. 'Call me if Jarrold needs...'

Looking at the nurse's meaty, besotted face, Kitty realised that 'Jarrold's charm' had been put to good effect here at the hospital. Perhaps now, Esme was not his only friend in the world.

Kitty nodded. 'Yes, of course, nurse,' she said with some sympathy.

She sat quietly beside the window for nearly an hour. Every few minutes he fell asleep and then woke up again, always talking, talking under his breath. Then he started to babble more clearly. '... not my fault, dear lady ... of course I do ... always, always ... have to move on ... love course love ... but carefree on the meadows ... too young ... just on the drum ...'

As Kitty strained to hear him, somewhere, perhaps in her own head, she could hear the thump of a cloth-bound stick on a drum. She had heard it before.

'... love you yes ... this too much, Maria, spoiling it, why must you spoil it ... woman? A woman on the vans ... nice clean woman ... take care of you ... drummer boy...'

She caught his hand and shook it hard. 'Jarrold. Jarrold ... what is it? Who are you talking about?' She shook him again, tears in her own eyes, growing apprehension in her heart.

But when he woke up he seemed not to know what she was talking about, and his friend the nurse came in to stop her asking.

When she got back to Merridew Court she asked Esme about Jarrold – where he had come from.

Esme shrugged. 'Well, you can tell from his talk that he comes from the West Country, but since then from all the fairs and hurdy-gurdies in Britain, so far as I can tell. And maybe one or two in America at one time. Always on the move. No time or place to lay down roots. Do you know he boasts he's never owned or even rented his own kitchen? Why do you ask, Kit? This sudden interest of yours in Jarrold is strange.'

But Kitty wouldn't be drawn on this. Not yet. But a terrible thought was building in her mind.

26

I Wrote a Letter to my Love . . .

'Papa?'

'Yes, Michael?' William looked up from the table, where he was attaching a fine gold chain to a small gold watch.

'That's a very fine watch.'

William held it up, turning it so that the acorn pattern seemed to shimmer and move in the light. 'It took a great deal of work, son.'

'Did you make it for someone?'

'I made it for Miss Kitty.'

'Uncle Toby says that we should not play with Leonora, and Miss Kitty should not visit here.'

William put down the watch. 'Why?'

'He said it was . . . er . . . *irregulated* or something.'

William's jaw tightened. 'Uncle Toby should not say such things for they are not true. He should stick to showing you how to shoot, so you hit the bird, not the tree.'

'So we can have Leonora to play?'

'Yes. More and more, I think, when Miss Kitty gets back from London.'

'Goody,' said Samuel from the hearth rug, where he was glaring glumly into an illustrated version of *Le Morte D'Arthur*.

William chuckled. 'So why are you great boys so pleased to play with a little girl?'

'She's not a little girl,' said Michael indignantly. 'She's a fair maiden and we can rescue her from dragons and giants.'

'If Leonora grows up to be anything like her mother, Michael, it will be the other way round. The fair maiden will be rescuing the gallant knights.'

The next evening William walked from his workshop to the house of Tobias Hunter.

The lawyer's old housekeeper showed William straight up to the drawing room. In the centre of the room, at a small table lit by a candelabra, sat Tobias Hunter. Opposite him was a swollen unkempt figure whom William recognised as Gabriel Gullet, brother of Esme and son of the formidable Mirella. Between them on the table was a half-played game of *vingt-et-un*, two wine glasses and a brandy bottle, and two piles of money, the larger pile being in front of Gabriel Gullet.

The two men stood up, and Hunter came across and shook his visitor's hand with uncharacteristic affability. 'William, old fellow!'

Gabriel Gullet swayed. 'Are you joining us in a game of chance, Mr Scorton? These evenings are lonely without the ladies, doncha think? I hear Miss Rainbow's ensconced in London with my little sister, Esme. Mistake, that, sir. C'n never tell what the doxies'll get up to in that swirl of vice called London.'

William stared at him, his face rigid with contempt. Gabriel subsided into his chair, muttering under his drunken breath.

William looked at Hunter. 'Is there somewhere we can talk?' he said icily.

Hunter led the way to his study and, when William refused a seat, remained standing himself.

William took off his gloves and pushed them into his greatcoat pocket. 'Is this a new crony of yours, Toby? Gabriel Gullet? I know he once worked for you but—'

'I am attempting some rehabilitation, William. Mr Gullet, as you know, was dismissed from our office. Subsequently he has been thrown off by his family and I am giving him shelter, trying to convince him to change his ways,' said Hunter smoothly.

William relaxed then, and nodded thoughtfully. Old Toby did get these religious bees in his bonnet from time to time.

'Anyway, what can I do for you, William?'

'I believe you told my son that Miss Rainbow and her daughter should not come to Purley Hall, Toby. That it is *irregular*, or as he put it, *irregulated*. May I ask why?'

'I discussed this with him because it is my moral duty as his godfather to guide him where obviously no guidance is being given. You are an innocent, William. Inviting this woman and her child to your house as you do will put you beyond the pale.'

William looked thoughtfully at his old friend. He had always been sorry for this dry old bachelor, for whom members of the opposite sex were a terrible mystery. He had been a kind and caring godparent to Michael, had bought the boy his first pony and his first gun. But Toby had no understanding of at all of the intimate aspects of life, living the life of a crusty confirmed bachelor.

'We will be married, Kitty and I. That will straighten it all out, Toby,' William said reassuringly.

Hunter shook his head. 'The damage has been done. You do not realise, dear boy, the damage has been done,' he said sorrowfully.

'Nevertheless, Toby, I must ask for your word, on your

honour as a gentleman, that you desist discussing these matters with my sons.'

Hunter shrugged. 'My word is given. The boys are a single light in a dark life, William.'

William relaxed. 'You should get to know Kitty, Toby. She is a fine young woman, clever and strong. I am certain you would like her.'

The older man inclined his head. 'Perhaps so,' he said unctuously, 'perhaps so, William.'

'Well,' William pulled on his gloves. 'I must be off now.'

'There is one thing.' Hunter leaned over his desk and picked up two letters; one newly written and sealed, the other open. 'I've had a letter from Lord Tipton's London solicitor. Apparently the clerical world, beginning with that vicar friend of yours in Brack's Hill, has been throwing up smoke signals across England, and some smoke has floated as far as Sir Marcus. He wishes to meet the woman who now calls herself Miss Kitty *Maria Tipton* Rainbow, at his solicitor's office in London. I have a letter here and I wish for her address so I can inform her. Do you have it?'

William was smiling. 'Good news for Kitty, I hope.' He reached into his pocket. 'I've a letter for her here myself. See, here's the address.'

Hunter held the envelope up to the flaring gas jet. 'Ah. Good! Perhaps I could post this for you as well, William? I will take my own letter for the nine o'clock post and it will be no trouble to post yours with it.'

'That's very good of you, Toby. Thank you.'

Hunter followed William downstairs and saw him out of the house, then came back up the stairs to ply the execrable Gullet with more brandy. Soon the fellow would be unconscious in his chair, his nagging, mocking voice would be silent. And he himself could get about his much more important business.

Jarrold was sitting up in bed now. His dressings were lighter and his colouring was returning to a more healthy ruddy normality. His small hands lying on the white coverlet looked soft and well cared for. Kitty wondered if the besotted nurse had been cutting his fingernails.

He asked eager questions about Esme and details of her continued success. He asked probing questions about the new deal she was fixing with Cullen, making suggestions that Kitty should pass on to Esme, 'to make sure Cullen doesn't do the dirty on her.'

Kitty shook her head at this. 'All this concern for Esme's well-being,' she said mockingly.

He stared at her. 'I admit I got carried away over the squeezebox player, but I've been taking care of Esme since she was twenty, haven't I? Made all her chances for her.'

'Huh,' said Kitty. 'Robbing her of her socks, more like. She was your little golden goose! She told me.'

Jarrold stared at her, his face hardening. 'Did she now? Our little joke, that, nothing more. Look, Kitty Rainbow, haven't you flourished yourself since you hooked yourself to Esme's coat-tails? No longer the little Priorton guttersnipe, are we?'

Kitty stood up, bright red. 'I flourish, Jarrold Pommeroy, because of the sacrifices made by my father, Ishmael, the skills taught me by Janine Druce, and my own hard work, thank you very much.' She grasped her umbrella and made for the door.

'Stop, stop, don't go away!' His voice was suddenly desperate, wheedling. 'I'm sorry. I'm sorry. You attack, I attack. It is my instinct. It's kept me alive more than once, but sometimes it bites back at me. Don't leave me on my own in this bleak place, Kitty. If you don't come I will be on my own. No one else comes. No one else cares. Sit here. Let us not talk about Esme.'

She still did not like or trust him but something, not just his beseeching tones, made her return.

She sat in silence for a moment, her brain tumbling with her old suspicion and dislike of this man. But no matter what the truth was she needed to know it. So she must bear with him, hateful as he was. He started to say something, then subsided. The clock high on the wall ticked the minutes away.

Then Kitty said, 'Tell me how you started, where you came from, Jarrold. I don't know a thing about you.'

He stared at her for a few moments, then smiled slightly. 'I was probably more of a guttersnipe than you could ever hope to be, Kitty. I was born, I was told, to a Romany woman who told fortunes with some travelling shows. Who my father was I don't know. Perhaps she did not. A circus comes through a town and the men there see these travelling women as fair game. The constables did nothing. Sometimes it was they who did the deed.'

'What kind of woman was she, your mother?' ventured Kitty.

He shrugged. 'I don't know. True Romany. Dark-skinned. Strong, they said. And clever. Not clever enough for these coves that got her in the end, mark you. When I was three years old, she vanished on one of these stopoffs. The show people said they looked for her for a whole day but she had vanished. Then they had to move on to the next stop. I don't even know her name.'

'And you were left? Who took care of you?'

He shrugged. 'I slept in the van of the man who had the monkeys.' He laughed: a hard bark. 'He more or less treated me like one of them. Regular feeding to keep my coat glossy, regular beating to keep me in line.' He paused thoughtfully. 'He had a tailor make me little outfits like the monkey's. I was part of the show. The pennies certainly rolled in.' His voice was dreamy now.

She hardly dare breathe. 'Then?' she said quietly.

'Then? Then, the wife of Ben Frankus, who owned a big show, took a fancy to me. She bought me from the monkey

man. I was about six, then. Ten guineas she handed over.
Worth more than any monkey, I was.'

'Jarrold!'

He smiled, enjoying her discomfiture. 'Told you I was
more of a guttersnipe than you could hope to be.'

'Was she kind? The wife of Ben Frankus?'

'Kind? Well, I did have to be the cunning little monkey
for her, do my tumbles and clamber up poles to entertain
her and her friends. And I could mimic any speech, from the
Italian monkey man, to the man who rode two horses and
who spoke like a duke. But she fed me well and she didn't
beat me. She gave me my name. Before that I was called
Monkey Jack. And she taught me to read and write. For that
I am eternally grateful.'

'And you stayed with her?'

He shook his head. 'When I was about eight or nine, I
think, I went off with a horse man from Plymouth – a man
called Jake Pommeroy who did horse cures, travelling from
racetrack to racetrack. Bit of a gent, really. He was a great
cove. I'd'a been with him always but he was killed one day
by a horse he'd just cured.'

'So you were on your own then? Did you find someone
else?'

He shook his head. 'I was a big lad, nearly twelve then. On
my own after that, as you say. Oh I was took up by people
now and then, but mostly I took care of myself. I went to
America as a sailor. Saw Blondin, the great acrobat. Saw
wild Americans riding horses in ways you would not believe.
I'd a dream once to bring a whole troop of them here.' He
laughed. 'Some dream.'

Kitty hesitated. 'Was there anyone you ... really ... felt
affection for?'

His eyes narrowed and he stared at her. Then he laughed.
'There were always women, but some of those ladies were
good. I learned much from then.'

'Was there no one special?'

'There was one.' He laughed. 'I sent her a letter and got a thorough beating for my pains.' He stared at the window, lost in his thoughts.

'When you were babbling you talked about Maria.'

His head whipped towards her, naked emotion on his face. 'How...?' Then he laughed. It was an ugly sound. 'No. No one called Maria.'

'Are you sure? You—'

'For goodness' sake, leave the matter, Kitty,' he drawled. 'Here you are, weedling my life story out of me, lulling me down. I'm telling you more than I've told anyone. What do you want of me?'

'What do you want of me?' she mimicked him.

'Just tell Esme that as soon as I'm out of this bed I'm coming for her.' He laughed harshly. 'Tell her I miss my little golden goose.'

That night Kitty reported back to Esme that Jarrold was much improved. 'Moving about, and quite talkative, to be honest.'

'And what do you and Jarrold talk about, Kitty?'

Kitty shrugged. 'How he thinks you and he belong together. How sorry he is that he hurt you. That he misses you. I think in his funny way he really does care about you, Es. As much as he can about anyone.'

Esme chortled. 'Ah! You're letting him get under your skin with his charm. I know Jarrold, Kitty. He is selfish and cruel and loves to hurt people.' Esme's tone was hard.

To her own astonishment Kitty felt herself leaping to Jarrold's defence. 'Maybe that's because of all those terrible things that happened to him when he was little.'

'What terrible things?'

'When he was an orphan in the travelling show. He must have told you?'

Esme shook her head. 'I heard of all his adventures in

America. Then drumming up for the big fighters over here later.' Then she laughed. 'I know what the devil's doing. He's telling a pathetic story to make you feel sorry for him. To win you over to his side so he can get me back.' She came over and shook Kitty by the shoulders. 'Don't take any notice of him, Kit. Lies are his second nature.'

'It sounded right. I—'

'What did he say?'

'He said ... Oh nothing. Don't take any notice of me. You're probably right. He lies before breathing.'

But she knew that, liar or not, Jarrold Pommeroy had told her the truth about those early days when he had been sold for more than the price of a monkey, and he had not been lying when he'd murmured the name Maria in his sleep.

Esme relaxed. 'Well, Kitty, will you come to the theatre with Tom and me tonight?'

Kitty shook her head. She was bone tired, and she needed time alone to think. Walking towards Merridew Court this afternoon, down the dank alleys, she had finally allowed the thought to surface, that Jarrold Pommeroy, whom she had hated all her life, and was in every way a despicable and cruel man, had been Maria Tipton's sweetheart. And if he was Maria's sweetheart, he was the one. The one she had been looking for.

All this had made her even more bone tired and all she wanted to do was sleep for twenty hours and then go home to Leonora and Ishmael. And William Scorton. As she lay her weary head on her pillow she thought, yes that was what she would do! She would go home. Tomorrow. She turned over again on the narrow bed. No. She would stay one more day. Go once more to the hospital and ask Jarrold straight out. Tell him what she knew about Maria.

It was quite late the next morning when she got up and dressed. The rooms were very quiet. She heard odd chunterings from Esme's room. Thomas spoke more words in there when he was alone with Esme than ever he did in the world outside. Kitty reflected that those two seemed to be getting closer and closer and neither seemed the worse for it. Esme, in her working life, endured so much fulsome flattery and provocative advances from other men in her life that Thomas's very childlike simplicity must be like a fresh mountain stream after stale well water.

Kitty was feeling happier this morning than in many days. By tomorrow night she herself would be home. Leonora would be in her arms and she would be listening to Ishmael's measured tones in response to her many questions.

She had decided to spend the morning taking a last look at the great shops in the West End, to inspire her for the changes she planned to her shop when she got back to Priorton. Then she would go for her final talk with Jarrold before buying her train ticket north for the following day. She skipped down the steps, her sore foot hurting less than it had for days.

At the bottom of the steps stood a postboy. 'Rainbow?' he said. 'I have two for Rainbow.'

She snatched them off him, checked they were for her, not for Esme, and thanked him.

Both envelopes were addressed in beautiful looped script, but she recognised the heavy vellum of one as from the writing desk of Purley Hall. She looked around and realised she was being observed by at least four interested onlookers. Post around here could mean money or goods. Robbery was common in these mean unguarded streets. She shoved the letters deep in her bag and hurried on out of the alley. She would read them on the tram.

She sat down on the hard wooden seat and waited for the tram to wheeze off and start to rock before she tore open the letters. The strange one first. It was a letter from a company called Skerne and Oliphant, Solicitors, of Essex Row, near The Temple. They had been instructed by Sir Marcus

Tipton to invite her to a meeting on the twentieth of the month at two o'clock. There she might hear something which might be of interest to her. They were hers most sincerely, etc. She read it again and again. It was addressed to her. She would hear something of interest. She felt herself smile and looked round, dying to have someone with whom to share such obviously good news. But she was in an island of empty seats, so she tucked the letter carefully into the side of her handbag. She would have to stay till after the twentieth. But now it did not seem such a penance.

Then she opened William's letter, settling down to savour its contents.

My dearest Kitty, it is too long since we met and talked and although I try to be patient I wait your return.

The shop is fine. Young Joan Wharton is shaping up very well and is a very strict taskmistress for her sister Kezia, whom she has running about all the time.

I have done the books for you and the turnover is excellent. I have good news about Long's Emporium. We have taken steps and the papers for the lease will be ready for you to sign on your return. Your return!

I have taken the liberty of showing your books to the bank and have obtained an assurance from them that any initial costs will be forthcoming from them in the form of a loan. You know, dear Kitty, I would have given you this outlay myself, but I can hear your protests regarding *that* ringing in my ears. I think you take this issue of independence far too stringently. In time we shall share all anyway.

I had tea with Mrs Gullet and Ishmael the other day and they were in fine form, contentment shining from them. Ishmael asked if I were writing would I tell you that you were much missed and you were to be 'bold, show no fear. Only when you show fear can you be bested.'

I took a present for Leonora, a hobbyhorse made by my servant Luke, from wood and leather. I may tell you she galloped away down across the yard of the Royal George, all that fizzy hair flying. She is fine and happy. I know you will need to know that.

Oh Kitty, this town is a ghostly place without your presence. Does your friend Esme still need your help and support? I hope you will always be such a fine friend to me. When you return I think we *must* take steps so that we can walk in the world as Mr and Mrs William Scorton.

Yours in utmost affection, William.

She smiled, and smoothed the letter with her hand, aching to be back with them all.

She was pushing the letter back into the long envelope when her fingers touched another piece of paper. William must have included a postscript. She smiled and pulled it out, and smoothed it on top of the letter, and started to read. It was not addressed. The words leapt out at her, written not in proper lines but in clumps across the page

I know thy works, and charity, and faith, and faith, and thy patience, and thy works; Notwithstanding I have a few things against thee because thou sufferest that woman Jezebel, to teach and to seduce my servants Behold, I will cast her into a bed, And I will kill her children with death; and all the churches shall know I am he which searcheth the reins and hearts: he shall rule them

338

with a rod of iron; as the vessels of a
potter shall they be broken to shivers:

Kitty cried out and the paper dropped from her nerveless
fingers. She took some deep breaths and closed her eyes.
Then, dancing before her were Ishmael's words about being
bold and knowing no fear. She took another very deep
breath. Two hundred miles away and Ishmael was still here
for her. She opened her eyes, leaned down and picked up
the paper. She thrust it into the deepest part of her handbag
without reading it again. Then more slowly she closed the
envelope and tucked it in behind the note.

Her brain was swirling. William would not write such
stuff. The words were biblical, she knew that. But the hand
that had written it was not Christian. Not William's hand.
Surely not William's hand.

She was still shaken when she arrived at the hospital late
in the afternoon. She was met halfway down the corridor by
Jarrold's nurse, whose face was swollen, and whose eyes
were red with recent tears. 'It is no good, Miss Rainbow,
he's gone.'

Kitty frowned. 'Where'?

The woman shook her head. 'He asked for his clothes
because he said they should be cleaned, and he would tell
me what to do with them.' She sniffed. 'He must have just
got dressed and gone.' She opened the door to show Kitty
the empty bed. 'See, he left one thing.' It was a rumpled
waistcoat in threadbare green sateen.

Kitty turned it over. Pinned to it with a very narrow gold
pin was a scrawled note: 'Kitty. You asked about Maria. She
made this, and gave me this pin. Can't think why I've kept
them all these years. Not much use to me. She was a silly
woman. Can't think why she or anyone would want
anything to do with a fellow like me. Love to Esme.
America, I think next. J.'

She held the waistcoat up to the light. Trimming the

breast pocket and the watch pocket was a finely embroidered border of acorns and oak leaves.

'Nothing for me,' said the nurse standing quietly beside her. 'And him disappearing off into thin air.'

Kitty looked at her and undid the coral brooch which held the points of her own blouse together. 'Here,' she said. 'And thank you for taking such good care of Jarrold. There's some trouble in his life so he has to flee. I know he liked you. He told me.'

'Did he?' said the other woman eagerly.

Kitty nodded vigorously. 'Yes. Several times.' Then she pinned Maria Tipton's gold brooch to her own collar, wondering if lying really was an inherited talent. Was that one of the things she'd inherited from Jarrold?

Later she plodded back through the narrow, dark streets to her lodgings. She ignored men who called out to her, barged through groups of men who tried to accost her, her mind full of the astounding certainty that Jarrold Pommeroy was Maria Tipton's lost lover. How young he must have been then, perhaps no more than eighteen, while Maria must have been thirty, even more! But he had kept the keepsakes; not sold the gold pin. They must have meant something. The fact that Jarrold was her father hammered itself into the centre of her brain. Jarrold! The man she had so disliked since she had been a little child; the liar and the cheat who manipulated, even injured, those who ventured near him.

She turned a corner and hesitated, catching sight of a man in country gear, his face shaded by a flat brimmed hat, accost a woman with tumbling orange hair and her dress half off her shoulder. The man caught the woman's arm and hustled her down the street ahead of Kitty. She caught a glimpse of a neckerchief tied twice around and with a bow at his neck. Ishmael sometimes wore such a tie; the day she watched him box there were many there with this showman's insignia. Jarrold sometimes wore one.

Kitty frowned, there was something vaguely familiar about the man, about the way he walked. The woman's voice rose into a high protesting whine and the man pulled her into the deep shadow of a cut between two houses.

Kitty had seen such transactions a dozen times now. She hurried on.

27

A Plait of Hair

Esme stretched her long legs on to a stool and closed her eyes, breathing deeply to rid herself of the fire that took possession of her, as the rounds and rounds of applause rolled towards her. Usually she relished all this applause but sometimes, when it was too noisy and laced with drunken *halloos*, when it went on too long, the pleasure seemed to reverse itself. At these times she felt that all these people were sucking her towards them, and in minutes they would be fighting over her, tearing her limb from limb, eating her flesh.

Her dressing room, a thin capsule of space with a ceiling which dripped slimy rainwater, was blessedly empty. Thomas was still playing his accordion out front, accompanying a group of Polish tumblers called the Flying Rajevskis. The Poles were enthusiastic about his playing, which reminded them of home. They sang their own songs to him, which he played back as they did their great leaps and cartwheels. He had the knack of playing in time to their tumbles without appearing to look at them.

A peremptory knock on the plankwood dressing-room door brought Esme's feet clattering to the floor. She pulled a face. She hated callers in the interval. It broke the special bubble she created round herself to perform, so she would have to recreate it to manage her performance in the second half. She set a white cap over her curls, pulled a wrap over her silk shirt and velvet knee-breeches, and putting a smile on her face, called, 'Come in!' She expected to see a 'gentleman' already within her widening acquaintance, or some new 'gentleman' eager to rustle up an acquaintance-ship.

However, here were a couple: the man short with powerful shoulders and a strong balding head; the woman was taller, very slender, with startling eyes and looks which must have been very fine ten years ago.

The man bowed low. 'Armistead Carrington, Miss Rainbow. And this is Mrs Carrington, whom you will know as Miss Henrietta Danson.'

They were dressed in the finest fashion and their manners were grave, but from Armistead's rolling resonant voice, and a certain thespian hauteur of the woman's demeanour, these two could only be people of the theatre.

'Ah.' Esme beamed her pleasure and grasped the man's hand, shaking it vigorously. 'You're the great manager, Mr Carrington. I'm always reading of you in the newspapers.' Even as she was doing it she knew she was being too hearty.

Mr Carrington extracted his hand and turned to Mrs Carrington (or Miss Henrietta Danson), who inclined her head to Esme, smiling very faintly.

Esme grasped the other woman's hand and wrung it with the same embarrassingly excessive vigour. 'I've read of your great performances, Miss Danson. Indeed my mother saw you several times at the Theatre Royal, Newcastle and came home entranced. I think it was Cordelia in *King Lear* which had her rushing for her Shakespeare and reading parts, to share with us her delight.'

The woman flushed slightly then and her smile this time had much more warmth. 'Ah. I see. You're from the North.

We have had good seasons at the Theatre Royal, is that not so, Armistead?' she murmured. Her voice was light and strong, clear as a bell.

'The Fact of the Matter is, Miss Rainbow,' he intoned, scattering capitals like seed corn, 'Miss Danson and I, and our Company, are between Tours and have had the delightful Opportunity to attend your Performance on three Occasions.'

It was Esme's turn to go red. She looked around the cluttered space in some embarrassment. 'I'd ask you to sit, but there's no room in this dreadful place.'

'Do not fear, Miss Rainbow, we have been in Worse Places on our Travels. It is the Burden of those driven by the Thespian Muse to endure such conditions for their Art,' Armistead resonated like a base viol. 'Now then, Miss Rainbow, Miss Danson and I are simply here to say how much we appreciated the Tone and Style of your Performance, yea! the Restraint, when excess could have been Engendered by those Roaring Boys in your audience—'

Miss Danson interrupted him. 'Have you ever performed drama, Miss Rainbow? In the classical theatre?'

Esme shook her head.

'Well, we have a Proposal for you,' said Armistead. 'But enough! You have to Gather yourself for further Excellences. And we have an Engagement with a Delightful fellow from Dublin who is desperate for us to fill his Theatre. Perhaps you will join us for Supper, later, at the Southampton Hotel? There we can sit down. We will await you there. No doubt you have another *tour de force* planned for the Second Half?'

Esme grinned. 'Yes, Mr Carrington. I am to be a cavalier, to defend my honour in a fencing scene, after which I will die with a mournful song and funereal splendour, midstage.'

'You can swordfence?' said Miss Danson, interested.

Esme shrugged. 'A few moves, taught me by the prompter,

who was a gentleman in a former life.' She paused. 'Some say he is the son of the old King.'

The couple exchanged glances. Armistead coughed. 'Well, Miss Rainbow, we await your Presence with Pleasure.'

He bowed deeply, his wife bowed slightly and they were gone, leaving behind them only the echo of swishing silk and a heavy perfume overlaid by musk.

'Well, well,' said Esme, removing her linen cap and her velvet wrap and buckling on her scabbard. 'Well, Blooming Well!'

Kitty sat with her feet tucked up under her dress watching the fire flicker and smoke, thinking about Jarrold Pommeroy. The story which had unfolded in the hospital had not made her like him any more. All it did was plunge her into further confusion. She *knew* Jarrold Pommeroy; she knew him very well. He was greedy and cruel, a chancer whose chosen companions were those on the edge of the criminal world. For him, lying was the least sin. He had done many unnamed wicked things, she was sure. He was a thief. He had certainly stolen Esme's money. He had nearly killed Thomas.

And now she was just about certain that he was her blood father.

She poked the fire to encourage a flame in the dank coal. But in the telling of his tale she had glimpsed a young Jarrold who might have been different. A Jarrold who, without doubt, had had badness laid down in his soul by beatings and torment. For a second she'd had a glimpse, a flicker, of true feeling from Jarrold, when she mentioned Maria, but that was all. She had never seen that before. Even his keenness on Esme was bound up in her role as the 'golden goose'.

Kitty smoothed the threadbare waistcoat on her knee and allowed herself a glimmer of heartfelt sympathy for the man she had hated for so many years. She pulled out her watch.

It was eleven thirty. Esme and Thomas were late. She went to the door and peered along the foggy deserted street, then, struck by the cold, hurried back inside.

It was only a few minutes later when Thomas came in on his own. Kitty moved to pour him a cup of tea, and he thrust something into her hand. It was a package wrapped in newspaper. She opened it on the table and there, coiled in the crumpled newspaper like a snake, was a swatch of gingery hair, tightly plaited and neatly tied with a black ribbon.

She frowned. 'Thomas! Where did you get this?'

But he had squatted down beside his accordion case and was carefully unclipping it. She put a hand on his shoulder and wrenched him round. 'Thomas! Where d'you get this?' She shoved the parcel hard under his nose. 'Who gave it to you?'

He struggled to get away from her but she held on. 'Who? Some woman? Did she sell it to you?'

He shook his head violently and then started rocking backwards and forwards until Kitty herself felt dizzy. She sighed, sat back on her heels and put the parcel on to the table. 'There's trouble attached to this, Thomas. I can smell it.'

It was more than an hour before Esme came bowling in, bubbling over with her news. 'They liked me, Kitty. They really liked me. Said I had presence. And they want me in their company, can you imagine? Classical theatre. I am to play hero to her heroines. They had one but she ran away to—'

'Whoa, whoa!' Kitty put a hand over Esme's mouth to stop the torrent. 'Slow down, start again. Who, who?'

Esme peeled Kitty's hand off her mouth and held on to it. She breathed in deeply. 'Well, Kit, Mr Carrington, and Mrs Carrington, also known as Henrietta Danson the great actress, came to see me perform. They want me to join their company and learn the classical repertoire. They're to go on a tour of Ireland and I'm to join them as a kind of apprentice. If I come up to scratch I will perform opposite Miss Danson, hero to her heroines. If that's successful I'll join them on their tour of America.' She hugged Kitty. 'What d'you think of that?'

Kitty hugged her back. 'Sounds wonderful, Es. Wonderful.'

They sat down and stared at each other for a few moments. Thomas came to sit with his back to Esme, his shoulders to her knees. 'I could be terrible,' said Esme. 'They might think I'm terrible.'

'How many times have they been to see you?'

'Three.'

'Then you're what they want.' Kitty paused. 'What about Thomas?'

Esme shrugged. 'He'll come with me. They heard him play and liked him. I said they could have him for free. He can do musical interludes. The drama programmes are always mixed. They showed me one playbill with Miss Danson playing Juliet, and in a later scene dancing the polka. Can you believe that? They always need music. And if I'm thrown off, Thomas can always earn some money, play for our supper. He's good.' She put a hand on his still shoulder. 'They did ask about the nature of our relationship. I told them he was my husband.'

'What?'

'Well, it makes it all regular. Keeps them happy.'

'Talking of Thomas . . .' Kitty leaned over and showed Esme the plait of gingerish hair. 'He brought this in and I can't get him to tell me where it came from. You try.'

Esme looked at the parcel then started to talk into his ear. He was unresponsive for some minutes. Then she stroked his face. 'Show me, Thomas dear.'

At that he reached to the hook in the corner to get his hat and scarf. He pulled the rim of the hat down and the scarf round his face. Then he led them both out of the lodgings. He made Kitty stay at the top of the steps and he and Esme walked along the street. He dragged Esme to a place under a struggling gas light, then walked even further away. He pulled his hat lower and seemed to draw himself in until he was shorter and narrower, his shoulders slumped forward, and he walked on quick feet, looked up at Kitty at the top of the steps, thrust the package into Esme's hand then raced off into the darkness.

Esme walked after him, took his hand and brought him back. 'That was very nice, Thomas. You're very clever.'

They trooped back up to the rooms, into the smoky warmth of the fire. 'What did all that mean?' asked Kitty.

Esme laughed. 'Somebody came along, saw you standing at the top of the steps, then stopped Thomas and gave him the parcel. Somebody not too tall and quite thin, with a slight leaning to the left and a hat pulled down over his eyes.'

Kitty struck her forehead with her hand. 'I saw him! He was with one of those unfortunate women, pulling her down an alley.'

Esme looked at the plait of hair, shuddering. 'Kitty, you don't think something awful . . ? Perhaps we should show the constables . . .'

Kitty rolled up the parcel tight and put it to the back of a fireside cupboard. 'Don't think about it, Es. If anything has happened to that poor woman, and we say Thomas brought this in, you know what they'll do? They'll drag him back to the cells and ask no more questions. Remember how he was blamed for everything in Priorton? This could put a noose round his neck,' she said soberly. 'I've something else to show you. I had a letter from William and this was sealed in with it.'

She showed Esme the paper with the ravings about Jezebel on it.

'Ugh!' Esme threw it on the table. 'Are you saying William . . . ?'

'No!' said Kitty, but her tone belied the uncertainty in her voice. 'He would never think such things. Someone must have unsealed the letter and put this in.'

Esme spied the other letter, and Kitty brightened at this, happy at least to share what seemed like good news, something about the connection between Maria and herself. This reminded her about Jarrold running away. It had been an eventful day.

Esme's face lightened when she heard about Jarrold. 'Good riddance, I say. Now at last I might feel free. And now you can go home to your Leonora.'

'Thank you I'm sure,' said Kitty drily. 'Come to the end of my use, have I?'

'No, no,' protested Esme. But in many ways that was indeed the truth of the matter. In these years away from home Esme had become quite accustomed to thinking of herself first, second, and last.

Climbing into bed that night Kitty felt totally alone. The sour events of the day made it impossible to relish the thought of the meeting about Maria Tipton, and Kitty's own possession of a battered waistcoat embroidered by her mother's own hand. Uppermost in Kitty's mind was the pathetic plait of gingerish hair. The best possibility attached to that was that some poor woman had been deprived of her crowning glory by some dolt. The worst possible story made Kitty shudder with dread and fear.

In the seconds before she fell asleep or the seconds after, she seemed to be struggling in water, treading on it and not able to find the bottom. Then towards her came a great, battered and scarred hand. She held on to it and for a second everything seemed all right. The hand released her and the waters were rising above her again.

'Ishmael!' She woke up in a sweat, breathing a sigh of relief when she saw where she was. All the thin blankets were on the floor. She pulled them up, tucked them round herself and snuggled down. She forced her mind to think of the warm body of William as they made love that first time in Maria's little room on the third floor of Purley Hall. Then she turned over and went back to sleep, this time without dreams of any kind.

28

The Jezebel Paper

It was not the custom in Esme's household to rise early, but next morning by ten o'clock Kitty set out to get bread and beef for their breakfasts. There were quite a few people buzzing up and down Merridew Court, and she was stopped on the road by a young woman who spent much of her day in her doorway, stitching linings for a nearby clothes manufacturer. 'Want ter watch yer step terday, darlin'!' she called.

Kitty came abreast of her and stopped. 'I beg your pardon? I—'

'Sweet pigeon like you wants to watch her step. There's a bad man walkin' these streets.'

Kitty glanced round. 'Far as I can see there are more than one.'

'Ah but this one went the course!' The woman drew her sewing needle gently across her own throat. 'Did for a poor gel.'

Kitty swallowed. 'Killed? D'you mean killed?'

'Dead as a plucked chicken, darlin'. Dead as yesterday's dinner.'

Kitty looked round. 'Who? Where?'

'Poor unfortunate they called Red Nora. An' 'e did the deed in a shed down that alley over there.' She used the same needle which had mimed the death to point across the way.

Kitty thought of the ginger plait stuffed into the back of the fireside cupboard. 'Red Nora. Did she have red hair? Is that why they called her Red Nora?'

'More rust than red. But she did 'ave lovely 'air one time. Dressmaker then, alongside me, before her husband was in prison and her kiddies taken of some new pox. Newspaper's full of it.'

Kitty ran three streets to buy a newspaper from an old man who had a stand on a corner. She glanced at the dramatic headlines and the thick columns of black print. Underneath these was a macabre illustration of a dark figure lurking beside a lamppost. She thrust the paper under her arm and ran back to Esme's lodgings.

She battered on Esme and Thomas's bedroom door and urged them to rise. A rumpled and yawning Esme came through, naked under her silk wrap.

'What is it, Kitty, what's all this babble?' She wrested the paper from her friend and spread it out on the table in front of her in silence. She looked up at Kitty. 'Ugh. He beat her with horse reins and killed her with an iron railing. He had grabbed the railing from a pile of new ones which were to be set in cement for a barrier by the canal.'

'Monster!' Kitty was staring at her with wide terrified eyes.

'It's just another murder, Kit. Not a rare occurrence around here. It's terrible, I know. But this is a bad place and there are murders here from time to time . . .'

'But, Es, can't you see? It happened not a hundred yards from here. Her name was Red Nora and she had long ginger hair.' Kitty scrabbled in the corner cupboard and pulled out the newspaper parcel. 'What if he cut it off, Es? What if this is her hair? That's where this comes from. I'm certain of it, Esme.'

Esme was still shaking her head.

Kitty took her friend by the shoulders. 'I saw him. I saw him pull her into the alley. A woman with ginger hair. And Thomas saw him, that man. He took the parcel from him.'

Esme clutched her silk wrap to her and sat down hard.

Kitty leaned down now over the paper and peered at the picture. 'Perhaps I'm wrong. This picture here doesn't look anything like the man I saw.' The drawing in the newspaper was of a man in a tall hat with a dark cloak, almost bat-like, very dissimilar to the man she had seen. He had looked like a farmer, his hat slightly flatter and wider, more like the tradesmen on Priorton High Street.

Esme nodded encouragingly. 'No, Kitty. You're right. Just some fortuity.' She, like Kitty, did not want to believe there was a connection.

But in the next couple of days the tightly woven plait nagged Kitty's consciousness, as did the recurring image of the man pulling the ginger-haired woman down the alley. Several times in the squares she came across two men who must be policemen, talking to bystanders in the street and entering the houses. She discussed with Esme the need to go to tell them what she had seen, to show them the plait.

But Esme forbade it, worried as always about Thomas in all this. 'Do you see, Kitty? It says "prodigious strength". You know what Thomas is like when he has one of his fits. People know about that.'

In addition to all this, something in the back of Kitty's mind kept presenting itself: the image of the poor shivering soul brought to the drapery by Gabriel Gullet – the woman dressed in a torn sheet with her head bound in a strip of it to cover her nakedness. She too had had her hair cut off.

And Kitty kept going back to the Jezebel paper, poring over it, wondering why it had been sent to her.

Words leaped at her from the page: 'I am he which searcheth the reins and hearts: he shall rule them with a rod of iron, as the vessels of a potter shall they be broken to shivers:'.

Kitty shuddered. Was that not what the newspaper said the man had done? Red Nora had been beaten with a leading rein: they had found it there caked in blood. And then she had been struck with an iron railing many times.

In the next few days Esme would not allow Kitty to stay alone at the lodgings. And twice, as they hurried through the streets, Kitty thought she saw the countryman again. Esme had a hard job convincing her that it was her imagination. The newspapers told of dozens of different sightings and the image presented by the newspaper artist varied from day to day.

One night Mr and Mrs Armistead Carrington visited Esme again backstage and Kitty had to squeeze her way out of the tiny dressing room to make room for them. She followed the sound of Thomas's accordion and found him in the wings, playing jigs with an Irishman with a penny whistle and the old handyman, who was playing the spoons. None of them raised his head to look at her.

She felt completely tired and, having determinedly put Leonora out of her head for days, she suddenly longed to feel her daughter on her lap, feel the child's small hands tugging her hair. She thanked God with all her heart that tomorrow was the twentieth. After her meeting about Maria Tipton in the solicitor's office, she would at last be able to go home. She was deluged with hatred for this drab foggy London and longed for the green hills of home.

She checked her money in her purse, then put her head round Esme's door. 'I'm off now, Es.'

Esme broke off her eager conversation with Henrietta Danson and protested in a distracted fashion. Kitty said crossly that she wasn't a baby and she had money, anyway, for a hansom cab.

However, she did not feel quite as brave when alighting from that cab into the dark foggy night. To get to the lodgings she had to face a ten-minute walk, or a five-minute run. She set off for their lodgings at a very fast pace indeed.

This night she was not stopped in the street, despite the fact that there were the usual crowds swilling in and out of the public houses. The 'unfortunate' women were in twos and threes, and as one went off with a man, another tracked closely behind the couple. Their earnings must be halved in these risky times.

Kitty had just reached the bottom of the steps when she heard a noise to her right. A light flashed in the entry opposite, the entry where the man had dragged the woman. She could make out the shadowy figures of two men. She raced up the steps and fumbled with the large key.

'Kitty!' The voice was familiar. She stopped and turned round. There at the bottom of the steps, their faces bottom-lit by their lantern, were William Scorton and his friend Tobias Hunter.

'William!' Turned to ice, Kitty stood there and waited for the two men to mount the steps.

'Kitty, how are you?' William was ahead of Hunter, leaping up the steps two at a time, his arms going out to greet her.

She shivered with remembered feeling at the sound of his voice, then went cold again. 'William,' she repeated, and put out her hand to shake his. His arms came down. The formality of her gesture was like a barrier between them.

She opened the door and ushered them in. The sitting room suddenly looked mean and poky, despite Esme's flowers and the shawls she draped everywhere. 'Sit down, won't you?' She livened up the fire and turned to face them. 'This is a surprise,' she said, forcing a smile on to her face. 'I'm certain Esme has some sherry wine somewhere. Can I offer you some?'

William shook his head and when he spoke his tone was

as cool as hers. 'No thank you, my dear. It is very late. We simply came to call on you, to ensure you had received the note about seeing Sir Marcus Tipton tomorrow.' He wanted to add that it was because he couldn't wait, but he couldn't bring out the words in this frosty atmosphere.

'You'll be there in that office?' she said. 'Both of you?'

'Sir Marcus asked us both if we would oblige him,' said William. 'I ... we will take you there.'

She turned her gaze on Tobias Hunter, who shuffled his narrow feet. 'I will be there in my legal capacity, Miss Rainbow.' His tone was icy. 'I have long been assigned the care of Sir Marcus's Priorton affairs.'

'Were you particularly invited to this meeting?' said Kitty, forced into being very direct.

He bristled. 'I resent your tone, madam. It is a matter of custom that...'

'Poor Toby's been here several days trying to organise a preliminary meeting before tomorrow, but to no avail.'

'Sir Marcus has been in France till this very afternoon,' interposed Tobias Hunter, 'or I am sure he would have seen me.'

Her head went up. 'I see no reason for any preliminary meeting,' she said hotly.

'Do you not?' Hunter put his elbows on the arms of his chair and placed the tips of his fingers together. 'May I ask you, Miss Rainbow, do you think a ... person ... who lives in a district such as this would make an appropriate beneficiary – if that is what you are to be – of Sir Marcus's goodwill?'

'Toby!' warned William angrily. 'That's enough.' In fact Tobias Hunter had inveigled himself into this meeting once he heard that William was coming down. William felt annoyed that this much-looked-for meeting with Kitty was blighted by this sour man who had tagged along.

William leaned forwards and looked directly into her eyes. 'As for myself, Kitty, I came down this afternoon. Sir

Marcus asked me to be present myself, as . . .' he hesitated, '. . . your godfather.'

'How does he know that you are my godfather?'

'He discovered it from the vicar who baptised you, being intrigued at the way you had named yourself. That's how this all came about.'

She nodded slowly. 'Well, it's good that I won't be on my own there tomorrow.' She turned very deliberately to Tobias Hunter. 'For your information, Mr Hunter, I live in this place with my friend Esme and my foster brother, Thomas Druce. Esme lives here because it is cheap. She saves her money: the theatre is very insecure.'

'Criminals and fallen women, slatterns and thieving children run here,' he said sourly. 'It is no place for . . . ladies.'

She stood up. 'Perhaps not for gentlemen either, sir. In this case you will feel quite at home.'

William stifled a smile and Tobias Hunter stood up, grasping his stick hard in his hand. 'Madam, I will go. I abhor this impertinence.' With that he barged out of the door.

William stood up. 'I'll have to go with him, Kitty.' At the door he turned. 'Am I not welcome here, Kitty?'

She stared at him, then shrugged. 'I am very, very tired, William. Bad things have been happening here, and all I want is to be at home with Leonora and Ishmael.'

His mouth hardened. 'And not with me, Kitty? After all we've been—'

She put her hand over her eyes. 'I don't know, William. I tell you I don't know.'

He turned and strode off. She followed him to the top of the steps and watched as he joined Hunter and the two men walked away. She noted that they were dressed in the country fashion – a broader flatter profile than that affected by city men of that class.

Again she was visited by the image of the man dragging

the woman down the alleyway. This time she recalled the necktie the man wore, tied twice round his neck, like boxers and showpeople wore. Ishmael sometimes wore his like that. As did Jarrold. Jarrold. What had led her to thoughts of Jarrold? Could these killings have something to do with him? Esme had said he could be violent towards her, and he had half killed Thomas.

She came back inside, and locked and bolted the door behind her.

The man who had given Thomas the parcel had a scarf round his face. He must have thought they would recognise him. So could it have been Jarrold? The man whom she had so recently decided was probably her father? She sat down with a bump, her brain racing with this new unbearable insight.

That night, when Esme came in with Thomas several hours after Kitty, she was all agog about the hullabaloo they had encountered in the streets. Apparently the district was in an uproar. It seemed the body of another woman had been found. This time it was a dressmaker, a woman who sewed linings, apparently, for a local manufacturer.

29

Sir Marcus Tipton

The next day Esme insisted that she should accompany Kitty to the lawyer's office. 'You'll be like Daniel in the lion's den there, Kit. Let me come with you.' She tried to persuade Kitty to wear a hat of hers, a rather flirty little veiled concoction, in deep purple. 'No one here knows that you're in mourning, Kit.'

Kitty shook her head. 'I know that, but I wear this black out of respect for Janine. It's just for six months. Not a lot to ask. Anyway,' she smoothed her skirt with her hands, 'I like this jacket and skirt. They're smart enough, aren't they? You made me go to the trouble of choosing them in that grand shop of that Monsieur Whatsit of yours.'

Esme had to content herself with the offer of a fetching bit of veil, and rather a fine filigree hat-pin to embellish Kitty's own neat velour hat.

Esme stood back and surveyed her friend. Kitty had lost weight while she was in London and had become rather pale, even delicate-looking. But the finely cut suit set off her graceful shape and made her paleness shine to an almost ethereal glow. 'You look absolutely beautiful, Kitty Rainbow, although you could do with some roses in your cheeks.'

She made Kitty squeal then, by pinching her cheeks to bring a blush to them. 'There, perfect.'

'Just one thing.' Kitty reached inside her jacket and pulled out the cornelian pendant, rubbed it with a linen handkerchief and let it fall. It glowed softly against the black broadcloth.

Esme grinned. 'Ha! Putting out the flags, are we? Telling the lovely William that we're all at home?'

Kitty shook her head. 'I don't know. I was horrible to him last night.'

'Why?'

'I don't really understand. To tell the truth, all the time I've been here I've hardly thought of William at all, just Leonora and Ishmael. When he came to Merridew Court last night, he seemed like a stranger. I couldn't embrace a stranger. And the two of them, him and that Hunter fellow, they loomed up out of the alley and I thought of this man who's . . .'

Esme put an arm round her. 'Nine-day wonder, these murders. I told you, things like this happen round here a lot. You have to harden yourself to them.'

Kitty shook her head. 'I'd never get used to them. All I want is to be back in Priorton behind my counter, planning for the new shop.'

'There's wickedness in Priorton too,' objected Esme. 'Murders. Beatings. Remember I grew up in the Royal George! And I've lived with Jarrold. Always on the edge of things like that, he was.'

Kitty glanced quickly at her. What had made Esme think about Jarrold? Was she too making connections in her mind between Jarrold and these murders? However, Esme's eyes were clear, untroubled by such thoughts.

'I wonder where Jarrold's got to?' Kitty ventured.

Esme shrugged. 'Signed on for some ship to America, I should think. He mentioned America in that note, didn't he? Always wanted to go back there. Always.'

Kitty left it at that and Esme shouted down and told a boy who was loitering below to run, get them a hansom cab and tell the driver to wait at the end of Merridew Court.

Few people took any notice of the two smart girls as they picked their way down the busy street, followed by a large handsome man wearing a bright necktie. A crowd of people clustered at the murdered dressmaker's door, their clothes advertising every station in life. Kitty noticed the burly policeman and his assistant she'd seen after Red Nora was killed, talking intensely to bystanders.

The police inspector was the only one to look up as Esme's little procession made its progress. His gaze fixed on Thomas, then he ducked his head and spoke to the woman next to him. When his eyes came up again the little procession had vanished.

They dropped Thomas off at the theatre to meet with his friend the penny-whistle player, and went on their own to the office of Skerne and Oliphant. They arrived twenty minutes early and alighted on the wet pavement, shivering at the wind that was cutting through from the river. William Scorton and Tobias Hunter were waiting in a hired carriage outside the lawyer's office, their breath visible on the air.

William jumped down. He took Esme's arm. 'Perhaps you'll sit in the shelter of the carriage, Miss Esme, out of the cold?' He handed her up. Then he took Kitty's arm and turned to the others. 'If you will excuse us for a few minutes...' he said grimly. 'Kitty, I wish to talk to you about something.'

Purposefully he hustled her down the street towards the Strand, conscious of the frozen face of Tobias Hunter and the amused smile of Esme Gullet.

'Kitty,' said William rapidly, 'I do not want to go in there with us being out of temper with each other. I was confident, when you came away, of the special affection between us. But now...'

They were beside the river and the tangle of masts and the gaggle of ships below receded, row upon row, into the foggy distance. The quays and landing stages nearer to them shimmered with the purposeful scramble and scamper of workers and loiterers of every kind and condition.

Kitty stopped and leaned on a rail. William stood quietly beside her. They watched all the activity for a moment.

'This is such a big place, William,' she said. 'You feel engulfed, overtaken, no more than a speck of dust here. Terrible things have been happening here. Terrible.'

'The murders,' he said. 'I realised only when we arrived that these occurrences are in your district. I had thought you would be in some respectable place, some small hotel. Esme should not have . . . You must not stay there, Kitty.'

She pulled her arm away from his. 'I choose myself where I stay. Now and in the future.'

There was another long silence. He leaned towards her. 'I see you're wearing the cornelian.'

She fingered it. 'Yes. I wear it. Now can we go? We'll be late for this lawyer.' If they had been friends, if they had been close still, she would have told him of her discoveries about Jarrold Pommeroy. But this did not seem possible and she gulped back the confidence. 'Come on!' she said. But this time she put her arm through his, and there was more ease between them.

The offices smelled of a combination of beeswax polish and lemon juice, reminding Kitty of the front hall of William's house. They were shown down a panelled corridor into a large office where heavy books were imprisoned in wire cages on the wall.

A tall portly man stood up as they were shown in. He shook their hands gravely and introduced himself as Mr Skerne.

In the corner, on a throne-like chair, sat a man who appeared so tall he made even William look small. However, when he stood up on short stumpy legs, Kitty found herself looking into the eyes of her soon-to-be-acknowledged kinsman, Sir Marcus Tipton. He shook hands with Tobias Hunter and then with William, who wrung his hands enthusiastically. 'Sir Marcus, I have the pleasure of presenting Miss Kitty Rainbow and her friend Miss Esme Gullet.'

Kitty was surveyed by small eyes, bright as a squirrel's, encased in withered greyish-pink skin. Sir Marcus did not take her half-offered hand and she did not proffer the half-expected curtsy. He nodded to William and uttered a strangulated sound which might have been a cough and might have been the word 'Yes'.

Then he turned to the plump lawyer and nodded. 'Shrunken version, of course. A foot shorter at least. But the child is like that dratted Maria Tipton. Spinster woman, turned out no better than she should be in the end, and like all poor relations, was a damn' nuisance then and continues even now to be a damn' nuisance. Should never have given her house room.'

He picked up his stick and pushed a battered leather-covered box across the desk towards Kitty. 'Yours, miss, I believe.' Then he picked up his cane and his gloves and swept out of the musty office.

Kitty sat down hard on a chair before she fell down.

'Now there's one who wants to mind his manners,' said Esme.

Tobias Hunter looked on in sullen silence as William explained their discovery. He had pursued his own convictions on this matter, to the point of corresponding with and finally talking to Sir Marcus this very morning. Sir Marcus had finally conceded that he did have further material information. 'Kitty, I am certain, as is Sir Marcus, as are you, that you are Maria's daughter.'

Mr Skerne pulled a chair up closer to the desk and said not unsympathetically to Kitty, 'Perhaps you would sit here, Miss Rainbow? You would like to peruse the contents, no doubt.'

She changed her seat and very slowly lifted the heavy lid of the box. It was stuffed with items; no great wealth but the gentle archive of an impoverished woman who had found at last something to live for: a baptismal certificate; letters from schoolmistresses verifying Miss Tipton's delicacy and scholarship; references affirming the virtues of Miss Tipton as governess; a leather-bound book of the poems of John Clare. In a manila envelope was the marriage certificate of Bertha Callen, dressmaker, and Gervaise Tipton, gentleman; tucked behind it were the death notices of Bertha Tipton, housewife, and Gervaise Tipton, workman. There was a letter, written close to death, from Gervaise to his beloved daughter, Maria, saying his cousin Marcus would watch over her as his own. He had obtained a promise. There were baby's gloves and baby's little kid boots, cracked now with age. There were battered, much-used dress patterns.

Kitty lifted tearful eyes and found herself looking into those of Tobias Hunter, who was watching her now with a strange, tight anxiety.

'Leave it, Kitty. You can look through all this later.' William was concerned at the grief in her face.

Esme leaned over, poked up a small cluster of embroidered collars and fished out a fragile folded paper. It was a cutting from a newspaper. It was faded at the edges but the print was still very clear. The story was headed 'BODY FOUND', and told the tale of the discovery of the body of a woman, so brutally battered as to be unrecognisable. She had been in a turn of the River Wear at Croxdale. It was thought that the death might be natural, but this was uncertain, because of the sinister fact that the woman's hair had been cut off, and the police were treating it as murder.

'Apparently there was no way of knowing it was Maria,' said William, 'but Sir Marcus tells me he thinks it was.'

'Who? Who did it? Who killed the poor soul?' said Esme sharply. 'Some dreadful man?'

William shook his head. 'Not caught. They never found anyone.'

Tobias Hunter looked Esme up and down, coughed and spoke for the first time. 'Fairground feller. Drummed up business for the fair. Went underground. Never seen again.'

His voice shook, and his friend put a hand on his arm. 'There now, old fellow.'

Esme put an arm round her friend.

William turned to Kitty. 'Sir Marcus Tipton had agreed that they should marry, Maria and Toby here, but Maria refused. This man from the fairground already had a stranglehold on the poor woman's affections.'

In the warmth of Esme's embrace Kitty felt for a second the arms of the woman who threw her from the parapet. She sat there in silence for many minutes, absorbing the terrible discovery of her parentage: the confirmation of the fact that her father killed her mother.

Esme poked aside a pair of darned gloves. 'Look, there's a letter.' She pulled it out and handed it to Kitty. It was addressed to Maria Tipton and had been resealed. Kitty laid it flat on the table. The lawyer pushed across a fine silver paperknife.

The writing was very careful and slightly jerky, the hand of a person not often called upon to write. Kitty tried to make the words out through her tears, but couldn't. Esme took it from her and read it in a low voice.

'My Sweetheart Princess,

'I wish from the heart to be with you and say sorry that I was hard about your news at first and am now pleased that the baby is arrived and well and you are to return to Priorton soon. It's no surprise to know Sir M. won't let you back but at least like you say he's made provision for you through the lawyers. I am a fool, wise princess, that knows no better but for all that wants to be with you, but it seems impossible the way we are both placed. I am sorry I said to "get rid". I'm pleased you did not do that. I will find some money some-where, princess, and come back and we will be together. Wait six months and I will come for you both. My love to my wonderful princess and the little princess.

J.P.'

Scrawled across the bottom in a different, unsteady hand were the words, 'but you didn't come, dearest boy and we are alone now. She will not survive. I will not survive. But still for a little time there was a rainbow in my life.'

Kitty sagged against the chair. Esme scrabbled in her bag for smelling salts. The door clicked quietly behind Tobias Hunter and one part of Kitty's mind acknowledged his surprising tact in leaving at this particular moment.

The grandfather clock in the corner intoned three, and Esme gave a squeak. 'Great heavens, I was to be at the Southampton Hotel at three to read Romeo to Henrietta Danson's Juliet.' She looked at William.

'I will guard her with my life, Miss Esme,' he said simply, and Esme was off with a flurry of shawls and taffeta and the scent of violets.

Quietly, Mr Skerne started to return the items to the box. He clicked the lid and looked at Kitty. 'There is no great fortune attached to this bequest, Miss Rainbow. However, there is a small amount deposited in trust by your great-grandfather, who was Sir Marcus's grand-uncle. He left this for his direct descendants through Mr Gervaise Tipton. The money was not to go to Mr Gervaise himself. This money realises two hundred pounds a year to be paid annually. You will understand your ... em ... poor departed mother was not able to gather this in the last twenty years. Therefore there is an accumulated sum of some four thousand pounds due. I have been instructed by Sir Marcus himself to remit this sum to you in anticipation of the proper legal settlement. Here is a banker's draft to that effect. Thereafter, on November the first each year, you will receive the two hundred pounds due to you as Maria Tipton's daughter. Not a fortune, I'll grant you, but it will oil some wheels, Miss Rainbow. It will oil some wheels.' He spoke as though he were reading it off a paper in front of him.

Kitty shook her head numbly, trying to slot all these facts into place.

William looked at the lawyer. 'Miss Rainbow has a great deal to digest here. If your clerk will be so kind as to lift the box down to my carriage I will take Miss Rainbow back to her lodgings.'

Bumping along in the carriage cloaked by the benevolent silence afforded by William's tolerant presence, Kitty leaned back on the cushions and thought of all the unfinished business: with William himself, whom she probably loved but did not want; with Ishmael, whom she would now be able to repay for all the generous love which, more than Maria Tipton or Jarrold Pommeroy, had made her who she was; with Jarrold Pommeroy himself whatever he had done, to glean more about Maria; and most importantly with the sturdy policeman, to tell him all she knew and to show him the crucial ginger plait. Things were not over yet. Not by some degree.

30

The Attack

When they were back in the lodgings, William, clumsy with lack of experience, attempted to put together a cup of tea while Kitty went into her small bedroom and spread the items from Maria's box on the bed.

She put the paper items together, and then all the examples of fine sewing in one pile, and the concrete flotsam like the silver buttonhook and the ivory shoehorn, in another. She picked up a bracelet of seed pearls with a tarnished silver clasp and put this around her own wrist.

In the very bottom of the box she found a miniature double portrait, executed by a fine hand. Inscribed on the back in a scrawling hand was 'Bertha and Gervaise Tipton'. Her grandparents looked timidly out of the picture, portrayed just about the time when the defeated Bonaparte remained the biggest bogeyman in the Englishman's cupboard. These two people looked ordinary, undistinguished.

There was a knock on the bedroom door. 'Kitty. Dear girl.' William's voice came from behind the closed panel.

'Come in here, William. Look at this and help me put it all back.'

He brought in her tea and made her sit in a chair while he,

with some comments and due reverence, packed the items back into the box. She watched in a detached manner while his neat craftsman's hands replaced these fragile building blocks of the life of Maria Tipton.

When he had finished he sat on the bed beside the box and fished something out of his pocket. 'I have here another treasure, Kitty, which you may or may not wish to keep in your mother, Maria's, box.' He dropped a tissue parcel in her lap. She moved the tissue aside to reveal a small gold watch on a fine chain. It was etched with a detailed copy of her oak and acorn design.

'You made this for me?' she said.

'I made the watch. Mr Goldstein did the etching. I filched one of your collars for him to copy the design. Open it.'

She opened it. Etched inside were the words *Semper Amans* and, underneath, KMTR and WS.

She looked at him.

'It means "always loving",' he said.

She put the watch in the pocket at her waist and tried to fasten the pin to her jacket, close enough to let the fine chain fall free. Her fingers were trembling. The pin fell out of her hand.

'Here, let me.' He kneeled before her and pinned it on properly. She kissed his busy hand.

'Oh my dear Kitty,' he said, clasping both her hands and kissing them. 'I've missed you so. I cannot tell you how I have missed you.'

She pulled his face to hers and kissed him with strengthening passion. Then they were standing together straining their bodies close, and he was at her hair, pulling out her pins, and she was unfastening his jacket and pushing it away from his linen-clad shoulders. He kissed her hair then, and moved his hand past the watch on its gold chain, into her jacket to feel her softness. 'Oh, Kitty,' he groaned. 'Did I tell you how much I missed you?'

Two hours later, slightly ruffled, they were seated in the

little sitting room, outwardly decorous but comfortable and intimate with each other, as they had not been since he arrived in London.

'Well, my dear Kitty, you know so much more about yourself now. You have antecedents!' He smiled at her.

She put a hand to her mouth. 'How could it slip my mind? I know more, William, even more than this.'

She proceeded to tell him her of discoveries about Jarrold: that he was the one who had signed himself J.P. That she was convinced that he was the fairground drummer who had been Maria's lover and was therefore, in all probability, her father.

'Have you told Esme about this?'

She shook he head. 'Nor will I unless it's impossible to avoid it. But it's worse than that, William.' She went on to share her suspicion that he may have been involved in Maria's death, the man from the showground. It was such a relief to say things that had weighed so heavily on her mind.

William put his hand on hers. 'But his letter to Maria, Kitty! That letter does not indicate any evil intention. In the letter he sounds, well, besotted with Maria.'

She showed him the Jezebel paper then, and the ginger plait. He frowned when she told him that the paper had come in his envelope, with his letter. 'You didn't think that I had written this filth?' He was flushed now, his jaw tight.

She passed a hand over her brow. 'I didn't know what to think for a little while. Someone must have opened the letter, put that in, I suppose. But it all seems so unlikely, for it must have been someone who knew I was here and wanted to frighten me, yet had access to your letter. Do you know I was at the top of the steps when that fellow gave Thomas the plait? All this business seems now to be coming nearer and nearer to me. I'd just spoken to the dressmaker, you know, the morning before the man killed her.'

William put his arm round her and held her to him for a moment. 'Come. We'll set off back home this very day. I urgently need to be at the workshop in Priorton. I have lost days of work and I am late for one of my deliveries. You will come with me, out of this mess!'

She pulled away from him. 'I'll do no such thing. There is a policeman who's been in and out of the dressmaker's all the time. We passed him as we came in earlier. I'm going to take what I've got to him: the paper, the plait, everything. This awful thought keeps whirring in my mind that the man he's looking for must be Jarrold, so it's hard . . .' She stood up. 'I'll go to him now. Ask at the police station.'

William nodded slowly and stood up with her.

At the station, she refused to speak to anyone until the thickset policeman she'd seen came. He introduced himself as Inspector Gilroy, sat down and listened to her story in silence.

Then he said to her, 'You live in those upstairs rooms on Merridew Court, I understand? I've seen you coming to and fro.' His voice was surprisingly light for such a heavy-looking man. 'You're staying with Miss Esther Rainbow who's performing at the Crystal Theatre?'

She nodded.

'There's a gentleman living there who's a bit shilling-in-the-guinea, so they say. Several people tell me he's not quite right in the head. I was just about to come and talk to him.'

Kitty shook her head. 'You mean Thomas Druce? He's my half-brother, and husband to my friend Miss Gullet who you call Miss Rainbow. He's a quiet man, Inspector. Wouldn't hurt a fly.'

He shook his head. 'My experience, miss, it's the quiet ones you should watch.'

She took a breath. 'I've come to tell you something. You should look for a Mr Jarrold Pommeroy. He is the former acquaintance of Miss Gullet, a violent man, and has always been angry at me. He came out of hospital the day of the first murder.'

He noted her comments but showed little enthusiasm. 'I'll still need to speak with this Thomas Druce.'

She shook her head. 'You can't do that. He doesn't speak at all. He's kind of dumb.' It was too hard to explain any other way.

He looked at her dourly. 'Then I'll come and talk *to* him, miss,' he growled.

Kitty spent the next day and evening with William in a kind of passionate daze. He slept on the floor of the lodgings, determined to protect her. From time to time Esme stepped over him, her face wickedly amused, but she restrained any inclination to comment.

Early on the second day, after breakfast, Kitty told William she had ordered a hansom for him.

'What? Why?'

'To take you to the station and then back to Priorton and to your workshop. You're cluttering the place up.'

'And you will come with me?' he said eagerly.

She shook her head. 'No. I've to wait for Inspector Gilroy, and make sure Thomas doesn't get trapped into anything.'

'It's dangerous. And I'm here now to look after you.'

She scowled. 'No you're not. I can look after myself. Ishmael taught me that. Face up, don't run away. That's what he taught me.'

'Kitty, it's different now. Now you know you're Maria's daughter...'

She took his face between her hands. 'You can love me, William Scorton, but you can't look after me. I didn't belong to anyone except Ishmael before I grew up. And a few scraps in a box do not change that. I want you to go home now, for me. Spend some time with Leonora and tell her how much I ache for her. Talk to Ishmael. And can you put Mr Skerne's draft in a bank account for me, and take real steps to get hold of Long's Emporium? Tell Ishmael I'm all right and don't breathe a word of all this trouble to either Ishmael or Mirella. That's what you can do!'

He straightened up, saluted and grinned. 'You remind me of a sergeant I had in the army. I can see that a lifetime with you'll be like being under permanent orders.'

She put her head on one side at this. 'Nobody mentioned a lifetime, William. Not yet,' she said gently. 'There's too much to think of here and now.'

At the station after she had assured him yet again that she would be home soon, she waved him off. His train steamed out and she turned back to go about her business with an undeniable sense of relief.

She went to a little shop by the station and bought a small notebook and pencil. Then she made her way to the West End and walked by all the great shops, peering into the windows and making notes. She walked through each one and bought a small purchase in many departments, making notes in her little book. It was a methodical, satisfying exercise. The plainness of the task was a great relief after the complications of recent days. It was exciting to think of her plans for the new shop, which involved nothing more frightening than the thought of an unpaid bill, or undelivered goods.

Her step was quite light as she jumped off the omnibus and tripped along through the afternoon gloom towards Merridew Court.

As she turned the final corner she heard screaming. She started to run and saw Esme's familiar cloak on the ground, alongside it the cloth unicorn which Kitty had fashioned for her. Esme's voice was rending the air like the screech of the peacocks in the grounds of Purley Hall. She was being dragged along by a man with a broad country hat who had an old-fashioned boxer's neckerchief pulled up over his face. She made out the glitter of a knife in his hand.

Launching herself at the man, Kitty grabbed hold of his

arm and pulled him off. 'Jarrold, you...' She wrenched at
the scarf.

But it was not Jarrold.

It was Gabriel Gullet.

'Get off me,' he snarled thickly, hanging on to the
whimpering Esme by the hair. 'Runt, bastard. They're
saying now your mother was a whore like my sister. Both of
them with a taste for rough lots...'

Kitty put down her head and butted him hard in the
shoulder. He let go of Esme, who jumped back, then came
piling back in with her umbrella, yelling, 'Murderer!'

The people seemed to run out from every doorway, from
the mouth of every alley. In minutes the two girls were
sitting on top of Gabriel with a circle of admiring supporters
around them.

'There y'are, gel, give it 'im good,' said one woman,
hitching her scanty dress on to her shoulder. 'Bleedin'
murderer.'

Sitting there, Kitty was almost crying with relief that
Esme's assailant was not Jarrold and therefore, she was
sure, he had not killed the dressmaker or Red Nora either.
And now there was the precious additional hope that Maria,
his lover and Kitty's own mother, had not been his victim.
Two constables came in through the back of the crowd, and
then one ran off for Inspector Gilroy.

Gilroy saw to it that Gabriel, battered and mumbling, was
dragged off to the police station, out of reach of the grasping
vengeful crowd. Then the first constable asked Esme and
Kitty if they were harmed in any way and requested with the
utmost politeness that they follow him, as the inspector
wished to see them.

In the station they waited in Inspector Gilroy's hutch of
an office. It was some minutes before Gilroy stopped his
fussing and sat down. Even then he tinkered with his pipe
for a while before he shot a question at Esme. 'You say you
know this man, Miss Rainbow?'

'Miss Gullet is my name. I borrowed the name Rainbow from my friend here. Seemed more appropriate for the stage than Gullet.'

'Ah. So you're not sisters?'

She shook her head.

'That must be a complicated setup, miss. Miss Rainbow 'ere says the daft fellow is her half-brother, and is,' he coughed, 'apparently your husband. And you two're not sisters though you share a name. An' you make your living singin' in gen'lemen's gear.'

She put up her head and glared at him.

He waved his pipe apologetically. 'I do not criticise it, miss. Seen your performance myself, Miss ... er ... Gullet, and not even in the line of duty. Comic but tasteful. I told my wife. Got nothing against it. Our boys do get some trouble at the Crystal from time to time with your audience, but that ain't your fault.'

They waited.

'Now, Miss Gullet. You seem to know this man who attacked you?'

'Yes. He is my brother, Gabriel.' Esme was very subdued now.

'Another brother? Entangled it is, miss. Entangled!'

'I didn't know it was Gabriel, till Kitty pulled off the scarf.'

'He was intent upon murder?'

'It felt like that.'

'Is there a reason your brother would wish to murder you?'

Esme grimaced. 'He's tormented me since we were little. Only Kitty could stop him.' She squeezed Kitty's hand. 'When she stepped in he couldn't do it any longer. He hates her.'

'My constable told me she was quite a scrapper.'

A thrill went through Kitty as once again she thought of Freddie Longstaffe, who had called her 'the scrapper'. She said quickly, 'Up in Priorton, where we come from, Gabriel once brought a woman to me, so I could help her. She was one of those "unfortunates". She was in a bad way. She'd been beaten and her hair'd been cut off.' She frowned. 'But to be honest I thought it was someone else who had done that, not he.'

Gilroy pulled on his pipe thoughtfully. 'This brother of yours doesn't fit with our description of the murderer, Miss Gullet. Too heavy. *Tallish and thin*, we have.'

'There was the other one, the one that was standing by the wall,' said Esme.

The inspector's head shot up. 'Other one?'

'He was the one called my name. Well, he called out, "Miss Rainbow".'

'He was taller? Thinner?'

Esme nodded slowly. 'He was in the shadows, but, yes, he was shouting to Gabriel. Something about God, and teaching and seducing servants and searching the reins and hearts.'

Gilroy shot a glance at Kitty, opened a file and pulled out the Jezebel paper. Then slowly he read the words out to Esme.

She stared at him. 'That's it,' she said soberly. 'That's it. Of course, the letter that was sent to you, Kitty!'

Kitty nodded, then she clapped her hand on her forehead. 'I know it. I know who it is!' She stood up and leaned over the desk. '*Tallish and thin*. I think I know who it is. It can't be, but it must be.' She took a breath. 'Gabriel shouted at me when I was beating him. Talked about my mother in horrible terms. Only one person thinks of her, and me, in those terms.' She sat down and digested her own information. 'It is Tobias Hunter. He could have interfered with William's letter. He has a down on those unfortunate women. And he hates me. Tobias Hunter.'

Gilroy put down his pipe. 'An' where might we find this gen'leman, miss?'

Kitty shrugged. 'I didn't know he was still here. He's been in London this week, but he lives in the town where we come from. Maybe he'll go back there now, out of the way of all this.'

'If you'll excuse me, Miss Rainbow, Miss Rain— Miss Gullet.' Gilroy left the women and went to the small room which had a grille but no windows. Gabriel Gullet was sitting slumped in a hard chair in the centre of it. Gilroy went and sat opposite him.

'And did you plot and plan this murder all on your own, Mr Gullet?' said Gilroy, almost pleasantly.

'There weren't no murder,' said Gabriel. 'We just thought—'

'*We*? And who might be the other half of the "we", Mr Gullet?'

Gabriel went a dull red. 'I don't think—' he said.

'So you planned and carried out all these murders on your own?' persisted Gilroy.

'*These murders?* Sir, there were no murders. This was a trick we were to play on my sister and that Kitty Rainbow.' He leaned forward confidentially. 'You know what these women are, sir. My friend and I would teach them a lesson, set them on the way called straight. My friend is very religious, sir. He wished only the good of their souls.'

'Well, then, Mr Gullet, if he is a religious man you will have no trouble telling me his name.'

Gabriel nodded very wisely. 'He is a very respectable man. A lawyer. Man called Tobias Hunter.'

Gilroy stood up. 'Thank you, Mr Gullet. You have been very helpful.'

Gabriel smiled his relief and stood up, dusting down his coat. 'Then I can go from this stinking place?'

Gilroy shook his head and said gently, 'I think not, sir. Not for a very long time.'

The door clanged after him and he was gone.

31

Incident at the Railway Station

Inspector Gilroy decided he would take men to the railway station to see if they could apprehend this fellow Hunter. If the two ladies would assist that would be most fortuitous, seeing as neither he nor no one else on the force had a blind bit of knowledge as to what the fellow was really like. On hearing this Esme begged leave to go to check on Thomas, who would be back home and would be distressed at not finding her. Goodness knew what those excitable neighbours would be telling him. Or trying to. And he would not understand a single word they were saying. But she knew he'd be upset.

Kitty assured Gilroy that it was she, not Esme, who would recognise Hunter. He did not need Esme.

Gilroy stroked his chin. 'But it was Miss Rainbow – this Miss Rainbow, I mean Miss Gullet-Miss Rainbow – you saw him by the wall.'

'Well, when you get back with him I'll tell you whether or not it was the fellow beside the wall. Trust Kitty, though, Mr Gilroy! You never saw a person so clever, so sharp. She has a nose like a hunt pup.'

He looked from one to the other. 'I'll grant you're

very persuasive, Miss Gullet-Miss Rainbow.'

Although Esme protested that she felt perfectly safe now, the inspector insisted on sending a constable back with her to Merridew Court. He, with some nod at ceremony, handed Kitty into his carriage, took the reins and set off, posthaste, for the railway station.

At the station the platform was cluttered with barrows and luggage and teeming with passengers, porters and attendants of one sort of another.

Kitty saw Tobias Hunter almost straight away through the bustling crowds, standing erect and quite composed beside a square pillar which supported a high arch. The soaring arch pulled her glance, reminding her of the viaduct at home, making her pause a moment.

'Well, Miss Rainbow?' said Gilroy fiercely. 'Do you see the fellow?'

She nodded. 'See? There by the pillar? *Tallish and thin*, you said. I told you he would be here.'

The policeman started forward and she pulled him back. 'No. Let me go and talk to him. You stay the other side of the pillar. Listen to what he says.'

She tucked a curl in her bonnet and sauntered forward. 'Mr Hunter, goodness me! Are you off home then?'

His light eyes blinked, then he surveyed her coldly and glanced behind her. 'You are returning to the North, Miss Rainbow?' he enquired frostily.

She shook her head. 'William Scorton told me that you might be returning today, and I took a chance that I might see you,' she lied.

He bowed very slightly but didn't reply, his eye going past her to a train, two platforms away, which was just chugging in. Then he turned his gaze back on her. 'And why would you wish to see me, madam?'

'I wanted to ask you about my mother, Maria Tipton.'

'If she is indeed your mother, and I suppose one must accept Sir Marcus's action in confirming that, then she has still little to do with you. You were nurtured by a vagrant boxer and your habit is to consort with idiots and actresses. And worse.'

Kitty folded her lips. 'Did you come to see me earlier at my lodgings, Mr Hunter?'

'Why should I wish to do that? The Gullet chap had business with his sister, that is all.'

'So you knew Gabriel Gullet was there?' She noted some rustling behind the pillar. Then she took Hunter's arm, impelling him to walk along the platform with her. She didn't want Gilroy breaking in at this point. Hunter's arm under her hand was rigid with revulsion. He tried to disentangle himself from her. 'You are acting true to type, madam, soliciting in a public place.' He said the words through gritted teeth, but he walked with her.

She clung on, talking up at him earnestly. 'Gabriel brought a woman to me some time ago, Mr Hunter. A woman who had been beaten and whose hair had been cut off. Was she anything to do with you?'

'Such women need to be brought to their senses or brought to their Maker,' he said briefly.

'Like my mother, Maria Tipton?'

'Your mother, madam, was a sweet, demure woman, God-fearing and chaste. Then she ate the fruit and was reduced to being yet another fallen daughter of Eve. For that she must needs be brought to redemption.'

'And you did the same to her? Brought her to her Maker, as with the others?'

He laughed harshly. Then he turned his hand over and she was held in a grasp of iron, being pulled along at a great pace. 'I will show you, madam. We will forget about the train and the way north. We will show you the process of being brought to salvation.'

She wriggled and almost lost her footing in his forward rush.

'Stop!' Behind her Kitty could hear the sharp tones of Inspector Gilroy. With all her strength she pushed her elbow sharply into Hunter's ribs and his grip loosened. Then she half turned and, curling her knuckles, she landed a glancing upward blow on his cheekbone. He staggered but did not fall. She was free.

'Stop!'

Hunter took a step back, saw the thickset inspector and the uniformed man at his side. 'Ah. How wonderful! You may arrest this woman for soliciting, sir. She has been harassing me for these ten minutes now. The streets, even the railways stations, are polluted...'

For one second Gilroy's forward rush was halted by the even, authoritative tones of the lawyer. 'It's you I come for, sir, begging your pardon. I believe you may help us with an important investigation. Miss Rainbow here was the only one who could recognise you...' Then he moved forward, putting an arm out to grasp Hunter's shoulder.

Hunter leaped back out of the policeman's grasp, ran along the platform and on to the second one, then jumped down in front of the idling train. Kitty followed, surrounded by others attracted by the mêlée. A woman on the platform shrieked and more people came, pushing Kitty right to the edge.

Gilroy had a word with one of the constables, then fought his way through the crowd to stand beside Kitty. He called down to Hunter, now standing before the idling engine like a stag at bay.

'Now, now sir,' said the policeman, 'no need for 'istrionics. Just come up 'ere and we'll go somewhere and talk about these matters.'

Hunter glared at Kitty and then drew a long sharp knife from an inner pocket and pointed it at her. Then he moved his gaze to Gilroy. 'Read your Bible, you ungodly snivelling functionary. Open it at Revelation and there before you, you will see the truth laid out for even dolts like you.' His voice went up a pitch. '"...thou sufferest that woman Jezebel ... to teach and to seduce my servants to commit fornication..."'

A gasp, a ripple of fully relished disbelief and horror flowed through the crowd.

'"I gave her space to repent ... and she repented not ... I will cast her into ... great tribulation..."'

'It's you who're the snake, you murderer!' Kitty jumped down to get at Hunter and felt rather than saw the heavy thump of Gilroy landing beside her. Hunter moved towards her and before he could reach her was grasped from behind by Gilroy's constable assisted by a heavy-shouldered railwayman with smuts of black soot on his face.

There were shouts of 'Bravo!' from the gathering crowd, and the knife clicked and clattered as it spun on and off the railway line. Then Hunter stood quite still in the clasp of the two men, his voice still droning on. '"I am he which searcheth the reins and hearts..."'

Gilroy mopped his brow with a grubby handkerchief and said wearily, 'Shut that man up, will you, constable?' The constable clapped a hand over Hunter's mouth, gagging the sound to a growling mutter.

The inspector turned to Kitty. 'You don't mind taking things on, do you, miss?' he said, holding his hands in a cradle so that she could hitch herself back on to the platform with the help of eager onlookers.

She watched as they helped the inspector up. 'That's because I was brought up by what that snake called a "vagrant boxer", who taught me always to go forward and face up to things.'

Gilroy settled beside her, breathing heavily. 'Boxer eh? An' what was 'e called, this boxer?'

'Ishmael Slaughter. It was a long time ago.'

'I've 'eard that name. Did he ever mention the great Richmond? Only a hundred and fifty pounds, but a great boxer. They say my grandfather saw 'im, an' always said now there was a fighter you'd bet your gold watch on. He was a great follower of the fancy, was my grandpa. Lost a few gold watches in his time.'

'Ishmael often talked of Richmond, who he saw as a boy. He thought he was greatly skilled.'

Gilroy nodded wisely. 'So he would, if he knew a single thing about boxing. So he would.' He brushed sooty spots from his greatcoat and then slapped the dust from his hand. 'Now, miss, I'll deal with the lawyer and you should go home an' rest, as you look pasty as an uncooked pie. I'll come to see you tonight an' put you wise to events. An' I'll get our learned friend here to the station and ask him a few questions. Make way, ladies and gentlemen, make way!'

Then he led her through an approving, cheering crowd and for a second she felt what Ishmael must have felt in the seconds after victory, before the pain hit him.

At Merridew Court Kitty was met at the bottom of the steps by Esme, who had obviously been watching for her. They lingered there, while Kitty told her of the incident at the railway. Esme grinned with pleasure when she heard of Hunter's capture. Then her face sobered.

'But there's more to face here, Kit. Jarrold's here and is sitting tight. He'll not go until he sees you.'

Kitty froze. She had thought she would not have to see Jarrold again. 'He hasn't been horrible to you, has he?'

Esme shook her head. 'Quite the reverse. Sober as a judge. Humble as pie. Even so, poor Thomas is hiding in the bedroom.' She caught Kitty's hand. 'And worse, I've to go to the theatre. It's my last night before I join up with Mr and Mrs Armistead Carrington. And I'm late already. I could leave Thomas here with you, but—'

'No.' Kitty pulled in her skirts, leaped past Esme, and tripped up the stairs. 'Don't you worry about me with Jarrold, Esme. Not any more.'

Jarrold was sitting hunched in a chair, more soberly

dressed than usual. Only the bright blue necktie betrayed his taste for flash colours. He nodded briefly when he saw Kitty.

She turned to Esme. 'You and Thomas go off to the theatre. And me and Jarrold'll have a nice little chat.'

They sat in silence as Esme arranged her feather boa and called Thomas from the bedroom. Jarrold stood up. Esme kissed Kitty. 'Now, Kitty, you take no nonsense from him.' Then she shook Jarrold's hand. 'I wish you well, Jarrold, with whatever you do. There were good times as well as bad times and I'll remember those.'

He smiled faintly at her and watched her leave. Then he turned back to Kitty. 'How old are you, Kitty Rainbow?'

'Twenty.' Kitty sat back in her chair and he resumed his seat opposite.

'Well, Kitty, after today you'll see nothing of me. I've booked passage to America and will stay there this time for good.'

She put her chin up. 'And what do you want with me Jarrold?'

'I want to tell you a story from twenty-one years ago. About this boy who wasn't bad and wasn't good. He'd had some bad beaten into him for sure, but he did no real harm.' He paused.

'How old was this boy?'

'Oh, seventeen, eighteen years old – he never knew his birthday. He worked the shows and fairgrounds, drumming up for the boxing, working in setup theatres, and the like. One day, in Priorton as it happens, he was returning from the station (where he'd been on an errand for the show-master), when he was run into by this runaway gig. No harm done, but he was a bit shaken. The gig was driven by a lady...'

'Miss Maria Tipton.'

'Miss Maria Tipton. She pulled him to his feet and dusted him down, all motherly concern, if you like. Then he looked into her eyes and it was as if the moon and the stars came out at once.'

Kitty glared at him.

'No, Kitty Rainbow, I'm not codding you. I was hit by thunderbolts and so was she. For minutes we tried to pretend it'd not happened but then we clasped each other and knew that it had.' Now he had dropped the pretence of the boy and his voice went lower, the West Country drawl more distinct. 'She was lovely, your mother, Kitty. Quiet, but such a shining face, such bright eyes, such hair. And such a soft voice.' He paused. 'We met every day during that stopover in Priorton. We passed time in the meadows and the woods. She would say it was ridiculous, she was twice my age, and I would cry and tell her to stop that.' He took out his handkerchief and blew his nose. 'She read me poems from a book in that voice, poems of the trees and the streams, and of love.

'Then I had to go, and we were both broken at the parting, but we promised we would meet and find a way.

'The next time I came by she had news of ... well I suppose it must have been you, a baby that we had made together. I did something terrible then. I told her she must get rid of it, and I broke the spell between us. She ran away from me, as though from a stranger.'

Kitty sat very still.

'I did try to make amends to her. I wrote her a letter. You must believe that, if you believe anything.'

Kitty nodded.

'But then I was caught by some men, sent by Sir Marcus Tipton, who beat me within an inch of my life. Both my legs were broken. Beating away, they told me Sir Marcus was incensed at her folly. And that she herself never wished to see me again. When I asked about the baby a thing came crashing on my head and I didn't wake up till two days later in a showman's van in Ripon.

'I took months to heal. But I did go back to Priorton,

nearly a year later. That's when I found out she was dead. I asked in a roundabout way regarding a child. But no one had knowledge of a child.'

He thrust his hands deep in his pockets. 'I'd'a thought she would have seen my mind in the letter, that I'd find some way to get together. That things would work out better.'

Kitty stayed silent for a moment then said, 'She did see your letter, Jarrold. It was in her box. There was a note on it in her hand mourning the fact that you did not return.'

A shadow fell over his face. Then he shrugged. 'Well, her dead and nothing to lose, you might say, Jarrold Pommeroy really went to the bad. Gambling, thieving, anything to get a bit of power and not be at the bottom of the heap for everyone else to kick you. To be very honest, Kitty, I might have been like that anyway. If me and Maria had really got together I'd probably have been as bad with her as you think I was with Es. You'd say that anyway.' He stood up and picked up his hat. 'I'll tell you one thing, Kitty Rainbow, you could have hit me with a mell-hammer in the hospital, when I finally realised who you are. And since then I've been thinking back and I can see Maria all the time. It's like she's whispering in my ear. So I thought it only right in memory of her that I should tell you the truth. You've a right to hate me, as does Esme, so I'll leave it at that.' He put out his hand.

She stood up and took it, holding on to it. 'I'm grateful for your story, Jarrold. I'll tell it to Leonora so that she too knows where she's from.'

He nodded.

'And my heart goes towards that battered little boy who had to make his own way. And I'm eternally grateful to be born in love, the love you and she shared. What life you must have brought for her!' She paused. 'But you must know that it's Ishmael who's my father and always will be. I choose him.'

He sighed and nodded again. 'You choose well. Will you tell him, tell Esme about all this?'

'No. I won't do that. But I do wish you well in America, Jarrold. A bare page. A clean slate. Perhaps you can be the man Maria would have wished for, there.'

He shook his head. 'A wonderful thought, Kitty, but I'm a hard, selfish, sometimes a bad man. I cannot change.'

She squeezed his hand. 'Well! Do a good deed instead of a bad one once in a while, and think of me and Leonora.'

He laughed out loud and clapped his hat on his head. 'A good thing I'm going away, Kitty Rainbow, or you'll have me behind a shop counter in a week, slicing bacon for the good of my soul!'

She bolted the door behind him and leaned on it, rehearsing Jarrold's extraordinary story again in her mind, and finding she was glad that she knew. Truly glad. She came to poke the fire, which was nearly dead.

Leonora next. Would the child recognise her? And Ishmael! Dearest and most loved father.

And – Kitty didn't know whether it was the most or least important – William Scorton. What about him?

She would go home tomorrow. Whatever happened here she would go home tomorrow. Nothing, not Inspector Gilroy nor the Queen herself, would stop her.

32

New Shoes

Armistead Carrington sat back in his chair and drew on his cigar with some satisfaction. 'Will you miss it, Miss Esther Rainbow, the adulation of the hoi polloi? The shouts and whistles of the natural exuberants in this bubbling city? Will you relish exchanging that for the patter of bucolic appreciation of the Irish gentry for your rendering of the works of the Bard?'

Esme stared at him, thinking that Kitty would have some comment about old Armistead swallowing a dictionary. 'I'll feel quite at home there, sir. I learned my craft to the sound of such gentle . . . er . . . bucolic applause.' A bit of poetic licence there, when you thought of the riotous atmosphere at the Windlass Theatre in Priorton.

After taking her very last curtain at the Crystal Theatre, Esme had been presented with a box of plums from the other performers, and a rather ragged second-hand-looking bunch of flowers from Mr Cullen. He said sulkily what a pity it was she was going off to the bogs of Ireland spouting Shakespeare, as he had it for certain that one of the princes, perhaps even the Duke of Clarence, was going to call in for the second half, one night soon.

Now, as Esme listened to the arch, mannered talk of the Carringtons, her mind drifted back to the image of her brother's face as Kitty pulled away the yellow scarf. Gabriel had always been heavy-faced, but this afternoon his colour had been high, his eyes glassy and too bright, his lids turned out, showing their pink fleshy underside. His mouth was snarling and he had smelled of the meaty, rotten stench of the street. Esme was still wondering why she had not felt afraid when she was grabbed like that, when her ears were assailed by Gabriel's profanities and the hypocritical exhortations from the figure lurking by the wall. Perhaps some part of her had known it was Gabriel, even in the yellow scarf mask; and in truth she'd felt no fear of *him* since the time she and Kitty had burned her counterpane and nearly set fire to the Royal George.

Still, she was not looking forward to seeing him tomorrow morning at the police station, where she was to see if that Tobias Hunter was indeed the 'man by the wall'.

'What will you do about him, Miss Rainbow?'

She came back to the present with a jolt. How could Mrs Carrington, the great actress Miss Henrietta Danson, know about Gabriel?

'About Gabriel?' she repeated, her thoughts confused.

'Gabriel? And who might he be with his socks on?' Mr Carrington cut in sharply.

'Gabriel's my brother, Mr Carrington. I was just thinking about him. I had some trouble with him earlier today.' She paused and returned them look for sharp look. 'What will I do about whom?'

'Your musician. Mr Thomas Druce. You did say he was your husband, did you not?' said Mrs Carrington.

'I did say that,' said Esme evenly.

'And is it inevitable that he accompanies you on this tour?' said Carrington brusquely.

'It is,' said Esme stubbornly. 'He and I are always together. I take care of him and he plays music for me. And others. His playing gives great pleasure. The musicians know him, like him.'

'Seems a strange kind of fellow to me. Never utters a word,' said Carrington.

'Thomas is just quiet and very reserved. He talks a great deal when we are alone,' she lied. 'Look, you don't have to worry about him. He'll not need a wage and he doesn't make a noise, apart from his music. If you happen to need music for one of the interval pieces, he'll play it. He can play any tune – and I mean any tune in the world – when he's heard it only once.'

Carrington stroked his moustaches, which he'd just had dyed to a fine deep brown by a barber in Jermyn Street. 'That could be useful, of course, and if he would cost us nothing . . .'

'And he's strong. He'll lift anything I ask him.'

'Now that would be useful. The boxes, the bags,' said Henrietta Danson smoothly. 'Armistead, dearest, leave the matter alone. Miss Rainbow will make her arrangements as she may. Just as we always have.'

Esme smiled faintly. She'd discovered from a peeved Mr Cullen that the Carringtons had only been *truly* man and wife for three years now, owing to the *inconvenience* of Mr Carrington having a wife. Tragically, albeit *conveniently*, the said wife had been run down three years ago by a runaway carriage and killed. This cleared the ground for a small ceremony in Aberystwyth which confirmed the legal status of this long-term partnership. Curiously, after this event, Armistead Carrington had become unctuously sanctimonious about the morality of the domestic arrangements of other people.

Later that night, over steaming cups of tea, Esme listened enthralled to Kitty's dramatic tale of the capture of Tobias Hunter at the railway station. Then, taking her turn, she told Kitty about the encounter with the Carringtons. She imitated exactly Armistead's grandiloquent phrasing and Henrietta's refined, almost mincing delivery.

Kitty laughed, then shook her head. 'Oh Esme, are you sure you want to go and spend three months in their company? Not just performing and listening to them, but eating with them, sleeping in close confines near them? They sound a queer pair.'

Esme laughed. 'Want to? I'm absolutely bursting to do it, Kit. Miss Henrietta might mince offstage but she is the most wonderful performer. On the stage since she was six months! Her mother carried her on in one of Sheridan's plays. Me? I suppose only time'll tell if I can do this straight theatre. The pieces I've learned for them seem easy enough. Strange to say Miss Henrietta thinks I'll take to it like ducks to ponds. Talks about my *natural projection*. And old Carrington? Well, he worships the ground *she* walks on and is rather good himself at the grand old parts. And he opens doors which'd have remained shut forever to a simple music-hall singer, no matter how many loud *huzzahs* she gets from the gallery.'

Kitty looked at her over the rim of her cup and sighed. 'I think you'll come back from Ireland a changed woman. Using long words and loud gestures.'

'So I shall,' said Esme. She put her hand on Kitty's. 'But you and I will know different, won't we, Kit? No pretences between us.'

For one second Kitty contemplated telling Esme about Jarrold: all the things Esme did not know. She turned her hand and clasped Esme's. 'You're right there, Es. Now, what about you? Are you all right now? After that thing with Gabriel today?'

Esme shook her head. 'I was thinking earlier that I should be troubled about it, I should be frightened but I'm not. Odd, that.'

'Good girl! Anyway, he's behind bars now. As is that Tobias Hunter. Gilroy said I was to take you to the station tomorrow morning to look at Hunter. There were things he said as well, which could only mean that he was lurking around here. And those holy words he shouted at you, he wrote them to me in a letter. So Gilroy's making connections already.' She put down her empty cup. 'Hunter keeps condemning himself out of his gabbling, profane mouth. Do you know, Es, that man has done some bad things. Some monstrous things. Worse than we can think,' she said soberly. Then she shook her head. 'Anyway,' she said, 'as soon as I've seen you to the police station I'm taking the first train north. Gilroy says I'll have to come back when there is a trial, but he'll write and tell me when to come.'

'I wonder what'll happen to Gabriel? Has he done such things? My mother'll have hysterics over this. I'll have to send her a telegram.'

'Apart from what he did to you there's no saying what he *really* did. He told Mr Gilroy that they were doing it as a bit of a lark, to give you and me a bit of a shake up, that's all.' She shrugged. 'Who's to tell?'

'That's just what some judge will do,' said Esme gravely, 'tell my dear, benighted, feckless brother whether he will hang by the neck, or not.'

Kitty! Kitty!'

Kitty threw off the shaking hand and made an effort to open her eyes. She had slept fitfully for the whole of the long journey, profoundly exhausted now by the efforts and exertions, both mental and physical, of recent weeks.

'Kitty! Kitty! The journey ends here!' The train had stopped but the motion from the long journey was still whirring through her body.

Her eyes finally snapped open. 'William!' His bright sharp face was above her. She struggled to her feet. 'Am I home?'

'Not quite.' He reached up to the rack for her small bag. 'This is Darlington. You change trains here.'

She straightened her hat, picked up her small satchel and followed him off the train. She looked around, disappointed at not seeing Leonora or Ishmael. She had sent a telegram to Ishmael, as well as William.

Catching her look, William said, 'The others are not here. There's only me. I came up to Darlington to bring you on the next stage. They'll be waiting at Priorton.' He took her hand. 'I wanted to see you myself before you were engulfed in people. How are you, my dearest girl?'

She took a very deep breath. 'Pleased to be home.' Then she laughed and squeezed his hand. 'Pleased to see you. Dying to see Leonora and Ishmael. Even Mirella, although I have terrible news for her.'

He cocked his head. 'What's this about Mirella?'

They walked along the platform. 'Wait. I fear I've black news for you also.' She put her arm through his. 'Come, show me the Priorton train, and I'll tell you everything.'

She waited till they were settled in their seat on the Priorton train and in whispering tones, so as not to be overheard in the crowded carriage, she told him the tale of Tobias Hunter. 'Do you know he was the one who put that piece of bad writing in your letter to me?'

He frowned. 'What?'

As the train chugged along and her whispered tale unfolded, his face grew blacker and blacker. 'The vile creature, who'd believe it?'

'Mr Gilroy thinks it was he who murdered Red Nora and the dressmaker. Gilroy doesn't say it, but he thinks all these events are due to Hunter's hatred for me. He says he'll hang. I think he did the same to Maria. And how many since? Who knows?'

Despite the fact that there were others in the carriage William put his arm round her. 'My dearest, dearest Kitty. The danger you've been in! If what you say is true, I have been negligent, even instrumental in that danger.'

'Oh it's true enough,' she said grimly. She moved away slightly from his encircling arm. 'How many times do I have to tell you, William. I can look after myself.'

He pulled his arm away, sat stiffly beside her for a moment and then relaxed. 'I thank God you can,' he whispered grimly.

After that they were silent all the way back to Priorton and as the train chugged, snuffed and whistled along, there built up between them a barrier as fine as mist, as impenetrable as glass. It was a relief when the chugging note changed and Kitty knew they were entering Priorton, so she could lean against the window to make sure that she got the earliest possible glimpse of Ishmael and Leonora.

They were there, towering above the rest of the crowd, Leonora on Ishmael's shoulders, her petticoats draping him like a shawl. Kitty leapt off the train, picked up her skirts and ran. 'Ishmael. Ishmael!' she yelled, sobbing at last, melting the store of pent-up feeling that had been building inside her in the weeks in London. Leonora tumbled into her outstretched arms. 'Sweetheart! Little girl! So good, good to see you.' She hugged her daughter close and for several minutes the pair of them were clasped in the circle of Ishmael's great arms.

'Mama! Mama! I'm choking . . .' came a little voice from somewhere about the region of her collarbone.

Ishmael and Kitty pulled apart, laughing, and Kitty held on to her daughter. Ishmael put a hand on Kitty's shoulder and surveyed her. 'Well, Kitty, I'd like to say you look well, but I am afraid the contrary is the case. You're white and drawn. And you limped down the platform.'

They both looked down at her feet, she raised the shorter one and they surveyed together the ruined shoe. 'I bought some clothes but I didn't want shoes from anyone else,' she said simply.

'And I've just the pair,' he said. 'I was working on them for you, on the days my hands aren't too bad, to keep you in mind. Leonora helped, is that not so, Leonora?'

Leonora pulled her mother's face round so she could look her in the eyes. 'I make Mama shoes,' she said solemnly.

Kitty looked around for the face she was dreading. 'Is Mirella at the George?'

Ishmael shook his head. 'Your trains would pass each other. She had a telegram from Esme and got the first train she could to go to Gabriel.' He frowned at Kitty. 'It all sounds a very bad business.'

'It is,' she said simply, and put one hand to her head.

William touched her arm. 'Let me take you home in my carriage.'

'We are to go to the George, Kitty. Mirella left instructions. Mabella has the kettle boiling. There I can take care of you tonight and you can go to the shop tomorrow.' There was no gainsaying the authority in Ishmael's voice. William Scorton noted wryly that there were no protestations from Kitty now that she could 'take care of herself'.

Ishmael turned to William. 'We will be glad to take your kind offer of a ride, Mr Scorton,' he said graciously.

As he handed her down in the yard of the Royal George, William whispered to her, 'I will call for you at ten tomorrow, Kitty. I have things to show you.'

'Well, William I . . .' Her voice was slurred, distant-sounding.

He caught her as she fell, carried her into the George and handed her over to the tender ministrations of Mabella, who said, 'Poor bairn, she's as tired as a ten-mile infantryman.'

Kitty slept for twenty-four hours, occasionally coming to, to find Leonora in bed beside her, or Ishmael and Mabella hovering over her.

She woke up properly at noon on the second full day, to see the late sun slanting through the leaded panes of the Royal George. She took a deep breath and stretched. She felt wonderful. It was as though the interior parts of herself, the inside of her, her head and her body, had somehow knitted themselves back together, had retrieved their lively tension. She leaped out of bed and peered out of the window at the busy street below.

The door opened behind her. 'Ah, that's my lass!' Mabella was beaming at her. 'Shed ten years in two nights.'

Kitty frowned. 'What time is it?'

'Twelve of the morning and a fine day too. You've a visitor down below. Seems he's been here every three hours in the last twenty-four.'

'William Scorton?' asked Kitty.

Mabella nodded.

'Oh, Mabella, what am I to do with him?'

Mabella narrowed her eyes. 'Yer want my counsel, lass?'

Kitty looked at her a minute, then nodded. 'Yes I do.'

'I say, keep him, love him, nurture him, for he's a nice man, a genuine man.' She folded her arms. 'But I say as well, to keep him at a distance. Dinnet marry the feller, for one thing. 'Cos far as I can see, once a feller gets you like that, you're the dirt under his feet that he walks over to get to others.'

Kitty laughed. 'Well, that's a surprise, Mabella.' Then she nodded slowly. 'There's certainly sense in it.'

'Anyway, feller's downstairs. Get yourself dressed and down to him. Put the poor soul outa his miseries,' Mabella growled, then flounced out.

Twenty minutes later Kitty was downstairs with her hair neatly dressed, wearing the skirt of the suit that Esme had bought her in London, and a fine grey silk blouse which she had made for herself a good three years before. She found brand-new black button shoes beside her bed with black silk stockings rolled up inside them. They fitted perfectly.

'Kitty! You're up!' He put his hands in hers and pulled her towards him. 'You look so well.'

She kissed him quite warmly on the cheek and pulled back, surveying him. 'You look very well yourself, Mr Scorton.'

'Are you fit for a ride, Kitty?'

'Fit for anything.'

'Then I have things to show you.'

She put on the black jacket and the little black hat. Leonora and Ishmael were nowhere to be found. Mabella shook her head when asked where they were.

Kitty tied her bonnet ribbons. 'Where are you taking me?'

'You will see.'

She sat back, happy to be in the fresh air, and happy to be in the company of this good man, whom she knew she loved even though she was about to tell him she would not marry him. They stopped first at Salvin Row, where he tied up the horse and handed her down, then led her round the back of the street along by The Green. They reached the spot where not so long ago William had dug up the stone which completed his Roman jigsaw. Where the hole had been now stood three sturdy saplings, with a delicate fuzz of green which turned out to be oak leaves.

Kitty touched one of the glossy surfaces.

William smiled at her pleasure. 'They're from the grounds of Purley Hall. It was as though old Luke had nurtured them for just this purpose. And he has said Hindu prayers for their growing so they're bound to thrive.'

'Why three?'

'He says we will watch them year by year and choose the one which thrives and take out the other two and return them to the park. A tree will grow here, Kitty, for a hundred years. A thousand years. Eternal like my feelings for you.' He coughed. 'But come. There is more to see.'

'Where now?' said Kitty, warming to the adventure. The dark images of Whitechapel were fading in her mind now. There had been a letter from Gilroy saying that Tobias Hunter had roundly condemned himself out of his own mouth and would hang for sure, unless his madman babblings rescued him to an asylum for wild men. Even Kitty's worry about poor Mirella, who must be just now meeting Gabriel in some dark cell, was starting to recede. She knew that Esme and Thomas, soon to be off to Ireland and places further afield, were moving into the background of her life too. She thought of Jarrold, on his ship to America, the memory of Maria Tipton at least restored in its place in his life, just as Maria now had some kind of existence in Kitty's mind and life.

Her life here in Priorton. Her place was here and she was staying.

'Where now?' she repeated.

'Wait. Just wait and see!' He clicked his teeth at the horse, who obligingly raised a trot.

Kitty watched as William's smooth muscular hands pulled this way and that against the constraints of the reins. She trusted him. She loved him. She relaxed against the creaking maroon leather.

He manoeuvred the gig right back to the centre of Priorton and drew up just off the Market Square beside Long's Emporium.

'Now, madam, will you alight?'

She laughed and took his arm. The shop looked much cleaner and smarter. Someone had given it a lick of maroon paint. He led her round the corner and there, swinging over the doorway was the sign from her little shop. *C. M. T. Rainbow*. 'William! You did it!'

'Not just that. Look along there.' He pointed to the fascia above the long window. There, painted in cream copperplate with gold edging was the legend *Rainbow and Daughter*. 'Joan and Kezia are in there at this minute unloading your stock from the little shop . . .'

She took a step forward. 'I'll go in there, give them a hand,' she said.

He held on to her arm to prevent her. 'It isn't over yet, Kitty. There's one more thing.'

He drove then at a cracking pace to the edge of Priorton, on the road which eventually led to Purley Hall. They turned off up a lane, through a gateway in a dense deep hedge which had run wild, along a wide earth pathway which lead to a stone house by the river. It was rather squat and designed in something of a manner of a child's drawing: a door at the centre and windows up and downstairs either side. A pathway led from it down to a slatted boat-landing with the river slopping about beneath it.

'See, Mammy! We're fishing!' On the boat-landing sat Leonora, trailing a fishing net in the water. On either side of her sat Michael and Samuel Scorton, who were sitting with fishing rods, staring at the water as though that would make the fish leap from it. In the near distance a train puffed its way across the railway viaduct.

'What is all this, William? What are you up to?' said Kitty suspiciously.

'This is a waterman's cottage which belongs to the Purley Hall estate.'

'Who lives here?'

'You do. You will...' He paused. 'Perhaps you will.'

'What have you done?' she said, forcing severity into her voice.

'Well, at long last I decided that I would not ask you to marry me properly for at least five years. I would hope in that time you would offer me the ... friendship and companionship as we discussed. This house is halfway between Priorton and Purley Hall. So I've taken it for you on a five-year lease. And acquired a little gig so that you can pursue the daily business of Rainbow and Daughter with the energy which it deserves.' He held up a hand as she started to protest. 'No, I'll not pay for all this; it is well within your means now, especially as the business is bound to flourish. There's space here, Kitty, for you and Leonora, and Ishmael and Mirella should they need to come; the hills and the river and your beloved viaduct are there for you to view. It's no palace, Kitty. There's much to do. We've been cleaning and sorting and lighting fires to dry it out.'

The door opened and Ishmael stood there. She could see the glitter of a fire behind him. He held out his great arms. 'Welcome home, Kitty Rainbow,' he said.

She walked into his embrace. 'Ishmael! This is amazing. A

real start. A wonderful start. I am the luckiest person, the luckiest.'

The children had abandoned their fishing and were running towards them.

'I say, Miss Kitty,' said Michael, 'did you know Mr Slaughter says he will teach me and Samuel to box?'

'And me,' said Leonora. 'And me.'